DAZZLING

Signed by Chịkọdịlị Emelụmadụ

WILDFIRE

DAZZLING

Chikọdịlị Emelụmadụ

WILDFIRE

First published in 2023 by
WILDFIRE
an imprint of HEADLINE PUBLISHING GROUP

1

Cataloguing in Publication Data is available from the British Library

Hardback ISBN 978 1 4722 8964 3
Trade paperback ISBN 978 1 4722 8965 0

Typeset in Plantin Light by Palimpsest Book Production Limited, Falkirk, Stirlingshire

Printed and bound in Great Britain by Clays Ltd, Elcograf S.p.A.

MIX
Paper from
responsible sources
FSC® C104740

Headline's policy is to use papers that are natural, renewable and recyclable
products and made from wood grown in well-managed forests and other controlled
sources. The logging and manufacturing processes are expected to conform to the
environmental regulations of the country of origin.

HEADLINE PUBLISHING GROUP
an Hachette UK Company
Carmelite House
50 Victoria Embankment
London EC4Y 0DZ

www.headline.co.uk
www.hachette.co.uk

For my parents Drs E. C. and O. F. Emelụmadụ,
and for my ancestors: Emelụmadụ, Obiọra,
Okereke and Irugbo, and all others unknown or
forgotten. Bịanụ welụ ọjị.

The Arrival

Long Before

They knew he must have been a slave, the stranger, because he bore proof on his wrists and one ankle, his back red and raw, buzzing with flies. Nobody flogged a grown man unless he was a slave – or a criminal. A runaway, as the manacle around the right ankle testified. Or a violently mad man? The lookout had sounded the alarm and now the village lay hushed, the elderly, the children and the infirm. Runaway slaves had a way of bringing trouble with them.

The town, named 'Oba-of-the-nine-brothers' after its founders, hid, her best warriors crouching in dense bushes, watching and waiting. They were lucky, these children of the goddess Idemili, and they knew it. Collectively, they were one of the smallest villages under her dominion. The same goddess who fed them from her river, encircled them with her totem, the giant python, keeping their enemies away. Sometimes, though, they were not so lucky, and the same river allowed their enemies to draw up under the cover of night and try to steal their children away. Hence, the warriors in the bushes, and the silent eyes following every shuffling, weary step of the stranger, to see how far he would go before one of them buried a spear in his back.

Presently, he stopped and sank to his knees, unable to continue. The warriors stepped forth, wearing their leaf-and-raffia camouflage. The stranger fell on his face, speaking softly, his breathing laboured. The boldest of them all, Ejimofo, drew forward, prodding the stranger in the back with his machete.

'I want to see the elders,' the stranger said, arms outstretched. He lay prostrate until he was sure nobody was going to take his head from his shoulders, then he finally risked raising his face. 'I want to see the elders,' he repeated.

'And who are you that you should demand anything from us?' The warriors were tense. This close, they saw that the man's eyes were clearer than they had imagined, and when he stood, the esoteric markings under his matted chest hair, which they could not see until he drew closer, caused further unease. They fell back as a group.

'What did you do, then?' Ejimofo asked, hefting his machete. It spun in the air, landing in his palm with a smack, the raffia-bound hilt crackling. 'Big man like you, in chains. You killed someone you should not have, is that it? I know your type. Drunk with power. Did you kill a white man?'

The stranger said nothing, but each of the men knew himself to be watched. The spears and machetes raised. The stranger licked his split lips. He stood stock-still so that the flies feasting on his wounds settled like anklets around his feet.

'We don't want you here. Go.' Ejimofo pointed back the way the man had come. The group hesitated. The stranger had asked for succour, after all. He had asked for the elders, as was his right. One did not turn away anyone seeking aid. And had he not come in the day, on his own two feet?

'Do you know who I am?' he asked.

Ejimofo's downturned mouth spoke his disdain. 'And who are you? We should fear to speak, eh? Because you bear markings we cannot fathom? Your sort do not speak so boldly. You hide and you whisper and plot in the darkness. How are we to know you did not do those to yourself?'

The stranger bristled. He stared at the warriors, and they

tensed, waiting for him to spring. Instead, he lowered his head. 'My sort. You think there are people like me. Here?'

'We do not know.' Another warrior spoke up. Ejimofo, eyes flashing, cut short the exchange.

'We can give you water to drink, but after that, you must go. You smell of problems. We don't want the kind of misfortune you are bringing with you.'

A gourd was brought forth and, hands shaking, the stranger took it. He drank, little sips at first, but the sweetness of the water overtook him, and he gulped it down, gagging and spluttering. He poured the rest over his head, and it trickled down his muscular body, soaking into his loincloth. He handed back the gourd. Ejimofo motioned again, pointing the way out of the village, but the stranger ignored him, sitting down on the ground. The warriors glanced warily at each other. The end of the day was approaching. Soon, the path would be full of people returning from a day in the market, or children going on errands or playing before night fell. They did not want the stranger's presence known. They had no wish to cause a panic.

'Get him up,' said Ejimofo. With the flat of his machete, he slapped the stranger's broad, broken back, which rippled threateningly even though the man did not move. The smack set off their hysteria, and, as one, the warriors fell on the man and beat him. When they dragged him off into the forest sometime later, the earth was disturbed, bloody and scattered. They left the youngest warrior in charge of sweeping it over with a branch from a palm tree, and hauled their prisoner into the hut used for manhood initiations and rites. They left him there while spies were dispatched to the surrounding areas, to see if the stranger had come alone or if he had brought company with him. They argued into the night about what to do with him, and took turns guarding him while they decided whether or not they would tell the elders of his arrival.

It was not the done thing to beat a stranger and keep him locked up, but Ejimofo was in charge – and had he not taken the most human heads during wars? Nobody dared defy him.

Until somebody did.

The youngest warrior was on watch that night, away from his new wife's bed. It was he who, feeling in his heart the wrongness of what they had done, ran on swift feet to call Isi Idemili, the goddess's priest. Together, they bore the stranger up from the cold mud floor of the hut and spirited him away to the shrine, where he could be treated with herbs and potions, chants and prayers, the priest begging forgiveness from the Mother Idemili for the breaking of the laws of hospitality.

By the time the warriors noticed his absence and traced him to the shrine, the stranger was on his feet, healing impossibly fast, even for what he was. Ejimofo's eyes burned, but the stranger was now under the priest's protection. Ejimofo stood at the threshold to the shrine, staring into the dim hut at the man whose wide chest filled and emptied as he breathed life-giving air.

Ejimofo spat. 'Oru!' he hissed. An enslaved man. And one with strange, unreadable markings. Who knew to what type of clandestine sect he belonged? Ejimofo could do nothing more than spit. Idemili was their mother, and the stranger, through her priest, had anchored himself to her waters.

'Do not shoot your saliva in this house before water drowns you where you stand,' Isi Idemili warned. 'What is a fly but a spot on the buttocks of an elephant?'

Ejimofo brushed past the young warrior on his way out, murder in his gaze, but the boy was freeborn, from a long line of titled men, already wealthy with land and blessed with yams. He feared only the gods' displeasure.

'I will bring you to the elders when you are properly recovered,' the young warrior told the stranger. 'I should have said something earlier. There will be a fine for breaking the laws of the land – may Ani forgive us all.'

The stranger stood. 'I am Nwokereke; many call me Idimogu,' he said with pride. 'When it is your turn to fight, I will stand with you.'

In the trees above, a hornbill trilled suddenly and took to the skies, broad wings blotting out the sun.

CHAPTER ONE

Ozoemena: Then

On the day Ozoemena's uncle Odiogo died, she developed an itch in the middle of her back that no amount of scratching could ease. She did not tell anyone. Ozoemena, at eight, was a girl who had learned to read a room and provide exactly what it needed; and in that moment, the room needed her silence. Her uncle had just been delivered to their house, shot multiple times by armed robbers.

The building filled with panicking and the heavy metal scent of blood. Her mother scurried this way and that, from the medical storeroom-cum-laundry room in the two topmost flats they shared as a family, pulling packets of needles and scalpels and bags of intravenous fluids off the shelves. She handed them to auxiliary nurses, who raced downstairs to the ground floor of the four-storey building, where her father's theatre was located behind swinging double doors. There was no wailing – that would come later. So Ozoemena sat and tried to scratch at the itch on her back, just beyond the reach of her fingers. Her sister, Mbu, smacked the reaching hand away, watching their mother pace, torn between being with her daughters and going downstairs, where she would certainly be in the way of the surgical team. Mbu cradled their sleeping baby sister on her lap, making a spiky sort of nest from her gangly twelve-year-old limbs and a cushion.

'Stop scratching,' Mbu said. 'I don't like how it's doing my ear.'

Mbu was sensitive to sounds, and found many irritating. Ozoemena stopped, but only for a moment. The itch seemed like a concentration of heat rashes without the soothing cool of mentholated dusting powder. She rubbed against the knitted antimacassar on the back of the settee, its knotty cobweb design bringing relief.

'Stop scratching,' Mbu repeated, her voice harder. It had been growing steadily so since they returned to Nigeria from the UK four years ago – a time Ozoemena could no longer fully remember nor appreciate. Mbu yearned to go back, Ozoemena to go forward. They remained at an impasse.

Baby, the baby, stirred on the cushion and Mbu patted her back absentmindedly. Their mother took the baby and sent them off across the landing to bed.

It would be morning before they discovered their uncle had died on their father's operating table before the first IV bag could begin its job. Ozoemena's nails were reddish crescents from scratching in her sleep. Her morning bath was hellish, and she cried, both for herself and her uncle, and the change she sensed but could not name. For the unmaking of her father, withered to a whimpering boy before her very eyes by the absence of his closest sibling. They did not go to school that day.

A few days later, they made the hour-long trip to their grandfather's house in Oba. For Odiogo's funeral, they wore an indigo wax print. It was the closest thing to black that was not. This was not Ozoemena's first funeral. At five, her best friend, Nnenna, had died from complications arising from sickle cell anaemia. A whisper-death, six other siblings having died the same way. Ozoemena had stood at the open graveside with her classmates, schoolmates and teachers, watching Nnenna's wailing mother, imagining all eyes on her, expecting

something that she could not make happen. In the end, she
had looked up into the harsh sun overhead, blinding herself
to the sight of all those eyes. The tears had fallen, and people
had made the right noises, patting her head and shoulders,
even though what Ozoemena felt was bewilderment. Her
father had tried to save Nnenna too, half-dead when they
brought her into hospital, a greenish fluid leaking from her
mouth. The family, it seemed, had dallied with herbal remedies first, until it was too late.

Her uncle's grave was wide and red, a hungry maw that
swallowed the coffin whole and had no more room for the
soil that came after. Its stomach distended high above the
ground of her grandfather's compound. The old man did not
attend and neither did her grandmother – it was anathema
for parents to outlive their children. The night before, during
the wake, her grandmother, M'ma, had sat in her bedroom,
receiving visitors silently and shovelling utaba into her nostrils
with one blunt thumbnail. The women of the village had kept
her company, comforted her, held her when she could no
longer bear the pain of her loss, and mourned for her when
her voice failed. Their ululation had carried into the night,
spattering anyone who heard it with chills. Ozoemena had
wandered amongst the canopies arranged in her grandfather's
compound, playing games with her many cousins. When she
tired, she had sat on a frigid metal chair and eavesdropped
on conversations – easy to do in a place where nobody regarded
children as people, until they grew up and proved their worth.
The gospel band had played songs of heavenly consolation,
the loudspeakers had blasted, and the generator carrying the
fluorescent lights rumbled somewhere in the backyard, belching
smoke. And then there was morning, and right now.

'Mbu? What's a hard death?' she asked her sister. The jollof
rice was hot. Too hot. It made the plastic plate soft and
malleable, like chewing gum.

'Where did you hear that?' Mbu's voice sharpened, and Ozoemena knew she held her sister's attention in a bad way.

'I just heard someone say it. What does it mean?'

Mbu scowled, her small eyes narrowing even further. 'Don't let Daddy hear you say that.' She walked away to join the big girls serving food, her Ventolin inhaler forming a small tent in the pocket of her dress. Ozoemena accepted that she should not ask again. One of her father's sisters, Aunty Edna, passed her, carrying the baby, who reached out salivary fingers, recognising her big sister. Ozoemena waggled her hand at the baby in return and headed off by herself towards the animal enclosures belonging to her grandfather.

The boy stood there, at the goat pen. At first, she wanted to turn around and wander off again, but she cleared her throat. The compound belonged to her grandfather, after all.

'Excuse me? You're not supposed to be here.' She did not know if this was true – after all, the boy could be a distant relation, as welcome as she was – but it felt true. Her grandmother's ewes nestled on some hay, their young shying away from the boy's outstretched hands. In the area next to the goats, the chickens darted around, pecking at pawpaw leaves tied to the posts to discourage them from pecking each other to death. The boy did not turn.

The pens were made from dried mud and wooden posts. The zinc roofing crackled in the sun.

'Excuse me?' she said again, embarrassment in her voice. Her mother drilled good manners into her, into Mbu. Ozoemena still often found herself on the wrong footing with her classmates, found them to be rude and unresponsive to her questions, which they deemed obvious. They mocked her lack of knowledge of certain games. They made fun of her snacks and accent, long after she lost it. She never knew what to do in the presence of rudeness except be ashamed, blame herself.

Ozoemena crossed her arms. 'I'm going to call someone, since you won't listen. If M'ma catches you there, you'll know yourself.'

She turned away, walked past the covered pit latrine on her left, radiating heat, and headed towards the back of her grandmother's kitchen, cluttered with tools of the woman's trade: hoes and machetes and empty jute bags, wooden carriers with chicken wire made for ferrying chicks. Everything was covered in red earth or caked with rich black loam. Through the slit in the back of the kitchen wall, Ozoemena saw a wire basket of dried fish suspended from the sooty beam over the spot where her grandmother lit the wood fire for cooking, blackened ears of corn keeping it company.

The back of the kitchen was to her left; the pebbled concrete cubicle that served as the bathroom for the compound was straight ahead and to the right. The steps that led up to the cubicle were broken, and moss grew in the cracks. The ground remained wet. The big tree shielding bathers from the sun was fruitless, having gulped its share of bathwater and soap. Ozoemena meant to round the bend to the left, to call the attention of the women stirring tripod iron pots outside the kitchen, talking, instructions and orders flying. She saw the smoke coming from their cooking. She saw the dog she meant to avoid, a bitch named Chuzzy, who got meaner each time she pupped, and her litter was seized and sold. But she felt something the moment the dog's ears pricked up.

It was what told her the boy was behind her.

Chuzzy rose, growling, and Ozoemena turned around, her eyes level with a black mark on the boy's chest. Too slow. The boy placed a hand around her back, on the itch clustered there, and it exploded into heat and pain. Ozoemena's mouth widened to form a scream, and Chuzzy went insane, pulling on her chain, which was tied around a metal stake driven into the ground. Saliva dribbled from her fangs.

Ozoemena thought she was screaming, but she was not. All she felt was pain, in her head, in her veins, shrieking, a salted-snail shriek. Eventually, the women would stop throwing scraps to appease Chuzzy and come and check what she was barking at. They would see Ozoemena crumpled on the floor, her funeral blouse torn open at the back and the beginnings of a welt on her skin; they would shout, and M'ma, her grandmother, would spring to her feet and leave her room, alerted by cries that contained more alarm than sorrow, and follow them. M'ma would take one look at her granddaughter's weeping back and laugh and cry, and the women would wonder if she had already lost her mind from grief, because they had never seen her act with such ambiguity, but they would do as she said and lift the granddaughter up, and fetch the girl's father from the front of the compound, where he received guests under his special canopy and allowed himself to be consoled by old friends and classmates of him and his brother – the Inseparable Duo, so named by people who did not realise the brothers were bound by more than just blood. And Ozoemena's father would come and look and go in silence, such grim silence that nobody recalled him speaking afterwards, not even to accept heartfelt words from the delegation of priests whom he always treated in his hospital for free. His wife would ask him what was wrong, and he would say nothing to her.

In that moment, though, Ozoemena's body shrieked in pain, and the bitch Chuzzy rattled her chains as she leaped and jumped, her empty flattened teats swinging like bunting, and the strange boy leaned over and whispered in her ear, his breath a cooling breeze: I am sorry.

CHAPTER TWO

Ozoemena: Now

The sun shines its malice straight into Ozoemena's eyes. She is a child of above average height for her age, most of her growth spurt occurring in her legs. This proves rather unfortunate on the occasions where she sits in the front seat next to her mother, her short upper half denied shelter from the car's sun visor. It is barely ten o'clock in the morning. Her face burns. Sweat prickles her top lip, and the inappropriate fur interior of her mother's Honda Prelude – much more suited to the temperate region of the world from whence it came – prickles her neck. She cannot risk scratching. Her mother, Prisca, is like a scorpion these days. Ozoemena does not wish to get stung.

'Did you take your medicine today?' Prisca asks.

Ozoemena nods before she replies. 'Yes, Mum.' She shuts her eyes, wishing she could have ridden at the back of the car. It is her space, a place in which she had once shared sweltering, scratchy journeys with her sister, poking their fingers into the crispy hole in the synthetic fabric that had been made by their father's carelessly discarded cigarette, before her sister grew too big and began to ride in front. She thinks wryly that the shadow of the visor never misses Mbu's face.

The chasm between the sisters has widened, Mbu abusing her seniority once she hit secondary school. She refers to Ozoemena as 'child' and delights in the keeping of womanly secrets. Now they are almost strangers, reduced to imperial commands from one and grudging obedience from the other. Sometimes, it irks Ozoemena how much Mbu and Prisca are alike, how her sister expects the sort of respect Ozoemena reserves for their mother, simply because she is older and privy to mature confidences. Thrice, Mbu has sent Ozoemena off to buy her sanitary towels. The packets of fluorescent yellow Simple pads, as thick as loaves of bread, seem to glow through the black polythene bag designed to camouflage them. Each trip to the shops down the street has been worse than the last, Ozoemena feeling all eyes on her, women and men, girls and boys alike, the contents of the bag announcing a fecundity to the world that is not hers.

Still, Ozoemena wishes her sister could have been on this journey with them. Anything to distract Prisca from—

'Recite your twelve times table for me,' says Prisca, and Ozoemena is off before she even has time to consider the request fully.

'Twelve times one, twelve; twelve times two, twenty-four; twelve times three, thirty-six; twelve times four, forty-eight; twelve times five, sixty . . .' She falters, begins to panic. 'Twelve times seven, eighty-four . . .' Ozoemena is sweating by the time she finishes, the perspiration gluing her cotton vest to her back.

'You should know it better than that,' says Prisca. She taps on her horn twice and gives an unruly driver a dirty look. 'You were too slow. What is twelve times thirteen?'

'Em . . .' Ozoemena adds quickly. 'One fifty-six.'

'Maybe you should have stayed behind one more year,' Prisca says, and Ozoemena's heart leaps out from behind her ribcage and into her throat.

One mark. One mark is what separates her from true freedom. Ozoemena had scored twenty-nine in the Common Entrance examinations, missing the cut-off point, and meaning she was doomed to stay on for Primary Six instead of leaving for secondary school from Primary Five as her teachers had predicted. The day she went to pick up her results from school, the best students were invited to the headmistress's office to view their scores first. Ozoemena can still taste the mouldiness of defeat on her tongue when she thinks about this: the involuntary gasp of disappointment from her teacher, Madam Ozioma, who went outside to wipe her eyes with a handkerchief.

'Ogbo m,' she said on her return. 'Don't worry, it's just one mark.' Madam Ozioma had called Ozoemena 'namesake' since the first day in class, when she had misheard the short-ened form of her name, 'Ozo', and assumed that the two of them shared the same first name. 'If not for everything that happened in your family . . . how can they expect that you will pass in flying colours? Just one! It is nothing. You are intelligent enough.'

Had Prisca not been persuaded to let her daughter try to get into a private secondary school, Ozoemena would auto-matically be returning the following term for another year of primary.

After the extended and celebrated farewell to all her teachers and friends.

Back to the pointing fingers and pitying looks.

Back to the gossip and taunts.

She has to pass this next exam.

Prisca slips a cassette into the player and turns it up. Jim Reeves's deep baritone comes through the speakers. She immediately ejects the tape, and winding down the window with her free hand, flings the cassette out into the dust, hissing. Ozoemena grinds down on her teeth. It had been one of her father's.

The sky has no clouds, only a relentless, cheery expanse of blue that fills Ozoemena with dread. She turns her head towards the window, watching her reflection as the car flitters in and out of the shadows made by trees, providing brief respite. The presidential elections are about ten months away, and posters cover tree trunks, gates and walls, despite many abodes being daubed with 'Post No Bills' in bleeding paint. The election touts have been busy, covering every spare inch of space, including buses and roadside stalls. Some traders use the posters to tie up wares for customers, to sit on, to create makeshift shade, risking a beating from whatever rogues are working for which party.

Ozoemena exhales. Her nose and forehead are oily. She pulls a handkerchief out of the pocket of her school skirt and dabs off the shine. Tucking it back into place, she attempts to drag the elastic waistband of her skirt lower than her stomach, where it sits squeezing her like a toddler with its hand on a full tube of toothpaste. Earlier, Ozoemena had tried to get out of wearing her old school uniform to what could potentially be her new, grown-up school. Along with the fresh patewo hairstyle on her head, its plaited fringe curving over her forehead and ending somewhere on her right cheek, Ozoemena thinks she looks like a baby.

Beside her, Prisca sighs and leans on her horn, a warning to the car in front of her, which has braked suddenly. She passes the offending driver, winds down her window, and splays her fingers at him.

'Waka,' she says, her wedding band glinting in the sun. The next cassette is in her hand, and she feeds it to the player. Paul Simon. Before her mother can snatch it up and hurl it out of the window again, Ozoemena ejects it.

'Why are all these tapes in my car?' Prisca asks, half to herself, in Igbo. *These* with emphasis, to show how little she thinks of them, their owner – her husband – and his taste in music. Ozoemena shrugs, refusing to admit she brought them along for the journey because she craves the comfort.

They fly into a pothole and out again. Ozoemena's teeth crash together, and she tastes bone. Her mother is like an extension of her car, small and quick. At ten, Ozoemena is almost her mother's height, which she loves, but is also horrified by on an innate level. In the side mirror, she watches the overladen bus behind them navigate the same dried-out hole, crawling around the outside of its rim, balanced unsteadily on two wheels. Its conductor alights, his button-down shirt open and flapping in the wind like a distress flag.

'They will just keep on loading and loading the vehicle, putting people's lives at risk just to make money. Look at that, how the chassis is dragging on the ground. Can you even see the wheels of the vehicle? Then when they get into an accident, they will bring their broken bodies to us and expect us to work miracles.'

Her father provided commentary on all their journeys: irate, despairing, humorous – or what counted for it in his dad-world. Prisca, on the other hand, can do entire journeys in near silence. Ozoemena swallows, unsticking a dry part of her throat. It hurts.

'Did you bring your rosary?' asks Prisca.

'No, Mum.'

Prisca sighs. 'Open that glove compartment. There is an extra one in there.'

This is another reason Ozoemena wishes Mbu was along for the journey – their mother's assumption that they are now Catholic by default, as she is. Their father was casually Anglican, which has never done for Prisca. Now, with him gone, she has free rein to initiate her children into the ways of The One True Church. Mbu has refused this encroachment, and Prisca, with her newfound respect for her maturing daughter, will not insist. She would not have forced Ozoemena to recite the rosary had Mbu been in the car.

'In the name of the Father,' Prisca starts.

'And of the son, and of the Holy Spirit.'

'I believe in one God, the Father Almighty, maker of Heaven and Earth . . .'

They pray, Ozoemena without paying attention to the words, content in the soothing ritual, the up-and-down of tones, the smooth wax beads linked by rough string. Her mind wanders and drifts; her vision is colour-bar bright and noises of traffic loud-loud, lorries belching smoke through sideways exhaust pipes. The heat sings in her ears. She is young enough that hours still feel longer than they are, stretching into something resembling days. Ozoemena busies herself reading the signboards to the various places they pass: Dikenafai. Isieken'esi. Isieken'asaa. Signposts advertising products, services and speed limits that nobody seems to obey.

In the months following their uncle's death, their father had grown increasingly paranoid and would make the sisters take note of everything – where they were, what the vegetation looked like, what cars were following, and if they were white Peugeot 504s. Count the people inside. Four or less? Any women or just men? Even now, in the starkness of daylight, Ozoemena watches and counts. Her uncle's murderers had driven a white Peugeot 504. Sometimes, Ozoemena cannot decide if it is a blessing or a curse that he regained consciousness briefly, only to relay this information to her father. What did it do? The robbers have never been caught, despite her father offering a reward. Despite her father's standing in society. That broke him.

'We should be getting there by now,' Prisca says. The hardness has vanished from her voice, leaving it lighter. Praying a chaplet always has this effect on her mother. Ozoemena notices there are fewer vehicles, and bicycles begin to appear. She has only ever seen bicycles in villages, not in the town in which they live. Where on earth are they all going? There are breeze-block bungalows interspersed with tracts of farmland and fallow land. Ozoemena sits up, craning her neck as her mother slows down to take stock.

'Is this the way?' asks Prisca.

Ozoemena does not respond because the question is rhetorical. Her mother takes off again, at a slower pace, winding up her windows against the dust from the earthen road, which stretches out wide and flat in front of them.

Soon, they pass a Catholic church, followed by a government hospital, and Prisca steps on the accelerator again, triumphant. She turns on the air conditioner. Its breeze is hot, almost scalding, and Ozoemena takes it full in the face without complaint.

'Don't worry, we will get there soon. They said after the hospital and church, I will keep going straight until I get to school,' her mother says. 'Drink some water.'

Ozoemena pulls out her water bottle. A quarter of water had been frozen in the bottle, to which Prisca had added boiled, cooled and filtered water before their journey. The water bottle sweats condensation as Ozoemena lifts it to her lips, thinning down the cotton wool consistency of her saliva. A finger of ice slips into her mouth and she sucks on it gratefully until it dissolves into a needle and slides dangerously down her throat.

The way grows narrower, and Prisca pushes forward, dried twigs clutching and scratching at the car like claws. A few riders dismount from their bicycles to let them pass, muttering as they are forced deeper off the path and into the bush. Prisca waves her thanks and apologies, but hardly anyone acknowledges her. A furrow appears between her brows.

The path spits them out again, and a dwarf wall appears on their right, keeping time with them, disappearing into dense vegetation only to reappear. Election posters form a cacophony of colour on the wall, plastered over each other in competition. The faces and smiles are composites of various candidates, some ripped off by rival touts and faded by the elements. They follow the fence to a clearing, where a cylinder with a handle stands glinting in the sun. The short grass around its concrete platform base is lush and green, the earth cracked in a way that says it is often muddy. In the dryness of the surrounding area, it stands out.

'Manual pump! Ehhh? When last did I see those?' Prisca exclaims, and they are there at last, by a gap in the fence through which they can see a vast compound, lined with buildings. To the right of the gap is a white signboard, higher than their eyeline, recently repainted and stencilled with the name of the school. There is no imposing gate to speak to the school's grand reputation, no security spikes on the walls, but there *is* a guard in uniform, and he waves them through, saluting and bowing as though they are royalty. Prisca waves back, pleased by this show of good manners, and the guard points with four fingers towards the four or so cars parked on a huge field opposite the classroom block. Prisca drives on.

'Mum, he is saying we should park in the field,' says Ozoemena.

'In the sun? You want me to cook. I am going to look for a tree.' But there are no trees near any of the buildings, and Prisca circles back to a sliver of shadow beside a long, low edifice painted the dusky pink of Mbu's Ventolin tablets.

A man approaches in the shirtsleeves and trousers combo of a civil servant. His shoes are thick and hardwearing, brown to match his trousers. The muscles of his jaw stick out at angles on his face. He reminds Ozoemena of a praying mantis.

'Welcome,' he says, pushing his glasses up his nose. Another pair hang from his neck on a piece of cord. 'Welcome to Novus College. You are Mrs Nwokeke? I am Basil Chiwetara Udegbulam. All the children call me BC. Please follow me.'

CHAPTER THREE

Treasure: Then

I see the woman dodge into the shop and know her immediately. Mummy and Daddy's friends them, have all vamoosed,
but me, I will never forget them. Mummy used to say I have
bad heart because if you do me bad, I do you back, God no
go vex. And this woman, she did me and Mummy bad.
Common shop cannot hide her keep. If she likes, she should
run to Kafanchan today, me I will follow her in her back-in
her back.

Her name is Mrs Mbachi, Mama Ujunwa. Me and Uju,
her last-born, used to be friends before-before. Mrs Mbachi
them would come to our house, she and her husband. I don'
know his name. I use to call him Uncle or Papa Uju. He like
to drink Seaman's Aromatic Schnapps and pour libation on
the carpet because he carries chieftaincy title. Mummy would
boil and mud her face, frowning. After they left, she made
Mercy, our housemaid that time, to scrub the carpet with
Elephant Blue and brush. She used to point in Daddy's face
with her yellow fingers like uncooked shrimps: 'Bia, this man,
don't be bringing these bush people to come and spoil my
Italian carpet for me!' And Daddy would throw his head back
and laugh because he liked when Mummy does as if she is
scolding him, even though they are always doing love. Daddy
would pinch her cheeks and call her 'Ikebe Super', his hailing
name for her because he said he can perch on her bum-bum

and she will just be walking and not know he is there. Then he will beat her on the thing, kpaa!, like that. Mummy will pretend to be vexing until he drops something for her, and I knew I was getting a new dress and shoes and bag to match after escorting Mummy shopping to spend the money, and maybe even Den's Cook for hamburger and ice cream for me and cream soda for Mummy. Mummy will tell them not to put tomato o, because I don' like tomato and they will say, 'Madam we know noooow,' and she will dash them money too because they behaved well to remember what me I like to eat.

Those were the days when things were sweet.

When we came back from eating his money, Daddy will now put turntable and play William Onyeabor 'When the Going is Smooth and Good', and he and Mummy will dance and dance, but I dinor know that something like that song is singing can do us as well.

That time, Mama Ujunwa used to give my mother cloth on hand, and she will pay after – George and Georgette and Akwete and plenty-plenty Hollandaise – fresh from Main Market in Onitsha, before any of the wives in our side had them. After Daddy died, she was among the first to come and collect her property back. I didin even see her at the burial. That's why she is hiding from me inside the shop like a rat in a food store.

I leave where am squatting and pursue Mama Uju. She enters a jewellery shop in Ogba Gold. I know this shop. Mummy used to come here before, when Mama Uju introduced her to Solo, the owner, because he don' cheat since he is a church person and can swear on Bible. Inside, all the showcases are lined with black foam so that the rings, earrings and all those assorted things shine like stars in the night sky. Mummy used to buy gold, not GL, as she told anyone who asked, but I don' know what is different between gold and

GL. It don' matter anyway. The whole thing is gone now, plus-including her wedding ring and the small ring made from Igbo gold that I used to wear when I was small. It's in all the pictures. Those ones too are gone, the albums and frames. Daddy's brothers took them. What is their business with pictures they are not inside?

Am leaning against the zinc walls of the shed, and people are looking at me with corner-eye but nobody chats to me, not even small 'How are you?'. My silpas are too big. Aunty Ojiugo said it is better to be big than small so that I will wear it a long time. The sun is entering innermost my eyes. It's afternoon. My eyelashes divide the colours into red and green and yellow and orange but me, am not going to find shade where will cover me. Let Mama Uju come and pass. I want her to see me here. I want to see the thing her face will do.

A mineral seller plays bottle music with his metal opener, sliding it across the red Coca-Cola crate on his head. Some of the bottles are empty. The others are black like heaven, sweating with cold. There are also Krest bitter lemon and the tonic water my mother used to sometimes drink, that tastes of malaria medicine. The soft drinks are what carry Mama Uju's legs out of the shop. Always a longathroat, this woman.

'Hey, mineral-person! Come!' It is her voice. The man stops and turns back. He don' even give me face and maybe that's what makes Mama Uju think that me I've gone. She steps out. 'You have soda water? Is it cold?'

'Aunty, good afternoon,' I say.

'Jesus!' She jumps. The mineral seller shows me warning with eyes not to spoil market for him. Mama Uju comes back to herself. Her chest is going up and down, up and down, like a dog that has chased its tail tire.

'Treasure? Is that you?' That is the name that everybody uses to know me because of my daddy.

'Yes, Aunty. Is me.'

She holds her throat as if her heart is jumping out of it. Her hand is full of chains and gold rings. When I was small, Mama Uju was black. Now only her hands and feet are remaining that colour. Her face is fair, but it's not fresh like Mummy. Mama Uju's yellow is forcing-yellow, like a mango that has been tied in a waterproof bag to ripe it quick before selling. Her cheek and eyelids have drawn red-red threads inside. She is wearing a blouse that sits on her shoulders, orange lace. English lace. The space between her breasts sparkles with sweat. There are hairs there and under her chin. Everybody knows only wicked women like Mama Uju have beards like men.

'Hewu! You poor child. How is your mother? Embrace me.'

'She is fine,' I say.

Mama Uju narrows her eyes. She is continuing to open arms to embrace me, but I refuse to move. The mineral-man's eyes are on her and then me. He hands her a bottle of soda water and also a bottle of tonic water.

Mama Uju waves him away, irritation doing her whole body. 'Go! Take that thing that is not cold and go.' She sucks her teeth. 'Idiot.' Mama Uju likes doing Big Madam. She thinks if she shouts at people it shows how important she is. She stares at me and I stare at her back and don' bite my eyes. I know she wants to leave me here and go, but shame is catching her. She shuffles her feet.

I feel like insulting her. I want to tell her the ancient and modern of her life. I saw it all. Nobody here gives children ear, so I saw everything just by being quiet and doing like I dinor see. I saw how she used to sneak eyes at my daddy when her husband dozed on the armchair, blinking like this and that as if there was something in her eye. She is his third wife and the man is old and rich and didin go to school. When they sat down to eat the food Mercy cooked, Mama Uju would use her toes to be touching Daddy under the table.

When Daddy smiled at her, she dinor see that he mercied her, but me, I did. After all, her husband was old and smelled like ogili okpei inside carton, and everybody knew he stored his money under the matras as per local man, and Daddy was the one that helped him use his money well, like importing and exporting and that kind of a thing.

Anyway, I need Mama Uju to dash me money, so I suck my words and swallow them.

'Aunty, how is Ujunwa?' I bend my head to one side. 'Long time I have not seen her eyes.'

'Hewu! She is fine, my dear. She keeps asking when she can come and see you people, but she is so busy now, as per secondary school chikito, you know. All those assignments . . .' She stops talking because she can see me standing in front of her and am not in school. Stupid woman.

'Do you know where we are living now? I can come tomorrow to your shed and take you to the place. Or now, sef. Did you bring your car?' I say.

Mama Uju looks around the market for somebody to call her name so that she will now go to greet them and never come back. 'Ah, my car is in the mechanic, my dear, but I will find the place and I will come, you hear?'

She fumbles in her bag and brings out one ten-naira note like this. It is rumpled and she straightens it, ironing it between her hands.

'Mummy is not yet well. She sleeps all the time. The other day, she was calling your name – "Nne Uju, Nne Uju" – like that. I haven't eaten since two days now, and Aunty Ojiugo hasn't come back since she left for Nkwelle-Ezunanka. You remember Mummy's sister? Her half-sister. Yes, the one that farms. Her husband don' want her to see us again.' I twist my face and my empty hands – the money is already inside my pocket. I see from her eyes, from the way she is looking at her watch, that she don' want to give me more money and am angry. After all, didin Daddy make them money? He used to gist Mummy what he did for them and me, I heard. Before everything happened, all of them used to come to him as if he was Jesus, now she wants to leave me in the middle of Eke Awka market with only one dirty ten naira that plenty people have touched?

'Please, let me follow you to your shop and sit for a while, Aunty, the sun . . .'

'No!' She clears her throat and smiles. The lines in her cracked lipstick spread. 'I'm not going to the shop.'

She don' want me there. Am the daughter of 'That Man' and she don' want people to remember that she knew him. I start crying loudly. People are beginning to look. It takes a few tears before she brings out another five naira. Stingy woman. Mama Uju takes her bag and walks away fast-fast. She don' even say 'Don mention' when I say 'Thank you' to her.

I cross from Ogba Gold into Babies and wander among the tinkling toys and tiny clothes. The whole place smells of Tenderly and Pears baby powder. The traders here, they like to rub their stuffs all over theirselfs and be smelling baby-baby. Who don' like baby smells? Before, when I used to come buying with Mercy, she hated to waste time, so it was put head-come out. Now, am just walking slow-slow in the market, eating with my eyes. Where else am I going today? Mummy is just sleeping sleep all the time. She will not know if me am there or not there.

The matured men and women selling, stare at me and the ones doing boyi for them in their shop, learning trading from the traders, stare too. Nobody walks like I do in Eke Awka, dragging their feet. You can do that in a supermarket with the things arranged fine-fine on shelves, with one door in and that same door out, but not in the market with plenty ways in and out. A man with a ring of powder around his neck uses his eye to poke inside my own. Just as am about to poke him back, I notice one pregnant aunty like this sitting in his shop looking at baby bath. She's on a bench, in the cool shade. I run towards her, but the man is faster, blocking me.

'Get out of here,' he says. I twist my neck around his potbelly.

'Aunty, please.' I put my hand to my mouth to act eating like I see the beggar-boys do. 'May you born boy, a big strong boy. May your house be full of boys.' The woman laughs.

'Don't give her anything. You can't see she is in school uniform?' He turns to me. 'Why are you not in school?'

I want to ask him can he not see that my uniform is too small for my shoulders? I have opened the armpit so that I can move inside it, but it don' matter sha. The man's question has nothing to do with the price of garri.

'You will born plenty-plenty sons, one by one, until your house is full,' I say. People like sons.

'And what if I want daughters, nko?' asks the woman. She is a small aunty, just past 'sister' level, wearing a starched boubou and scarf that tells me her marriage is new. Her outfit looks like to-match, one for her and another for her husband from the same cloth. She has a big open-teeth on top and a smaller one below. Her body jiggles like hot agidi jollof. She gives me five naira and I pocket it as well. I sing for her:

'Your marriage will be a blessing, your children surround your table, you will see your children's children, so says the Lord of Hosts.'

The woman gives me a packet of four biscuits from her bag. The man shaas me away because he don' want beggars to think that his section is where it's happening.

Twenty naira. Allelu-alleluia! I wander around Ogba Cosmetics but the men there are young and are afraiding me with their shirts open at the neck. A lot of them have plenty chest hair and wear chains. Some of them bleach like Mama Uju. One or two have Jheri curls, shiny and bouncy, curl activator melting on their necks. I used to have Jheri curls when I was four. By six, Mummy started plaiting my hair for school – not by herself because she don' know how to plait hair. She paid someone to come to the house every weekend. By ten years, it didin matter what me I did with my hair. Mummy started sleeping and Daddy was not there to say, 'Ikebe, ah-ah change this girl's hairstyle now, has she not carried this for one week?' Aunty Ojiugo got me that comb that you put razor inside and when you comb, it cuts the hair. She had to use scissors first to get the whole thing down.

The men in cosmetics look after theirself like women to bring women in. They stand at the door to their shops and gossip to one another across the passage, and when girls come, they eat them with their eyes, pulling at their hands, gently-gently. They sing, 'Ifeoma, I want to marry you, give me your love,' in case one of the girls is called 'Ifeoma'. They shout out common names too: 'Bia, Chi-Chi, come and look at my shop,' or, 'Ngozi, I've got just what you need.' Sometimes they pull hard, and someone's wristwatch will cut, then the girls insult them, but the men like that, so they laugh more. I like the smell of cosmetics the most. There is Cleopatra piled by my elbow, the soap Mummy used to use and baff. I would like to buy but food is greater than Cleopatra.

In Kwata, the meat side, I find intestines. When Daddy was alive, he loved to celebrate by slaughtering animals. A ram for Mummy's birthday, a goat for mine, a cow for Christmas, which he shared to our neighbours and the less fortunate, the motherless babies and widows them. Now, am the less fortunate and I know that everything is food, is just remains how to cook it. I haggle how Mercy taught me, when the traders would grow saucy and ask why she was being stingy, after all, the money she was saving was not her own.

They would ask out of the corners of their mouth, half-joking because they wanted to do customer with her.

Mercy. They came to collect her like property too. The man that came was the same man that brought her to our house. She use to call him Uncle Joe. He was an agent and his job was to be carrying girls from the village to do maid in town. Mummy was not sleeping that time and she begged Joe, that he should please let Mercy stay. She told that man that me and Mercy were like senior and junior sister.

'What kind of life will she have in the village?' Mummy asked. 'Let her stay here, two years she will take WAEC, by then her value to you people will rise. She will be able to do any job she wants, even employ plenty people if she has her school cert.'

I was just looking at Uncle Joe as Mummy was begging, and I could see the begging was sweeting him. His own was just to find houses for the girls he brought from the village and collect finder money, which was already much. Mercy told me that she and her friends thought Uncle Joe used to throw all of them far from each other so that they would learn Igbo fast-fast. The truth was that he did it so they didin talk about how much they were paying them. That was how she saw another of the girls in the market that had left her madam, and the girl told her that Joe was chopping their money and sending kobo to their parents in the village. Chicken change. Mercy reported to Mummy and Mummy now started sending her money to Ikot-Ekpene, cutting Joe out. We didin see him again oooo, until after Daddy died.

After Daddy died, Mummy told Mercy that she cannot pay her until things were better, and Mercy said anywhere me and Mummy go, she will go. That if we are eating palm nut, she will follow us to eat. Until Uncle Joe landed.

'Dem don already pay bride price,' said Joe. 'She be pesin wife. Wetin you wan make I do?'

'Let me speak to her father,' Mummy said.

'Her papa no too wan talk, Madam. E talk say make I return im property with immediate alacrity. Wetin una wan take the pikin do? She no too dey useful to una in town, and the old man no dey chop anything for im hand.' Joe pulled himself up until his head reached Mummy's chest, and changed to English. 'Please Madam, let us not make this difficult.' Joe looked Mummy inside her eyes as if they were mates. No more bending neck.

I saw Mercy cry that day as she picked up her things. When she came to our house, she only had one waterproof bag with comb, Vaseline, two dresses and toothbrush, but when she was going, her things fulled two suitcases. Mummy really tried for her. This was before the uncles now came to clear the rest of our property and Mummy started sleeping. Before she left, Mercy now blew her nose and washed her face well. She didin want Joe to see that she was crying because he will tell her father. What kind of child was not happy to go back to their parents? Me, I dinor cry. Crying don' do anything for anybody.

The butcher coughs.

'Should I tie?' He puts the intestines for me in a santana waterproof. It is warm and slimy. I ask him to please double-waterproof for me, but he wants to collect money for extra bag, so I leave him and go away.

Someone jams my body, hard.

'Sorry!' A group of boys in tear-tear shorts and vests. The one who bumped into me is wearing monkey coat. His arms are bare and thin but strong like a village boy's. He pulls me up and they surround me, dusting me, brushing off the dirt and animal hair, plus pieces of bone that break off when the butchers chop up the animals into cooking chunks. I push the boys away from me. Their hands are everywhere.

'Get out from my face!' I say. They troop off like a swarm

of locusts after something to destroy. My packet of intestines is intact, and I pick it up and follow their path into the food section, hills of garri and ground corn in sacks and basins, fine cassava flour for mixing nni oka, fingers of okro, heads of green and ugu. I approach the friendliest-looking seller, a mama that looks as if she will put hand after she has measured out what I need.

It's after the garri is tied in its bag that I search my pant for my money, but don' find it. My hand is in my pocket, through the hole, deeper than any pocket can be, and the woman is eyeing me one-kain as if I am doing bad-bad things in front of her shop. Something holds my throat and squeezes it and all the blood in my body goes into my head.

'Are you buying or not?' says the mama. I can't answer her. She takes the black polythene bag and pours the garri back inside her basin, piling it high into a mountain top.

I know when the first tear leaks out of my eyes. I don' want to cry. I want to look for my money well, but my eyes are not agreeing.

'Ha! Please leave the front of my shop before you bring me bad market. Did I tell you I am doing salaka with my garri? It's not for free.'

My body is shaking me. Those boys with their monkey-coat leader stole my money. Where did they follow me from? When Mama Ujunwa gave me that fifteen naira? When the shining pregnant woman dashed me the five naira? It's as if somebody has cut the rubber holding me and now everything is falling down inside me. Through my eyes-water, I follow the way the boys have gone. Am like a mad person, opening my eyes waaa, looking inside shops and down roads and people are shouting 'Comot there' but my money is gone. Soldier ants are stinging me all over my body.

I sit on the floor and wait for the boys to pass again. Don' thief have the same places they like to go? Agaracha must come back. If I wait, they will return. The ground is wet and muddy even though is dry season. The women here spray their vegetables with water. Carrots are crying like Judas, añara and cauliflower heads, round and white like boils full of pus. There in the mud, under the trays of raining vegetables, I finally allow myself to cry, hoping that all the water will hide the ones coming from my eyes. I don' stay long. Nobody likes idleness. After they check to make sure I am not dying, the women chase me away again. I won't go home. I find a dry spot around the men selling yams. They are old men with those line-line mazi caps falling over the sides of their faces, weighed down by the ball at the end. They drink palm wine and salute each other, blasting Chris Mba from the radio. They don' chase me.

The sheds are closing when the feet appear under my nose. Brown, leather 'pons, with the mouth of the shoes pointing to heaven. The man's hands are long and thin and he's holding an open bag. I know the smell. It's ugili. I hate ugili fruit, it's stinking and only bush people eat it, but my stomach makes a loud noise as if it forgot. I look up into the man's face. Thin like lizard, with moustache. He chews the ugili and his moustache moves like he has two mouths. He swallows and the ball on his throat moves up, up and down again.

'If you give me your mgbilima afo, you can have some ugili,' he says, pointing at my packet of intestines.

When I blink, my eyes click camera noises in my ears. My face is tight-tight from the salt I was crying in my tears.

'Is there mango there?' I ask.

The man sighs, disappointed but not vexed. 'You children don't know good things.'

'If you want my intestines, I bought them, seven naira.'

He laughs. 'I'm not giving you money.'

'Okay, I want the whole bag of fruit, then.' I don' know what me I will use ugili for, but this is business. After much-

much, I will see someone that will give me something for it, or I will ask somebody how to bring out the agbọnọ from inside and how to cook it as soup for Mummy.

'You're not serious,' says the man, but I know he will give me. He was the one to ask for trade-by-barter first, and . . . there is something else. He looks straight inside my eyes. Daddy used to look at me the same.

'Well, do you want this juicy intestine or not? Think of how they will look in your wife's soup, curled up like shrimps.' Intestines was what Mummy used to feed our dogs, over-salted so that they would drink lots of water.

The man stops chewing. He smiles and the moustache smiles, but I can't see his mouth. 'Ngwanu, bring,' he agrees. He hands me the bag of ugili and I give him my packet of intestines. One of the fruits rolls out of the bag. I run and pick it up.

Is then that I see his shoes and his feet properly.

'You negotiate just like your father.' He tears open the santana waterproof that sees-through, pulls out one pink tube and sucks it into his mouth like supageti.

His feet. They are not touching the ground.

CHAPTER FOUR

Ozoemena: Now

BC Udegbulam is a man who takes his time. He teaches English language, he says. Ozoemena will be in his class. Slowly, slowly, he leads Ozoemena and her mother to the school office, the first room in the long bungalow that houses the girls' classrooms.

'Yes, we are boys and girls, but even though we are under one umbrella, there is no mixing. If you come here, you will learn that.' He says all this to her mother while looking through his desk drawers. Prisca nods, appreciative. BC pulls out an office flat file, fitted with green tags through its perforations. It is marked 'Examination Questions'. Ozoemena, sitting opposite him on the imitation leather chair, feels her heartbeat in her wrists. She focuses on her hands, and her white knee-length cotton socks, with their elastic bands biting into her brown flesh. The ceiling fan above them is stilled – there is no electricity this afternoon. On the bench and to her left, the powder-blue wall bears oblong marks of oily dirt imprinted by many sweaty backs. Behind BC is a door that reads 'Dr Vincent S. Udegbulam', and underneath that, 'Proprietor'. BC's desk faces the open doorway through which they have just entered.

When their host leaves the office clutching the file, Prisca turns to her daughter and says, with barely moving lips: 'I hope this is a real school o, not some family business. It's

a lot of money to spend.' She points with her lips. 'First
there is no gate, now we have one Udegbulam as proprietor
and another as English teacher. Is he qualified, or is it just
favouritism?'

Ozoemena does not mind. She observes herself acting as
if she has gained admission, and it terrifies and pleases her
in equal measure. If her mother expects it too, then she must
attend secondary school this year. She simply has to. Her
maths set is in her hands. She is prepared. When she moves
her fingers, their pads have left wet marks on the cardboard
sleeve.

Presently, BC returns with foolscap sheets in addition to
his file. 'Follow me,' he says.

'God's grace,' Prisca calls after her.

Ozoemena's knees creak when she walks, as if she has not
used them for ages. BC leads her across the pale peach sand,
towards the pink building where the Honda is parked.
Ozoemena notes that the sun has moved, and the driver's
side is no longer shielded. They mount the steps. BC's shoes
land with a dull clunk, like the sound a coconut makes after
it has been smashed, echoing towards the end of the veranda
a split second after his feet hit the concrete.

'These are our computer labs,' he says, lowering his voice.

Ozoemena nods, picturing somewhere pristine with light-
coloured walls like her father's surgery.

'Next door is physics and next to that, chemistry, then
sports. All students here do the core sciences from year one,
as well as economics, agric and introductory technology. Here
in Novus, we believe in starting young.' He sounds like a
prospectus. Ozoemena thinks to herself that he does not need
to sell her on anything, when she has been fully and thoroughly sold by the distance alone, which will take her away
from the twin terrors of Prisca and Mbu. Her very own world,
no hand-me-down friends or forced bonds with younger

siblings of Mbu's mates, and nobody to pull up her family's history as evidence of any perceived wrongdoing.

BC pushes the door to the chemistry lab and steps down from the veranda into the room. Ozoemena pauses after the first step to allow her eyes to adjust after the glare of outside, and follows, realising once she is indoors that they are not alone. BC appears temporarily nonplussed, stopping abruptly in the aisle.

'Oh, yes,' he says, checking his empty wrist. Ozoemena recalls him taking off the heavy leather wristwatch in the office and wiping his moist wrist with his handkerchief. Thinks of saying something. Changes her mind. 'Ah,' he says again, spinning around and staring above her head.

'That clock is not working,' says one of the girls, pausing in her scribbling. She checks her own watch. 'We have one hour, five minutes more, sir.'

'Very good, very good,' says BC. 'Nwokeke, you sit over there.' He motions. All through this, the second girl, who is yet to speak, watches, chewing on the lid of her Biro as if it is made of something delicious.

Ozoemena pulls out the lab stool as indicated by the teacher and hoists herself up, nervous about the equipment clamped on to the ends of the benches: the rubber hoses for the Bunsen burners; the beakers, test tubes and pipettes lined up in their wire mesh stands. She does not know the name for any of them, only that they are foreign and, therefore, important. BC places the foolscap sheet in front of her, and then the examination questions, pulled with reverence from the folder and placed downwards.

'There is to be no talking. These are exam conditions. We expect you to conduct yourself as befitting potential students at this school. No expo. No cooperation. The time is . . .' He tries to check his watch again, grunts when he encounters an expanse of hairy flesh.

'Twelve forty-five, sir,' says the same helpful girl again. She seems closer to Mbu's age than Ozoemena's, her skin is dark, and she has tight, blond-tipped sandy curls that Ozoemena wishes to somehow dust off.

'You have two and a half hours to answer questions in English, maths and general knowledge,' BC says to Ozoemena. 'You may begin.'

Ozoemena is only vaguely aware that he is somewhere in her periphery, observing them. She does not hear him when he leaves, mounting the steps almost comically on tiptoe and shutting the door to the lab softly. She tackles the English language questions first, breezing through them before she has registered each question. English has always been her favourite subject. Next comes general knowledge. Ozoemena pauses before each question as she has been coached by teachers. 'What is the tallest mountain in Africa?'

She writes: 'Kilimanjaro'.

'First woman to win a Nobel Prize?'

'Marie Curie'.

'For what?'

Ozoemena writes: 'Chemistry'. Thinks hard. Crosses it out and writes 'Physics' instead.

'Name of the UN Secretary General?'

'Boutros Boutros-Ghali'. Here, she pauses to thank her father for all his corny jokes, which helped to affix this name in her mind. Thinking about her father lowers her spirits and distracts her, and by the time she looks at her own – Mbu's old – Roman-numeral watch again, ten minutes have passed.

'What is the capital of Gongola State?'

It is a trick question. Ozoemena's smile is quick and sure. Trick questions are her way to show off her intelligence. Gongola State had faded out of existence the previous year, and her teachers made the entire school recite 'Thirty States and Capitals' every assembly after prayers to make sure they memorised the new states.

In a hand made shaky with excitement, she writes: 'Gongola State does not exist in the present Nigerian reality' – just to show that she knows how to use big phrases.

The maths questions bring her down to earth again. The first few are easy, but soon she is forced to stop and crack her knuckles. The numbers and letters buzz around her head like agitated flies. She notices the room, the double blackboard in front, the laboratory apparatus lining the walls on the side, arranged on one long, unbroken countertop. A huge periodic table provides colour and focus beside the blackboard. The walls have posters on them about things she cannot make out. In the gloom, the squares of window are overly bright, white. She scans her exam sheet again, attempts a few more questions, dragging her pen reluctantly from line to line.

'You were writing fast before. Why have you stopped?' The question is accompanied by a smell of boiled eggs. Ozoemena wrinkles her nose. The girl standing next to her is not the one with the watch. She has short, permed hair, slick with Pink Oil, combed back and flat over her scalp, and is wearing a huge chequered shirt over some jeans. She stabs a stubby fingernail down. 'That answer is wrong.'

Ozoemena covers her sheets and says, in what she hopes is Prisca's stern voice: 'You're not supposed to be standing up. Or talking.'

'That one is wrong, too,' says the girl, craning her neck. 'And that. Don't you know maths? I can help you.'

'No, thank you. I don't need your help.' Ozoemena casts an anxious glance at the door, nostrils flaring in fear and annoyance. This girl is going to get her in trouble. 'I have to finish.'

The girl shrugs, but makes no move to budge. 'I've finished,' she says. Behind them, a stool is dragged against the concrete floor. Ozoemena, with an arm still over her sheet, turns her head towards it. Will the watch girl report them? She wipes her top lip with the back of her hand, determined to say no more to the girl beside her. Keeping her shoulders still and straight, she ignores them both and starts writing again, formulae jumbling in her head, the confusion spilling out across the blank pages in blue ink.

'My name is Obiageli,' the girl in the chequered shirt says. 'I heard Teacher call you Nwokeke. Is that your father's name? What is your baptismal name?'

Ozoemena clears her throat. What she really wants is to tell the girl to get out of her face. To shut up! Sit down! Go away! Instead, she bends over her sheet until her nose grazes it.

'Well, Obiageli, you sef, your answers are wrong,' says a soft voice behind them, and Obiageli, incredulous, hurries over to the watch girl. They begin to argue, while Ozoemena's worry rises. Her shoulders shake and, when she can take it no more, she whips around.

'We are taking an *exam*!' she hisses. 'Do you want us to get in trouble?!' Ozoemena cannot believe how lackadaisical they are being. A stickler for rules, this rebellion astounds her, turns her world on its head. The watch girl approaches, looking at her wrist.

'You still have time,' she says.

'I haven't finished.' Ozoemena bites her words out.

'My name is Ifenkili Persyfone Ozondu, but you can call me Nkili,' she says, squinting at Ozoemena's barely legible scribbles. 'She is right; you got these wrong.'

'Have you ever heard such a masquerade name before?' asks Obiageli, flanking Ozoemena on the left again. 'A name that has phone inside it, and "Ifenkili", like you are only good for looking at.'

'It's because I am beautiful. See,' says Nkili, snatching Ozoemena's pen. 'Like this. You do the same thing to both sides, so . . .' Before Ozoemena can stop her, Nkili is writing fast, workings covering the paper. Ozoemena squints at the alien-looking things.

'I'm sure they didn't teach me this,' she says, exhaling in exasperation. Nkili says nothing. Her tongue wiggles in the corner of her mouth, peeking out as she writes. Her nose is high and straight, and each exhaled breath flutters the edges of Ozoemena's sheet.

'Wait . . . wait. No, no, no,' says Ozoemena, trying to snatch back her pen.

'Oya, check my own,' says Nkili, plonking her answer sheets down in front of Ozoemena. 'I'll finish this.'

'They'll know I didn't write it!' Ozoemena says. Her chest rises and falls. 'Stop.' But her eye catches the top of Nkili's sheet, scanning of its own volition. Of the twenty questions in English, Ozoemena notes that Nkili has got six right.

'Your English is wrong,' she says.

'Ngwa correct it now, I'm helping you,' Nkili replies without pausing.

'What about GK?' asks Obiageli. 'Do fast, let me see what she wrote. She was writing fast for that one as well.'

'I'll dictate for you,' Ozoemena says, resigned. Her heart still thumps, and of the three of them, she casts her eyes to the door the most.

'Let's all go back to our seats,' Nkili says, noticing her trembling.

'But how will I hear?' whines Obiageli.

'No, that's enough.' Ozoemena snatches back her sheet, covering it with her arm, and sighs. She corrects a few of the answers on Nkili's sheet and hands it back. Nkili scans it.

'Will that be enough to make me pass?' she asks.

Obiageli raises Ozoemena's arm off the paper, squints, mutters, 'It's true!' and writes something on her own sheet.

Ozoemena packs up her maths set and puts her things

together. She still has time, but her stomach roils when she
looks at her sheet. She has ruined her chances. She cannot
ask for extra sheets to redo her maths by herself without
explaining why she needs them, and she does not want to
implicate the two girls by revealing what has happened. Besides,
Nkili seemed sure as she wrote Ozoemena's paper. Does she
really want to risk her chances of going to boarding school
this year? Has she not, after all, answered all her English and
general knowledge questions by herself? She is still standing,
deliberating, when the door opens with a puff of air.

'Time's up . . . Nwokeke, you have finished too?' asks BC.

'Yes . . . yes, sir,' Ozoemena stutters, walking up the aisle
and handing over her sheet. Footsteps behind her as Obiageli
and Nkili do the same, then they are out on the pavement,
into the open air, while BC locks the lab behind them. In the
sunlight, the contrast between Nkili's dark complexion and
gold hair is stark and marks out her mixed heritage. She has
pale pink pearlescent polish on her fingernails and toenails,
and wears a pair of leggings sparkling with silver vines and
purple flowers underneath a short linen shift with a very high
neckline. Her watch is a Casio, one with a mini calculator.
Ozoemena knows calculators are not allowed during exams.
Did she use it? Her shoulders fall further.

Seeing her defeated gesture, Obiageli claps her about the
shoulders. 'Don't worry,' she says. 'My brothers are in this
school, and they say the exams don't really matter like that
if your parents have money. Your parents have money, shey?'

'This Obiageli girl!' Nkili says, and her tone has developed
a familiarity borne of their recent shared experience. 'Bite
your words before you speak them, ah-ah.'

Ozoemena brushes Obiageli's hand off.

'Unless you're a dundie, there's no way you can fail,'
Obiageli continues. She looks Ozoemena up and down. 'Better
not be a dundie after I copied from you.'

Despite being wrung out by emotion and guilt, or perhaps because of it, Ozoemena begins to laugh. 'My name is Ozoemena,' she says. 'And you're a very stupid girl.'

'You're the friend of a stupid girl,' Obiageli counters. 'So, what does that make you? Double-stupid.'

'Obiageli!' Nkili shouts again, but even she begins to snort. BC passes the girls on the pavement, doubled over. Ozoemena recovers herself first.

'Sir, when will we know if we've passed?' she asks, the cloud returning to her voice.

'In a few minutes,' he says. His jaws work in the pauses between his words. 'I'm going to get the papers to the right teachers to mark. They are waiting right now. I, of course, will do the English.'

They spend a little longer chatting on the pavement, but Ozoemena begins to grow more and more anxious. BC has returned to the classroom block. Prisca will be wondering where she is.

'Do you want to come to my car?' asks Nkili, smiling. She has a peculiar way of smiling, with the top lip dipping over the bottom one in the middle, her eye teeth showing instead. 'I have food and mineral and juice. The driver parked on the other side of school.' She points past the classroom block. They will have to walk in front of the office and her mother.

'Let's go,' Obiageli says.

Ozoemena shakes her head, no. 'My mum brought something,' she says, seeing the girls through her mother's eyes. They are too free. Prisca will say they have no home training. Ozoemena already feels protective of them, even though she does not know if they will meet again.

She is finishing up her sardine sandwiches when Prisca, sitting in the shaded passenger's side of the car, turns and says, 'He's calling us. Hurry up.' Ozoemena, in the backseat, slips the last bit into her mouth and chews fast, trying not let her cheeks bulge. The margarine in the filling has melted, and her face feels even greasier than before. She wipes it with her handkerchief, tripping over her own feet as she tries to keep up with Prisca. Her new friends are there, Obiageli with a bored-looking older boy who barely pays attention.

'You've all passed. Here are your lists of things to bring, textbooks, provisions, the important term dates and school fees information.' BC hands A4 typed sheets around to the adults and Nkili, who is by herself. She gives her new friends a thumbs-up. Ozoemena pretends not to see, peeking instead at the sheet in her mother's hand, illustrated with sketches of the school uniform and daywear. Her heart begins its triumphant thumping from where it had ceased moments before. The partly chewed sandwich makes an agonising descent down her throat and into her stomach.

'Congratulations. See you in September.'

On the drive home, Ozoemena begins to fall asleep, but not before she hears Prisca say, 'Yes, but why didn't the man say who came first out of the three of you?'

CHAPTER FIVE

Treasure: Then

The bag of ugili is in front of our door the next morning. Afraid is doing my whole body from my head down to my toes. My left eye is pulling by itself, and I pluck hairs from my eyelashes to stop it because is bad luck.

I remember the spirit eating raw intestines, and saliva fills my mouth. The way I ran from him, leaving the ugili fruits behind, leaving everything. I ran and ran o, until my chest wanted to break open and the air rushed into my mouth tasting bitter. It don' matter, he has found me anyway. I pick up the bag of fruits and throw it in the compound dustbin. I spend the day watching the children in our yard go to school and wishing me, I could as well. At night, I don' sleep well. Every sound wakes me. The mosquitos sing in my ears, and when I slap them, I shut myself deaf. Mummy talks in her sleep, but she don' wake up. Small time after Daddy died, she started sleeping for many many months. Sometimes it is long – one, two, three, four weeks – and sometimes short. Her sleep has lasted three days this time, and even when she is awake, she will be doing sleeping-mulu-anya, talking to people in the dream, because her eyes will be open, but she will not be there.

The noise my stomach makes keeps the rats away from where they chew chewing stick at the bottom of the door.

Come morning and there is a carton by our door. It's

closed, sealed with Sellotape. I can't smell any smell from the box. I don' touch it. I want to wake Mummy, but when it has not reached for her to wake up, is hard. Only Aunty Ojiugo used to manage it, and even that used to take all her power, but anyway, me I try because am feeling that whatever is happening is bigger than me, and I need my Mummy.

'Mummy. Mummy, wake up.'

She says Daddy's name and turns but don' open her eyes.

I hear Landlady talking. She sits in front of her house on a bench, shouting at everybody. Her voice is loud but also, inside her throat, the way that masquerades speak, as if something is stuffed there and air is shifting through to get outside. Under the bench, her dog Captain bites its tail and flies are disturbing his ears. It takes me immediately-immediately to notice that the carton is no longer by our backdoor. And too, Ifeanyi, Landlady's grandson, is walking away quickly. He has the box.

'Give me my thing!' I shout, running after him. Ifeanyi jumps the last few feet to Landlady and sits next to her on the bench, holding the box. Am breathing fast from chasing him. I don' even know why I am going for something that me I don' even want, except that Ifeanyi is a goat who takes what he wants all the time, and the rest of us in the compound are supposed to just close our mouths and let him misbehave anyhow.

I greet Landlady. She don' give me face. She shouts something across the compound to Omalicha, her daughter-in-law that she hates because anything Omalicha touches turns to money, but she cannot born children for Landlady's only son, Chuks. Ifeanyi unpacks the carton as I watch. One loaf of Goodwill Buttered Bread, a tin of Bournvita, Nice biscuits, evaporated milk, and a packet of St Louis sugar. The rest of the box holds mangos, ripe and unripe.

My life wants the carton box. I want it.

Ifeanyi selects one mango and bites, leaving uneven marks from his detty stinking teeth that are big and covered with something like cotton wool painted palm-oil colour. I squeeze my face. Landlady turns.

'Where is my money, Treasure?' Her voice is low and quiet, full of dangerous things. I don' like it.

'Landlady—'

'What? What nonsense story are you going to tell me now?'

'Landlady, please. My aunty is coming this Friday . . . No, the next one. She said she will bring money then.'

'This Friday, next Friday.' Landlady clears her throat and spits on the floor. Captain pounces on the something and licks it up. 'Why can't you follow your aunty to her own family, eh? Isn't she your blood? Go with her now, and free my house for me, let me rent to someone that doesn't waste my time. Your hands and legs are strong, you can run maid for someone.'

I stare at the ground, following a line of ants with my eyes as they are disappearing into a crack between the sand and the concrete pavement.

Landlady will never chase us from her house. She knows she will get her money, and too, she likes having us there because of the plenty gist that me and Mummy bring. People want to know. Are we not, after all, the family of 'That Man'? They come to the beer parlour that Omalicha operates in front of the compound and Landlady feeds them stories, all sorts of things, plenty lies. They gist and drink and eat. I don' go out at night. One time like this, it was my turn to throwaway the rubbish, and when I came back, all the men were looking at me and talking. One of them asked Landlady that all this market and she is not selling? pointing to my breasts. Now I sleep with the rubbish when it's my turn, and the rats play outside the door to our room until morning.

Ifeanyi's teeth scrape the mango seed loudly, kraa, like that. His mouth is bleeding juice and saliva in the corners.

I use my mind to say, 'Teeth like a hoe' to him.

Landlady looks at the things Ifeanyi brought out of the carton. 'No money, and yet your mother has boyfriends bringing her things. Or is it for you?' She eyes me up and down as if she wants to haggle for my price. 'Anyway, go. The box is now my own. Consider it payment for what you owe me,' says Landlady. 'And I am giving you till Monday, you hear me? Or una go sleep for bus stop. I no wan tori o.' Landlady switches from Igbo to Pidgin when she wants to show how serious she is.

Ifeanyi sucks the mango seed until it is white. He licks his fingers, picks up another mango and bites into the orange flesh, crunching the reddish-green back of it, hard. It makes a sound like biscuit-bone. The juice drips to his elbow. Landlady cleans his mouth with her wrapper and tucks it back in at her waist. Ifeanyi is my age mate, the son of Landlady's dead daughter. His grandmother treats him like an egg.

The sun is hot. Hunger makes it burn hotter. The water in our buta is low. I don' have strength to fetch more. Sometimes, the big men on High Court Road and Works Road who have boreholes, they allow the taps on the outside of their fences to run so that we can fetch without going to the stream. Am afraid to check. I wish it was rainy season so I can put bucket outside under the roof.

Am not bold of going to Eke Awka to see if I can get anything. What if I jam the spirit again? I don' want to see it, the thin face like something drawn by a child in baby school. How could I ever think it was a man before? Everyone knows that the market is full of humans, spirits, angels and other beings, buying and selling. Spirits are easy to find. They don' like people looking at their feet. Everybody knows of one person, a boy, a girl, who looked and got conked on the head by a spirit, only to get sick and die after. Is that why it followed me home, because I saw its legs? I am lucky, but I don' want to try my luck. No market today.

I sleep. In the afternoon, I soak garri and wake Mummy. She sleeps a lot. Three spoons and she is asleep again. I eat the rest. The garri is bottom-bag, full of sand, exploding innermost my ears when I chew. Sweat soaks my dress. The floor is cool, but the curtains are not closing well in the middle. I move away from the strip of sun. I sleep again.

My dreams are more real to me than when I am awake, but I know when me, am dreaming. Daddy is waiting for me at the gate to our old house, wearing his packet-shirt and the black trousers with lines that make noise when I scratch them. My daddy is handsome and the gold chain on his neck is twinkling kilikili stars. I run to him and he carries me up, turns me around as if I am not heavy at all-at all. When he puts me down, my cheeks are paining me because I am smiling too much. My eyes are full of sun and the breeze he made spinning me around is on my skin. I hold his left hand tight. His wedding ring is cold. I remember the taste of it when I was a baby. Tasting of salt and iron metal.

'You came late,' he says, but he is not angry. 'Food is getting cold.'

Food? In my other dreams, we used to sit and gist, no food. Saliva fills my mouth. Daddy laughs and hurries me inside.

The table is set for Sunday lunch. Mummy's precious Pyrex is out, the white ceramic with fruit and vegetables drawn on the side and a glass cover. There is white rice, puffy and swollen, blood-red stew with chicken drumsticks packed, no space for serving spoon sef.

'It's turkey,' says Daddy. 'We always have turkey on Christmas Day, you remember?'

I can't remember talking outside my head, but yes, is turkey drumsticks, not chicken. The neck of my dress is scratching. Is pink chiffon with sliver shine-shine that traders call 'sequence' plaited inside it. The underskirt of my dress is made stiff from net, so that when arranged, it spreads from the waist like wedding gown. My socks are knee-high with bow-ribbon and pearl button on the sides of their elastic tops. I turn around helicopter in my buckle white shoes that squeak. Daddy claps.

'My dazzling one,' he says. 'Shine-shine baby.'

I look like Anna in *Prince and I*. Me and Daddy used to watch it when I was small. It's my favourite film. All those big-big dresses turning, turning.

'Ngwa, sit, sit,' Daddy says. He starts dishing food. 'Eat, eat. The food will get lose heat.' He piles rice on my white plate, puts two large laps of turkey, stew, and reaches for the giant salad bowl. The salad is definitely Christmas salad. Lettuce, onions and tomatoes, sweetcorn, cucumbers, baked beans and sardines. I reach over to the serving dish of fried plantain and pick up one slice.

'Wait! Is Mummy not joining? And where is Mercy?'

'Your Mummy has a headache,' Daddy says. 'She will soon come. Do you want chicken curry?'

I dinor noticed the other serving bowl, but now it comes to me as if I called it, light yellow and oily, swimming with vegetables and potatoes, the way Mummy makes it. The only thing she makes. My stomach grumbles, begging me to eat, but I leave it alone and don' put my mind in it.

'You're not my daddy,' I say.

'What kind of talk is that, Dazzling?' Daddy is talking to me and looking at me, but his hands, the one holding the plate and the other dishing the food, work as if he is not controlling them. 'You look thirsty, let me make some Tree Top for you. Sit down, sit down. Mercy will be angry if you waste all this food.' The bottle of Tree Top pours itself into a jug and the water follows, the orange drink getting lighter until it is just the right colour.

'You can stop pretending now.'

Daddy laughs. 'You are a very stubborn girl, you this Treasure. I'm very proud of you, but aren't you tired? Don't you want Daddy to look after you?'

'You are not my daddy!' Am not even raising my voice, but the whole room shakes, as if we are inside a carton that someone is carrying.

'Please, don't shout, my love. Your mummy has headache. Be considerate.'

'He doesn't talk like that. He won't say "your mummy". He calls her "Mummy" too.'

The Daddy-pretender stops. He rearranges his face and picks up the glass of Tree Top he poured me.

'All this just for you and you don't want. No wonder you are in the market begging for ten-ten naira.' He drinks. The juice is now some funny colour that is not like a thing people drink.

I open my mouth and scream. My dress tears off my body. The table is heavy with too much food. It bends on the ends. It breaks. Everything is in the air, the plantain, salad, the minerals and Tree Top. The stew stains the ceiling red like blood. The rice falls to the floor. Many grains are on my skin and hair, tickling. They are maggots. I scream again, brushing them off. Some of them burst, leaving their mess on my arms. The fake-Daddy throws more rice in the air. It crawls everywhere it touches.

My nose is pressing inside the hard concrete when I wake up. The saliva in my mouth is too sticky, sour, like old okro soup warmed on the fire many times. I listen for noise in the compound. The light under the door is not that bright. Evening, maybe. I allowed sleep to carry me too long. The room is hot, stuffy from two people sleeping inside it. My lower lip is cut. I am tired.

I am tired.

CHAPTER SIX

Ozoemena: Now

The clippers nip the nape of her neck and Ozoemena winces but does not move. She is used to painful hairdressing; hair pulled too tightly into plaits and wraps, sprouting a crop of blisters as soon as one stands up from the plaiting stool. She has heard of children being beaten with the fisted handles of afro combs by hairdressers to keep them sitting quietly, but that has never happened to her, luckily. Sometimes they are bribed with treats, but Prisca would never allow such pampering.

Nevertheless, she keeps still as the barber staunches the blood from the cut with some toilet roll, muttering, 'Sorry, sorry. Your skin is too soft,' as if it is her fault. His creased brow in the mirror shows how worried he is about Prisca finding the cut. Ozoemena wants to tell him not to worry. She will not tell.

The last of her hair comes off, gracing her shoulders and carpeting the floor of the barbershop thickly. Ozoemena shudders in delight, gooseflesh breaking out over her skin at the sudden coolness on her head. This, the last vestige of her childhood, is gone, marking her as a serious secondary school student. She wants to stroke her head with its three inches of hair left.

'It's fine, abi?' asks Brother Ali, the barber. 'I will make it style, carve it here like this,' he says, gesticulating a complex pattern over her scalp, probably to make up for the injury.

'No, Uncle, my mummy will not like it. I'm going to secondary.'

'Really? Where?'

'It's boarding. In Imo State.'

'Federal in Imo State? Wonderful,' says Brother Ali, brandishing the clippers like a wand. Ozoemena does not correct him. Smart girls and boys end up in federal government colleges, and he has assumed that Ozoemena has as well. He makes a few more passes at her head, stops and surveys his handiwork with some regret. 'Let me just carve the back small,' he says.

'Okay, but don't give me "Punk" o,' she says, forgetting in her anxiety that a 'Punk' requires more hair than she currently possesses. Ozoemena, having tried her best to dissuade his artistic proclivities, shrugs and lets him get on with it. Brother Ali brushes some of the hair off her neck and begins to work. He keeps turning her head, his thumb painful against the tender point under her earlobe. It is almost as though he forgets she is a person, not one of his practice dummies.

Brother Ali's shop is on the main road, next to the popular supermarket, Jordinco, and, a few metres away, its rival, Thompson's. It is this same lengthy Achalla road that has the ancient Eke Awka market at one end and the modern banks at the other, each keeping the other alive, loans and profit flowing in and out in a loop. Foot traffic is heavy, and through the dulled, spotty mirror on one wall, Ozoemena watches the constant procession of laden orange lorries, pick-up trucks, and the state-registered buses and taxis, yellow with double black stripes running vertically from bonnets to boots, a hive of exotic bees. The barrows jostle with pedestrians for what little space there is on the concrete kerb, which also doubles as cover for the gutters. Some of the slabs have been hoisted to the side by the Saturday sanitation crew, the algae within drying to a crusty green-brown smudge. In the rainy season, these gutters and their missing covers are often treacherous, filled with rubbish, stagnant and stinking, teeming with microscopic activity and bubbles popping intermittently on a slimy surface. Occasionally during floods, they are able to suck down unsuspecting passers-by, who mistake the surface for wholly even, cradling them in muck and laying them down at the bottom of the river.

'I've finished,' says Brother Ali. Ozoemena looks up and is confronted by an image of her father looking back at her. Brother Ali, smiling, picks up a hand mirror to show her the back of her head. 'It's good, isn't it?'

Ozoemena makes a sound in her throat, suddenly wanting to cry. Brother Ali has given her a daddy's cut, *her* father's style. 'You gave me Punk,' Ozoemena says, suddenly upset. She turns her head, watching all angles between both mirrors. It is a masculine cut that does nothing for her head or face.

'It's not Punk,' says Brother Ali, patting her head. 'You look studious.' He pats her head, every coil in place.

Ozoemena's lips feel hot. They tremble, and she knows she is in danger of sobbing. She jumps off the chair, ripping at the cape around her neck, the towel underneath.

'Easy! Easy!' shouts Brother Ali. He furrows his brow and his nostrils flare, shiny and bulbous. 'Don't manhandle my property.' With obsequious care, he takes off the garments, shakes them gently and brushes Ozoemena down.

'Thank you.' Ozoemena forces the words out, lowering her eyes so that he cannot see the lie. She is not thankful for this atrocity perpetuated against her person. Prisca is supposed to pick her up, but she cannot abide the shop anymore with its penned-in state, the broken-waisted chairs and the padded bench by the window covered in needles of hair, the illustrations of men on the walls, glistening afros of various heights, side parts, moustaches. The shop is a museum to the eighties, and she feels an artefact with her daddy-cut.

'When Nwanyi Chemist comes, please can you tell her I have walked home?' she asks, using her mother's nickname. Brother Ali nods his agreement, whistling and slapping a rag around the chairs haphazardly. Ozoemena senses his relief – it will be easier to get paid with the liberties he has taken if Ozoemena's hair is away from Prisca's sight.

Ozoemena steps out into the warmth, glad to be leaving. A breeze blows about her newly exposed neck, but she cannot enjoy it for self-consciousness. She imagines that people stare at her, at her prominent forehead, at how large her lips appear. As a much younger child, she had been inordinately pleased with the dark blotch of hairs on her top lip, because her father had worn a moustache and she had wanted to *be* him, but now, now . . .

Now what?

The urge to weep does not dissipate, and when a woman snaps at her for dragging her feet and raising dust, the stone in her throat grows even larger. She waits until she has passed the woman before she drags her feet again, but stops after the dust begins to coat them.

At Ogbugba Nkwa, the square, she turns right into Amikwo Village, and her prevalent curiosity dampens her self-pity. The village is a popular habitation for northerners, the Hausa and the Fulani. For Ozoemena, it is like stepping into another world. The radios blare Hindu music and Hausa news. The Mallams sit in front of their houses and shops – often combined – talking loudly to each other, laughing, and jesting, drinking fura da nono, and eating kola nuts. To her left is a madrassa, from which chanting can be heard. It is dark and cool, although some of the ends of the students' mats extend past the awning into the road and the sun. The students write on slates, and Ozoemena wishes, not for the first time, that she was fluent in Hausa and could communicate. The only northern influence that has made it into their household is that every other Saturday, their breakfasts of akara and akamu become bread and dawa.

A gaggle of Fulani girls pass her with otangele around their eyes and colourful beads in their thick hair and around their necks, limbs, waists. To Ozoemena, they are very like the prevalent film posters glued to walls in Amikwo Village, of much-admired cow-eyed beauties with fluttering eyelashes and flittering veils, the ubiquitous red dot in the middle of their foreheads and stacks of gold bangles on each arm. She stares at them, envious of their ease, their camaraderie. The girls giggle together, balancing trays and baskets on their heads without holding on to them. Ozoemena feels regret at the loss of her hair, despite her earlier celebration. With her head down, she takes bigger strides, her slippers slapping against the soles of her feet. It is the same route home she has taken from her primary school for the last year, and her legs follow the twists and turns through the village without her being aware of it. Here is the shop where she bought Go-Go and ButterMint sweets, using the money she had been given to take taxis at the end of her extramural lessons and trekking home instead. Opposite, a dressmaker's shop, where apprentices learn how to sew on empty cement sacks before they graduate to the customers' expensive cloths. Out of habit, she hurries past the shed where the mother of one of her teachers runs a brisk business grinding people's beans for mai-mai and peeled cassava tubers into pulp to be roasted into garri. She takes a sly peek at the storey building next to it, where her teacher, Madam Ozioma, can often be seen lounging and marking maths papers on the balcony. Ozoemena likes Madam Ozioma, everybody does, but she avoids calling out in greeting as most students do. She does not want to answer any questions about which school she 'passed into'. Her recent cheating continues to sit uneasily on her conscience.

Ozoemena looks left, right, and left again, before dashing across the crossroads into a dirt path that will lead her home. No more glossy film posters; instead, the exterior walls of people's homes are back to the dull harshness of ripped and glued-over election posters, a trailing smear of brown where children have wiped their behinds. She quickens her footsteps.

A nun sits on a tree stump by the side of the road, fanning herself forlornly with a bare palm.

'Good afternoon,' says Ozoemena. At the greeting, the woman's bleary-eyed look sharpens. She stands and sniffs the air with a bony nose. Ozoemena hurries along, wondering what she has done to offend her.

'Little girl,' says the nun. Her Igbo is stilted, stresses placed on all the wrong syllables. Her voice crackles.

'Yes, sister?' Ozoemena answers. She wonders to herself if this could be one of her mother's acquaintances; thinks how odd it is to see a lone sister burning red by the side of the road when nuns often travel in packs and by air-conditioned vehicles. This woman is the colour of a Julius Berger contractor. Her skin is tough and pitted like an old cocoyam.

The nun draws closer. Ozoemena looks into eyes coloured the sea-green found in picture books, set deeply in a peeling face. The nun stares back, those eyes devouring Ozoemena.

'I see you.' The nun is beatific. She stretches out a hand towards Ozoemena, and the latter, associating the gesture with the Sign of Peace, holds out her own palm. The nun grips her wrist, tight, pulls her close so that Ozoemena can smell the woodsy odour of her breath.

'I want to go home,' she says. 'Show me the way. Where is it?'

The pain travels up Ozoemena's arm and into her elbow, spreading in a sensation of ice as if she has just banged it. She freezes, a numbness that ripples outwards like a drop of ink in a bowl of water, tainting Ozoemena from within. She watches the old nun shake her until her teeth clash in her head, and yet she does not move; she cannot.

'Tell me!' says the nun. 'You see me. I know you are one of them.'

The hand clamped about her arm tightens, crushing bone, and Ozoemena thaws, searing pain and nausea hitting her in the stomach. She writhes, and the skin of her arm twists like a wrung-out towel.

'Don't fight me,' says the woman in her stilted tone. 'I am tired, I want to go home.' There is a red dot in her veil. Ozoemena thinks, *Strange, a sister with a bindi*, but simultaneously, she sees it for what it is: a ragged hole, sinking deep into the nun's head.

Ozoemena kicks out. Her leg connects with voluminous folds of cloth and then, nothing. She jumps, makes a grab for the woman, for those fierce eyes sitting in the unnaturally brown face. Instinctively, she jabs at the hole in the veil. The nun rears back, releasing her grip, and Ozoemena whirls and takes off, faster than her chubby body is used to moving.

'Wait!' cries the woman as Ozoemena flees. 'Little girl, wait! Show me the way. I want to go home!'

Ozoemena looks back as she runs. The woman is rooted to the spot, arms outstretched. She does not give chase.

Her legs are water when she gets home. Ozoemena climbs the stairs, hanging on to the metal bannisters and dripping sweat all the way up to her room. The nun has left marks on her wrists that swell to blistering. They smart with the intensity of Nsukka peppers. Prisca is almost on her heels.

'Did I not ask you to wait at the barber's for me? Who asked you to leave? In this climate of danger everywhere . . .' Prisca breaks off, noticing her daughter's bleary eyes, tinged with the beginnings of a fever.

'Something was chasing me . . .' Ozoemena begins, panting. She stops as Prisca's face furrows. There will be no revelations of ghosts, of possible dead people sitting by the roadside, grabbing at her. Encounters with ghosts are commonplace enough; everyone knows someone who knows someone who once saw or spoke with or was visited or pursued by a ghost, but Prisca cannot abide such talk. Instead, Ozoemena tells her mother that she was chased by a mad dog and fell into a bush.

Drawing a breath, Prisca continues. 'Serves you right for being stupid. Setting off without telling anybody where you were going.'

Ozoemena does not dare correct her or defend herself. Mentioning that she had informed the barber would further irritate her mother.

'Don't you see children your age going missing in the news?'

Ozoemena swoons. Panicked questions flash on her mother's face; Ozoemena already knows what she is being assessed for. Malaria? Typhoid? A poisonous plant from when she fell in the bush? What was this bush and where exactly was it? Ozoemena reads her mother's face until the latter shuts off all expression, keeping her thoughts within. Further scolding will have to wait. Ozoemena does not know if her mother believes her explanation.

Prisca confines Ozoemena to her bed, treats her, spoon-feeding her medicines. Prisca's favourite is a large coral tablet that she crushes between two spoons before mixing the powder with droplets of water. Ozoemena's special vitamin. She suffers in silence, not speaking, her eyeballs burbling like boiling eggs in their sockets. She hears things. Sometimes, they sound like snippets of conversation from Mbu and her mother or babbling from her baby sister, Baby. They slip into her fever-riddled dreams, swirling and taking on a form of their own.

The voices do not disappear after she gets better, not

entirely. Sometimes Ozoemena swears somebody is whispering to her, and if she only focuses, she will be able to hear. She develops a strange stillness when nobody is watching, listening for the whispers and trying to decipher them. She becomes frightened of what she will hear and tries to tune them out, singing loudly in her head. Mostly, she succeeds. Encouraged, Ozoemena begins to sing aloud, frequently jumping from verse to verse of various popular tunes to keep her mind working, to stop herself from relaxing into the whispers, from listening out for them.

'Shut up,' Mbu yells, unmoved by Ozoemena's status as recuperating patient. 'Why can't you just stick to one song and finish it? You are annoying.'

It is three weeks before Ozoemena is well enough to make the journey to her new school; three weeks during which school has started without her. Her uniform is adjusted to account for some of the weight she has lost. Her hair has grown. Prisca sends her off to Brother Ali again.

'And none of that funky haircut nonsense again, you're too young for that,' she says.

Ozoemena takes the long way, sticking to the main roads where the cars honk and the boys hoot, where handmade carts drag flexible construction rods on newly repaired roads to building sites, their discordant music setting her teeth on edge. She strides briskly, keeping her eyes open but averted, avoiding looking anyone in the face.

She feels exposed. There will be no stopping to greet anyone this day, nun or no nun.

CHAPTER SEVEN

Treasure

At night when the spirit comes, I wake up. Simple and short. Is like somebody tapped my leg. I crawl on the floor to the back door of our one-room and open it. The moon's stomach is not yet full but is enough to see inside the night.

'What are you finding?' I ask. Fear is trying to catch me, but if me I allow it, I will be stuck inside trouble.

He is no longer pretending to be a human being. I can see the space between the ground and his shoes. He don' have shadow. He takes his cap off to scratch. His hand looks like one giant spider like this, sitting on his head.

'What do I want?' He puts the cap back on his head. Is black like Nnamdi Azikiwe's own, but designed with gold coils that shine. It's the same cap he wore the last time me and him talked. That's how I know it's not silver like is looking now.

'I brought you a gift,' he says. 'I was going to give you before, but you ran away. What was chasing you?'

I want the something he's holding. It smells like ọkpa wawa, steamed with pepper and spices. The saliva in my mouth is pouring spring water down my throat.

'Thank you. I don' want.'

He sighs. The breeze is cold and dry from his mouth. Deep freezer air. It smells of stockfish and sawdust. Can spirits breathe? The man unties the knot of the ọkpa, holding it by the end of the bag. It dangles in the air and spins open. He caresses it.

'Warm as a mother's breast,' he says, and takes a bite.

I don' like how he says this. I want to spit. The whole place is smelling delicious. I can't bear it anymore.

The spirit blows as he chews, pushing the smell towards me. He swallows. 'You called me. I came. The question is, what do you want from me?'

'Me? I dinor call you.'

'Yes, you did.'

'When?'

'When you were sitting on the floor cursing those boys that stole your money. You wanted them to pay, didn't you? You've forgotten all the things you said?' He bites more of the okpa until what is remaining resembles a shadow smile in his hand. 'It doesn't matter. You called me and I am here, and now, we bargain.'

'Hia! Bargain, kwa?' I think for a moment. 'If I really called you, then where is my money?'

His face is dark from the moon, and I can't see his eyes, but his body becomes straighter. 'You want your money back? Is that what you want?'

I don' trust him. Yes, I want my money back, but the way he is behaving makes me suspect something. I don' answer him. He don' eat the remaining okpa in his hand and the smell of it is twisting up my inside.

'Before I answer, I want another okpa. A big one . . .' The thing is in the air between us before I've finished talking. Looking back into our room, the bed is dark. Mummy breathes softly on it, shallow and fast, as if she's running in her dreams. Everything she has taught me is at the back of my mind: Don' talk to strangers. Don' eat food in your dreams. Don' collect things from people's hands.

I take the okpa. It's hot, the waterproof bag sticks to my

palm. I tear it with my teeth and the okpa sticks to the soft parts of my mouth and burns them. My tongue is on fire. Palm oil is all over my face. I suck my lips, pulling all of the sweetness into my mouth; even the bag follows.

'You want more?' the spirit asks. He comes down slowly, a leaf on the wind, until his feet almost touch the floor. His moustache moves. He is smiling.

I don' answer him. I am thinking what I will do to pay for the okpa. It was sweet, but—

'You can't be coming to my dreams anymore,' I say.

'You pulled me in. Such a sweet dream. Do you miss him? Your daddy?'

I don' give him ear with this question as well. My mind is telling me that I should not have got up from where I was sleeping, but I had to. I don' know why. Like he is pushing me button and I must be answering him.

'By the way, you haven't thanked me for my other gift. Did you not like it?'

The carton with the bread and things and things.

I should just say, 'Thank you.' Instead, I say, 'Ifeanyi took it.'

The moustache falls. 'And who is this Ifeanyi?'

I tell myself to shut up. 'Ifeanyi is Landlady's grandson.'

'Eh-ee. Taking something that I called your name over? Anyway, leave him to me.'

'He is mannerless,' I say.

'I can get you another box. Anything you want, I can give you. I just have one small request. Very small. It's not a big thing at all.'

My stomach is bubbling as if I have eaten spoiled egusi soup. The okpa wants to come out, but I know that one is what Daddy calls 'forgone conclusion'. I have eaten the spirit's food and now I must kuku obey him. Sebi that's how it works in all the stories?

'I want to live again. My first life was . . . taken. You will
help me. You will be my wife.'

'Your wife? Who is your wife?' Fear drums in my chest.
'Please, I can't be your wife. I am a small girl.'

The spirit is silent. His body moves dancing-dancing like
fire. If he was breathing before, he has stopped now. He's
waiting for me to do something that me I don' know. A spirit
wife? God forbid bad thing. I can't be anybody's wife.
Husbands that walkabout chasing woman, that leave their
wives and children to suffer. Every time you see them
answering Papa-this and Papa-that, but they will stay in
Omalicha's beer parlour until morning. Talkless of longathroat
men like my uncles? No way spirit husbands can be better.
Only my daddy was a correct man, and he went and died.

After much, he laughs. 'If you know you're a child, are you
still a child? Hmm. Okay, you don't want to marry me? You
don't want me to look after you, to give you all the things
that you lost? No problem.'

'Wait!' I know he is about to leave even before he moves.
His head bends to one side. I still can't see his eyes. 'Are you
going to bother me?'

'Bother you? No o. I'm going. There are many other girls,
but you called me, and I answered. Now you say you don't
want me again? It's okay. You said I should go, so I will.
Consider my okpa a gift. I will bring you many more things
if you let me. Shoes for your feet. Cream to keep your skin
shiny. New clothes. Food. All you need to do is agree to be
my wife. Simple. I can give you the world—'

Am thinking: *If you can give me all these things, why do you
resemble a starving lizard? Why can you not give yourself life?*

'Can you bring someone back that has died?' I ask.

The spirit pauses and the way he is moving tells me that
he is happy. 'Your daddy? It will take a bit of work. Only
mature spirits like me can come and go to the market with

what resembles our bodies. I will find your daddy and teach him this, even though it is not yet his time. I will prove it to you.'

His body moves like fire again. My hands are cold, colder than how my room used to be when I had AC. They are aching me.

'Teaching this skill takes a while, but I will find him and bring message to you. Then you will marry me, and you will help me. Yes.'

Inside me I am thinking, *Is that how people in your place use to marry?* I want to see Daddy. I want him to come back and use his power to work miracle, beat my uncles, wake up Mummy to be happy again, everything. But fear is catching me, because the spirit can come into my life when I am sleeping and when I am awake.

'No, I don' want,' I say.

The spirit is rubbing his face, rubbing, rubbing. He says, 'Okay, what if I bring you those boys who stole your money, mm? Will you agree for me then?'

My belly starts to sweat. I am thinking what I will use that money to buy. I am thinking that I will throw the boys stone, make blood to come out of them somehow because they used kindness to deceive me. Do me, I do you.

I tell the spirit, 'Bring them first and we will see,' making mouth like I am not afraid true-true when I am. It's like when I want to relax, my mind will tell me again, 'You and a spirit are gisting in the night.' My heart is knocking kpum-kpum-kpum in my neck.

I close the door. Ice blocks are under my cheek. When I turn, Mummy is sitting up on the bed, a dark patch in the grey light of the moon.

'Treasure?' She croaks like a frog. 'You and who are talking there?' She don' wait for me to answer her. 'Come and lie next to me,' she says. 'The cold is feeling me.'

CHAPTER EIGHT

Ozoemena: Now

'Ozoemena Nwokeke!'

The use of her full name gives her pause. Ozoemena has barely enough time to react before Nkili flings herself into her. The girl is taller than she is, and it is a hard embrace filled with ribs and collarbones, and knees in the wrong places, but Ozoemena feels the warmth behind it, and it pleases her. She begins to grimace out of habit – they are not a family that deals well with physical affection – before she catches sight of Mbu scornfully watching this display from the front passenger seat and returns her new friend's hug. Prisca has stopped the car in front of the tuck shop, and, with a bent head, checks off items against a printed page in her lap, its corners flapping in the air stream coming from the AC. Ozoemena knows it for a time-buying tactic. Prisca will not address the girls until she is ready.

Obiageli, following Nkili at a more leisurely pace, punches her in the arm. Ozoemena punches back. Her cheeks hurt from keeping back the smiles. It feels amazing fitting in, happiness like supping on bubbles.

'Where have you been? We thought you were not coming again,' Nkili says. She talks with her lips, the way Prisca tries to get her girls to and fails. This is why Ozoemena notices.

'Your daywear is not correct,' Obiageli adds.

'I was sick,' says Ozoemena.

'Thank God. You are lucky you came on a beans and plantains night,' says Nkili. Ozoemena's mouth waters. Beans with fried plantains is one of her favourite dishes.

'Don't eat it, sha. You will purge. Maybe wait till your home stomach disappears.' Obiageli addresses her statement to include Mbu, who has chosen that moment to exit the car, slamming the door as hard as she can. Prisca cuts an exasperated eye and taps on her horn once in warning, before turning off the engine. Mbu, leaning insouciantly against their mother's car, feigns disinterest at Obiageli's generosity. 'There are all kinds of things in the beans: weevils, maggots. Sometimes stones.'

Ozoemena makes a face. Her mouth waters for an entirely different reason, imagining grains of sand stuck in the cusps of her molars.

'Don't give Obiageli any of your provisions o.' Nkili wags a finger in warning. 'Can you imagine? We have barely started, and she's nearly finished all her stuff.'

Obiageli shrugs. 'Food is for eating. It's not as if I stuck it up my bum-bum.' They giggle, Ozoemena covering her mouth.

Prisca exits the car and walks towards the tuck shop and Ozoemena wonders if she should follow her mother's determined exploration of the school grounds. Normally, she would go with her mother and await further instruction, but now Ozoemena hesitates, torn between her duties as a daughter and showing responsibility for her new possessions. Ozoemena does not trust that Mbu would stop anyone wanting to make off with her things.

Nkili pokes Obiageli playfully. 'And too, she is lazy. When it is her turn to fetch for our school mumsie, she dodges and leaves it to me to be fetching.'

Obiageli shows her palms. 'Yes, now. You like doing it, why should I follow?'

'Because it will make it fast, lazy baboon,' Nkili chides.

'Ozoemena, sebi you will be our school sister? That way we can all stay in our school mother's corner, and nobody will send us on errands.'

'Our school mumsie is the deputy senior prefect, Senior Ijeoma. She doesn't have wahala,' Obiageli agrees.

'At all!'

Watching them is like watching a game of ping-pong. Ozoemena's neck moves from girl to girl, but her eyes do not tire. She feels extremely lucky to have a ready-made clique. The trip down to school had gone faster than the previous time, perhaps due to Mbu's presence or their mother's more informed navigation. Maybe a combination of both. Yet, Ozoemena could not relax in the car. She worried all through about being so late to start, the notes and classes she must have missed, the stories and games, the friendship circles that would have formed without her. It is bad enough that she is being forced to use Mbu's gear, abandoned after her one-and-a-half-year stint in a famous all-girls' boarding school. Her sister passed her time there in a rash of suspensions before Prisca decided that the boarding school experience was not for her first daughter and enrolled her in a day institution nearer home.

'Let's get people to help us carry your things!' Nkili cries.

Obiageli jiggles the boot handle and Mbu glares at her without speaking. She need not have bothered. The boot is locked.

Prisca motions to Ozoemena. She has been joined in front of the tuck shop by a tall, commanding senior girl.

'That's Senior Nwakaego,' Obiageli whispers. 'She is the senior prefect.'

Ozoemena approaches timidly, trailed by her new friends. She greets the senior girl, 'Good afternoon, Aunty,' and behind her, Obiageli – who else? – sniggers.

'You say "Senior",' the prefect corrects.

Ozoemena mumbles her apologies. Prisca formally hands her over to the senior prefect. As is her way, she offers the senior prefect gifts – a loaf of bread, a bottle of roasted groundnuts and two boxes of Lucozade ready-to-drink – which the girl rejects, only to accept after a little persuasion. Prisca nods, satisfied. The senior prefect has been brought up well. Too quick to accept and she is a greedy longathroat with no home training who will come to no good. Reject the gifts outright and she is stuck up and will come to no good. The senior prefect is flawless and worthy of further attention.

'Nwakaego, what is your father's name, dear?' asks Prisca.

Ozoemena listens to her mother's probing. This too is normal. What village are you from? Who are your parents? What do they do? Questions designed to unearth a connection, one that she can exploit. Prisca tries to get Senior Nwakaego to take a particular interest in Ozoemena, perhaps a school daughter? But Nwakaego has a whole school to care for, and the most she does for Ozoemena is to assign her a room in which she also lives. This is how Ozoemena becomes the new girl in hostel four.

Senior Nwakaego reiterates what they already know. Novus is not a 'mixed school'. There are two separate colleges under its umbrella: Vincent for boys and Dorothea for girls, named for the proprietor and his wife. Senior Nwakaego touches the crest patch sewn into the fabric over Ozoemena's left breast, pointing out the Gothic 'D' in the middle. There is to be no consorting between girls and boys, apart from chapel – and even then, contact is kept to a minimum. The only other times they will be together under one roof would be for labs (mostly mixed for seniors taking exams) and school events like Christmas shows.

'What about PE?' asks Ozoemena. She is not a great athlete, not even a good one, a fact that would be made worse were

boys to witness it. She is growing self-conscious around boys
and wants nothing to do with them.

'It depends. But we have a large field. Four teams can play
on it, and they wouldn't even meet each other.' Senior Nwakaego
is delighted to state this, as if the school belongs to her.

Prisca nudges Ozoemena and makes a face as if she is
impressed, which is the reaction that Senior Nwakaego had
been hoping to elicit with that statement. Prisca does not, in
fact, care for such things as large playing fields. Ozoemena
knows her mother would rather there was minimal play
between school and church activities. Ozoemena wants to tell
her mother to stop acting, but that is Mbu's role, not hers.

'Last but not least.' Senior Nwakaego brings her palms
together in a clap. 'You never, ever cross the school gate
without permission. And never by yourself.'

A cloud passes over the sun and Ozoemena shivers, involuntarily searching the skies.

Prisca snorts. 'Where does this one even know she is going?'
she asks, gesturing towards Ozoemena with her chin.

Senior Nwakaego brightens, showing her eyeteeth in a
smile. 'Exactly. There is nothing out there. Things are more
interesting within school than outside.'

The boot is finally cracked open and, under Senior
Nwakaego's orders, a flock of junior girls carry Ozoemena's
things to her new abode. She joins them, lugging her suitcase
in solidarity.

Back at the car, Prisca hands Ozoemena a plastic wallet
from her pharmacy, containing a handful of small white pills.

'Daraprim. Sunday-Sunday medicine. Make sure you take
this every week, so you don't have malaria.'

'Yes, Mum.'

'And these,' she hands over another plastic wallet. 'Your
vitamins. One every day. The minerals in it will keep your
brain peaceful. You'll sleep better.'

'Yes, Mum.' Ozoemena has no intention of doing this. They are the same coral pills that Prisca crushed, oblong and hard to swallow.

'Pray your rosary.'

'Yes, Mum.' She will not be doing this either.

'Study hard.'

'Yes, Mum.'

Prisca lowers her voice. 'And no more talking nonsense about . . .' And here, she falters. '*Those* sorts of things – do you hear me? Nobody knows you here, this is a fresh start. There is madness in your father's family. If he had told me all this before, I would not have married him.'

Ozoemena cringes inwardly. Her index finger works the cuticle of her thumb loose. Her mother says that a lot these days. Ozoemena is aware of the criteria for marriage in Igbo culture: no kleptomaniacs or thieves, no poisoners, no people who have borne false witness to steal land, no murderers and definitely no madness. Every Igbo girl knows this, just as they know they exist only as an extension of their families. Ozoemena hears the implied question: '*Don't you want you or your sister to get married?*'. Marriage hangs over every girl's head. Bad genes can rot whole branches of family trees. She does not need to be told to keep schtum.

'Yes, Mum,' she says, looking around. Mbu, in her cropped top and baggy trousers, is attracting attention from the boys. They ogle her as they meander from hostel to class and back, talking loudly as if to woo her with the bass in their voices. She is a statue. Flies would get more attention from her.

The compound is busier than it was when Ozoemena came to take exams. Outside the tuck shop, some students stand in a haphazard line, partly buying snacks and partly staring at the newcomer. Her mother had timed their arrival for the end of the school day, after lunch and towards the end of siesta. Windows extend all along the side of the hostel building, wooden shutters open to let in a breeze behind a grid of thin anti-burglary bars. A few heads look out, curious, faces pixelated by the small squares. Ozoemena pretends not to see them. She will be in the hostel soon enough, and they can get their fill of her then.

To the right is the boys' hostel, similar to the girls', and separated only by a wire fence. The hostel areas are the only place where there is a physical demarcation, but even this does not extend past the rear of the building. It makes no sense. Behind her and to the left are the labs where she took her exams, while the classrooms are to the right, with a wide, green patch of grass lying between the boys' and the girls' sides. Nevertheless, when the bell for prep rings, the students file out, heading for the classrooms, neither looking over at the other. It is as if the chicken wire fence is made of impermeable material.

'My daywear is wrong,' Ozoemena tells her mother. There are buttons running down the front of her blouse where the other girls have none. Three buttons have turned Ozoemena's purple chequered blouse into a shirt.

Prisca smiles at the girls who greet her and turns back to Ozoemena. 'Nothing I can do now. You'll just have to wear it like that. At least nobody will steal your clothes.'

'Some girls have long hair here,' she says, mimicking her mother's chin motion. It is only an observation, and she does not know why she says it aloud.

'Those are half-caste girls,' says Prisca dismissively.

'Not all of them.'

'Are you coming here to study or to do your hair?' asks Prisca, in the kind of voice that tells Ozoemena how close she is to being cracked on the head. Mbu struts around the car, opens her door and folds herself into the passenger's seat.

Prisca sighs. She looks at her watch and adjusts the strap of her bag, which is slipping off one shoulder. 'Remember, one of the drivers will bring your provisions locker with the van. And the poles for your mosquito net. Either tomorrow or next.'

'Yes, Mum.'

'Until then, just manage.'

'Yes, Mum.'

'And write me a letter if you need anything. I put the stamps in your Bible.' Prisca slams the car door, fastens her seatbelt, and starts up the engine.

'Gbado anya,' she says, turning the car around in a cloud of dust.

Some of the boys lean out of their class windows, applauding, but if Prisca hears them, she does not react, a behaviour her first daughter takes from her. Ozoemena is certain she has heard, but pride is a sin her mother takes as seriously as murder. She shoots out towards the gap in the fence, tyres dipping into the dried pothole in the middle of the driveway. Her lights blaze red as she brakes before hitting the narrow dirt road. Ozoemena watches the top of the car over the dwarf wall until it disappears. Mbu does not so much as glance at her sister, and Ozoemena's throat knots up.

'Was that your sister?' Nkili has returned with Obiageli. Her voice is low, careful, as if she recognises the presence of something big and fragile in the air.

'Yes,' says Ozoemena. 'Sometimes.'

'What's doing her sef?' Obiageli asks, but the question is exceedingly complex for Ozoemena to answer. She has insight, but not the right language to explain her sister's disdain. Ozoemena has never been dear to her sister, despite all she has done to ingratiate herself; she has had to bear the brunt of being born in a way that Baby, who came after her, does not. And then, there are 'those sorts of things', according to her mother. How on earth will she explain that? The whole thing is complicated, and when she thinks about it, it makes her dizzy and breathless, hot, as if she has been stuffed in a box.

Nkili puts her arms around the both of them. 'It's okay, we will be your sisters. Senior Ijeoma said yes! Me, I'm the first born because I senior both of you so, I get less jobs to do.'

Obiageli is quick to speak. 'Guess what, Ozoemena? It's your turn to fetch water for her today.'

'Maybe you think I'm a goat.' It pleases Ozoemena, this retort. Already she feels herself changing. She would not have been this fast to respond at home.

By the door to the porter's lodge, a girl coming the other way shoves Ozoemena backwards.

'Move from the way!' She makes to hurry past, accompanied by three girls identical enough to be indistinguishable.

With newfound boldness, Ozoemena blocks her. 'Don't you have any manners?' she asks. 'You should say "excuse me".' She holds the girl's gaze, even when her eye begins to itch, when it prickles, a precursor to watering. Her neck is rigid from holding what she hopes is a fearsome stance. Quick, minute jerks in her body threaten to undo her hard work.

The girl squares up to her, chin jutting aggressively. The stink of a fight is strong on her, hot and musky. She looks Ozoemena up and down, going faster and faster, sizing her up from head to toe so that the whites of her eyes are a blur. Ozoemena knows how hard this is to execute and is grudgingly impressed. The girl, finding Ozoemena wanting, hisses and brushes past, followed by her entourage.

'Hah,' says Obiageli, clapping her hands. 'You've not even landed and already you've gone to pull a snake by the tail.'

'Wonderful!' Nkili agrees, but her smile does not match her tone and her eyes are worried as they track the departing girls. Ozoemena's shaky breath escapes out of her mouth. Her bravado is swift to ebb.

CHAPTER NINE

Treasure: Then

Mummy says, 'Tell me again.'

I tell her. I tell her everything that happened from the day she started sleeping again till now when she wakes up. As I am telling her, she is waking up more. Mummy breathes out. She smells like stale meat. I have talked and talked. Landlady's cock is going koo-koo-ro-koo and Mummy is not allowing me to close my eyes. She is asking plenty questions: When did you meet him, what was he wearing, what did he smell like, what did he bring as he was coming?

She says, 'Good girl,' so I know she is happy now. I lie on the pillow. Mummy don' talk. She is just looking and thinking. The gist is much for her.

'It's good you didn't agree for him. If he comes back, I will deal with him. Imagine the guts! When your daddy was alive, would a cockroach like that have dared look at you, talk less of opening his mouth in your direction?'

She is getting sad again, thinking about Daddy. I lie on her chest. Her breathing is loud and far at the same time. Mummy shifts me off and gets up. She walks but small time; she is tired. I hold her hand and escort her back to the bed.

'Has Ojiugo come since last time?'

I shake my head. Mummy sucks her teeth loud.

Mummy was so tired the day we came to live in Landlady's yard. In the bus, Aunty Ojiugo sat in the back, carrying half of Mummy's body like baby. Aunty Ojiugo is always doing baby-baby for Mummy because she seniors her with almost twenty years. I don' want to tell Mummy how Aunty Ojiugo left, what happened that very Monday her husband, Uncle Ngozi, came to get her. The things he said. Mummy was on the matras that time, sleeping, her mouth open. Uncle Ngozi gave her one kain dirty look. I went and closed her mouth properly. I packed her legs together and put wrapper on her. Uncle Ngozi grew his mouth long.

'So, now she knows you're her sister, okw'ya? When there was money, did she call us to follow and chop? Did we see shishi from the money that her husband stole from here and there? No. Instead, she left you to be breaking your back on the farm, while they slept on waterbed and ate food with gold spoons.'

Aunty Ojiugo waved her hand, begging him with her eyes to stop talking. Uncle Ngozi cleared his mucus and spat outside the open door. 'What? I should not talk true because their child is here? She is old enough to know the truth about her parents, that man she calls Daddy. Her own day is coming when she will do like them. After all, a snake will always give birth to what is long.'

I knew he was saying bad things, but me I was looking at him with my full eyes because he is a stupid somebody. What is waterbed? Me I have never seen it before. Was it not the same matras we are using to sleep that he too is using? Daddy use to say people like Uncle Ngozi, their eyes are too big. The man, even if Daddy shared his money into half and gave him one side, his belly will never full. He is just that kind of a person, always cutting eye for people because he wants what they have. It is a terrible something that Aunty Ojiugo married him, but that is what lack of schooling can cause. Me, I must return back to school, before I start to think small like him.

Aunty Ojiugo started making chicken noise as her husband

was purging the bitterleaf water in his stomach, in the name of talking. She said me I should go outside, let him and her discuss. Uncle Ngozi now started shouting so that his voice could follow me, and I would hear what he is talking. The things he said stung me in the ears, but what Aunty Ojiugo's face did was worse. I wouldn't have given her husband mind and too, he prepared me for all the bad-bad things people said, but Aunty Ojiugo trying to cover his mouth with her hand, begging him to talk softly-softly, was worse than all the things I heard about my mummy and daddy combined.

I knew she believed all those bad-bad things. She just didin want Uncle Ngozi to shame her family by saying them.

I sat outside the door and listened to them, Uncle Ngozi's voice pounding like a pestle in a mortar and hers low and slow. After much, I didin hear anything again, until Uncle Ngozi shouted as if he wounded.

When they finally came out, he was cleaning mouth as if he ate food. Aunty Ojiugo retied her wrapper on her waist, but her eyes and my own dinor jam and my mind told me she was leaving us and following her husband home. That night, as I came to lie down, I saw Uncle Ngozi had used anger to spit his mucus or nose on the floor and just left it there. It was plenty, but I managed to clean it with paper and went to bed. That was the first time that I slept on mat, because even if the matras was enough for me, Mummy don' know how to sleep next to somebody and she used to kick. That is why she and my daddy bed that time was as big as football field, and they went to factory to have foam made for it special. My uncle Obi collected the bed first, as per he senior the rest of the other brothers. I heard the thing could not even enter his house sef so why carry it and go?

Mummy puts her hand inside her head. She pulls her hair and it breaks where I dinor comb it well when she was sleeping. She says, 'I need to retouch my hair.'

Am thinking how we will manage. I don' have relaxer, but Aunty Lucy in our yard is a hairdresser. Maybe she will agree if I clean her room, because she does like everyone is her sister and brother from her village.

Mummy's hand starts to shake. She's tired, but her eyes are happy. She yawns, squeezes her face tight.

'Is there chewing stick?'

I shake my head. Sleep is catching me. 'I will try and get tomorrow.'

Daddy used to laugh at Mummy and call her Bush Woman because she always used chewing stick in the morning before toothbrush and toothpaste, but Mummy's teeth is the whitest, whiter than a dog's. After a while, Daddy now started using chewing stick, then Mummy laughed too and called him Husband of Bush Woman.

Mummy pats me on my back. 'You've done well, managing everything,' she says. 'Mama Ujunwa owes us more than twenty naira, but forget it. You've learned that lesson now. It's the ones that are always smiling you need to watch out for. If your back is turned, they will bury their knife inside it and still show you their empty hands.'

Her voice is angry, but she smiles one smile like this and touches my one cheek. Mummy don' really touch me. She don' really touch anybody, only Daddy. She would rub cream on his face or Robb balm on his chest when he had cough and catarrh. She would cut his nails, or, if his back was paining him, Mummy would do him massage. She uses her hands like the advert women on TV, softly-softly.

In the evenings, everybody takes turn-by-turn in the kitchen in the middle of our yard, beside the mango tree. I mean the women. The men sit around in the evening and gossip, 'koo de taa' this and that. Babangida is like tendon in their mouths; they chew and chew and cannot swallow his name. They think someone will push him out of his seat soon, but they don' talk this part loud because people can be sabo and you never know who's listening.

Before Mummy woke up, me I would have been helping Nne Chinenye to do small-small things so that she can give me something, or I will help Aunty Lucy. Now that Mummy is awake, I can just sit down and be looking and listening, because she said she will bring food. From where and with which money, I don' know but she said it so me, I believe her – after all, she has been bringing food for two days now. Am still angry at those boys that slapped their hands inside my pocket in the market. They are baskard and if I catch them, they will hear trouble.

I am sitting in front of our own room, in the doorway. The sun is resembling Fanta Orange in the evening sky. The curtain covers me small so the men cannot really see me and too, some of them are drinking because they sent one of the children to buy them beer from Madam Rose's place, so they can't really see anything again. Sometimes, when they vex for Landlady, they buy from Madam Rose so that money don' enter Omalicha's pocket, because then it will go to Landlady somehow-somehow.

Ifeanyi walks by the front of the curtain. He stops. After looking like Lucozade, he passes without saying anything. I don' know if he sees me or not. He is scratching the ground with his bare foot like a chicken and his toenails are black with dirt. He has been shitting for days now, his stomach is washing itself. Landlady locked the tank so that only her can use the water inside. That's why the men vexed for her. Chinenye my neighbour said she saw Landlady where Ifeanyi squatted, and she was washing his anus as if he is a small child. Her doors are open, and I can see inside her room. There is a table with a small TV and cassette player. There is another small radio on the hand of the chair. There are too many chairs and cushions in her room, upon even the standing fan in the corner, and it's scratching my eyes to think how hot it is in the night. There are pictures all over the walls, old-old ones. The floor is linoleum and wet. Landlady has been mopping and scrubbing everywhere. She hasn't said anything to me and Mummy about her money, but I know it only remains small before she starts beating that matter like drum.

Mummy walks out from the bathroom behind our yard in her wrapper. She has washed her hair and it is on her back. It has grown. Mummy has always had full hair, but it is fuller from undergrowth and reaches below her shoulders. She don' talk to the men when she passes, stamping on the pavement to remove the sand from her wet silpas. Our neighbour, Papa Chinenye, points at her with his mouth and the men them start laughing until they see me by the door looking; then they stop.

'Close the door, darling,' says Mummy.

I bring my legs inside. Mummy pulls on her nightgown quickly. It's clean now, because she washed it and spread it at the back fence. If you come out of the back of our house, two steps and it's the wall, so Mummy sits out there small because nobody can see her unless they come out from their own rooms or they are finding her.

'What time did you say he usually comes?' she asks.

'At night.' My fingernail skin is dry, and I put it in my mouth and eat it.

'Don't bite your nails. It's not ladylike.'

'Yes, Mummy.' I take my hand away and pluck the dry skin instead, and we wait. Mummy slaps at her legs. She is even fairer in complexion because the sun has not touched her in a long time. People used to say Mummy resembled Bianca Onoh, but she is too thin now, bony like dried fish. The laughter of the men is louder than Landlady's radio.

Somebody is frying meat – probably Omalicha's maid, to sell to the men that come to drink in her place. I can smell fio-fio, onions and crayfish. Mummy sits outside until it's dark, and the mosquitos come out.

'Go and baff,' she says, but the water remaining is not enough. I tell her so. 'Why did you leave me to use all of it? We could have shared.'

'I will fetch tomorrow, Mummy. Is okay.'

'No, Treasure. You have to baff, morning and night, just like we used to when Daddy stayed with us. We cannot allow mourning to take away the pride of our womanhood. A woman must wash herself, always. Have you started seeing your sacred?'

I shake my head. Aunty Ojiugo collected pieces-cloth from tailor for me. She taught me how to wash them and boil them and to make sure no man touches them.

'Good. At least sleep did not carry me to miss your first one,' Mummy says. 'In a few months, you will be twelve years. In our family that is around when it starts, but no later than thirteen.'

My stomach is paining me, but it don' feel like hunger. Mummy puts my head on her lap and starts to plait my hair, dividing it with her fingers. Is not real plaiting because my hair is too short, and she cannot really plait. She is just looking for something for her hands to do. 'You got the thickness of your hair from me, you know.'

'I know,' I say. Everyone used to talk about Mummy's hair. Plaiters in the market dodged me because my hair took too long to make, or better, they charged double or three times the amount they used to make other people's hair.

'Daddy used to call me Mami Wata, do you remember that?' Mummy asks.

I swallow the stone in my throat.

'You miss him, shebi?' she asks.

I nod.

'Me, too.'

My nose is tickling me because there are tears coming, but I don' want them to come out. My uncles and their wives called Mummy all types of names. They said she killed Daddy. They said she was a witch. A prostitute. That a woman as fine as her only brings bad luck to men. Mummy dinor allow one single tear to come out, even though she looks as if eats tears for morning, afternoon and night food.

The noise in our yard is coming down now the men are going off to their rooms and their night food. Landlady's TV is on and the nine o'clock news music comes on. She leaves her door open with the mosquito net frame over it so that she can have breeze before bed. There are other TVs too, but Landlady has the loudest one, as if anybody is dragging position with her.

Mummy is singing, 'Police ee, is committing suicide o, the blackman wey dey here is committing suicide o.' She sings slowly, not like Bright Chimezie sings it, fast-fast, dancing like a lizard on hot zinc. It used to be joke between she and Daddy too, whenever Mercy cooked ogbono soup. Daddy would make big-big balls in his garri and swallow them, kpurum down his throat, then he would say, 'I have committed suicide,' and he and Mummy would laugh and laugh.

They were always laughing. I didin understand half of what they were laughing at and the ones I understood sef were not even funny.

CHAPTER TEN

Ozoemena: Then

Ozoemena did not remember much else about the burial after the incident with the whispering boy whose touch burned her back. She stayed in her grandmother's room while the majority of the family left for her late uncle's final Mass on the third day. It was a Sunday. Time for the family to thank God for a successful funeral rite, for not losing one more person, even though her uncle had died a bad death, murdered, before he had the chance to marry and beget offspring.

She must have nodded off after her family departed, because her grandfather's dry coughing from the next room woke her. She listened to him singing under his breath, something in an Igbo dialect, so ancient and particular to their village as to be nearly extinct. She understood barely every three words out of ten. Ozoemena often had trouble understanding the old man, born as he had been late in the previous century, but the song felt familiar, and she allowed it to soothe her. It sounded to her like a lullaby.

Everything about her grandmother's room smelled of snuff, dry and herby. The sheets beneath her were soft and thin from frequent washings, and Ozoemena felt the bedsprings beneath the flattened Mouka foam, a second spine on her back. She winced and turned over on her side. How did M'ma sleep?

Another single bed was jammed against the wall on the other side of the room, made up for whichever aunt joined her grandmother in her nightly vigils for her grandfather's care. Antique clothing hovered on suspended rails over the beds like ghosts. Floating shelves were piled with boxes and cartons and all sorts of things. Shoes in suede and cracked or worn leather were stuffed under the bed, abandoned for the latest styles by owners too nostalgic for their youth to let them go completely. At the foot of the bed in which she reclined stood a wooden dresser made from a tree that had probably existed and been cut down long before Ozoemena was a conscious thought in her parents' minds. It was covered with intricate carvings of animal and plant life, its recessed handles shiny from regular use. On the top of the dresser stood three woven raffia heads adorned with various wigs. Ozoemena considered their eyeless observation of her and turned away.

'You're awake,' said M'ma. She approached the bed from the doorway leading to the parlour-cum-dining room, bearing a steaming bowl on a tray. 'You slept a long time.'

'M'ma, good . . .' Ozoemena paused, unsure of the correct greeting. Morning or afternoon? The light coming from the window seemed bright and strong, but robust sunlight was a constant and consequently no indicator of time.

'Sit up. I brought you akamu.' The steam made M'ma's black skin dewy.

Ozoemena obeyed, wincing. 'Did you find the boy? The one that hit me?' she asked.

'He's gone now,' said M'ma. 'Your father saw to it. Come, eat.'

'But why did he attack me?' Ozoemena persisted. 'I didn't look for trouble. I just told him he wasn't supposed to be there, and he ignored me anyway.'

M'ma placed the tray on Ozoemena's lap. A thick slice of

buttered bread lay beside the bowl. Ozoemena fell to. She was hungry, and cherished the combination of bread and corn pap, creamy with liquid Peak milk and a sprinkling of crunchy granulated sugar. M'ma sat on the other bed, watching her and tapping a plastic Mentholatum bottle with her thumb.

'Tell me about the boy you saw,' she said.

Ozoemena tamped down a shudder. 'He was tall, dark . . .'

'Dark, like me?'

Ozoemena thought for a moment. 'Yes. Maybe a little darker. He didn't have a shirt on, and he was not wearing any shoes.'

M'ma nodded. 'What else did you see?'

'He was feeding the goats. No, he was looking at the goats and they were running away. I told him not to stand there, but he didn't listen.'

'So, he was just wearing nika?'

'Yes, but a long nika, not a short one.'

M'ma nodded again. She twisted the cap off her Mentholatum bottle and tapped out some snuff into her hand. 'Did he have a mark anywhere on his body?'

Ozoemena started to say no, but an image of the boy stopped her. Before the pain started, when he had first touched her and Chuzzy had barked, she had turned. The mark on his chest – a black bump shaped in a broken circle.

'Eh-he? Speak child. Did he or did he not?' M'ma asked.

Ozoemena sensed that something important hung on her answer. She replied slowly. 'It looks like the mark my daddy has around his shoulder, but not the same.' She frowned. 'The boy had a big one.' As a young child, she had played with her daddy's scar, which he told her was left over from a battle he had had with smallpox in his youth. Ozoemena relished the puffiness of the small patch of skin on his collarbone, three dots in decreasing sizes, as though his chest was having a thought, brown-black the colour of a velvet tamarind.

'M'ma?'

'Mmh?' replied the older woman, sniffling fiercely.

'The boy, I think he was crying.'

M'ma sneezed, blew her nose into a brown handkerchief, and crumpled it in her fist. Her eyes watered. 'That was your uncle Odiogo,' she said. 'He's given you a gift. That's right. A big gift!' She laughed, showing her pointed teeth.

Ozoemena's blood froze in her veins. Grimacing, she shifted position on the bed. What gift? She told herself she could do without any present that hurt, that burned, that unravelled something in her that made her howl. She was terrified to the point of speechlessness at the thought of interacting with a ghost, of having the boy, her dead uncle, touch her as surely as her grandmother did. Ozoemena wanted to ask M'ma questions, but was afraid of the old woman's answer. Her mouth went dry.

Ozoemena knew there was no life without the dead; some at rest, others wandering, lost, having been deprived funeral rites for one reason or the other. There were stories of brooms that swept compounds clean without hands wielding them; birds flying into high-tension wires and dropping to the ground as people. She knew not to take things from anyone for fear of being turned into a tortoise or chicken to be used in money ritual sacrifices. Ozoemena had watched her parents' brows crinkle during the nine o'clock news when another child was announced as missing. Kidnappers. Whether these practices worked or not, people were taken. They must work, Ozoemena reasoned with herself, otherwise why would people keep on going missing?

'Are you afraid?' asked M'ma, staring into her face.

'No,' Ozoemena said, tongue tripping, exposing the lie.

M'ma smiled her sharp-toothed smile. 'That is good. You

must never fear your dead kin. If you see them, speak to them. You and your cousins will pour us libation when we are gone, after all.'

Ozoemena wiped the sweat off her forehead. She told herself it was the hot pap making her sweat, and nothing else. The wound on her back stung.

'Let me see it,' M'ma said.

Ozoemena handed over the empty tray and flipped over, presenting her back to her grandmother. The old woman grunted. She rattled around in her bureau, and when she returned, swabbed something cool on to Ozoemena's back. Savlon. The smell relaxed Ozoemena.

'It will soon go. It's getting better.' M'ma nodded to herself. Her amber eyes were dull with fatigue, but to Ozoemena's mind, M'ma looked much better since she'd learned about the boy. She rearranged things absentmindedly, smiling tiny, secret smiles. M'ma had been a great beauty, and because of this, her father, Ozoemena's great-grandfather, had allowed her to get her teeth chiselled to better bring her beauty forth. Ozoemena saw it, this magnificence. Her grandmother resembled a bird of prey. Although she and Ozoemena were of the same height, nobody could mistake the woman for a child. Her arms were sinewy, muscular from farm work, and when she spoke, her voice travelled, shaking the whole compound with the force of it.

M'ma stopped moving things about. 'There is someone we should go and see,' she said.

Ozoemena was slow to rise, confused by the change in her grandmother's demeanour. Fear and food hampered Ozoemena's movements, made her sluggish. Did this so-called gift mean her uncle would appear to her now, whenever he pleased? What for? Ozoemena already felt squeezed between her two sisters: Mbu in her lofty position as Ada, the first daughter, and Baby being . . . well, the baby. She had no room for ghosts disturbing her, hurting her. Could she give the gift back, whatever it was? M'ma pulled her up by the wrists and Ozoemena made herself comply.

'Hurry, child,' M'ma said. 'We must be back before everyone returns from church.'

All rural areas look the same, thought Ozoemena. Bumpy gravel roads and red-earth pathways. Lots of trees and men gathered under them, gossiping, drinking, playing nchọ. Chickens scratched at the earth with chicks in tow, dyed garishly to dissuade hawks, wings tagged with strips of coloured rags denoting ownership. Here in Oba, village life revealed itself in the way people walked, leisurely, the women swaying their hips, balancing baskets or basins of foodstuff on their heads, with babies tied to their backs. The children on errands, playing chase. It did not matter what they did, people chatted to one another: across the road, greeting, making appointments to meet, asking about ill health, and tossing remedies the way people in the towns and cities hurled insults in traffic jams. Afternoons in villages are unhurried, and Ozoemena slowed her footsteps. As she passed an old Ford pick-up resting on its rusty rims, a monkey lunged and she started, forgetting that she had seen the animal chained to the truck before. The monkey, a small grey thing, bared its teeth at her.

M'ma rushed ahead, her small feet in their foam rubber slippers raising minute dust storms with each step. She grunted to acknowledge greetings, said, 'I am coming,' or 'Let me see somebody,' by way of explanation. Ozoemena watched people watch her grandmother. She wondered how much of what had happened the previous day they had heard, but then she realised they were not bothered with a child. Children were unimportant by themselves. M'ma's presence outside her compound so soon after the burial disturbed and titillated them. Ozoemena saw the start of gossip in their wide eyes.

She worried for her grandmother. Whenever she lagged, M'ma forced her to lengthen her stride by squeezing her hand, until Ozoemena was almost dragged along.

'It's remaining small,' said M'ma. 'We have nearly reached.'

The midday sun shone bright and blinding, but in the presence of many trees to filter it, the light fell green and softly on the body. Branches rustled with creatures too hot to fly or too scared to break cover – it was a bold squirrel that often ended up gracing the soup pot. Lizards dashed around on the ground, nodding, seeking the warmest spots in which to lie undisturbed, occasionally pausing to lick at ants and swallow hurriedly. Ozoemena saw all these things and her mind lingered on them, resisting the panic transmitting through M'ma's many keep-up squeezes.

A compound appeared to their right, separate from the rest, amidst land left to go fallow. It was as if every other homestead gave it a wide berth. Its wide, flat face lay open, uncluttered by the usual signs of human habitation. A hut squatted in the middle, and the edges of the yard still bore the wavy marks from recent sweeping.

A rustling, and M'ma stopped. A man appeared from the side of the house, near an empty hutch. He was old like M'ma, perhaps older, and tall but not yet stooped. His earth-toned Akwete cloth was knotted in a big bulge under a shirt of a similar hue. It reminded Ozoemena of the way her father wore his Abada on Saturday mornings when he sat in the parlour drinking his coffee and reading the weekend *Champion* newspaper.

The man approached them, completely ignoring M'ma, who stood beside her, holding her hand. His face filled Ozoemena's vision and time seemed to skid and slide. A breeze whispered through the trees, ballooning her T-shirt and kissing the sting of freshly pearled sweat from around her wound.

'Idemili told me you were coming. Daughter of Nwokerekè Idimogu, I salute you. Welcome, young leopard,' the man said. Then he waited, expecting something that Ozoemena did not know to give.

Nwokereke? Ozoemena was puzzled, noting the extra syllable. It was not the way her family pronounced their surname. In the awkward silence, she turned towards her grandmother for reassurance, confusion morphing into distress when M'ma did not meet her gaze. She did not wish for any gods to know her whereabouts. The man's words were frightening, his manner bizarre. Why did he greet her? It should be the other way around, her grandmother making introductions, Ozoemena curtsying traditionally. It felt to her as though, even without bending, the old man had just bowed to her.

M'ma cleared her throat. 'We haven't got long, Oruke,' she said.

The old man – Oruke – nodded. 'In that case, come in. There is much to say.' He paused in the act of folding himself in two to slip under the low eaves of the hut. 'Take off your shoes, daughter of Nwokereke. We do things the old way here.'

Something scurried on the roof, dropping dried pieces of thatch on Ozoemena's shoulder. She jumped, caught herself and sat back down on the dwarf stool, hoping nobody had noticed in the gloom of the hut.

Oruke, standing over her, smiled. 'Don't be afraid. Soon you will become the thing that all other beasts of the night fear.'

Ozoemena's heart skipped a beat. 'Beasts of the night' sounded ominous. What cause would anything have to fear her? Nothing Oruke had said so far was reassuring. Her eyes slid to M'ma again, who sat not refuting anything the man said.

He inclined his head. 'I salute you, Ozoemena, daughter of Emenike, son of Irugbo, son of Nwokereke. Nno. Welcome. Oruke Nwosu welcomes you, daughter of leopards.'

Ozoemena, teeth clenched nervously to stop the unexpected chattering, tried to figure out his meaning. He mentioned her father, Emenike, but her father had not as yet taken any titles. He was not known as a leopard. He was valued for his skill with a scalpel – could that be what the man meant? Ozoemena knew she was missing something quite obvious. She cast her mind back to M'ma's earlier talk of gifts, of dead uncles, of their swift trek from the house to what could only be a shrine. What were they doing here? Ozoemena regretted coming. Prisca would have her head if she found out Ozoemena had set foot inside a pagan place.

The man's greeting was irksome, but his manner of searching out her gaze bothered Ozoemena the most. She looked down and away again, but felt his eyes following, drawing hers. Ozoemena unlatched her jaw behind closed lips, trying to relax.

'What do you want to know?' Oruke Nwosu lowered himself on to a seat. 'There are some things I can help with, but you must understand the Leopard Society was a mysterious and secret one. What I know applies only to your family, as much as your great-grandfather, a leopard, revealed to my father, who revealed it to me. My job is Isi Idemili here in this town. It is me the goddess speaks to, and I relay to Oba people what she has said, what she wants. I am the mouthpiece of her shrine.'

Ozoemena breathed out shakily. The more Oruke spoke, the worse things became. *Leopard Society*? Oruke Nwosu used the Igbo words 'Ọtụ nzụzo' – 'hidden sect'. Secret societies were bad news.

'I don't want to know anything!' Ozoemena spluttered. 'Sir,' she added afterwards. The thought of her family being part of a secret society rankled and disturbed her.

Oruke Nwosu stared at Ozoemena's grandmother.

'Emenike and his wife did not teach them anything,' M'ma said, clicking her tongue, derisive.

Oruke Nwosu touched M'ma's shoulder, his eyes sorrowful. His knee stuck out through the folds of his cloth. An old knee, knotted and lumpy, the ochre-coloured skin thin and smooth and speckled with white dots. He pulled out an enamel bowl from the shadows under his wooden bench and offered it to her grandmother.

'We broke kola before you came,' he said. M'ma took a piece of the lilac nut, scraped it off on her lower teeth and chewed. Ozoemena looked around, searching the gloom for the other party making up 'we'.

'You as well,' Oruke said, offering the bowl to Ozoemena. She paused. The hollow in her throat trembled with the force of her pulse. Ozoemena, a child, had never been offered a kola nut. Slowly, hesitantly, her fingers picked up a piece. She held it in her palm until Oruke Nwosu motioned for her to take a bite. The kola nut was bitter, chalky when she bit into it. Ozoemena swallowed. The saliva stuck to her throat.

Oruke began. 'A long time ago, when my father's father was alive, a man came here asking for protection. This man was a leopard – your father's father's father, Nwokereke Idimogu.'

Ozoemena relaxed further. Stories, she could deal with. Stories, she enjoyed.

'They don't know from where he came, but there were marks on his body, deep ones that should have killed a normal person. Other marks, too, that told them he had deep knowledge. He came here when the influence such societies had was beginning to die in some areas. The missionaries were destroying them on the right hand, the white soldiers on the left. We don't know whether they tried to capture him, or even kill him, but obviously, his enemies failed.'

M'ma took over, a smooth relay. 'There was some trouble where he came from, is what your grandfather told me. Do you know what "Ọchụ" is?'

Ozoemena shook her head.

'Ọchụ is a taboo, something bad. Your ancestor gbulu ọchụ, he committed a grave offence. Someone took his wife and children and sold them to slavers when he was away farming – in those days, they used to travel for days to get to farmland. When he found out, the leopard overcame him and—'

'He could change himself into a leopard?' Ozoemena blurted out before she could think. It was rude to interrupt elders and completely uncharacteristic for Ozoemena.

M'ma gave her a warning look.

'He slaughtered the ones involved, even killed a slaver, someone important to one of the whites,' continued Oruke. 'He had to run, you understand, to go as far away as he could so that nobody could find him; that was what your grandfather told me, and what his own father had told him. He walked for a long time, eating in the bushes like a complete animal. And when he sought help here—' M'ma paused. 'The watch people also did a bad thing. They beat him up.'

'Why?' Ozoemena's brow creased. A stirring within her. 'Did he try to kill them, too?'

'No, but they were afraid of him.'

'Why?' Ozoemena asked again. She pictured it, a fatigued man, eating grass like Nebuchadnezzar in the Bible. There did not seem to be anything particularly fearsome about it.

'He was big and tall, formidable. That's what I was told. Who knows? I was not there. Maybe he fought them,' said M'ma.

Oruke continued. 'Whatever happened or did not happen, Idemili gave him her protection. Idimogu was grateful and so, he used his gift to protect this Oba, the village-of-the-nine-brothers, and many other villages surrounding this one.'

'My great-grandfather killed people,' Ozoemena said, awestruck. 'How many?'

M'ma bit off another piece of her kola and crunched it rabbit-fast between her teeth. 'It is ọchụ. We do not mention such things, not without reason. That is why we are telling you now. Listen carefully.'

Chastised, Ozoemena stared at Oruke Nwosu's feet, slender and delicate as a woman's, the nails long and square. There were strings around each of his ankles, limp and brown with dirt.

'Yes,' Oruke added, kindly. 'A leopard's work is crucial. It roams all over this world, and the next, and whatever other worlds exist. Wherever there is time, it can go, even if it is something that happened before-before.' Oruke clicked his fingers for emphasis. 'No doors are closed that a leopard cannot claw open. A person cannot commit a crime and die, thinking they have escaped. A leopard, if it decides, can hunt them to the afterlife. You can do all this.'

'If we are not really from here,' asked Ozoemena, picking up on his earlier story. 'Where is our real hometown?' It explained the different pronunciation of a common enough surname. The extra syllable had obviously disappeared to help the family name fit the local manner of speaking. Ozoemena, in her head, felt lost.

'This is our real hometown,' M'ma said, sucking her teeth. 'This is where Idimogu's destiny led; this is where he stayed. He used his leopard to protect these lands. Nobody can chase you away, especially not now.'

'Indeed. You have his might.' Oruke looked proud. 'In the

time of our foremothers and fathers, the leopards are the ones that kept the rules of the land.'

'Like army,' M'ma interjected.

'Like secret service,' Oruke countered. 'They were strong and powerful. Nobody crossed them and came out alive.' He nodded, agreeing with his own assessment. 'They tangled with the British, scattered them. Those white men, they would have taken more of our people if the leopards were not fighting them hand and foot.'

Ozoemena's eyes widened as their meaning became apparent. They had lulled her into a false sense of security with their stories. She recalled Oruke's earlier greeting, M'ma's excited talk about gifts.

His might.

Ozoemena had put it together too slowly for her own liking. The stool was painful on her bottom, the hut by turns chilly and sweltering. Distaste. Distrust. Fear. Nausea. Ozoemena was beset by myriad reactions. If her great-grandfather was so admirable, why had Emenike kept him a secret from her and Mbu?

'There are things I know, and things I do not know,' said Oruke Nwosu, oblivious to Ozoemena's discomfort. 'And what I know is that we have lived in peace here since. Did you know that even during the war, we were never in the hands of the Nigerian soldiers? Never. Odiogo, all by himself, saw to it.'

War. Beast. Murder. Ozoemena began to shiver slightly. Nothing about the leopard sounded pleasant.

M'ma wiped her nose on her handkerchief and tucked it back into the front of her blouse.

'Odiogo has nominated you,' said Oruke Nwosu. 'But you have to decide to eat the leopard for yourself – that is what we call it – but it is up to you and your chi. You must agree, otherwise, it doesn't work.'

M'ma nodded. 'That's right.'

'What if I don't want this gift?' Ozoemena's voice was small, and she stared at M'ma, speaking to her and only her.

'If you don't want, then you don't want,' said M'ma, shrugging, but Ozoemena could tell she was disappointed by her response.

Oruke appeared startled. 'Nobody has said no before.' He bowed his head, deep in thought.

M'ma sighed, hands folded on her belly, at ease in the quiet.

Oruke cleared his throat. 'Well, if you say "no", then your chi must also say no. The leopard is strong, and only the strong may eat it.'

Ozoemena's overwrought mind drifted. Can leopards change form? she wondered. And why did her uncle not choose Mbu? Her sister was stronger, more ferocious – and the firstborn to boot. Surely, her uncle had made a mistake. Relief flooded her body briefly, until she was arrested by the image of her sister as a wild animal. She knew without a doubt that Mbu would turn her into minced meat given half the chance. The thought made her feel insignificant. To remain powerless, then, or to become capable of killing? Her ancestor was overcome by his leopard; a child did not stand a chance. She cleared her throat involuntarily.

'Uncle Odiogo was big, and you said my great-grandfather, he too was big, and . . .' She stopped, waiting for Oruke to agree, to free her from the obligation of an answer.

'She's a girl,' M'ma said. 'Has this ever happened? What does it mean?'

Oruke Nwosu sighed. 'There is nothing new under the sun,' he said. He patted Ozoemena on the head gently. 'I will ask questions on your behalf, little one. We will follow the matter and see its head.'

Ozoemena coughed again. Her throat was dry, and a pain had settled inside it. Oruke scooped some water from a clay pot to his left, poured it out into a cup and gave it to Ozoemena. She looked to M'ma for permission, and when the woman nodded, Ozoemena took the cup from Oruke and thanked him. She allowed herself only a little sip. The water might not have been boiled, and her parents were particular about typhoid. Oruke sat forward, holding Ozoemena in a sorrowful gaze.

'There is something you must do if you are to become the leopard.'

'I have to say yes so that my chi will also,' Ozoemena said in a low voice.

'Yes,' replied Oruke Nwosu.

M'ma tied and retied her wrapper, readjusted her blouse. 'And you will have to find your tether quick. It is the person that keeps you tied to your human mind when your animal takes over, so that you do not become a beast. When you find them, you will know.'

She had not agreed to be leopard, but a tether sounded comforting. Somebody else would be responsible for keeping the leopard in check. But why had the tether not stopped her great-grandfather from committing murder?

Her worry returned. Ozoemena tipped the cup and drank quickly. The water was icy cold and sweet after the bitterness of the kola nut.

Oruke's face wore a grave expression. 'You will also have to die.'

The walk back took longer. Ozoemena dragged her feet. As they approached Ngo, her grandfather's compound, they observed it was alive with mourners once more. Cars pulled out, people leaving for their homes after a brief stopover, the last chance to commiserate with the bereaved. The Sunday-after service was usually for relations and close friends.

In the compound, most of the canopies were being disman-tled, the hollow bonging of metal tubes reverberating through

the afternoon. The awnings dropped like great birds, primary-
coloured in broad stripes, dirty, on their way to the next
funeral, the next wedding, the next ofala or August Meeting.
Workers chatted and sang loudly as they worked.

Some of Ozoemena's cousins ran to M'ma, glad to see
their grandmother, curiosity clouding their delight. Where did
they go? They stared at Ozoemena, wondering about the
previous day, about her absence at the church, and now this.
Ozoemena avoided their eyes. M'ma did not look at Uncle
Odiogo's grave as they walked past the ube tree under which
he had been buried.

'I don't want to die,' said Ozoemena quietly. The tears that
had been threatening to fall slid down her cheeks. M'ma
knuckled them away fast.

'Don't worry about all that. You just find your tether, and
we will decide what to do afterwards. All will be well.'

It all sounded overly simplistic. Ozoemena was preoccupied
with the thought of staying alive.

I don't want to die. I don't want to die.

Ozoemena's tears came faster than her grandmother could
wipe them away. Her shoulders shook, her chest heaved. M'ma
paused to fold her into her small frame, a quick squeeze-and-
release.

'Stop that. Nobody is killing you.' Her grandmother's
callused palms were sandpaper on Ozoemena's face. 'Do you
imagine you will have just one life? As leopard, you will have
many. What is one small death compared to all the lives you
will live?'

But her uncle was dead, Ozoemena thought. Killed for
nothing. Before he died, Odiogo had told his brother that the
robbers wanted his car. The same car they had left behind
when he put up a fight. They had opted for taking his life
instead.

Ozoemena saw Prisca emerge from the back door, walking

towards them, nostrils flaring. Her mother's glasses caught the sun, and her face was aflame.

M'ma drew Ozoemena in for another hug, whispering, 'Remember, keep everything a secret.'

CHAPTER ELEVEN

Treasure

The spirit is wearing his Nnamdi Azikiwe cap and showing teeth as if me and him are pallies that have not seen each other in a long time.

'My wife,' he says. I don' like the spirit calling me his wife, before Mummy will now think am a bad child that is following men around even if is only a spirit-man.

'What is it? You don't want to embrace me?' asks the spirit. 'Hug me, wife.'

Mummy moves fast and pulls open the door. She points at the spirit's face. 'Eh, stop that rubbish there.' She unties the wrapper round her waist and reties it. 'Just hold it there, you hear me? Treasure, light candle.'

'No need,' says the spirit. He don' vex. From somewhere inside, a blue light is coming out of him. It resembles the fire that Mercy used to cook on the gas cooker, clean and quiet, not the yellow smoking fire from the empty kerosene stove in the corner of the room. At least the kerosene lasted small. In rainy season I would have used it to rub on the floor so that mosquitos won't finish us. I am lucky that Mercy taught me many things about how she grew up.

The spirit glows some more, from his shoes floating just on top of the ground to his hat. I don' know how me I could have thought he was ever a living person, but maybe the sun is merciful on the eyes. Mummy hisses, eyeing him up and down as if he is a rat that has crawled out of a rubbish heap.

'So, this is the thing that thinks it can marry my daughter.' She laughs, claps her hands, kpam, kpam, kpam. Mummy is acting. Her laughter is the type of play laugh that women in home videos laugh when they want to insult men or each other. The spirit hears this, and he swells like a sack of soaked garri, covering the whole doorway.

'It's me you're talking to like that? Do you know what I can do to you? To your daughter?' As its middle grows, the light dims as if there is air coming from somewhere, trying to off the flame. Mummy folds her hands and stares at the spirit. I have never seen her so angry before.

'Regardez!' she says, pointing at the spirit with four fingers. She claps again, the pink inside her lower lip showing from where she turned it out. She says other things in French that me I don' know. Mummy talks French from when she worked as a secretary in one French-West Africa company like this, but she didin teach me French. The spirit stretches and stretches. I can see the door through his middle part, the bottom of the wood still splintered and chewed from when rats used to try their power, before Landlady now got Captain to be chasing them.

'I can make sure you don't find rest in this world or the next,' says the spirit. His voice is so deep, I cover my ears. The door is shaking as if the spirit is sucking it by growing, moving the air with his body.

'You can't do nothing more than a hanging pant,' Mummy says, looking away. Her eyes are half-open, but she is not tired. She is not sleepy. Mummy don' look sleepy. She is awake and then, she is asleep. This is part of her acting for the spirit to show him that he has not even started.

The spirit gets smaller and smaller until he is the same

size again, tall and thin but also different. His light is lower and . . . something else. Is as if he is shy, a small boy.

'What do you want, woman? Did I do a bad thing in waking you and returning you to your daughter?'

'You don't have the power to do anything, so stop boasting. Look at you, see the shoes on your feet, see your clothes. These are not in vogue. There is no way you could have been an important somebody in life, talk more of death. And you want to marry my daughter? Me, Akuabata?' She taps her chest gently, as if it will break. 'I did not raise her to give to pigs.'

She is not talking to me, but I feel her insult inside my stomach, a knife wound. What if it is too late and I am already tied to the spirit?

'Listen, Madam, I will not let you abuse me. I am spirit and you are common flesh and I can do things to you . . .'

'Eh-he. That's the first time you've addressed me properly,' says Mummy. She straightens her bony shoulders. Her neck is too long, curved like banana, but she is Mummy. This is how I have always known her. Speaking softly and strong. Mummy is in charge here, not the spirit. I move close to her and touch her wrapper with one finger, but only small. The spirit's eyes follow me. He's not happy. I am feeling bad because he did something good for me by waking up Mummy and all the plenty things that he gave me. I am doing him bad, but me, I don' want to be his wife. No way.

'Mummy, it's okay, he's sorry,' I say.

Mummy stares at me, considering. 'You're lucky my daughter is begging for you,' she says to him. 'Her heart is soft, that is why she allowed you to try and deceive her with ordinary okpa, five naira.'

'I looked after her! Without me, she would have died.'

'Since when? I raised my daughter better than that. We survived without you.'

I don' say anything, but a shame thought enters my head that me *I* survived by myself.

'She took my okpa. I did not force her. She came willingly with her own two legs. She belongs to me.'

'And you belong to someone. You will bring your oga here or take us to them. They are the ones we will deal with.' There is silence, and then Mummy says, 'Look at you, you can only be a servant. You can't be the one at the top.'

My heart starts to beat all over my body again. This is not the way I thought everything would go. Mummy supposed to fight for me, tell the spirit to get out and never come back, but now she wants to meet the king of spirits? For what? Is there even a king of spirits? This is bad market.

As I am thinking these things, I look up and the spirit is watching me. I can't see his eyes, but I know. The blue light in his body glows like electric shock.

'You want to cheat me,' he says. 'After everything we agreed. You said you will help me to be born again. I want to live again. You promised.'

I am saying, 'I didin promise you—' but Mummy takes the words out of my mouth.

'Then you know what to do,' says Mummy. 'Gerrout. Vamoose. Shaa!'

He goes.

Mummy's hand falls on my shoulder. Her voice was strong talking to the spirit, and am forgetting that she is not yet properly well. Now, sweat is sweating her hand. I can feel the bones, like the ends of broomsticks. I help her lie down on the bed.

'And that is how we deal with subordinates!' she says. 'Now, he will bring us something worthy or he will take us to his oga. But something tells me that he doesn't want anyone knowing what he is doing . . . whatever is on that their side . . .' The last few words roll out around her open mouth. She is already sleeping.

CHAPTER TWELVE

Ozoemena: Now

After a shortened afternoon prep in which the girls spend more time chatting than studying, they return to the hostel. Ozoemena unties the blue nylon rope binding her mattress in a roll. Sheathed in a calico covering, it is stencilled all over with Mbu's initials in bright blue paint. She makes her bed quickly with a bobbled plum bedsheet and slips on a matching pillowcase. Her pillow is new and plump from the shop. Her own initials are sewn into a corner in red knitting yarn. She lays a wrapper down over her bed and a blanket on top of that, as she has seen the other girls do, folding the top down. Despite all her efforts, her corner without an accompanying locker looks bare, unfinished. Ozoemena pushes her buckets under her bed and chains her big jerrycan of water to the springs at the foot of her bed as Nkili instructs.

'It's home water, so it won't give you typhoid. If you see that tank eh, disgusting. They haven't washed it yet,' Nkili says.

'You can even drink it and use the tank water for baffing and washing your clothes only,' Obiageli says.

Ozoemena makes a face. Drink it? The water has not been boiled yet. 'I have my drinking water here,' she says, pulling out a small jerrycan.

'That one enters your locker,' Nkili says. She pauses. 'But

since you don't have yet, I can hold it for you. Come let us show you everything.'

Ozoemena's fresh haircut and wrongly sewn daywear are a dead giveaway. As Nkili and Obiageli introduce her to fellow classmates and friends, senior girls call her over to gauge her suitability as school daughter. Who is her father? What does he do? What does her mother do? How many senior brothers does she have? None? Has she ever been abroad? Can she Flex? Ozoemena sees from their faces that they cannot place her. She has lived abroad, but not for a while, and she has lost her accent. Her father is a surgeon, but without big government ties like a lot of the other students, some of whose parents are diplomats. And for her to have no brothers? They vacillate, but let her go when Nkili informs them that Ozoemena already belongs to their school mother. The girls continue the tour.

The compound is laid out in a rectangle. From the porter's lodge, rooms one to eight lie on the right-hand side while numbers nine to sixteen lie on the left. The first room is the matron's quarters, which she shares with a young woman of about twenty who mans the tuck shop operating out of matron's front window.

'Her chin-chin is . . .' Nkili pauses. '. . . Not correct.'

'Like, not tasty? Or stale?' Ozoemena asks. At Nkili's questioning look, she explains. 'Old?'

'Yes! Exactly.' Nkili mutters 'stale' to herself three times.

Obiageli pulls a face. 'If you try to sell old food in Main Market eh, touts will sack your shop and dump everything into the mud.'

'You live in Onitsha?' Ozoemena asks.

'Yes! You?' Obiageli asks.

'Awka, state capital.' Ozoemena puffing out her chest, observes Nkili's eyes widen slightly. 'What?' she asks.

'Oh, my driver is from there,' Nkili replies, smiling. 'He will be happy when I tell him my friend lives in his place.'

'Onitsha is the real state capital. Everybody knows,' Obiageli says.

'Anyway, as I was saying. . .' Nkili taps Obiageli to quieten her. 'Matron is not around now, but when she comes back, you should try and greet her with something. Maybe one of your Bournvita or milk. Or maybe keep one bread for her.'

'Okay.' Ozoemena nods, but does not think it likely that she will be parting with her hard-won provisions. They are a symbol of her freedom, her ability to do what she wants.

'She eats enough out of us,' Obiageli says, lowering her voice and looking around. 'Not just the girls, either. My brother says that she makes money from students, especially towards the end of term, when provs are finished and hunger is wiring everybody.' Obiageli picks her nose and examines its contents.

'Don't pick your nose!' Ozoemena is aghast.

'Why not?' asks Obiageli. 'The hair there is for catching all the nyama-nyama, but it's your job to pick it out.'

'Then use tissue!' Nkili takes a packet of pocket tissues from her skirt and flings them at Obiageli, who shrugs, pockets them, and continues cleaning out her nose with the finger.

'You're dashing her the whole packet?' Ozoemena has never had a packet of tissues to herself, does not know anyone their age who does. Tissues, like paper and toilet roll, come from trees and should not be wasted on children – just enough, and no more. Posters and newspapers are recycled by street food vendors and market women, and latrines. Why, in her grandparents' toilet in Oba, squares of newspaper hang suspended on a rope from the ceiling, despite the toilet roll mounted on a nail on the wood wall. A lot of people felt more comfortable using the papers that would have gone to waste anyway. The soft rolls are too precious. And here is Nkili, throwing away a packet as if it is nothing.

'If you keep doing that disgusting thing that gives somebody shivers, you can't come with us,' Nkili says to Obiageli.

'Okay, find me later then.' Obiageli goes off, flicking the gunk from her index finger. On the pavement to her dorm room, a senior girl gives her a thwack at the back of the head. They cannot hear what the senior is saying, but her jabbing finger practically screams.

'Do you want to see my corner?' Nkili asks. They are on Ozoemena's side of the compound, in front of room eight, right next to the dining hall. 'It is very useful for when it's time to pass plates in the hall. See, I have Obiageli's own here.' She shows Ozoemena a yellow enamel plate and bowl, marked with what looks like red nail polish. 'I can take your own plates to be passing for you, after your home stomach goes.'

'Thank you.' Ozoemena smells the plantains frying. Her stomach grumbles. She would risk the purge for some plantains.

Nkili's corner of the dormitory is pristine, and her locker is nearly twice the size of everyone else's, covered in white paint. Ozoemena takes in the flowered sheets, the tightly tucked ends. There is not one grain of sand on the floor of Nkili's corner. Girls lounge on their beds, half-heartedly cheering two girls play-wrestling in the aisle.

'Do you want anything? Biscuit?' Nkili asks. Her keys are in her palm. Ozoemena is aware of the noise dying down. The other girls in the hostel are watching. She had not been going to accept Nkili's offer of snacks, but the added scrutiny makes her self-conscious.

'No, thank you,' she says.

'Are you sure? It's no problem.' Nkili cracks open her padlock. The door swings open, and a dictionary narrowly misses Ozoemena's foot.

'Sorry.' Ozoemena bends to pick it up, but Nkili gets there first. She searches the ground and retrieves a toothpick.

'I don't want to lose the page I was reading,' she says, slipping the toothpick into place. Returning the dictionary, Nkili snatches up a packet of biscuits and thrusts it under Ozoemena's nose. 'Here, take one.'

'Em, okay.' Startled, Ozoemena obeys, working a disc up from the packet and taking the tiniest bite. 'Thank you.'

'Let's find Obiageli,' Nkili says, suddenly shy. She padlocks her locker again and, linking hands with Ozoemena, tugs her gently up and away.

At the other end of the compound, opposite the porter's lodge, are two rectangular concrete enclosures, embedded with pebbles. The bathrooms: one side for seniors and the other for juniors. They are open to the elements and a wall with a fist-sized hole at its base separates them. Along the lengths of both stalls are shallow depressions.

'You have to hurry up in the morning. Once the seniors begin to baff, their dirty water enters our side.' Nkili pinches her nose.

'What time are we supposed to wake up?'

'When the bell rings. I like to go before everybody wakes up, but if seniors ever catch me . . .' Nkili lets the sentence hang. Ozoemena wants to ask why she would risk breaking the rules. The thought of her new friend being a lawbreaker is unsettling. Nkili starts speaking again and Ozoemena lets it go.

There are WC toilets that do not flush behind the bathrooms – 'Don't even think of going there if you value your life' – but Ozoemena can already smell the heavy scent of human faeces, the low hum of flies fattened and undisturbed in the dim coolness. Room nine is empty, a storage room of sorts. Mops and cleaning buckets lie against its walls, catching the sun. They find Obiageli in her corner, in hostel ten.

'Come and eat,' she says, making no move to offer up her bowl. She is eating a bowl of garri, groundnuts and powdered milk. 'This is the best room, abi? Even if it's on B-side.'

The sun is over on Ozoemena's side of the compound. It has only been a few hours, but she has already developed an affinity for her dorm room, its low, even pavement. Obiageli's corner is cold, as is her half of the yard. The pavement disappears almost under soil. The last room, nearest to the bathrooms, has only a sliver of concrete separating them from the deluge of sand. Ozoemena imagines they must get flooded during the rainy season.

'Why does that matter what side?' Ozoemena might have made up her mind, but she is still curious. Obiageli's bed is untidy, but Ozoemena does not refuse when their host gestures for her to sit down.

'That back of B is where people go to shit because it is full of bush,' says Nkili. 'You're lucky we are on A.'

Ozoemena takes it all in, their busy corners, laid out side by side, demarcated by provisions lockers of all shapes and sizes. Socks, pants, bras and bath sponges hang from metal headboards, drying or airing. The senior girls are permitted posters on the walls above their beds. The juniors are not.

'So, if I want to ease myself, nko?' Ozoemena asks.

'You go behind the bathroom in the daytime. If the seniors catch you in the bushes, you will serve punishment.'

Ozoemena thinks about the humming she heard coming from behind the bathrooms and is determined to hold her bladder until it is dark enough to go to the bush.

'You think you can hold it? That is how you end up with yellow eyes,' says Obiageli, reading her mind. 'And shitty breath.'

Ozoemena throws her head back to laugh and feels it, a shrieking building in her head. She holds her breath, saliva filling her mouth at the nails-on-chalkboard sensation.

Not now, she thinks. *Please, not now.*

Saliva bulges her cheek. She hears colour, the buzzing iridescence of the late evening flies clustering around the rusty metal dustbins under the tree in the middle of the girls' compound, the huffing pink of the sky at sunset, as steam escaping from an opened pot. Ozoemena impales the soft meat of her palms on her fingernail.

Stay, she tells herself. *Stay, don't go.*

A bell tolls, faintly building in volume until it cuts through the bad transmission in her ears. The intensity of her surroundings fade, muted and subdued in comparison to just moments before.

A hand falls on her shoulder and Ozoemena looks into Nkili's eyes. Her friend's caterpillar brows are furrowed in concern. Students scuttle like soldier ants around them both, including Obiageli, holding on to her half-eaten bowl of food.

'What happened?' Nkili asks in a soft voice, and Ozoemena stops short, wondering what Nkili senses, if there is something on her face that shows itself as strange or bizarre or terrifying. Something that will lose her friends before she has even begun her stay in school. She also wants to tell Nkili everything. It is funny, she thinks, that a stranger should show such inquisitiveness about her condition after a few hours in a new place, when her own sister would not. However, she relents, perturbed by what her face must have just revealed, the fear of rejection if she tells her secret too soon or to the wrong person.

The saliva in her mouth is cold and abundant, impossible to swallow. In spite of how bad it looks, she steps out and spits towards the sandy mound, miscalculates, and embarrasses herself. A huge globule lands at her own feet, having dribbled ineffectually off her chin.

'I smelled something bad,' she lies.

'Oh.' Nkili's brow clears. Her eyes dance with mirth. 'Don't worry, in a few days, even the smell of poo will be good to you.' The bell ringer keeps going, summoning girls for the next event of the day – dinner. The bell's deep sound is made by banging on one of the poles holding up the roof in front of the dining room attached to the end of hostel.

Another senior girl walks up to them and slaps Ozoemena on the back of her head, hard. Ozoemena doubles over, clutching her head. She grits her teeth, tears rushing down her face.

'I saw you spitting,' she says.

'Sorry, Senior. She didn't know. She is new,' Nkili explains.

'And so?' the senior answers. Nkili says nothing else. 'You are supposed to tell her how we behave.'

Obiageli rushes back from the dining hall. 'Are you people coming?' she shouts, and gets a smack from the same older girl for her trouble.

'This is not a market,' says the senior. 'You three, see me during night prep.'

As they walk away from her, Nkili mutters darkly, 'These ones think they own the whole school.'

Ozoemena nods. Senior girls are already proving a pain.

CHAPTER THIRTEEN

Treasure

Mummy shakes me and shakes me until I wake up behind my eyes. I already know the day will be bad.

'Get up, Treasure!' she says. She is talking up-up, her voice high and excited, the way she used to talk when Daddy buys her something she likes. I allow her to shake me more, but when my head is feeling like it will break off my neck, I open my eyes. I sit up.

'See? What did I tell you?! *This* is how you do business.'

I am breathing through my mouth and my nose. The air is souring my tongue.

There are cartons all over our room. Plenty-plenty cartons. Mummy has opened some of them. There are packet-cereals and tea, tins of milk and coffee. There is Omo detergent and body cream . . .

'Cleopatra soap!' says Mummy. One whole carton full. The perfume is much and our whole room smells of it. My heart lifts to see Mummy so happy. My heart falls to see Mummy so happy.

'Mummy, does this mean I am going with the spirit now?'

Mummy puts down the soap fast. She is looking more and more like herself before-before, even though her thin resembles bonga fish own.

'For where? No, it means nothing like that. Did you promise him anything? If somebody wants to spend money on you,

you let them. Don't refuse, but don't pledge them anything either. Look at you. Your hair curling without chemicals, your teeth white and straight like mine. You know book. Why would you settle for a spirit? No, he should bring what he wants, and you take. It is your due. It's what you deserve. You hear me?'

'Yes, Mummy.'

I hear Daddy's voice in my head. *My Dazzling, you deserve the world.* He used to say that whenever his poke-nosing, jealous brothers questioned any of the things he bought me: shoes and clothes from China, Indian skirt with little bells in the tying-strings, the tape recorder I used to record myself singing.

Mummy takes her chewing stick and navigates around all the boxes, laughing small to herself. When she opens the door to the back yard, she screams. I run to her.

Yam tubers are lined up, row upon row like the thighs of men. There are new yams, full of hair and heavy with clay. There are bundles of ụgụ and spinach, an open bag of egusi seeds spilling in the corner. Mummy's exclamations have attracted Landlady, who is counting everything stacked by the door with her eyes. The more she counts, the more her mouth turns down o, until her chin sags like one turkey neck.

'I did not see the truck that carried this in,' she says. 'The people bringing you gifts, ọkwa they brought my rent money as well?'

When I leave them, Mummy is giving her things as if she is a poor relation, pointing here and there. 'Landlady, oya take this one, I know you like big yams like this, and you people are plenty. No, no. We will never finish it.'

My stomach is boiling me, and my mind is not peaceful. I go to the market to see if me I can find the spirit there.

By the time I walk round my usual area three times, the sun has woken up, burning my head with fire. I want to sit inside

someone's shed, but I don' yet resemble someone that has
money, so nobody will let me in. I tell myself that I should
go home. Someone hisses my name.

'Ey-iss! Treasure.'

The spirit is eating roasted groundnuts from a funnel paper,
standing under one empty shed that is broken. I can smell
them, the type where the shell is roasted in san-sand. He don'
get the seeds out but throws the whole thing into his mouth
and chews with the sand and everything inside.

'Do you want some?' he asks.

I want, but I shake my head. 'Thank you.'

'Did you like my gifts?'

'No,' I say.

'No?' He looks as if I slapped him; then he starts laughing.
He turns the funnel paper into his mouth like cup. I don'
know how all the groundnuts can enter his mouth at the same
time, because the paper is newspaper and big, but he pours
all of it inside. He chews and swallows without his cheeks
fatting.

'Side effect of being here-but-not-here. Hunger is always
flogging me.' He pushes all the newspaper into his mouth
and chews it. Nobody looks at him. Is like people can't see
him. Fear is catching me. If people can't see him, and I am
talking to the air, they will think I am mad. They will flog me
and pursue me from the market so that I don' spoil something.
I move to the side and walk out of the market, into one small
road with walls from other fences. I don' see the spirit move
but he is there, smiling at me as if he knows all my in and
out.

'Ah, my wife . . .'

'Why did you bring all those things?' I ask him. My body
is scratching me because I don' like knowing something is
happening but not what.

'All which things? That little something I did?'

I tell him, 'I dinor agree for you.'

'No wahala.' He waves it away. 'I said I will look after you – and your mother, even if she doesn't like me. Tell me, did she like the things I did? I showed her that I am not small. She likes it, okw'ya?'

'No,' I lie.

The spirit's face grows serious. The sun hits his shirt, and I peep his body through cloth. Do spirits have bodies, even the parts we can't see?

'You forced me to involve other . . . colleagues of mine, you and your mother. You nearly made trouble for me.'

I want to tell him that I was not among, but what kind of daughter will I be? Mummy is only looking after me, the way a mother should.

'I know you didn't do it, my Treasure. You're too pure. It doesn't matter. You forced my hand, and to bring all the things I did, I had to involve others. Now they too want wives. And Treasure, these ones, they are not like me. I told them you will find them wives, and you must. Or they will do terrible things to you. Many-many things. If you were my wife, I could protect you, but since you've refused . . .' He shakes his shoulders.

'Ngwa, go and collect everything back! I didin beg you for things. Take it all back. After all, our first meeting was trade-by-barter. I gave you something and you gave me something else!' I am angry now. I am angry at him and at Mummy. I am vexing for her. I don' want them to do her bad thing. I am happy she is alive and okay and not sleeping. I am happy she is happy. But I . . .

'All my friends need are three more girls. Three pure girls to be their wives. Pure, do you hear? They must not have seen their first menses. My friends want wives to bear their souls and help them live again. This life is not just one go, but to come back, somebody from your family, from your

lineage, must give birth to you again. My friends and I . . .'
The spirit clears his throat. 'You see, we all died before we
could have children. We cannot live again if there is no lineage
to carry us on. We will be forgotten, nobody to pour us libation and say our names. You can help us, shey? If you help
them, I promise, I will leave you alone, but the blood that
does it must be new and fresh. Pure – that is what I hear.
That is the only way it works outside the family line.'

'How am I supposed to know who has seen their menses
and who has not?' The way he is looking harmless, my mind
is turning it and suspecting cunning. 'If I get wives for your
friends nwanụ, you will just leave me to go like that?'

'Ah, that's where I am different to the others. I can't marry
someone that doesn't want me. I cannot force you. I will find
someone else.'

'Then why did you say three *more*?'

'It's just a slip of my mouth. I won't touch you. As for the
others, you have to find wives for them o. I will stay around
you until you do. I won't let any problems occur. In fact, to
show you that I am serious—' He reaches into the air near
his head and pulls out something. It shines in the sun, and I
cover my eyes. 'Sorry,' he says, and puts his hand down so
that my shadow covers it.

I stare at the something he is holding.

Is gold, cool, like plaits of hair in my hand.

Daddy's watch. We buried him with it.

Immediately-immediately, I start crying. Am missing my
daddy. My nose is scratching me. Everything is too hard and
heavy on my body. Am tired of always thinking, looking for
who wants to cheat me, for who is finding my trouble, dodging
Landlady. Is plenty-much. When I put the watch to my nose,
it even smells like Daddy. I cry more. My throat is paining
me and am having headache.

'Did you take this from my daddy's body?'

'No o,' says the spirit. 'I found your daddy as we discussed, remember? He was in the line of lost souls, the line going to see the Bone Woman. I saved him; I'm looking after him. The Bone Woman will not deceive him like she deceived me. I told you I would look after him. It was going to be my present to you, bringing him to see you. But now that you've refused me, sha, keep the watch.'

'Who is this "Bone Woman" sef?' I am cleaning my eyes, but more tears are coming out.

The spirit twists his mouth like this. 'A wicked person, believe me, you don't want anybody you love going to see the Bone Woman. She has a warehouse of bodies and can bring people back to life without them starting from the beginning again.'

My nose is coming out too and I bend down and clean it inside the end of my skirt so nobody will see. 'So why not go to her?' I ask. 'Why are you disturbing me, "my wife this, my wife that"? You and your friends should beg and the kain woman will help you.'

'Nothing in this life is free.' The spirit throways his face. 'All that woman wants is to have slaves that she can keep for years and years, turning them about with promises.' He shakes his head. 'No, I won't wait anymore.'

He starts humming one song and I am trying to stop crying but my shoulders are trembling, and my nose is pouring innermost my mouth.

Ada eze, nwata ọma, biko bịa. Ka m kuru gị n'aru, k'obi juọ m oyi o. Ọkwa ịmara, na-aga m anwụ, m'irapu mụ laa, Ada, Ada biko bịa oyoyo m o.

Daddy used to sing it to me when it was time to sleep. From when I was small, till the night he died. Only the two of us know.

The bell for Angelus begins to ring. The market stops around us. Only the non-Catholics are walking, and there are few of them, moving small-small with respect. The market has turned into church. Everybody respects church. Everybody is standing up, customers and traders, doing sign of the cross on theirselfs. Barrow boys lean their barrows on their bodies, on people's sheds. In different areas, people are leading prayer and others answering them answer. The spirit stands there looking at me and not going. This is the first time I have seen him standing quiet, like pole.

I blow my nose into the sand. I wipe my eyes. 'I will help you,' I say.

The spirit nods as if he already knew before I opened my mouth. I put Daddy's watch inside my pocket, thinking where I will hide it when I go home so that Mummy will not see.

THE ANGELUS

> *And the angel of the Lord declared unto Mary*
> *And she conceived of the Holy Spirit*
> *Hail Mary, full of grace,*
> *The Lord is with thee,*
> *Blessed art thou amongst women,*
> *And blessed is the fruit of thine womb, Jesus.*
> *Holy Mary, Mother of God,*
> *Pray for us sinners,*
> *Now, and at the hour of our death,*
> *Amen.*
> *Behold the handmaid of the Lord,*
> *Be it done unto me, according to your word,*
> *Maria dị asọ, nne nke Chukwu,*
> *Yọbalu anyi bụ ndi njọ ayịyọ,*
> *Kita ma n'onwu anyị,*
> *Amen.*

There is another something on my body when prayer finishes: one long detty string. At the end is a bead, big and brown.

It resembles udala seed. I didin see the spirit when he vamoosed. The necklace is smelling dry, spoiled meat odour after they have offed and cleaned the deep freezer, just like the spirit smells. I remove it from my neck and hold it in front of my eyes to look it properly. In the sun, it don' resemble ordinary udala. There is something drawn on it, carved and shining. No, inside the seed, moving small-small like worm that is dying. Looking at it swells my head and gives me bad feeling.

I put it inside my pocket. It is heavy like cement, heavy in my stomach.

CHAPTER FOURTEEN

Ozoemena: Then

From the beginning of the new school year in September, everything changed for Ozoemena – and not in a kind way.

Oruke Nwosu had told her to be vigilant, to search for her tether, but he had not informed her how to go about the process of searching. Ozoemena was bursting at the seams to tell someone, anyone, but the Leopard Society was a secret one. And unlike Mbu, she was more interested in fitting in than standing out.

Oruke Nwosu also did not tell her how to use said leopard powers, or when they would materialise. What to do about bullies. Whether she could retaliate or not. And how? Ozoemena remained a target because of her slight fleshiness, which many perceived as weakness, and for the way she kept getting drawn to the outcasts, like Anulika, the girl who drooled constantly. With one side of her body paralysed, Anulika dragged her left foot through the sand, staining her white socks. Kind-hearted Anulika, who gave her an orange segment that she had pains-takingly peeled, its tough green skin yielding under her persistent fingers. Ozoemena, grateful, popped it into her mouth, and hell broke loose. Lost in her own world, Ozoemena was unaware the bullies had been watching. They pointed, horrified. Surely Anulika's drool tainted everything; why would Ozoemena take food from the girl's hand? They clicked their fingers until Ozoemena spat the orange out. Instantly, shame came, especially when Aṅulika stared at Ozoemena, a flash of knowledge in those wide-set eyes. She tried to say sorry to Aṅulika several times afterwards, but the girl's eyes never returned the flash of awareness they had in that moment. Ozoemena suffered under the burden of guilt. A leopard would surely be stronger and pay no mind to bullies.

At night, Ozoemena became afflicted by nightmares, incomprehensible things filled with danger and anxiety. She woke up sobbing most times, until she began to stay awake, only falling asleep during the day, in the classroom, snuggling on the sun-drenched pavements at breaktime, and difficult to wake after her siesta at home. The nightmares followed, traversing the boundaries of sleep. Ozoemena began to wet the bed.

Mbu, disgusted, demanded and got a separate bed from her sister, which she pushed to the opposite wall in the space they shared. Ozoemena watched Mbu's curved back rise and fall all through the night. The shadows in the room took on life animated by what she thought was her imagination. Once, she watched a catlike form crawl in from the window and stalk the ceiling before melting away into a corner of the wall nearest to the door. Ozoemena lay frozen until dawn. She checked her hands for claws, her teeth for elongated canines, her skin for spots.

'You are so vain,' Mbu spat. 'Get out from the mirror, I want to see myself.'

Ozoemena did not challenge her notion. She bore her insults, watched while she slept and tried to carry on as close to normal as she could manage with the search for her tether and bullies and Mbu and school.

A ball bounced off Ozoemena's head, jolting her. It was partially deflated, but hurt, nevertheless. Ozoemena glared at it, rubbing her head, and wishing she could melt it into a smear on the ground with her vision.

'Throw it here,' yelled Benjamin, her main bully, a squat boy with the rough skin of a toad and thick white clouds marbleising his teeth. Normally, Ozoemena would oblige, but this time she remained sitting on the pavement in the sun, staring at him. Several sweaty boys shouted commands, but it was Benjamin who waddled up to her on his bowlegs.

'Didn't you hear me say you should pass it?' he asked. Ozoemena purposefully looked away. Benjamin made a noise in his throat, incredulous. She sensed him turn away to elicit support, and Paul, his half-brother, was there, as dirty as his sibling, shovel-hands and giant flat feet. The boys came from a polygamous household, the children of a medicine man in Nibo-Nise, a fact they used to their advantage. They had not been baptised, and teachers often wondered aloud why they had biblical names when they were not churchgoers.

Ozoemena rose from the pavement and went into the playground, seeking the company of classmates, hoping to diffuse the trouble she could sense brewing. But the brothers were not so easily dissuaded by a crowd – not when they could smell blood.

Paul struck next. 'Leave her. You know her family are osu.'

Everybody gasped. Her friends covered their mouths. Ozoemena halted, turned around. 'What did you say?' she asked, not because she did not hear, but because she knew that even though Paul had used the wrong word, he had meant the deepest insult to her family. Is that what her family were? That is not the story her grandmother and Oruke told. Her family were not enslaved. They were the heroes, protectors. Mbu had told her that people mixed up the Igbo words over the years, confusing the word 'oru', those born slaves, for the word 'osu', those venerated servants of the gods, tarring everything with the same brush because of Christianity – but surely the children of a medicine man knew that? Ozoemena now had another problem tossed at her feet. How would Paul know anything about her, anyway? She eyed him, trying to think her way out of the situation.

And so? she thought. *Why should either be shameful?* Nobody was responsible for how they were born. Before she could speak, Benjamin did.

'I heard your father is going mad. That he cries all the time. Like a woman.'

Another gasp. Ozoemena heard the whispers start up. She glanced around her. Her father had returned from the funeral silent, and over the past few weeks, had been steadily turning into someone else. People were beginning to notice the cancelled surgeries. Prisca told everybody he was 'depressed', and had prescribed medication for her husband that he did not touch. She had started taking over management duties at her husband's hospital, redirecting patients to his competitors for a cut of the profits, risking more talk. Surgeons were terrible gossipmongers, but Ozoemena could not bear for her father to be further unmasked, on a playground of all places.

She snapped. 'That's a lie!'

'It's true,' said Benjamin, dismissively. 'He cries like a baby every day. My father told me.' He crossed his arms, as if that alone made it irrefutable.

'How would your father know anything?' one of Ozoemena's friend's interjected, coming to her aid. 'He doesn't use hospitals. He goes to the bush to cut green leaves and tree bark to chew.'

'Doesn't matter. My father knows everything, even things that are unseen,' Benjamin boasted. 'That's how I know your father is going mad.'

'Your father is a grass-chewing goat and a liar. Your mothers are liars! In fact, everybody in your family is a liar!' Ozoemena breathed hard. Already she regretted her words, regretted causing the flaring of Benjamin's nostrils, the violence that was sure to follow. Her palms turned cold, and her heart rattled, a ripe avocado seed within its fruit. Her female class-mates congregated around her. It was how schoolyard battles were fought, boys against girls. Ozoemena sensed as much of the crowd were on her side as were against her. Mothers and fathers were off limits in verbal spats, but Benjamin had cast the first stone.

Another friend took her hand. 'Let's go,' she said. 'We can report him that he was saying bad things about your family.'

'Go where? No, she has to beat him once and for all,' chirped the first, skipping from foot to foot. 'After all, they insulted her father's name.'

Everybody hated and feared the brothers, but nobody was willing to tackle them head-on.

'I won't fight anyone,' said Ozoemena, deflated. 'Let's go.' But it was too late, the circle had formed, and a boy pushed her towards Benjamin. Ozoemena resisted, shoving back, trying to get out of the band of arms and legs, the chanting, and the jeering. Benjamin glanced towards the classroom, and Ozoemena read his thoughts in the gesture: if there was to be a fight, he ought to make it fast before the teachers noticed. He lunged towards Ozoemena, but she side-stepped him, more out of luck than any technique. From the corner of her eye, she noticed several girls tucking the hems of their school dresses into their pants. The fight would proceed whether she wanted it or not. The best she could do was land a few blows of her own.

She turned, squared off to Benjamin, with his snapping cloudy teeth, Paul by his side, grinning. Even though the latter was older by two years, he had always followed Benjamin's lead. Paul bent down and scooped a fistful of sand, clutched it. He meant to pour it in Ozoemena's hair, earning her the ire of her mother and many market women. Every girl was taught from babyhood to avoid getting sand in her hair. The thick kinks and curls held on to every grain despite washing, ruining many elaborate hairstyles. The waste of money from taking out plaits, having them done all over. Paul meant to get her in serious trouble.

Paul danced up, blocking Ozoemena. He threw the sand. Paul was a good head taller, with a long reach. The sand, clumped from being held together in his palm, landed on her forehead, and exploded on impact.

Benjamin's mouth opened in an 'o' of disbelief. He had been looking forward to thrashing her, but this was something else. Ozoemena turned her eyes on both of them, hot, blinding fury rising within her. She gritted her teeth, and some of the sand that had invaded her mouth crackled and popped in between its bony peaks. Benjamin backed away.

Ozoemena screamed at him with all the fury in her, her body taut with rage. A shrieking, decibels higher than she was capable of producing, filled her ears, as though she had turned a knob and was caught between radio frequencies.

You will have to die.

Ozoemena wondered if this was how she died: filled with rage, her own screams blowing her head into fragments, the leopard taking her over afterwards.

The world through her eyes tilted, shifted. She was aware of a sudden darkening, a hand passed over the sun. Rain, coming to add to the mess on her head, she thought, but looking up, it was a different sky entirely, big and violet, lit up with stars as far as the eye could see.

Ozoemena stood by the edge of a huge swathe of farmland, watching a girl of about her own age sitting under a tree, stridently weeping.

Despite her desire to stare at her surroundings, and the strangeness of how she came to be in another place while only moments before she had been in a fight, Ozoemena

approached the girl. She felt a pull towards her, strong in the
middle of her chest, as if from a cough building. There were
salt trails covering the girl's face. The girl looked up, startled,
and rose to her feet. As she looked Ozoemena over, the relief
spreading over her face changed to dread. Ozoemena
perceived the girl's anxiety, and it infected her.

'Who . . . who are you?' Ozoemena asked.

The girl opened her mouth and shut it again. She raised
her hand to Ozoemena's gaze. An illuminated necklace around
the girl's neck shone brighter than any earthly source of light.

Ozoemena shielded her eyes. 'What is it?' she asked.

The girl opened her mouth again to speak, but a sound in
the distance caught both their ears. It was the tumult of the
earth's bones falling apart, boulders smashing one into the
other, the discord of rusted gears crushing masonry. Ozoemena
clapped her hands over her ears. The sound, whatever it was,
drew nearer, and the girl took off running. Ozoemena came
seconds behind, stunned into action. The girl fled and she
followed, disregarding everything telling her to stop, to take
stock, and the overpowering logic informing her that she must
be dreaming.

'Stop!' Ozoemena shouted. She was not a runner. There
was a ferocious stabbing in her chest, a burning in her lungs
that was spreading to her limbs. The girl stumbled but she
did not fall. She turned, pointed, mouthed something, the
veins on her neck popping with the strain of making herself
understood. Ozoemena could not hear the girl. They ran
through rows of cassava in raised mounds, lengthy leaves of
maize slapping their faces, other unidentified plants catching
Ozoemena's hair. The stone-crushing machine followed. A
thinning in the lush vegetation told Ozoemena they were
coming to the end of the farmland. A tug in her chest, and
she turned right.

'Take this way!' she shouted, but the terror-stricken girl

did not heed. Ozoemena picked up a stone and hurled it with all her might, surprised at her coordination when it hit the girl's retreating back. *This way,* Ozoemena beckoned. She took off again, knowing the girl was following.

She heard the roar of water. A river. *Idemili.* The thought came unbidden into her head. Crossing the river would lead to safety. Ozoemena knew this with the assurance of someone in a dream.

The waterway, when they got to it, was rough, churning and beating. Ozoemena was frightened, but the tugging in her chest continued, and she was certain that even though she could not swim, she would not drown. The girl halted next to her, eyes wide. She looked at Ozoemena, but whatever she said was lost in the same high pitch that blocked Ozoemena's ears with pain, feedback from a misconfigured microphone. Ozoemena grabbed the girl's hand and pulled her towards the water, but the girl dug her heels into the soft mudbank.

'Let's go!' Ozoemena screamed. The girl shook her head, no. She pointed the other way, the path she had wanted to take before Ozoemena stopped her.

'No!' Ozoemena insisted. 'This is the way, trust me.'

The water whipped itself into a frenzy, rearing up serpentine, its great coils churning. The girl backed away, trembling. Another roar from the stone crusher proved her undoing. She snatched her hand away from Ozoemena and sprinted off in the other direction.

'No, no, no!' yelled Ozoemena, starting after her. From the long grass, a trumpeting, loud and jarring. A great bundle of feathers flew into her face, knocking her back. Ozoemena fell backwards, and the twisting waters snatched her from the bank, tumbling her into their depths.

Mbu peered down at her and Ozoemena read concern in her bearing, which surprised her and quickened wakefulness. Her sister should not have been present, having gone off to secondary school the year before. Mbu's face tightened into its familiar slit-eyed fury. She hauled Ozoemena up from the table in the bare room that served as a nurse's station, shook her, and dusted her off roughly. Her sister's palms stung Ozoemena's bare skin. Ozoemena knew punishment when she felt it.

'Can't even fight properly,' Mbu snarled under her breath.

Ozoemena looked around, dazed. Her classmates were nowhere to be seen. The bell for the end of the day was going.

Recently, Mbu had been getting into fights at her new school, the last one triggering an asthma attack so bad that she had been carried home to recuperate for two days. It did not stop her getting into another as soon as she returned to school, though.

'Don't start anything if you can finish nothing,' Mbu said.

'I didn't do anything. It was Benjamin—'

'So, you just lie there and have a siesta till the end of school?' Mbu hissed. 'Get up! And why are your clothes wet?'

Ozoemena took over dusting herself off. Her clothes were indeed wet, sodden with earth that did not easily budge, staining her chequered uniform a deep reddish-brown. She wondered which pupils had brought her in from the playing fields. She hoped they had not seen her pants. Had they tried to wake her by pouring water over her?

The river.

Ozoemena pounded the thought into pulp before it was fully formed. The girl, the river, the violet skies; she had fainted and dreamed, that was all. Fainting was embarrassing, but Ozoemena could deal with that over the thought of slipping out of her own life and into another place like a greased catfish. A place real enough that it had returned her wet and dripping. A place with monstrous sounds that pursued her with – she was certain – no good intent. She wondered what would have happened if it had caught her. Did dying in a dream affect real life?

Ozoemena stared in dismay at her clothes. Prisca was going to kill her dead, deader than death in any dream. Her socks were soaked and heavy, and with each stamp of her feet, they lopped their way out of the front of her open-toed school sandals, like the tongues of thirsty animals. She pulled the socks up her legs. They itched.

The air was filled with playful shouting and the thudding of balls. Children swarmed towards the gates, to the car park under the old ukpaka tree and beyond, to the buses, roads: to freedom from another day of educational drudgery. The Nibo-Nise kids left through the back way. Ozoemena hoped Benjamin was not waiting to finish the fight. Her legs were weak. They struggled to hold her up.

'Go and get your bag from class. Hurry up.' Mbu's mouth turned down at the corners.

'Okay.' Ozoemena tripped and nearly faceplanted.

'I can't believe you're the leopard of our family,' Mbu said. Her face crinkled as she walked away.

Ozoemena did not ask how she knew. Mbu knew everything.

Ozoemena daydreamed throughout their journey home. Where had she gone, and how had she got there? Who was the girl? Terror seized her and she quivered in the sun. She had lost half a school day. In this world, and in any others that happened to exist, she seemed not to be in control of her life.

The First Bride

It was not that Chinenye was a thief sha, and it was not that she was not. Chinenye preferred to think of herself as a collector.

She did not steal big things. She did not take things that she could be caught carrying. Chinenye took small-small things, shiny objects. And try as she might, she could not bring herself to take anything that benefitted her parents. Once, when a neighbour's new bra had gone missing right out of her drawer, street urchins with their all-seeing eyes had fingered Chinenye as the culprit. A mob had surged to their compound, and a select few searched her corner of the room. They had found the bra, too big, too sequined. More burlesque than undergarment. What did she think she would do with that? her father asked, but as always, Chinenye had no answers to give. Only that she'd *had* to take the bra. It sang to her, called to her, quickened her blood until she took it. How did she know it was there? Chinenye could not answer either. The neighbour's sister had just sent the bra down from America and it was still snuggled up in its drawstring bag when Chinenye had pilfered it, leaving the packaging behind, but none of this mattered to her father.

That night, he had taken his belt and decorated her back with stripes. She entered the house – her father said, catching his breath between thrashing his daughter – did she not see anything better to steal? Could whatever impish spirit whispering in his daughter's ear not lead her to where the gold or dollars were kept? He said this bit in a low voice. The walls were thin, and he did not want the neighbours to think he was the one sending his daughter to pilfer. It was just poverty making him run his mouth so. The kind of poverty that had him gambling with his earnings whenever he could. The kind of poverty that saw him dreaming of finding money on the ground: a note, a wallet, a whole bag of the stuff, dropped by bank robbers fleeing the law. The kind of poverty that saw him stop by not one but two girlfriends on his long months away as a lorry driver, getting his ego massaged and the women's bellies swollen, before he returned to Nne Chinenye's caustic tongue.

Chinenye tried. She really did. But when she saw the jewellery in her friend's palm, her mouth watered and her blood pumped hard in her head, making her dizzy.

'You like it?' Treasure said. 'My uncle gave it to me. I won't wear it till we leave this place. It doesn't fit here.'

Chinenye feigned disinterest, but the necklace, with its bizarre gold and green striations that seemed to move with the eye, blazed in her mind. She helped her friend clean up the room, manoeuvring expertly between the boxes stacked high with food.

That night, she tossed and turned and could not sleep. Behind the curtain, her father sexed her mother into grudging silence, his frustration at another gambling loss apparent in the scrape of the bed's wooden legs on the naked concrete floor. Chinenye lay in the middle of her siblings and the necklace glowed brightly in her vision. She never needed to plan; opportunities just presented themselves.

Two days before her friend moved out, Chinenye saw her chance. There had been rumours regarding a change in the fortunes of Treasure and her mother, but Chinenye paid no

mind to any of them. What use did she have for whispers
when something real was within grasp? She watched and she
waited, and when the time came, she pounced. Chinenye had
seen Treasure slip the necklace into the pocket of a dress
she'd tossed over the back of a chair. A quick dip, and it was
ensconced within her palm. The dress slid off the back of the
chair, and Chinenye snatched it off the floor, rough concrete
embedding itself under her nails and drawing spots of blood.
She sweated with joy and accomplishment, picked shards of
ground-up stone from underneath her fingernails and bore
the pain, sucking her fingers to soothe them. That night, as
the family slept, she stroked the necklace's stone, gazing at
its flowing pinprick of light within until she too fell asleep.

The wind upon her skin felt sticky, like a smear of honey,
and the sky, when she awoke she had a strange shade, the
start of an ache that encompassed her entire being. Chinenye
looked around her and understood at once that her soul was
lost. There was a pulsing at her throat. The stone had
embedded itself in her skin, writhing and spreading dishar-
mony in her body. She tugged at the string bearing the stone,
and the skin came with it. Chinenye sensed herself being
cleaved, peeled away from who she was. She attacked her
chest, the flesh, almost to the bone. She could not get the
stone out. Her blood was saccharine, a bitter aftertaste. She
smelled putrid to her own nose.

Chinenye sat and cried for her mother, for her siblings,
for the friend whose bizarre jewellery she had stolen, now
knowing the rumours about the girl and her family's sudden
good fortune to be true. Sitting under the purple sky, she did
not notice from which direction the girl appeared, only that
she had. A child, really. Chinenye tried to ask, to find out if
she knew the way out, but no matter how loudly she screamed
her questions, the girl did not seem to hear her.

And then they were running, and the girl was going the

wrong way and Chinenye was fleeing from her, determined not to get caught by whatever it was that sounded like a cement mixer on legs, that scraping and tumbling of rocks in a metal throat that filled her stomach with water, water that ran down her legs and made her slip as she sprinted.

The ground pulsed through her feet with the force of the noise. She ran, and the roar followed. Chinenye was a strong girl, the first of all her siblings, used to hard work, used to moving fast enough to avoid blows from both of her parents, but no matter how hard she ran and how fast, the roar hounded her until her legs grew heavy with fatigue and Chinenye could run no more.

CHAPTER FIFTEEN

Treasure: Then

My conscience is not chooking me about Chinenye, because everybody knows she used to follow boys to uncompleted building and allow them to do alụlụmana with their hands inside her pant for five-five naira. That one, is it life? And too, her father is useless, always pregnanting women all over the place, so me I know that he will be one kain happy because he will not have to bring money to feed another child again. Not as if he used to bring before. Every time he comes back from driving lorry, Chinenye's mother will tie wrapper, off her earrings and greet him with, 'Wetin you carry come?' Every time they will be fighting.

Is not as if me I now deceived Chinenye. I said, if she steals that one seed, then is because is her destiny to marry a spirit. She stole it and now she has gone with them. They are saying she followed one of her boyfriends. Chinenye used to steal from everybody. I don' pity her.

Is Nne Chinenye that me I pity, because Chinenye's father has been insulting her up and down, shouting for everyone to hear that it was Nne Chinenye that taught her child how to prostitute, and that if it was not for her, Chinenye would not have tasted boys and learned to like their flavour. He said he will now sack Nne Chinenye, and our neighbours them were begging him.

'Wherever she is, that girl better-better stay there!' Papa Chinenye likes making noise.

Nne Chinenye is cleaning groundnut in front of her house and the pity inside me is heavy. Chinenye used to do all these petty-petty jobs for her. She used to sweep and wash all the clothes and baff the younger ones when her mother prepared all her roasted groundnut and ukwa and things. Is just that Chinenye follows boys and does hand-picking, but her mother trained her well. Anyway, is not as if me, I dashed her to spirit husband. She is the one that took his something by herself, so how is it my consign? We are leaving this place sha, so bye-bye Landlady. Mummy settled her all her money and plenty things sef, and is Landlady herself who was now telling Mummy, eh, are you sure you want to go? You can stay here now, in fact, I can even give you Omalicha-dem's room, is not as if they need all that space, after all where are the children that she is supposed to born kwanu?

Mummy didin even have time to say, 'No, don't worry,' before Omalicha now started singing all her vex-songs, direct at Landlady, and Landlady started talking to the air, insulting Omalicha, and that was the drama that we watched that night.

'I'm so glad we are leaving this rubbish heap,' Mummy says, sitting on the bed and combing her hair. Aunty Lucy relaxed her hair and is now so long, is touching where her bra hooks. Mummy combs it and the comb passes through it like they are not quarrelling. Her hair is shining with Pink Oil like white people's hair, and she is beginning to resemble Bianca Onoh again. She packs it banana on the top of her head and ties scarf over it so that it does not cut all over the pillowcase or dry in the night.

I touch my hair. I poured water on it well, since Landlady opened the tank for us to use and baff, and Mummy put the

oil in it too, but it will take a while before my hair is long
enough so I can relax it again.

Outside, the men are discussing before the news again,
arguing if they were ruling Nigeria, they will do this and that.
Mummy hisses.

'Some of them will live the same life, going round and
round like jangilova until they die. As for me and you, eh?
We are made for better things.' She pats her hair and looks
into the mirror she is holding between her legs. I don' know
where she got mirror from.

'Yes, Mummy,' I say.

'Just keep doing what I tell you.' Her voice is low now so
that nobody but me can hear. 'We will have that spirit dancing
awantilọ. Promise him nothing. Give him nothing. It's when
you give men small that they start to misbehave. Like that
fool outside.' She points with her chin and puts the mirror
away. The bed makes noise when she lies down on it. 'No
more hard beds after this. We will live like we used to; better,
even.'

'And I will go back to school,' I say, but Mummy is already
dozing. I lie on my mat and dream of new school uniforms;
pinafore, because I will be a junior girl. Daddy wanted me
to pass federal, maybe Onitsha, but me I wanted Enugu. When
I was starting Primary Six, that is when everything happened,
and now my mates are finishing JS1. It is paining me small
that I did not even do Common Entrance, that my mates will
pass me in class and senior me by two years in secondary,
but at least I will be in school again. Thank God.

The next morning, someone is sweeping outside. Is
Chinenye's turn to sweep, and I am thinking maybe I dinor
understand, maybe the spirit them released her, but when I
open the door, is Chinenye's small sister Kelechi. She is
carrying her baby brother on the back and his legs are dragging, and she keeps stopping to adjust him. She kisses her

teeth and backs him to the pavement, but as she is trying to remove the wrapper, she releases the top part that holds his shoulders, but the bottom part remains tight. It holds the boy's legs together and he falls back. His head hits the floor – gbim! – and he starts crying.

'Close that door,' says Mummy. 'I don't want to hear that noise.' She sighs.

Outside, someone slaps Kelechi hard, and it sounds all over the yard.

The pick-up was supposed to come in the morning, but twelve noon has passed by the time the driver comes.

'Only you? Who is going to carry our things? I can't help you o, I'm sick,' says Mummy. The driver came only him so that he will not share his payment.

'Ah, Madam, is this not your child here? She can work now, okw'ya nne?' He asks me, even though he is looking at Mummy like she is Father Christmas.

Ifeanyi joined to be carrying all the yams and cartons. There are more, I swear, and the pick-up driver is saying, 'Ehhhh,' and looking at us with new eyes. Mummy gives Ifeanyi a packet of Choco Milo, but he don' even look at her or thank her. He is only looking me with goat eyes. He don' look well. His eyes are bringing water, and when he was helping us to carry, his legs were shaking like izaga masquerade. There is an open sore on one side of his mouth. A fly circles it, but Ifeanyi don' use his hand to shaa it away.

'Ifeanyi!' Landlady shouts, and is then that he wakes up and carries himself back to her.

I sit in the middle of the pick-up, between Mummy and the driver. Am on the engine and it licks the back of my legs and my bum-bum shining-hot through the seat, and the driver says sorry and puts towel for me to sit on. He's trying to talk to Mummy and say this and that, but she says Mm, Mhm, and after a small time he stops.

I don' look behind me as we drive off. Forward ever, backward never.

The only thing I'm thinking is, Chinenye, is she pure enough for the spirit to collect and count as one bride, or has she started seeing her menses?

CHAPTER SIXTEEN

Ozoemena: Now

Buoyed by her friends, Ozoemena slips almost seamlessly into boarding life. Dawns are characterised by early morning prayers, held outside in biting Harmattan winds while the girls huddle, half-asleep, under their wrappers and blankets. Some of the seniors refuse to join in, preferring the warmth of their beds to mutual obeisance to the creator. Obiageli had caught sight of Ozoemena's chaplet, and presuming her to be Catholic, registered her with the Catholic prefect, Senior Chikodiri. The Catholics have more religious activities and rules than the Anglicans do, at moments inconducive to relaxation. Ozoemena does not wish to rock the boat with her new friends, who are Catholic, in a place where those groupings are clearly and utterly delineated. Besides, she knows how to pray a rosary; how hard could the rest of it be?

After morning prayers, there comes the inevitable scramble for the bathroom. The first two mornings, Ozoemena waits her turn, but it never comes. Girl after girl, mistaking her orderliness for disinterest, pushes past her to use the stall, lathering and rinsing in impossibly fast times before the bell for breakfast goes. Ozoemena learns to jostle like the rest. In the early days, she uses the water in her big jerrycan to bathe, contrary to Obiageli's suggestion that she save all water from home for drinking. Ozoemena copies the girls' running start, the jog they do on the spot both to warm up and gain some courage before pouring the frigid bowlful of water over their bodies. Even with this, the water is icy enough to make her teeth chatter for nearly an hour after her bath.

When her home water runs out, she fetches water from the red metal water tank outside the kitchen. One scoop of that on her body and the chill causes Ozoemena's vision to become unfocused for a few seconds. Her skin goes numb.

'Hey! Hey! Stop urinating in the bathroom, are you stupid?' It is the girl with the entourage from her first day, Ugochi. She skitters away from the yellow gliding over to her, a few places down from Ozoemena. The other girls, who had not noticed before now, complain and hiss. It is bad etiquette to urinate in the stalls. Ozoemena had not meant to.

'Sorry!' She scoops up her water, drops the cover of her soap dish, which serves as her scoop, picks up it again. The delay makes her hands shake as she collects some water in a cupped palm, rinses the soap dish off before dipping it in the bucket again. Ozoemena begins to sluice the urine.

'I mean,' Ugochi fumes and spouts, 'it's like you people don't know how to baff in your village or something, where did you even come from sef?' The triplets, Ugochi's perpetual audience and muscle, make secret signs to each other with their hands and titter. In addition to Ugochi's jutting jaw, her shoulders are broad as a swimmer's. Her entire face is creased with disgust. Even her body is angry, Ozoemena thinks as she rinses. She is nearly completely flat-chested except for hard, prominent nipples, scrunched up against the cold wind. Ozoemena's bucket of water is at the halfway mark, and yet Ugochi does not cease her tirade.

'Better don't splash that on me, if you don't want my trouble.'

'It's okay, now, haba. Do you want me to finish my whole water on rinsing the bathroom floor?' Ozoemena asks. Her face floods hot with embarrassment. A few girls are focused on the task of bathing and leaving to get dressed, and Ozoemena is aware that at this rate, she will be late to breakfast, risking punishment. 'I've rinsed it enough.' She pours some water down her back and not over her shoulder, to save as much of it as she can. Lathering her sponge, she gets to work, aware of Ugochi and co., towelling off and staring. Ugochi's towel is pink and fluffy, like something a child would possess. Ozoemena muses that it must take a lot of water to wash. Sensible parents, like her mother, buy their children the 'Good Morning' range of towels for boarding school; thin, absorbent, and tasselled for style. They take next to no water to wash, and in the Harmattan, her towel starts drying before it hits the line.

Ozoemena has just worked the soap over her face when she hears Ugochi swish past her, stepping carefully so as not to get any bath water on her feet. There is a whisper and a giggle that turns into a throaty chuckle as the girls go outside. Ozoemena had been involuntarily clenching her tummy from the cold, but she exhales and bends over to scoop up some of her water.

There is no bucket in front of her.

Panicked, Ozoemena feels around her feet for the plastic pail, her soap dish lid floating on top of it. Nothing. She moves her feet, hoping to connect with a satisfying thud from the bucket. Nothing but space in front of her.

'You guys, it's not fair o,' says a voice in the stalls. 'She's new. If it was you nko?'

More laughter from outside the bathroom. Ozoemena rubs the soap from her eyes as much as she can and opens them. Ugochi stands on A-side pavement, rinsing off the sand that has clumped together on her slippers from the walk across the quadrangle using water from Ozoemena's bucket. She passes the bucket along to one of the triplets beside her, and that one rinses her feet too and passes it back. Ugochi kicks her feet one after the other. Droplets fly out into the sun, sparkling prettily before soaking into the sand.

Everything within Ozoemena grows immobile and quiet. She cannot feel her flesh, only hate erupting, rising up from somewhere deep inside. Soap suds pop upon her skin, radio static in her ears. Ugochi waves to her and drops the bucket on the ground. It rolls in the sand.

Ozoemena shakes herself loose as the bell for breakfast begins to ring. 'Please.' She turns to the only girl left in the stalls. 'Can you . . .?'

'Sorry, my water has finished.' Queeneth is usually the last person to bathe in their year. Rumour has it, she has repeated their class so many times that the seniors generally leave her alone. Queeneth does everything at her own pace. As Ozoemena pleads with her eyes, the girl ties her towel around her chest, unties it, ties it again. She flicks her knotted nylon sponge in the air to dry it. Droplets mist and shimmer in the air between them. Ozoemena is desperate enough to nearly ask if Queeneth would flick the sponge over her own body.

'When you go out, can you ask Obiageli or Nkili to please bring me small water?' she asks. There is pressure in her bladder again, this time from fear.

'Okay, I will ask them,' says Queeneth, but she still bends over, pouring water over her legs so that the hairs fall exquisitely in one direction. She picks her soap off the ledge of the wall and pops her washed and wrung underwear into the bucket. Ozoemena's hands around her body are tight. She squeezes, and the Harmattan squeezes back. She watches as Queeneth sashays away. The soap crackles and flakes off her body, drifting to the ground like dandruff.

The older seniors are beginning to rise from their beauty sleep. Ozoemena cowers, shaking in the corner of the junior cubicle, praying that none of them will decide to use it. Outside, the compound pulsates with activity, white blouses and navy-blue skirts flashing from one activity to the next. Ozoemena waits for someone to come until her body is as dry as bone. She rubs off the sudsy marks as best she can and dashes into her hostel, to slather cream all over herself and try to forget the whole morning ever happened. Tears sting beneath her eyelids. Ozoemena snaps the claps on her suitcase with more force than is needed, throwing it open. She hates herself for crying, for being weak. *Mbu would not have cried*, she thinks. Her sister would have stepped out of the bathroom and given Ugochi a fat lip, even if she would have had to pay for it later. That is what Ozoemena should have done. Why didn't she? How can she be the leopard, protector of Oba-of-the-nine-brothers, when she is so feeble, so pathetic?

The bell rings for lining up, and she grabs her school bag, an old, tan leather doctor's bag that belonged to her father. She has missed breakfast, her bed is not made, and her skin itches from the soap in spite of the lotion she has rubbed into it. With a twinge, Ozoemena realises that she misses her sister Mbu and Baby, the toddler. What are they doing now, preparing for school? Eating breakfast? Ozoemena longs for hot water in the mornings like many of the senior girls have, warming a full bucket with a heating coil and mixing it to their desired temperature, sharing with a few of their darlings and friends. Ugochi uses warm water; Ozoemena has seen her exchanging bowlfuls with the triplets. She wonders who the girl's school mother is – somebody powerful, no doubt, given her stinking attitude. Were it not for Mbu crowing at her in triumph from now until eternity, Ozoemena would go to the admin office and ask to be sent home. Her sister has done many things, but she has never, never taken away the opportunity for Ozoemena to cleanse herself thoroughly of yesterday's body. Her sister has never made her start her day filthy.

Obiageli slips into the line for the JS1 students behind her.

'Do you know there is soap behind your ear?' She licks a finger and wipes it off. Ozoemena jerks away. She begins to sniffle, overwhelmed by wistfulness, sucking in the sorrow that engulfs her. She is preoccupied with holding it in when their matron, checking uniforms on the line, approaches. Ozoemena swallows and splutters, 'Good Morning,' a wet, choked-off affair.

Matron frowns. 'You cannot greet?' she asks. Matron is a small, wizened woman of indeterminate age, eyebrows drawn in thick black smudges as if by a child's wax crayon. Her lipstick is extremely red and harsh, bleeding into the lines around her mouth. Her eyes are grey, one of them cloudy with cataracts.

'I said, "Good Morning, Ma,"' Ozoemena replies, but Matron, snarling, boxes her in the chest. It surprises her more than if the old woman had hit her cheek, and has the opposite effect on her emotions. The tears dry up and her homesickness ceases. Ozoemena puts steel in her spine. Matron moves on. The whistle goes and they march arrhythmically to class.

'Did you not find Matron anything again?' Obiageli whispers. 'Give her o, even if it is small money or soap. Anything, that way she won't find your trouble again.' She rubs Ozoemena's shoulder and withdraws her hand before her friend can shrug it off.

Ozoemena does not answer. The fire has returned, blazing inside. From the front of the line, Ugochi, unaware of the chaos raging within her, turns around and blows Ozoemena a kiss.

'We should get her,' says Nkili. She flaps a wet T-shirt in the air to shake out its creases. 'Just say yes, and we will get her.

By the time we finish beating her, lips will be as fat as a tipper tyre.'

The girls are doing their midweek washing; that is to say, Ozoemena is. Nkili has one complete set of uniform for every day of the week, but she helps, rinsing out Ozoemena's garments and spreading them on the tall grass. The Harmattan sucks the moisture off the clothes before their eyes.

'No, leave her,' says Ozoemena. 'She will see herself.' It is something Mbu says right before she decides to thrash someone. Ozoemena has never done this, but it feels good to say so, to release the pent-up anger pulsating in her blood. She rubs at the armpit of her school shirt with the green Truck soap, pops the soap down on a breeze block and scrubs the fabric between two hands. She repeats at the collar, cuffs, submerges the whole garment, then wrings it out and tosses it into the rinsing bucket. Each time Nkili picks it up, Ozoemena thanks her.

'What does that one even think she is?' Nkili asks.

'It's because of her brother, Ambobo.' Obiageli cleans under her nails with a broomstick until they shine white like crescent moons on her fingertips. 'Brothers are market here, sebi you know.'

'You have brothers. You don't behave like a stupid cow,' Ozoemena replies.

'Ambobo is popular now; football captain, always taking first in hundred metres and four by hundred, excellent in science and maths, and everyone says he will be SP when Senior Emeka graduates next year.' Obiageli wipes the broomstick and begins to pick her teeth with it.

'Your brothers are popular,' Nkili retorts. 'Sebi the oldest one – Senior whatshisname – is labour prefect?'

'Nobody likes the labour prefect abeg. It's only how to give us clean-up and grass-cutting that my brother does.' Teeth cleaned, Obiageli worries under her big toenail. 'Ambobo is handsome. My brothers' heads resemble loaves of bread. And I mean Agege bread o, the one that you press like this, and it changes shape.'

Obiageli's manner of speaking often dissolves the girls into puddles of mirth. She usually makes the tightness in Ozoemena's head and chest evaporate, and while this was welcome in the beginning, Ozoemena resents it in this moment. She wants someone to stoke this new fire of vengeance in her. She wants Ugochi to suffer. She is tired of bullies, but she is afraid to lose her temper, to let the anger take over. The last time she felt such anger, it was at Benjamin. Her leopard snatched her away to another place, and she has no desire for a return visit. Not until she finds her so-called tether.

Around them, other students wash their clothes, bending over in the large clearing made out of white construction sand next to the water tank. It is a favourite spot for laundry, not just for its proximity to the water, but because the sand does not stain clothes. If they drop a wet item of clothing by accident, they only need to pick it up and shake for it to be clean again. The common red earth everywhere else on the compound stains as badly as palm oil. Ozoemena washes a pair of socks next. The cotton fibres turn hard and ropey in the water.

'Help me wash one of my shirts now, please,' says Obiageli. She does not wait for an answer, but dashes off to her hostel to retrieve it.

Nkili grins, showing off the grey tooth in the middle of her face, which she normally hides. 'You wait, she will come back with more than one shirt.'

Ozoemena pulls her hand from the dirty water. They are puckered, and her cuticles are raw and raised away from the nail after having the coarse fabric scrubbed against them.

'I'm only going to wash one shirt,' Ozoemena says. 'The water is too dirty anyway.'

'You should tell your mum to buy you those white powders

that are new. They don't change the colour of the water that quickly.'

Ozoemena makes a noncommittal noise in her throat, keeping an eye on her full water container. She made sure to fill it first before she began her laundry.

A gust of wind starts up, blowing loose building sand up from the edges of the clearing into their faces. Nkili shrieks.

'My shirt!' cries Ozoemena. She plunges into the sea of grass rippling around her and chases after the item. Her school blouse soars kite-like against the smoky evening sky, its front ruffles flapping wings. It lands on the grass. Ozoemena reaches for it, brushes it with her fingertips, and away it goes again. The grass is in a frenzy of motion, and Ozoemena has the sensation of water, as though the next step will suck her in, drag her under. She creeps towards the blouse when it lands again, slowly, stealthily, as if it is a living thing. She does not trust herself to get too close. The shirt seems to be waiting for her to reach out. It quivers with the breeze, taunting. The spears of grass sway their heads under its weight. Ozoemena remembers, as though from long ago, catching grasshoppers in her primary school. It took skill to identify the insects camouflaged against the green, to hover over them without casting a shadow, to launch oneself with speed, palms cupped together to trap the prey. She remembers the tickle on skin as the grasshoppers struggled, the ripping and tearing as she and her friends pulled the stalks of green from the earth in an effort to preserve their catch.

Ozoemena does this now, propels herself, heedless of how stained her shirt could get. She flies through the air and closes her hands around it, just as another wind kicks up, threatening to tear it from her grasp. Whooping, she holds the shirt up triumphantly and turns to present it to Nkili.

Her head hisses and pops like droplets of cold water on a scorching stovetop. The screeching has returned, and she clasps her hands to her head, ineffectually trying to block out the sound that comes from within and all around her.

The fibres of her muscles strain, drawing her forwards into the forest that has appeared where the clearing should be. The popping sound dies off. Ozoemena darts quick glances about, checking the sky for violet, listening for grinding noises, for crying. This is not the same place she visited; for one, the sky is a normal colour. The blood in her body pumps with a force that almost throws her face-down on the ground. She plants her feet. She cannot bring herself to yield to the power pulling her forwards. Nor can she go back – *to where?* All she desires is to get out, however she came to be in this place.

The shrieking again. Ozoemena begins to identify when it is coming, even if she does not yet know what it means. There are no tears; now is not the time for weeping, even though she wants to crumple up and cry for her mother. A shout slashes forth from her throat, loud and startling, unsteady under the weight of barely suppressed fear. She grips the lobes of her ears tightly, wanting to tear them, bleeding, from her head. Anything to make the noise stop. Saliva pours freely out of her mouth.

'Stop!' she shouts. 'Stop!'

The sound does not stop, but there is a kernel within it, one she senses rather than hears, a question from the earth and the sky, the rippling grass like waves around her knees:

Are you still sleeping? Is it not yet early day?

With a supreme force that Ozoemena has never before mustered, she tears one hand away from her ear, and forming a fist, punches down into the earth, breaking the connection, breaking the noise. Breaking everything.

'Ozo?! Ozoemena? Where are you?'

Her knuckles are abraded. Her wrist throbs, but the world is hers once more. A movement draws her gaze. Something scuttles away from her in the grass. Slowly, she gets to her feet, taking tiny swallows of air, afraid to wake the shrieking again.

'Here.' She waves the shirt, lumbering through the grass to her friends.

'Where did you go? You just vanished!' Nkili tips some water out of Ozoemena's jerrycan and into its cover. She gargles, spits. 'There is sand in my mouth. Sorry I'm taking your water.'

'There was a hole,' Ozoemena lies, but that is all she can manage before sitting down heavily on the ground.

'Ah, you need to be careful of snakes o, and animals that live under the earth.' Obiageli has returned. She helps herself to Ozoemena's soap and water. 'Why do you think Mr Ibe makes us inspect the field before games? People break their legs if they step into a hole. You're lucky.'

Ozoemena does not feel lucky. She is certain that before the scuttling, she had seen a very human pair of eyes at ground level, watching her.

CHAPTER SEVENTEEN

Treasure: Then

My father's brothers come to visit. The K-leg they carried to our house to take everything is the same leg they have now used to be knocking on our gate in the old Government Reserved Area where Mummy moved us. The place is not as fine as the house we had when Daddy was alive, but compare-and-contrast to Landlady's house, is heaven. Maybe I should be thanking the spirit for making it so that we can move up in life position again, but I still have two more girls to find before I can be thankful – when I will see Daddy again. At least now Mummy is no more sleeping.

The gateman does not open for the uncles. I am in my new room's window looking at them outside the gate, where sun is thrashing them well. I know they can see me through the white curtain, but me I don' move.

'Come! You girl! Open the gate for us!' It's Uncle Obi, my father's senior brother, commanding me as if he gave me the house to keep for him and he's come to collect it back. Am just looking at him inside his eye from where I am standing but I don' move, talkless of even saying anything. They stand there, having meeting like someone gave them chair to sit, and after, when the sun beats them tire, they carry their nonsense, craw-craw legs and go to home.

I ask Mummy, 'Why did you leave them outside?' Not as

if me I want them to come. I want to know why she, she didin allow them.

She says, 'They will come back. Their throats are too long. You won't remember, but their eyes were always paining them when it came to your daddy. They could not wait to take everything he owned. Even that fool Obi was saying, "Eh, by rights, you belong to me, after all, you have had no sons."' Mummy is putting rosy cheeks on her face, and her hair is permed with waves inside it. She blows the head of the brush before putting it inside the make-up case. 'As if that one can ever afford a woman of my timbre and calibre.'

True-true, the uncles come back, and this time, Mummy allows the gateman for them to enter. She keeps them waiting there o, while she chooses and chooses what she will wear. The wardrobe in her room is not as full as it used to be, but it's fuller than it has been since Daddy died. She wears long-shimi and bra that is shining soft. Me I want the thing that is going to happen to do now-now, but Mummy don' care. My leg is dancing-dancing on the floor where I am sitting waiting for her to finish, and she says, 'Treasure, if you cannot sit in one place, maybe go to your room,' so I stop.

She selects one buba like this and ties the wrapper with style. The blouse is off-shoulder and when she goes down the stairs, she is like a TV person. I follow her behind in her back.

'Oh, did you people come?' she asks.

In the parlour are my Uncles Obi, Amos and Shuwa. Uncle Obi is standing up, looking at all the things in the parlour. He picks one thing, looks at it, puts it back down before he turns to salute Mummy back. He has grown his mouth long and pulled it tight. His wife, Aunty Chinasa, is here too. She is short, and we used to be the same height, but now I am taller than her. Aunty Chinasa used to tell me to bring my shoe so that she too can wear because we were the same size that time, and then she will collect it and not bring it back.

Uncle Obi them greet Mummy, but it's like their mouths don' know how to move again. They stand up, counting their hands and legs with their eyes. They don' know where to put face. I greet them and they greet me back. I don' let them remove their eyes from my eyes, but Aunty Chinasa don' have shame.

'Eh,' she says. 'Look at how big you have grown; your shoe will not size me again.' And she laughs.

'Please, there is seat,' Mummy says. My uncles sit down as if there are soldier ants biting them on their bum-bum. 'Treasure, please bring mineral,' she says, but the salaka is too much for Uncle Obi.

'Don't worry,' he says. 'We only said let us come and greet you.'

'Don't worry ke? Ah, no now. You came to my house, you must have kola. Treasure, please add kola, love.'

I run and leave the parlour, but my style and Mummy's own are not the same. I know Mummy will give them drink and kola so that they will choke on it, but me, I will never. They should drink their saliva. I don' bring anything, I just stand by the wall in the corridor, looking at everything that is going on inside.

Uncle Amos and Shuwa are just looking around and around, counting things with their eyes: TV, home stereo, speakers. None of these things is what I want, but Mummy said if I tell the spirit, he will bring, and I told him, and he brought. She says these are the things Daddy likes, and that is true. But inside me, my body is paining me, because I am thinking if she thinks that her style is working? Does she think that all the things plus-including our house is for free? It's me buying it with the life of people, and I am owing. Am not saying that me I don' like having a bed again, but all the other things on top is jara, and I just want Daddy to come back.

'We heard the good news . . .' Uncle Amos neck is long like a giraffe. He swallows as if he's eating and looks at Uncle Obi.

'News?' asks Mummy. 'Did something happen?'

'We said let us come and greet the man of the house. Is he around?'

'Which man again?' Mummy asks.

'The man that has put you in this house now. He did not do well. You were somebody's wife, so if he wants to marry you, then he has to come to us, is it not so?' This one is Uncle Obi talking. He is still pushing this his agenda but where he is going, there is no road.

Mummy throws her neck, and her hair reaches down her back. She laughs and she claps, and when she finishes, she stands up and calls the gateman. 'Please, show them the way out,' she says, and my uncles are looking at her like frogs, and Uncle Obi is trying to choke something out of his throat, but the gateman is from Awusa-Hill in the North, and they are afraid of him when he starts speaking his language and pushing all of them to the door, so they go. Uncle Obi sees me where I am standing in the corridor and opens his teeth.

'Ah, our daughter. You don't ask of your cousins again. You have to be asking of your sisters and brothers; after all, we are one family. Eh-he, take this, you hear?' He gives me one dirty ten naira like this.

I look at it. I say, 'Thank you, Uncle,' and I put it in my pocket. Money is money.

'We will come again to see you, you hear? It is not good for women like you to live alone without the protection of a man from the family. This kind of life . . . there are many, many bad people that will be looking at you and your mummy. Okay, we are going, eh? Look after your mummy, inu?'

He is trying to save face so that it's not as if Mummy has
pursued them out, but me, I am not even listening to him. I
am nodding like agama and saying yes because Mummy is
here. Aunty Chinasa is smiling, smiling like something has
gone wrong in her head. These are the same people that left
us without anything, that took all the fat envelopes during
the funeral, even the ones that people put inside Mummy's
hand, they took it from her. Just shameless behaviour. If not
for Aunty Ojiugo hiding envelopes in her pant, me and
Mummy would have died since, like my uncles wanted.

Uncle Obi is wearing a new red cap on his head. I hear
he used money he made from Daddy's properties to buy
himself chieftaincy title, but his hair that is bearing the cap
sef is not combed, and that tells me that he cannot maintain.
Is it only to buy title?

As usual, Uncle Shuwa does not say anything. He just
came and looked and went.

Mummy arranges her buba on her shoulders after they
have gone. 'These people have not seen anything yet,' she
says. 'It's me they tried to maltreat. Me? A whole Akuabata?'

I don' like it, but am thinking in my mind: *No, it's Treasure.
A whole Treasure.* But I don' say it out.

'We showed them pepper,' Mummy says. 'They think I am
the same woman. They should try me and see. Look at their
greedy throats. They think they can consume me. With which
mouth? I am bigger than them!'

I am bigger. Me, me, me.

CHAPTER EIGHTEEN

Ozoemena: Now

The night is awake, and so is Ozoemena.

It does not matter how quickly she nods off; the middle of the night nowadays finds her awake and listening. She has never heard so many sounds in the night time – every emission of gas, every dreamy murmur and sigh.

Sometimes at home, when it rained and the potholes on their old street filled with rainwater, the bullfrogs would bellow through the night. Other times, there were crickets, but nothing like this, this orchestra of insects, bats and other creatures. She is aware more than ever of being in the middle of the forest. Ozoemena tries to follow the rhythms with her human mind, to make music out of the noise. Her mind drifts. She thinks of her father, where he must be, what he is doing. Has her mother forgotten him already? Her parents had separate bedrooms: he for always being up at odd hours once the emergency bell in the hospital rang, and Prisca for all the childrearing she has had to do with her children. After their father left, Ozoemena returned from school one afternoon to find his bed gone as well. She had loved its crushed red velvet upholstery, inlaid with gold strips. When times were good, she and Mbu used to lie on it and pretend to be Egyptian pharaohs. Just like that, the dream was over. Her father's wardrobe had been emptied of whatever he did not take, leaving behind his musky scent and one holey sock, where his hard, big toenail had pierced through the fabric. Ozoemena had snuck it into her pillowcase.

Tonight, it is the sudden absence of noise that wakes her properly, shakes her, so that she holds her breath the way the night does, waiting for something to happen.

There is a clatter from the metal dustbins under the tree in the middle of the quadrangle, followed by a low yowl.

'Jesus,' a hostel-mate whispers in the darkness.

Ozoemena exhales. A cat. Her grandmother M'ma has cats: striped creatures, grey, black and white, a bit of brown on the face and speckled in their green eyes. The cats keep rats out of her grandmother's bags of rice and beans and off her tubers of yam and cocoyam. They sometimes get overzealous and present M'ma with a clutch of bloody, downy feathers belonging to her chicks, which they have killed. Cats, Ozoemena can deal with. Cats, she likes. She pulls up her cotton wrapper, covering her shoulders and neck, and turns around to settle into sleep.

But there are footsteps that do not belong to the night. Footsteps that fall hard on the concrete pavement, knock, knock, knock, moving slowly and deliberately, coming from the bathroom end. Ozoemena has not heard any doors open, not here, in a compound so silent that every sound is amplified. She would have heard something. And no students wear hard shoes; they are not allowed.

Each step is a nail, hammered into the concrete. Her imagination runs away with her, and she sees it in her mind's eye, the sizzle of sparks, as though from a welder's torch. Ozoemena's breath in her ears is loud, and she is certain that whoever is walking outside can hear her.

Whatever. Not whoever.

In her heart, Ozoemena recognises that it is not a person who walks outside. She has no way of knowing beyond the feeling in her gut, but it is one she is learning to trust. The footfalls stop outside the door of hostel four.

'Jesus. Jesus. Jesus. Jesus.' Ozoemena recognises the voice now. Senior Joy, a class four girl who sleeps nearest to the window opening out on to the pavement. Her voice quivers. Hearing it, Ozoemena becomes even more afraid. She swallows, but the saliva will not go down. It dribbles out on her pillowcase.

The hairs on her arms rise, pressing against the sleeves of her pyjamas, aching where they are anchored in her skin. The thing standing on the pavement behind the door is looking in, searching. *For her.* She feels the heat of its gaze and wonders if it is not already in the room, unseen and waiting.

Senior Joy must have had the same idea. The silence, the waiting, proves too much for her. She snaps. 'Jesus!' she screams. 'Blood of Jesus! Holy Ghost fire!' Her shout rends the stillness of the night.

People begin to stir in the hostel. 'What is it? Why are you shouting?' asks Senior Nwakaego. Ozoemena notices the senior prefect's tone is low, and that she does not leave her bed to investigate the commotion. Senior Joy shouts, but Ozoemena can hear beyond her screams, beyond the bed springs twanging under impatient bodies, angered at being woken up and eager to get back to sleep.

'It's outside the door,' Ozoemena says, but her voice does not carry. As if waiting for her to acknowledge it, the footsteps start up again. This time, everybody hears. They quieten down. The footsteps grow fainter, heading out the right way, towards the locked porter's lodge and beyond.

Senior Nwakaego strikes a match and lights her kerosene lantern. Her fair-complexioned face is almost bloodless by the orange light of the flame.

'Was that Madam Koi-Koi?' she asks, and the name lies in Ozoemena's mouth like a dirty coin.

★

'I can't believe you heard her,' Nkili whispers the next morning in class.

'You're lucky it's only hearing you heard,' says Obiageli. 'She conks people that see her on the head, and they die.'

'I know.' Ozoemena shudders.

Every boarding school has their own version of the ghost woman: she is a jilted teacher who died by her own hand; a beautiful woman replaced by a senior student who vows revenge; she was marking scripts in the night when someone came behind her and strangled her and she never saw her killer. Many versions, none logical, all terrifying. Ozoemena can now attest to the skin-crawling wrongness of hearing those heels tapping away into the night. For the one-and-a-half years that Mbu went to boarding school, she had terrified Ozoemena with stories of Madam Koi-Koi and her ilk. No matter what Ozoemena believes, she had not expected this to be true. What does it mean? Are *all* the stories true? She nibbles at the Harmattan-desiccated skin of her lower lip. If an entity such as a leopard-person can exist, why can't anything else?

If such a creature exists.

Ozoemena shrugs the thought away. What proof does she have of being a leopard anyway, besides her sister's contempt, the words of an aged priest and her grandmother? Yes, she slid into another place and had an altercation with a deceased nun, but what decisive action does she take? She runs from noises. She flails about or is held, rooted, against her will, utterly useless. Completely afraid. Totally vulnerable. Ozoemena tamps down a shudder.

In class, none of the girls can talk about anything else. They lounge at their desks, textbooks open, waiting for first period to commence. Their teacher is late, but even the bookish students show no signs of concern.

'How come we've never heard Madam Koi-Koi in this school before until you joined?' asks Ugochi. Her compact mirror is open in her hand. She lifts up the top of her desk and takes out a pocket-sized tin of talcum powder, which she applies to her face to get rid of its shine.

'What is that supposed to mean?' asks Ozoemena, teeth gritting involuntarily.

Ugochi moves her shoulders up and down, feigning nonchalance. 'I'm just asking o, don't bite me. After all, the Madam Koi-Koi came to your hostel.'

'She didn't come to her hostel, is something wrong with your ears?' Nkili snaps. 'She stood outside.'

'Outside o, inside, it is the same thing.' Ugochi's fingers flicker over her cheeks, as smooth as boiled eggs in her round face. 'And I wasn't talking to you anyway, so mind your business.'

'If you talk to me like that I will Jackie Chan your whole face,' Nkili says.

'Aunty, go find your mates,' Ugochi snaps back, 'since respect is worrying you so much.'

Nkili rolls her eyes. 'You don't know the things I know. My mental capacity is better than your own because of what? Development. I can be in JS2 or 3 if I want—'

'Liar!' Ugochi retorts. 'Bo-bo gister! If you're so brainy, BC would have put you there after your entrance exams.'

Nkili hisses, and turns away with an exaggerated motion to show what she thinks of that. Ozoemena is grateful for her friend's intervention, more so when Ugochi's mouth tightens. The girls murmur, bits of gossip passing around the class.

'It's probably the villagers' fault, anyway,' says Thelma. The class quietens to hear her. She is one of the bookish ones who seems to know everything.

'Sweetie, we can't hear your back,' says Ugochi. 'Turn around if you're talking.' Her cronies talk with their hands and laugh, the same wide-jawed laughter. Ozoemena cannot yet tell the triplets apart.

Thelma turns, repeats herself. There is pink chewing gum in her mouth, which she slips around her tongue as she speaks.

'Villagers?' asks Ozoemena. Nobody else seems perplexed.

Thelma stares at Nkili, forming and cracking small bubbles in her gum as she chews. 'You didn't tell her the story? It's the story of our school.'

Obiageli stretches her hand towards Ugochi for some scented powder to dab on her oily face, but is ignored. She huffs. 'They say that the villagers are angry because we stole their school.'

'Stole? How do you steal a school?' asks Ozoemena.

'That's what they say o.' Thelma claps her hands, warming to her subject. 'Because our founder, Dr Udegbulam, is from this village, but he was brainy so he gained scholarship to study abroad and he now stayed there. He's been an educator in America tay tay.' Thelma clicks her fingers to denote the passage of time.

'Okay, so how did he steal the school?' Ozoemena asks again.

'Wait now, I'm getting there. He came back and now wanted to build Novus to compete with the rest of the world in technology and scientific . . . you know . . . all that stuff.' Thelma waves her hand, casting it around to ensure her audience is held captive. 'But he didn't have enough land. So, he went to ask the elders here. The village elders and the Igwe now—'

'Can't you take that gum out of your mouth, for god's sake? You look like a masticating goat,' Ugochi interjects.

Nkili rolls her eyes again. 'Yes, you know the meaning of big words. Please close your mouth and let her tell her story.' Her tone is soft, but the words hit their mark. Ugochi begins to say something, but one of the triplets touches her arm. She glares at them, but leans back in her seat.

'As I was saying,' Thelma continues pointedly. 'The elders

and Igwe then now discussed with all the villagers, and they agreed to give Dr Udegbulam the land, that when he finishes building, he would let all their children come to school free of charge. Dr Udegbulam said yes, but when he finished building the school, he refused to let their children go for free.'

'That's not fair,' Ozoemena says.

'He took only those that did well in primary school, the best ones, and they are not even plenty. And even sef, they had to take exams like we all did. They are less than ten that have that scholarship: Senior Delphine in class six, Mildred in class two, Senior Ogom, the boys' deputy prefect, Bobby in class three – the one that rings the bell.' Thelma punctuates each name by cracking of tiny bubbles in her chewing gum.

Ozoemena sees, in her mind's eye, a picture of Senior Delphine openly walking and talking with Bobby the bell-ringer. At the time, Ozoemena had assumed it was because Senior Delphine was in the topmost form, and Bobby was, well, Bobby. He went everywhere. Now she is not sure. It appears defiant. Nkili's comment about *'these ones'* at the start of school begins to make sense. Ozoemena had wrongly assumed she meant senior girls.

'That's why the villagers hate us,' Nkili adds. Her nod is old, wise. What a difference three weeks' lateness makes, Ozoemena ponders. She is being lectured to, like some sort of . . . non-member. A familiar and discomfiting sensation opens up in her stomach. She squirms, pursuing composure.

'Yes.' Thelma nods, sticking a sharp pencil into her ear. 'That's why they send witches and wizards after us. They want Novus to close, so they can get their land back.'

'Yes, but what does that have to do with Madam Koi-Koi?' Ozoemena insists. 'She visits many schools. My sister said—'

'You have to *invoke* her, stupid,' Ugochi says, rolling her eyes. 'They are *obviously* using her to scare us off.'

Ozoemena tosses her head, flippant. 'This is not *Scooby-Doo*, please,' she says pointedly, and is rewarded by a group chuckle.

Ugochi's jaw tightens.

'Haven't you seen the tree behind B block?' someone pipes up.

Ozoemena shakes her head.

'She is new,' says Ugochi. 'Wait till you start packing shit, you will see it.'

Ozoemena grimaces. 'We have to pack shit?'

'No, just *some* people.' Ugochi simpers. 'People with a shit-packing face. For example—'

'One ugly tree like this, it looks like it has a mouth that is shouting. That's a shrine,' Thelma continues, heading her off. 'They used to sacrifice people to it in the olden days.' She smiles the smug smile of master storyteller.

'Thelma, you're adding salt and pepper to your story now o!' The girls protest, many voices babbling. Ozoemena hears the fear running in an undercurrent through the sea of jeers. Its cadence is familiar.

'It's true, my brothers told me,' Ugochi says. Behind the classroom, someone snorts, and they turn to see Queeneth sleeping. Ugochi hisses. 'Always sleeping,' she says to no one in particular. 'That's why she is repeating the class.'

'They really didn't raise you well,' Nkili says, shaking her head.

'But why can't Dr Udegbulam do something, now? Maybe let them come and be doing their worship things at the tree?' Ozoemena asks, undeterred.

'Are you mad?' Ugochi's disdain for Ozoemena, for her question, is palpable.

'I mean,' Ozoemena explains, trying to dampen the spark of heat rising in her chest, 'Maybe let more village students in?'

'You're clearly stupid. This is not a motherless babies' home. What money will they use to run Novus if students aren't paying?' Ugochi whips the class into susurration again.

'Stop calling me stupid,' Ozoemena growls.

'Teacher is coming!' someone yells, and the girls scramble for their desks, knocking books to the floor in their haste. Thelma takes the gum out of her mouth and sticks it on to her wrist. Ugochi, lifting the tin of powder, tips it over Queeneth's sleeping head, giving the teacher a visible target for when he walks in, knuckles at the ready, to crack the sleeping girl on the skull.

CHAPTER NINETEEN

Treasure: Then

I am practising social studies composition practice when I start to be smelling that dry rotten meat smell again. I look all over the dining where I am sitting, in the side cupboard with all the new-new plates Mummy bought that have golden all around the corner, the glasses that shine straight from factory. Is looking more better than anything we are having before. My mind is telling me to ask where all these things are coming from, but me I don' know if I am ready to hear something that is bigger than my ears, so I just face front for now. Let me not drink Panadol for headache that is not breaking me. The time is coming when me and Mummy will have to talk, but it have not reach.

The rotten meat smell is strong around the fridge and when I open it, I see the bracelet there. How can something be smelling from fridge that is not open? I know me I am now getting used to seeing the spirit, but at times he will just perform something, and my mind will be turning with fear small. This one is also made with detty string, plenty-plenty small beads, black colour, brown colour, and reddish like laterite, but the middle bead is not bead at all and unlike the one before, that is what is making this bracelet to not be fine like that.

The middle bead is big and brown, like the nail of my thumb. It is also wrinkled like the body of an old woman, like dried aki awusa. Who will take this one now?

My problem now is that since we have moved, I don' know anybody and it will be hard to get another person for the spirit to collect. When Daddy was alive, we lived very well, but our estate was people like us too that lived there. Now Mummy has carried us to the acada-side, full of professor this and that, doctor this and that. Their kind of money is different. I know the kind of eye they look people like Daddy, as if he is a bush somebody. Why is here Mummy wants us to stay, me I don' know.

Children are singing outside. I sharp my ears. I didin use to like the game 'Fire on the Mawntin'. In primary school, we use to play it where everybody will sit in a circle, and we will be clapping and singing for the person who will be walking outside the circle. Then when the main singer will shout 'The fire is out', the walking person has to touch one of us on the back and run, and the person they touched must pursue them until they complete the circle round one time. If they don' catch the toucher before she sits in their space, then the pursuer will now turn into the walker.

Why I didin like that play is because of the running part. I can walk from here to Kafanchan, but to be running when nothing is pursuing you is hard for me, please. I like to play suwe and ọga because you have to be fast and think fast, or even Ludo and nchọ because it's for sharp minds, tortoise minds, and you can chop plenty of other people's okwe in the games if you are the best. But what is smart about touching somebody's back and running anyhow? Nonsense. Anytime they are playing 'Fire on the Mawntin', I will just find something else to be doing.

This time is the children in the next yard that are playing it with their friends. It's around two-thirty, three, so school has fallen apart, but instead of these children to be doing siesta or lessons, they are here playing. I want to tell them they should shut up, but is to shout and GRA is quiet. Nobody shouts here like that, and me I will not be the first. But then I am thinking something that makes sense. I peep over the wall from my window upstairs and see them, one, three, four children, girls, but is like one of them is a boy? What if . . .? I cannot take all even if temptation is doing me, but if I take one, then me I will only owe one girl. In a time that is small, Daddy will come back, then we can all move to somewhere and start life all over again.

I say, let me go and try to see if I can try my luck. The bracelet is in my hand. I'm not putting it on because me I don' know what will happen when I wear it. The gateman salutes me but he does not want me to pass, until me I give him the twenty naira inside my pocket and point him where I am going.

'Stay where I can see you, you hear?' he says. Mummy has not even paid him one month salary and already he is loyal. When she is in her full Bianca, all men must bow.

Outside, the kolo tar on the road is smooth like TomTom sweet and there are hot pink flowers everywhere falling on the road. Everybody has these flowers growing from their yard and falling their long hairs over the fence and into the road. Boganvila, they call it, the flower of richness. The gate of the house neighbouring our own is made from bar-bar and I say, 'Eyis,' to the children playing inside.

'What do you want?' The one talking must be their play-head. She stands up and the hair tie-tie in her big-big son-ga's are shining in the sun. When I was small, I used to use hair tie too. She comes to where me I am standing by the gate.

'Am your neighbour. I wanted to play with you.'

She looks me up and down like me and her have known each other before and I stole something from her. 'You are not our age mate. How old are you? Go away, we are not allowed to talk to anybody.'

I am telling myself if this girl reaches my hand, I will give her the slap of her life because she don' have respect. I senior her by two or three years, and this is how she is shaping her mouth to talk to me?

'I say am your neighbour.' I point at our house.

'Oh. You people.' She sucks her teeth.

'What does that mean?' I am telling myself to be smiling at her, but she is still looking at me like my head has spoiled.

'I am *definitely* not allowed to talk to you then.' She puts her hand on her waist, standing with her bum-bum out as if she is trying to lead a dance. 'My parents say you are bujwaa.'

I don' know what this word means, but from the way this small girl did her mouth to say it, I know is not a good thing.

'We are not . . .' I can't remember how she said the thing.

'You don't even know what it means!' She and her mates start laughing me. 'Your parents are OMATA market traders. You think living in GRA gives you panash.'

I turn to go, but I remember what me I came for. I hope when her spirit husband comes for her that this small girl will shit herself from fear. Then she will know how to talk to people that senior her properly. I pretend that something is on my leg and bend down.

'Is this yours?'

The girl twist her neck from where she and her friends are drawing something with chalk on the ground. She comes closer to the gate. When she reaches me, she snatches it, don' even say, 'Thank you,' but what's my own? She belongs to the spirits now.

The rude madam lifts the hand ornament up, turns it like this, like that.

'I would never wear such a hideous trinket,' she says. Then she throws it on the floor and marches it hard into the concrete, kpam! kpam! I am shouting at her to stop that, what is she doing, ngwanu she should give me since is not her own, but she stamps it until the thing starts to change colour to black, until it breaks, and smoke comes out like it is burning and flies away into the air.

CHAPTER TWENTY

Ozoemena: Now

Just after siesta, as the girls prepare themselves for an evening of games in the field, a student comes to the door. 'Nwokeke, they've come for you,' she says before vanishing.

'Pardon?' Ozoemena looks around, but everybody is busy making beds and putting on sportswear. She is already in hers – a calico tennis skirt with shorts underneath, and a pink shirt that used to be white until Mbu threw one of her red vests into the bucket in which Ozoemena had soaked her whites. Ozoemena wishes for the umpteenth time that she had had the foresight to soak her whites with bleach.

'You have a visitor,' Senior Akudo translates dryly. She is a senior who has not taken to Ozoemena, and has wondered aloud in her hearing why literal babies were being let into boarding school. She always finds fault with the way Ozoemena does chores, once yelling, 'Waist down! Aren't you female, for god's sake?' when Ozoemena volunteered to sweep her corner. Ozoemena detests her.

Ozoemena walks through the porter's lodge, trying not to break into a run. Her feet bang down on to the flexible metal sheet bridging a large dip on the way into the girl's hostel, and it twangs. She catches sight of the white van bearing the logo of her mother's pharmacy.

'Uncle Fred!' The chunky, moustachioed man has been in her parents' employ for a long while.

'Just these few days and you're already gbatịala like rubber band,' says Uncle Fred. The appellation is one of respect. Uncle Fred has known her since she was almost a baby.

'Did you bring Gala?' she asks.

'E butelu m gi your locker. And I also brought you more water. Go and get your jerrycan and ka m fill lụọ ya.'

Ozoemena smiles widely. She has missed the way he speaks. He is the master of blending English and Igbo together in the same sentence.

Uncle Fred opens the back of the van and grapples with the locker, sliding it to the edge. From the ground, he lifts it, grunting, leaning back to bear its weight. Ozoemena winces and rushes to help him. 'Go and get your container,' he says through gritted teeth.

Ozoemena grabs Nkili and Obiageli on her way back out of the hostel. The three of them wrestle with the heavy locker, carrying and dragging it inch by painful inch to the girls' hostel.

'We need one more person,' Nkili says, eyeing Uncle Fred. He has his back to them and is funnelling water from a massive fifty-litre jerry into Ozoemena's container. He fills up her drinking water too.

'We're beginning to line up for games. Come, let's carry it,' says Obiageli.

'Then put your hand under it well, now, Obiageli!' says Nkili.

'Let's not stop until we are inside,' says Ozoemena. 'Okay? One, two . . .' They lift. The locker is heavy, and in seconds it begins to hurt again. Its foot comes down hard on the sand.

'Obiageli!' Ozoemena is unintentionally sharp from being out of breath.

'Don't shout at me,' says Obiageli. 'Or I will just leave your locker here. It's not as if you're paying me sef.' Her breast rises and falls from the effort.

'Sorry, now,' says Nkili quickly, apologising before Ozoemena can say anything else. 'Obiageli oya just put hand and we will—'

'Tell me what you will give me before I help you,' Obiageli says to Ozoemena.

'You can't just do it because we are friends?' Ozoemena retorts.

'After you finished abusing me?'

'I didn't abuse you!'

'I'll help.' A voice cuts in. The girl who speaks is standing suddenly near them. Ozoemena does not know her, and looks to her friends for confirmation. Nkili shrugs. Obiageli has turned away, eyeing her escape route. Ozoemena seizes the offer in both hands.

'Thank you very much!' she says. They each take a deep breath and lift, working together, taking small, quick, ant-like steps. Ozoemena and the girl direct Nkili and Obiageli, who walk backwards. Up into the porter's lodge, shuffle, shuffle, down into the compound, and across to the pavement in front of hostel four, where they stand, stretching. The sickly-sweet smell of varnish coating the locker makes Ozoemena ache with nostalgia for home, for her mother's pharmacy, which shares a fence on one side with a carpentry workshop: the hiss of spraying tubes, the pounding of hammers and nails. The fascinating softening of sound that comes from being entombed in sawdust. Ozoemena loves sawdust for this reason. Mbu, naturally, does not.

'Thank you for helping me. My name is Ozoemena Nwokeke.'

'I am Chinonso Eke,' the girl says, clutching a polythene bag to her person.

Nkili smiles a wide welcome without showing any teeth.

'Have you just come?' she asks.

Chinonso nods. 'Please, help me?' Her English is stiff, the

way people speak when they are unused to talking in the language. They return outside to get Chinonso's things – a broom, a cutlass and a hoe, plus a zipped canvas bag and another heavy-looking black bag – which are leaning on the short wall of the lab buildings. There is not much, and Nkili and Chinonso share the load between themselves.

'Who brought you?' Nkili asks.

Ozoemena is already walking across the compound back to Uncle Fred and does not hear Chinonso's answer.

From her place by the vehicle, Ozoemena and Uncle Fred watch the girls troop out in sportswear just as the bell goes. Even heading to the same field as the boys, they keep in separate lines, the width of a classroom block between them. Ozoemena has never been to the games field, having been excused the previous week to catch up on schoolwork, and is anxious to get moving. She stays, however, as she does not want to be impolite to Uncle Fred, who has come all the way to see her and will probably be driving back in the dark. Her friends join the queue of girls, the last to arrive. Nkili and Chinonso appear to be bonding at the back of the line. Obiageli trails behind them, examining a new scab on her outstretched arm. Ozoemena observes her friends, a pang of possessiveness twanging in her gut.

Uncle Fred observes the line, leaning against the van. 'Ọnwere anything ị chọrọ ka'm gwa your mummy?' he asks. 'I dere ya letter? I will deliver it. No need to wait for NIPOST.'

Ozoemena shrugs, her earlier homesickness and terror forgotten in the light of day. Her mother will not tolerate stories of things walking about in the night, stopping by her dormitory. Ozoemena does not want to give her a reason to withdraw her from school. Any sign of auditory hallucinations would be one such reason.

They talk some more, and Uncle Fred fills her in on petty gossip. He is skirting around the obvious, and she knows it.

Even if Uncle Fred does not live with them, surely, he must know—

'Has my dad come back?' she asks.

He shakes his head, turning away from her hopeful, probing eyes. 'Eh-he, before m forget-ia. I brought you something.' The bag of Gala he pulls out of the cab of his van must contain twenty or thirty sausage rolls. They are hot from the sun, malleable and smelling of spiced beef. Normally it would be enough to make Ozoemena dance in ecstasy, but she manages a small smile, thanks him. 'The padlocks for your locker are in that bag too. Welu your keys.' He hands her a telephone coil keyholder-belt with two keys at the end and two other spares.

In the hostel, Ozoemena takes out three sausage rolls from the bag. She pauses a moment, adds a fourth, then slips them into the baggy pockets of her sportswear.

The cheers inform Ozoemena of the direction in which she should be heading, but once she steps off the end of the pavement, she is in uncharted waters.

A pebble gets into one of her plimsolls and she stops by a sooty old building, the earth around it soaked a permanent, oily black. It is the generator house. A fug of diesel hangs in the air, and a metal exhaust pipe shoots out of the side of the structure. She breathes in the fumes and the feeling of homesickness returns, swamping her. Her father had a generator like this, a big green Lister plant that rumbled like thunder and shook the foundations of their house when it was turned on.

Muffled cheering travels on the breeze. What game are they playing? She is missing it. Ozoemena shakes the tiny stone out and jams the shoe back on to her foot. The sausage rolls in her pockets sway when she stands, and she has a slight headrush. She burps and tastes the remainder of her lunch, garri and a watery soup made from elephant-grass shoots, which is fast becoming a favourite of hers.

Someone whistles her name, but as Ozoemena turns, the earth sways. A force slams into her chest and her body flies in the air, smashing into the ground. She coughs, stunned and in pain, and tries to get to her feet, scrambling up in terror. It happens again. Her legs fly out underneath her and her teeth rattle in her mouth, bone grinding against bone. She tastes salt.

The force pins her face down on the ground.

She has felt the leopard before, trying to take her over from within, waiting until she gave up the reins of her life via sleep before it emerged, tempting her with displays of its power to make her let it in. This feels different, insistent.

In vain, Ozoemena struggles, her right ear filling with the oily, grimy sand and sharp grit. She clutches at the ground, at the few straggling blades of withered grass. Whatever has her fastened is spreading. She could move her shoulders before, but now they are immobile. Her windpipe flattens like a plastic straw. She begins to choke on her own saliva, tearing at her neck, until her arms too can no longer move.

Ozoemena's teeth are clenched, imprisoning the sound of her screaming. She fights with every moving muscle from her waist down, kicking, thrashing about like an animal in its death throes. She is aware of wetting herself, but feels no embarrassment. The fear is greater than everything, pounding in her blood, filling her nostrils with the dusty smell of cockroaches crushed underfoot. Her right eye tickles. The sand is rising up as her head grinds further downwards into the ground.

'Hey! You! What are you doing there?!'

The tension over her body breaks, snapping her spine back into position. Ozoemena takes a deep breath, and her lungs fill with dust and diesel. She coughs hard and turns over on her back. She is still coughing when someone takes her hand and pulls her to her feet. Ozoemena doubles over. There is a slight streak of red in the spittle that funnels out over her tongue, but it might be the skin of a pepper from her earlier soup. Her throat prickles; she retches at the sensation. Her saviour claps her hard on the back.

'What are you doing here? Why are you not at games?' asks BC. His eyes behind the thick lenses are massive, concerned.

Ozoemena wipes her eyes with the backs of her wrists. Swallowing sets her off again. She coughs, hacking painfully. It is a while before she can answer. 'I was going . . . I fell down,' she says.

BC gives her the once-over. Ozoemena is glad that he found her; she does not know how long she could have lasted under the onslaught. She is even gladder to have been found by her favourite new teacher. Her *absent-minded* favourite teacher. Already she can see his eyes glazing over as his usual trance-like state returns. He waves her away. 'Hurry up, before Mr Ibe catches you here,' he says.

Ozoemena runs faster than she ever has before. The cheering grows louder.

She pauses outside the entrance to the field and rubs dirt all over her legs, hoping to disguise the urine trail. Her face is oily from the diesel and her shirt is stained. The hostels are usually locked during games to dissuade truancy, otherwise she would have run in to change into her spares. Ozoemena finds her friends in the crowd, sitting on the carpet grass at the edge of the field, cheering two classes in a game of football. She slides into place beside them and hands out the squashed packets of sausage rolls. Chinonso, the new girl, thanks her shyly.

'You have dirt on your cheek,' says Nkili. 'And your ear . . . did you fall down?'

Ozoemena dusts the places she has dictated, avoiding the question.

'What happened to your sportswear?' Nkili asks again.

Obiageli hits the snack on her thigh, pushing the sausage roll up and popping the packet. She takes an enormous bite. Sniffs. 'Why does this smell of urine?' she asks.

'If you don't want to eat it, give someone else and stop talking nonsense,' Nkili says, but Obiageli crams the other half into her mouth.

Ozoemena pretends to follow the game, and when the girls shout, she applauds with them. Inside her, questions are churning. Her chest throbs, and her cheek burns from being pressed into soil. Ozoemena's mind swirls. What if Ugochi is right? What if *she* is the reason weird things are beginning to happen in school? What if she is some sort of beacon?

The ball flies into her intertwined legs. Grimacing, Ozoemena picks it up automatically and throws it back, just as a senior player walks over to fetch it. The ball smacks into his nose, and he glares. The games master, Mr Ibe, blows his whistle sharply, pointing at her.

'I didn't do that on purpose, now.' Ozoemena cringes, sinking into herself.

Nkili is joyous. 'That was Ugochi's brother.'

The group turn as one to see Ugochi wearing an identical expression to her brother. She spreads her five fingers at them.

'I think she is officially your enemy,' Obiageli says to Ozoemena. 'E-yi, is that another Gala in your pocket?'

CHAPTER TWENTY-ONE

Ozoemena: Then

Ozoemena looked down on the world from a great height and then began to fall. She recoiled within herself and tried to break her descent, but the ground was a long way away, and gravity and the wind whistling past her ears flowed with her body, instead of against it. She found herself surrendering, and in that one moment between heavens and earth, tried to recall all that was. Ozoemena knew herself. She was the same, and not the same. Ozoemena was new and old, torn from nothingness, dripping celestial afterbirth, eyes open, eyes shut against the approaching earth, eyes open.

The ground welcomed her softly, silently, muffling her footfalls, cushioning her bones. Surprise widened her eyes, and when she opened her mouth to speak, a bark, short and authoritative, shattered the space. Within, Ozoemena tried to recoil again, to pull herself back, but regardless of her wishes, the body containing her spark of life moved without her. She could do nothing but go along.

Ozoemena's leopard shook itself off, shook from head to long, proud tail, shook off the muck of its rebirth and let its fur dry. The night and all that are in it belonged to the leopard. Regent of jungle, of swamp, of grassland and mountain. Regent of all the places in between, slipping through worlds to protect and mete out justice. That was its design, but not without a human mind to drive it. The leopard stretched, yawned, looked around, stretched again.

The tug, when it came, was faint. The leopard had a will of its own; unshackled, unbound, it could choose to answer, but hunger gnawed at its belly, and it decided to hunt for sustenance instead. Eyes aglow, it stalked its prey a while, its liquid form pouring through the dark. A pounce, and it had it: a juvenile antelope. The rest of the herd scattered. Its mouth watered. The leopard clambered up a tree, bearing the rapidly fading animal up into its highest boughs. The feasting went slowly and deliciously, rich and warm and wet. The leopard draped itself deliriously on a branch, but the night was not over. Sated, other calls now tugged at its senses. The leopard descended gracefully. It peered, found the right joint in the world's bones. One swipe of its claws and it went in and through, rushing like wind through a tunnel, and it was there, here, everywhere.

The ground near the metal gateway smouldered. The leopard slipped through the bars as if they were made of permeable tissue and sniffed the scorch mark. One long tongue tasted the sooty residue. Ozoemena within, and yet separate from the leopard, also tasted the bitter, sour flavour on her tongue, delayed as if through layers of dry fabric. The leopard raised its head to the air, searching out another join. This one already lay half-open, exposed by the ruined object that did not belong in this realm. It followed the odour through to another plane.

At the sight of violet skies, Ozoemena began to struggle, trying to plant her feet, to stop the forward movement of the beast, but it was powerful, stocky with muscle. It seemed not to heed – or even sense – her objection. Cushioned though she was, insulated from direct contact, the world appeared clearer, brighter, full of detail and sounds and smells she had missed on her previous involuntary visit. Ozoemena lashed out, kicking her feet. The leopard halted briefly before continuing on its way forwards.

Without warning, it suddenly crouched, pupils automatically dilating, its view panoramic. Ozoemena's breathing grew panicked, but she was not in control. The leopard stayed still, every hair, every whisker, poised and waiting. Before them, the rough outline of a man, dancing like a flame in the wind, feet floating off the ground. He glowed, blue, growing now brighter, now dim. The leopard crouched lower, smelling acutely the same sour bitterness. The dancing man was the threat. The leopard needed no other conviction, no juror. It coiled, prepared to spring, gathering up all its energies. Its claws unsheathed.

Wait! Ozoemena thought, trying to discern what the blue illumination could be, but it was too late. The leopard sprang, all claws, teeth and fury, slashing the figure to pieces.

Ozoemena woke up barking, crouched on the floor, her feet tangled up in her bedsheet. Her knees throbbed from smacking hard into the ground. Her hands burned as if she wore pepper gloves. She wiped the saliva staining her chin and lowered herself wearily to the floor. Her mouth hurt from dryness.

The silence in the room she shared with Mbu seemed unnatural, and when Ozoemena's eyes adjusted to the gloom, she saw her sister watching her intently. Without any words, Mbu turned her back, pulling her wrapper up over her head. Ozoemena saw her back rise and fall exaggeratedly. She got back into her own bed, holding her painful hands out in front of her. The pain grew, and she could not sleep.

By morning, she was weeping openly, as were her blistered hands.

Prisca stared at them in horror. 'What did you do to yourself?' she screamed. 'When did this happen?' Prisca examined Ozoemena's hands, making incredulous, dismayed noises.

'It wasn't me; I was dreaming, and a wild animal took me and my hands became claws—' She broke off, remembering what M'ma had said. 'I think it was a ghost, and maybe when you touch a ghost's body, it hurts you because we are not meant to touch it.'

'What is this you're saying? Stop talking this nonsense,' Prisca snapped. She stared at Ozoemena's eyes, held the look for a moment. She sighed, felt Ozoemena's forehead. 'You don't have a fever.' She held up Ozoemena's hands gingerly. 'Mbu, did you not notice this? Why didn't you call anyone?'

Mbu stretched languidly on her bed, the alertness on her face belying her lazy sprawl. 'Am I my sister's keeper?' she asked.

For the second time that morning, Prisca's eyebrows touched her hairline. Ozoemena observed the silent showdown with bated breath.

'Get up from that bed and go fetch the first aid kit before I slap the my-God out of your mouth,' said Prisca. 'And wake your father; he has slept enough.'

Ozoemena shivered, determined to stay awake. Her arms were beginning to weep. Prisca cleaned and dressed the wounds. Ozoemena's arms remained unhealed.

CHAPTER TWENTY-TWO

Treasure: Then

I know there will be wahala, after that stupid shaid in the compound next to our own spoiled the spirit's something. As I am baffing my morning baff, next thing, something holds my hair upon and pulls me up, up until I am nearly touching the offed ceiling light.

The spirit is like something that have gone to war. His cloth is torn, his Azikiwe cap is not there again, and I can see that some of his hair and scalp is uprooted, hanging but no blood. He is not young like me I used to think he was, but as I am thinking these thoughts with my mind, he is dragging me in the bathroom, hitting my head on this wall, that wall. I don' want to shout, because if Mummy hear, what will I tell her me and him were doing? How will I say I took Daddy's watch from the spirit and promised him things after she said me I should not? I hold my head with my hands.

'Foolish girl!'

I find myself on the cold bathroom floor. I have knocked the wing of my hand on the baff, and it is paining me cold up to my shoulder. My whole head is heavy like I am carrying iron pail of water on top. I can see assorted colours in my eyes. I am seeing the spirit's face, his teeth – he used his teeth to bite my hair and some of it is inside his mouth. He spits, tueh, at me like me I am a forbidden something.

'What did you do? What did you do, you foolish female?

Where is the seed I gave you? How did you destroy it? Do you know what kind of trouble you have put me in? Do you?'

He bites me again, this time, at the back of my neck. I don' know when me I start shouting. Is like pepper and salt inside wound. When my hair tears, I hear it inside my head. He spits again.

'Look at me! Look at what they did to me, because of you!'

'It's not me, is the girl—'

'I said look at me!'

The shouting is much, and the window of the bathroom breaks in the middle, one line, like somebody is cutting it with knife. I look at the spirit. He has four finger-hands lost on one hand, leaving only thumb. His one leg is facing back, his feet near his bum-bum. In his stomach is nothing, just breeze blowing his shirt inside one hole like this.

'They thought I betrayed them, that I destroyed our associate's seed on purpose, and they did this! Confronted me after, pretending not to know how I got mauled. Imagine what they can do to you!'

I jump up. Everything is pepper. 'I dinor do it, can't you hear what am talking? Is that girl, she is the one. She marched it into the ground, destroyed it kpata-kpata! How was I to know it would burn to nothing? I was trying to get you a wife!'

'They are threatening to reveal all to the Bone Woman. Do you know how difficult you have made things for me? I should eat your father for this.'

'No!'

'Yes! Eat him up. He is weaker than I am, new. I have been looking after him for you. But this, for making them send a beast after me? I will suck your father dry and use him to replenish myself.'

'Don' touch my daddy, Ọsịsọ!' My body is shaking me. If

he eats my daddy, he will not remain again. He will be forever lost. I put my hand to the back of my head. The new hair that had grown has gone, finish. It is shocking like electricity when I touch it with my finger, empty like the flesh inside my arms.

The spirit is not giving me ear. 'Maybe it was she, the Bone Woman. Maybe she found us out and the beast is her punishment, her avenger. No, no. I must think. Somebody is after me, after us.'

The spirit is doing nwi-nwu, coming and going like light offing and onning, but I know it don' mean he is not strong. Is it not my head that blood is coming out?

'I will get you another one,' I say.

He sits on the toilet. His bad leg is looking like the handle of something, turned like that. 'I have used up too much.' He hisses his teeth. 'They took my stomach. I earned that stomach, with hard work. How am I supposed to eat now?' He turns his face to me and in that time I see that half of his moustache is gone, and too, he don' have up-mouth on that side. His teeth are expressway open.

'Oh, my Dazzling. See what anger made me do.' He opens his hand as if me am a dog that will come after being flogged. That's when I see my open nakedness. I take my towel and cover myself. He is sad-sad, as if me tying towel is doing him bad.

'I'm sorry, my Dazzling.'

I agree with my nodding head, but inside me I am remembering how his face was when he came, his teeth full of my hair. He fears something, and me, I want to find that thing he fears and use it. Do me I do you, God no go vex.

'It will take me a while to recover – I don't know how much in human.' He is thinking. 'I must get my stomach back first.'

Headache is doing me from the wound in my head,

knocking on the front like carpenter with hammer. 'You will wait for me, won't you? You owe me. I have brought you a lot, enough to last you these months; more, even. Your mother is a smart woman. She is already managing what you have, bringing more from admirers. But me and you, we have our own deal. Don't forget.' Inside his mouth, he puts his hand at the back, opening wide, wide, wide like korokodai. He brings out something that resembles one seed of corn, shining.

'This is where I hid your father, see? In my mouth. Don't make me do something bad to him. Now, hold out your hand.'

Two more seeds: very simple, not hiding in necklace or bangle. One is like glass or ice block, but the other side of it is rough sandpaper. The other one is brown and long. I don' want to hold them, because the smell is strong, and they are drawing small like somebody blew them out from inside nose.

The spirit's hand is shaking after he puts the seeds in my own. 'These two souls here, they helped me fight her beast. They deserve to be born again. Do not mess up. These souls have important people on the other side too, so if they disappear, you will know the kind of calamity that I am preventing from befalling you. Once they are all progressing, then it will be my turn, with you.'

Me? One of the girls will be *me myself*? God forbid bad thing!

He continues to speak as if he cannot see the face am making. 'And soon I will have another seed to give you. You owe me three brides. Not two. This soul is crucial to our plans, but first I must get him to trust me.'

'But I brought you someone already! How am I now owing you three?'

'Ah, Chinenye is very good. Very hardworking. We will keep her, but not as a bride. She was not pure.'

'How is that one my consign? I am owing two.'

'And I say three, or do you want me to be angry again? Three plus you equals four.' He smiles with his jaga-jaga face. 'Don't worry your head about the maths. And don't think you can just be lackadaisical either. I have someone who will be watching you.'

Me I understand I supposed to pay for my mistake with the seed that that stupid girl marched, but for me to start from the beginning again as if he did not kuku take Chinenye? The spirit wants to cheat me. And too, to collect me is wickedness. Do I look like I want to pregnant for anybody talkless of a spirit?

I look the seeds in my hand. My head is banging me to burst, but my anger is worse than pain. He must suffer. Once I get Daddy, I will find the thing that he is afraiding and I will use it to destroy the spirit. He will see.

He stands up and puts the daddy-corn back inside his mouth and covers it, as if a star has gone under the cloth of the sky.

'Sorry about wounding you.' His voice is soft-soft. 'It was just the devil. Anger. Just do what you promised, you hear? Everything will be alright.'

After he goes, I bring out scissors from the cabinet-cupboard and cut the rest of my hair. I have luck that I did not throwaway Aunty Ojiugo's combing razor. I use it to barber my head and flush it in the toilet. I will find something to tell Mummy so she don' start thinking things, because Mummy knows sense.

Three girls increased from the two that am owing. And too, The Spirit will *not* take me. If he likes, he should be calling me wife up and down. But I will get Daddy back and then we will see.

My mind is turning about how I will get all the girls, one blow, seven akpus. The sooner, the better. First, that wicked neighbour girl that destroyed my property and brought wahala for me this morning. She must collect one spirit, whether she likes it or not.

I dress myself and begin to plan.

CHAPTER TWENTY-THREE

Ozoemena: Then

When Ozoemena thought of her father leaving, there were two things she remembered, even though she was unclear on the order in which they occurred.

The first: it was morning, and her father was packing a suit bag, the same bag he packed for conferences, when he was not inclined to iron or not certain there would be one where he stayed. Ozoemena watched him, a list in her hand, waiting for the right time to present it. It was a ritual they had, the sisters and their father. Ridiculously long lists. Wish lists, which they presented with the hope their mother would not find out. Mbu was absent, though, and Ozoemena's father did not look up when he packed, did not speak, the tension in his jaw deafening. Ozoemena remembered the sick feeling in her stomach as she chattered to him, ignoring the sensation of wrongness in her bones.

She recalled her mother sitting on the bed in a trance. Her ankle-length cotton nightgown, with piping around the neckline and short-sleeved cuffs in delicate lace like the froth from fresh palm wine. The front of her nightgown was spotted wet with holy water, which she had drizzled on herself from the white plastic bottle in her hand, marked with a sticker of a blue crucifix. The moisture deepened the faded pink and blue flowers on the nightgown, refreshing its worn green stems and leaves.

When Ozoemena thrust out her list, her father barely glanced at it before saying, gruffly, 'Go and help Aunty Comfo in the kitchen.'

She heard the car start up. Puzzled, she raced to wave to her father. She was too old to act in that way, and Aunty Comfo, their housekeeper, shouted at her to finish chopping the vegetables, but Ozoemena did not heed her. Out the door and on to the veranda, she shouted and waved and waved, but her father did not return the gesture as he drove off, the green Mercedes Benz fading away in the golden light.

The second memory was this: night time, and Ozoemena woke to see her father standing by the burglary-proofed windows of their room. They had electricity that night, and all was calm, bereft of throaty generators. The ceiling fan knob pointed to 'High', making short work of any frail mosquito bodies that managed to enter the house despite the green netting set into the window frames.

'Dad?' Ozoemena called. On her bed by the opposite wall, Mbu turned, snuffling. She slept with a pillow over her head, deaf to repeated warnings. Ozoemena climbed out of bed and stepped over to the window, where their father stood motionless, staring out into the town with its patchwork of lit and unlit sections. He put his arm over her shoulder and drew her close without turning towards her.

'I must go and look for your uncle,' he said. Ozoemena froze. Her father's strangeness lasted longer each time, and she feared to tell him that her uncle had died. Ozoemena was no longer certain to which version of her father she spoke. She fidgeted. Her father patted her shoulder.

'Where are you going?' she asked.

'I will try to get to the last place I think your uncle was. I might find him if he has not already moved on.' He rubbed his face and turned to her. 'When you find your tether, you will understand. A leopard and its tether are not easily parted.'

Ozoemena gasped. 'You were Uncle Odiogo's tether?' She glanced at Mbu, warily. 'Will that happen to me, too?'

'If that was the case between you two, you would know by now. I am still Odiogo's tether; death has not changed that,' said her father. 'I feel him, out there, somewhere, but I am not a leopard. All the worlds are not open to me to go and come as I please.' He exhaled. 'And you are not yet one.'

The light from a passing car illuminated his face. Ozoemena saw his dark skin was greasy. There were white hairs in his beard. New white hairs.

'Maybe I feel this way because he was also my brother. There is a lot of mystery to being leopard even now; so many questions.' He stared outwards and Ozoemena stared at him, even after the car had gone by and the light dimmed again. 'Odiogo tried to find answers,' he continued. 'We wondered if we were the first siblings to be leopard and tether. And now, there is you. We never heard of a female leopard.' A half-smile bunched his left cheek.

'I'm afraid,' said Ozoemena, examining her arms. The painkillers Prisca had given her were strong, but despite feeling minimal pain, the arm remained sticky after a week.

Her father sighed. He turned his head again and looked at Mbu, her legs hanging off the edge of her bed. 'You must be strong for the family,' he said. 'I'll be back soon.'

'But where are you going?' Ozoemena asked.

He rubbed her cropped head absentmindedly. 'You cannot come with me,' he said. 'And if your mother asks, don't tell her where I went.'

But Ozoemena's mother did not ask. And her father stayed gone.

She could not tell which came first. She did know, though, not to speak of either to anyone in her family.

CHAPTER TWENTY-FOUR

Treasure: Then

'When can I go to secondary?'

Mummy is eating pawpaw, her mouth opening wide so that her lipstick does not spoil. Inside, her teeth is scraping the fork and leaving the pawpaw on her tongue before she closes the mouth again. She don' chew. The pawpaw is ripe and too I know is juicy. She presses it on her tongue and mashes it before swallowing.

'Why did you cut your hair again?' she asks. 'You are making me look I-don-care. I'm the woman whose husband died. If my hair is long, and you are cutting your own, what do you think people will say?'

'Am not doing because of that, Mummy.'

'Then what, now? Because Daddy liked our hair to be long, like women. If I was not sick, Ojiugo would not dare touch yours.'

I breathe inside my chest and Mummy begins to vex. She says, 'Who are you breathing like that for, eh? Between you and me, who is a widow? If anyone should be sighing like that it should be me, not you. What do you even know that is suffering? Because of small-small hardship you saw when I was sick, you think you know what I know, eh, Treasure?'

Anger is angrying me small. Why is Mummy talking to me like this? Me, Treasure, who cleaned her body and everything when she was sick? Me that used my two hands and two legs to buy food that we eat, to cook it, to look after myself and herself? Why is Mummy talking to me like this? In short, it's because she still thinks the person she left behind, is the same person she woke up to jam here. Who is the one that—

'Come, let us go to the market.' Mummy normally will anger and forget because she likes to be happy. 'You are drawing face like your womanhood is upon you. Ngwa, wear better cloth and let us go.'

I don' want to go to market. Am tired of markets, all the things that I know is inside there, but going to market with no money is not the same as going to market correct – and too, what will I say I am staying at home to do? And all my biting my finger and planning for that useless girl is not yet having result. I wear cloth and follow Mummy. I am thinking we will be going to Main Market, but Mummy takes car and we drive back to where we used to live in Awka. Is that time I know is not ordinary market we are going. Mummy wants to show herself.

When Mummy is walking in the market, she is a masquerade that people come to watch. They call her 'Nwanyi Ocha' and 'Oyibo' and 'Fair Beauty', but nobody is holding her and pulling her, because she looks like Madam and they are finding her money not her trouble. This same market. Before when me and Mummy will come to buy cloth or gold, I will just follow her straight to where she is going, but after everything that happened, I am walking on the ground small and remembering that yesterday-yesterday, things were not the same. Then I remember spirit legs don' march the floor and look up well. Me I don' wan to see something that is bigger than my eyes when am still trying to remove my head from the rope of problem hanging around it.

We are going towards New Market, where all the bootik shops have now opened, and they have air conditioners and tile floors. Mummy enters the shop of the person that is not calling her, even though others are hailing. The man that greets us is forcing-yellow with Jheri curl hair and chain in his shirt. He gives Mummy his own chair even as there are plenty-plenty chairs there.

'Welcome, Aunty,' he says. 'Which one can I bring for you? We have Coke, Sprite, soda water . . .'

'Don't worry,' Mummy says. The light inside is blue-white and everything is shining. There are girls there, too, ASUTECH girls, maybe. One of them is drawing her face like she and Mummy are dragging something because the oga of the shop is selling to us, leaving her for his boys. Quick-quick, they pack her things for her – she buys plenty things – and she leaves, giving Mummy dirty eye, but Mummy don' even jar her face because she didin see.

'I came to buy clothes for my daughter. I only want sample.' Sample. That means only me will have the clothes. It's like Daddy used to buy for me when his partners them send container and put things for me inside.

The man rubs his hands together as if the AC is too cold. 'No wahala.'

'Proper sample o. I don't want after selling to me, I will now see someone else wearing what my daughter is wearing. Look her well, you can see how beautiful she is.'

'Very beautiful, Aunty.' The man is older than Mummy, but with his forcing-yellow and Jheri curl, he is forming young. 'Everything you see in other shops are reigning, but it's here you will find the fashion that is coming.' He is boasting, but the thing is sweeting Mummy and I will not lie, it is sweeting me too. One mind is telling me to be careful, that after eating comes payment, but is it every day suffer?

The man tells us to follow him to the back. He opens one velvet curtain like this and there is another shop.

'This one is real VIP,' he says.

Mummy buys me belt, shoe, bag, bras and pants to go

with all my new-new clothes. On our way out of the market, somebody pushes me, as in, to push me so me I can fall, but I dodge and stand well.

'Sorry o . . .' He is already talking and walking fast, trying to brush me as if I fell down, but I dinor fall so I am looking him because he is idiot. Our eyes jam and as I see him, I'm seeing the others, the boys moving around me as if they want to help me. It's the monkey coat boy.

Mummy reaches the end of the road and when she feels me I am not there with her, she turns and sees what is happening. I cannot see her eyes now, behind the sunshades, but I know what me I will do. Monkey Coat is begging me with his face, turning, trying to run, but his chi has entered hot water today. If you do me bad thing, I do you back. And this boy, he did me bad.

I point at him. I shout. 'Tief! Tief o!'

The whole market stops breathing. The other boys are doing buusu-bussu, sneaking away like cats, but it is not them that me I am pointing at. Monkey Coat starts to run, and everybody's eyes follows to him. I am shouting and pointing him. I know how me I look and how him he looks. I look like somebody, mala head or not, I look like somebody's daughter now.

One man puts leg for Monkey Coat, and he falls to the ground. Everybody is now shouting:

Tief Tief Tief Tief TIEF TIEF TIEF TIEF TIEF TIEF TIEF TIEF TIEF!

They are beating him to bring out what he tiefed, but other people are saying it don' make if they don' find it because tiefs work in gangs, passing all the things they stole to each other so when you catch them, you won't see your property. People are tired of tiefs in the market. There is too much hunger. Hunger has a way of sharping people's eye and mouth, of making it so that their stomach will dry all its water. Hunger is not good, and this boy wanted to kill me by collecting all my money. His own is coming.

We are already driving back to our house when they bring the tyre, but we see the smoke burning thick and black in the air. That's what they do to thieves and too, is not as if Monkey Coat he didin steal. He stole from me, and I know is not today he started stealing – every day cannot be day of tief. One day, it will reach to pay. Just see what happened to me, the spirit man tearing my head like that.

My hands are shaking me. The smoke is scratching my eye, my throat, my inside chest, even though we are far and there is no way. Mummy puts her hand on my own. She don' ask me anything, what I saw, what the boy stole.

She don' ask if me am okay.

CHAPTER TWENTY-FIVE

Ozoemena: Then

It was M'ma who saved Ozoemena's arms, or so she said. Ozoemena liked to think it was a combination of cures from the two powerful women in her life that did the trick, that Prisca started the healing and then M'ma finished it.

Before this time, she lay in bed for siesta and did not go to sleep. Her arms itched. Mbu had given up siestas, so the bedroom was calm most afternoons for Ozoemena, who counted the stripes on the curtains, forwards and backwards, noting how much time passed before a breeze lifted them up again, flashing sunlight from outside.

Ozoemena commandeered her father's radio and chose to play it at this time because she could. It was all discussion shows and news, interspersed with DJs talking over popular music instead of letting the tracks play, and election campaign jingles. She could tell which party, SDP or NRC, had paid more, based on how much airplay their individual ads got. Sometimes, it was back-to-back, causing a soporific effect on her senses. But then the news would come on, shattering any semblance of calm she felt.

She was not familiar with adults going missing. Children did often, having fallen prey to kidnappers or ritualists, but it seemed that with presidential elections on the horizon, the fever of the military transition to democratic leadership had tipped the scales. Now the missing announced over the radio

seemed to be as adults, men and women, as often as they
were children.

Of her father's disappearance, however, nothing was said.
There were no photos in the paper, no announcements on
the radio, no aunties and uncles gossiping and clapping their
hands in disbelief at the calamity – at least, not anywhere she
could see. Her father was there one day and gone the next.

Prisca seemed to accept this with her usual Catholic stoi-
cism, going to work and returning to her daughters. The
entirety of Mbu's being contorted into a giant frown. Aunty
Comfo initially picked up the slack with her usual fervour,
but it was no mystery that their father was her favourite, and
she simply stopped coming to work.

Ozoemena remained silent. The moments without the
radio were hardest, when she sensed the voice, not entirely
her own, speaking into her mind, prompting her to act in
ways she normally would not. Not quite a voice, for if she
spoke consciously into her mind, it would be her own voice
she heard, her patterns of speaking. What pushed her seemed
to be a *will* other than her own. She paced often, ran through
her chores, had a surfeit of energy to burn. At night,
Ozoemena shuffled around in bed, her skin dry and tight
as though she wore socks that were a size too small over
her entire body.

A heavy blanket of dread and apprehension settled over
their household. Her father did not come back. It was only
when his friends began to pay surreptitious evening visits that
Ozoemena realised Prisca had been secretly worrying, putting
the word out. They came with news: her father's car had been
sighted at his old college at Afikpo, Abakiliki, Abiriba. Some
professor reported seeing him at the library in Nsukka, rifling
through tomes in a hurry. The friends drank beer and
Guinness stout to show how at ease they were, told stories
about Emenike the Swot, cracked jokes about what topic he

could be researching. Their desperation to maintain a sense of conviviality only made Ozoemena anxious. They patted her head and talked how she was *only this small* yesterday, why, as small as Baby was right now. They remarked on how tall Mbu was, and her face stretched so tight in a huge smile that Ozoemena could not recognise her.

M'ma's arrival was a huge relief. She arrived one evening not too long after Ozoemena's father had disappeared, bearing a basketful of delicacies from the village. Ozoemena, delighted, threw herself into M'ma's body and hung on like a limpet.

'You this girl, leave me alone; you are fat and will squash me if I fall,' said M'ma, overjoyed. In answer, Ozoemena pushed against her even more. Mbu's greeting was slightly reserved, but she seemed happy. Prisca was not pleased, but her good manners always prevailed.

'Your father sent me. Let me see your arms,' said M'ma, when Ozoemena came into her grandmother's room to wish her good night. The woman dug into her handbag and pulled out a cellophane bag.

Ozoemena's eyes widened. 'My father?' she asked. 'You've seen him? Has he been with you all this time? When is he coming back?'

M'ma ignored her questions, concentrating instead on untying the bag. Inside it was a clear plastic tub with a screwed-on lid, filled almost to the brim with yellowish globules swimming in oil. M'ma unscrewed it.

Ozoemena drew back. 'That smells,' she said, trying not to gag.

'It's abuba eke. Breathe through your mouth,' replied M'ma. 'And hold out your hands.'

Ozoemena tasted the fetid stench in her throat. 'I thought we are not meant to kill pythons?' she asked, struggling not to inhale. 'How did you get its fat?' She retched again.

'I'm not from Idemili, I was married in.' M'ma chuckled at her weak stomach. 'Besides, I bought the fat from the market. How they acquired it is not my concern. That's why your father sent me. It's not taboo for me to handle.' M'ma screwed on the lid again, but the smell had escaped. It hung about the room and clung to everything, especially Ozoemena's damaged skin. She marched to bed with her hands held out in front of her. She was nearly asleep before she noticed that the skin neither itched nor felt tight.

The sound of Prisca and M'ma's voices greeted the dawn, and Ozoemena knew without rising that Mbu had something to do with it. Her bed lay tousled. A rank odour permeated the crisp morning like a worm through a rose apple. Ozoemena went along the corridor to the dining room, following the voices.

Prisca cracked the egg sitting in its cup with the back of her spoon. 'And I'm saying it is unhygienic and unsafe. How could you bring that into this house? How could you apply it to my daughter's skin?' Prisca spoke in a level voice, but Ozoemena knew all the hues of her mother's anger.

Mbu leaned back in her chair with a clothes peg dramatically holding her nostrils closed. It was obvious it was she who had reported the strange smell to her mother, leading to this tension.

'I am a pharmacist; do you think I don't have medicines that can make her better?' continued Prisca.

'Okay, okay, shorry,' said M'ma, jokingly surrendering. 'I am a village woman, I did not go to school, I am only doing the one that I know, that my mother taught.' But Prisca was not mollified. Abandoning her breakfast, she marched past a cowering Ozoemena to prepare for work. Ozoemena looked back at M'ma and Mbu where they sat at the table, wanting to lend her support to her grandmother. Mbu, insistent, said something in a low voice to her grandmother, which M'ma ignored, tucking into her slab of bread and butter, and washing it down with a giant mug of Lipton tea.

Ozoemena flexed her arms at the table. They felt perfect, and looked even better. She turned around and chased after her mother, determined to ask Prisca to examine her. Perhaps if she saw, there would be no more anger. But Prisca slammed the door to her bedroom before Ozoemena could reach her. Ozoemena knew better than to knock on her mother's door when she was upset.

M'ma paid Prisca no mind. Ozoemena shook when her grandmother called her that night for more ministrations with the stinking animal fat. She glanced fearfully at the closed bedroom door, wondering how she could sleep in the same room as Mbu for another night without repercussions.

'I have been thinking,' said M'ma, taking her sweet time. 'I know I am not meant to know anything about leopards and their society, but Odiogo was my son. A mother has her ways.' The last part was delivered slyly. Ozoemena wished she would hurry. 'Anyway, what I am saying is, if leopards are born when there is war, you need to be careful. The country right now is going through something hard; it's serious. If there is going to be war, like before . . .' M'ma cleared her throat, and patted the last bits of fat into her own skin. 'We don't want war again. We have seen what it can do. That is why you are called "Ozoemena" – may another not happen. But if there is to be war because the military are changing hands to democracy, if that is why the leopard has been passed on, then I will do what I can to help. I still have a voice in the village. War will not take us by surprise. Never again.'

'M'ma, you said Daddy sent you. Is he alright? When is he coming back?'

'When he finds what he is looking for. Go to bed.'

M'ma left the next morning, before Prisca could ask Uncle

Fred to drive her back to the village. Prisca was furious: M'ma was making her look as though she was a negligent daughter-in-law. Fuming, she stripped Ozoemena's bed and arranged for her soiled, rancid mattress to be disposed of. She washed Ozoemena's arm, in preparation for her daily dressing. The skin was flawless.

CHAPTER TWENTY-SIX

Treasure: Then

I know me I can try to find someone else to collect one spirit-seed. As we have started going to church in estate, and people are knowing us, I can just plan for one of the girls there. The spirit said they must not be touched by boyfriend/girlfriend matter, they must be pure and not seeing menses, but me I don' know if that one is a lie. If not for Daddy, I would have just left matter for Mata as they say, but Daddy is worth it because his heart is good for people, and he don' deserve to be dead.

We are going for nine o'clock Mass. Mummy likes to go late to church, and when we enter everybody is looking her, from the priest and Mass server down to even the people begging outside church. She has added more body and her face is ripe like sweet mango. After church, Mummy stays to greet the fada, but after he shakes her hand, he don' even talk to her, because somebody now touched him and he turned to face them. Mummy muddies her face. I can see the thing is paining her.

'Can you imagine, upon all the money I put for offering, the priest could not spare five minutes to talk to a new member of the church?' she says. We are using our new car to drive back to our house, and Mummy offs her shoes because her hand is not that strong in the steering. Daddy taught her how to drive, but upon that, it was him that used to drive us everywhere, even when we were going on outing. When it was just Mummy, or me and Mummy, then the driver will carry us.

'I can decorate that church one thousand, one million times sef, it's just that I know what I am using my money for, not like all these useless professors, upon they don't even pay them salary on time.' Mummy is very angry; her mouth is long. 'When Daddy was alive, could they even clean my shoe, talkless of holding my handbag?'

'Yes, but did you see how everybody was looking at you in church?' It's not as if me I am lying and too, Mummy knows what I am doing that I don' want her to be vexing, because she can vex and draw her face, and me I don' have power that Daddy use to call her sweet names and make her not to vex again.

Mummy is still frowning, but her mouth is no longer talking bad talk. 'I saw them, now. Looking and removing their eyes as if they did not see. But I know they saw.

'How many of them can buy this cloth I am wearing? Or the gold in my ears? Or is it the ones on my fingers?' As Mummy is talking, I am using my eyes to call result for her. Is it only things the spirit brought that has born all these other ones? Did Mummy sell some things to get money? The spirit said Mummy knows how to manage, but how manage? I don' want to talk, but my mind is turning me.

Mummy marches hard as she is driving and pulls the gear of the Volkswajin that resembles tortoise, as if the thing is stubborn. When the car parked inside our new house, Mummy said it's a gift from a friend. I ask her which friend is that one again, because me, I thought all their friends ran away after Daddy died, but Mummy said I should mind the business that is minding me. The car is supposed to be Tokunbo, but it is red and shining new-new. I haven't seen new Volkswajin in my life.

She says, 'It has been long since we did strong things, that's the issue. People don't know us in this town. We need to show them who we are.'

There is small go-slow on the road, because everybody is coming from church and going home. Mummy's hand is tight on the steering, but she is smiling, and one man like this is looking at her from his own car, over his own madam who is sitting in his front seat. His madam is talking, I can see her mouth moving, and the children are in the back playing and laughing, but the man is still looking at Mummy, and me I know she knows that somebody is looking at her, but she didin turn her head to give him face. I look the man up and down and cut eyes for him before I remove my face. The go-slow is clearing again.

We are nearing our house when Mummy talks again. 'We should throw a party. A big one.'

'A party?'

'Yes, a birthday party for me and you. It has been long since someone killed cow for me. We will throw a party and invite all our neighbours. After that, they will know I am not their mate. Invite the reverend father too.'

I know we are having some things, but do we have money for a party? And too, I don' think doing party is correct. Daddy used to do party for us. It's Daddy that kills cow for Mummy and goat for me.

'I don' want party,' I say to Mummy. 'Daddy is not here.'

'And he can never be here again. Are we supposed to follow him to the land of the dead, eh, Treasure?'

I don' answer her, but I cross my hand on my chest.

'Oh, oh, oh, wait. Don't tell me you are still dreaming of what the spirit told you? Nobody can bring somebody back from the dead, talkless of a pauper like that. Nobody, you hear me? We have to do things for ourselves.'

'I don' want party,' I say. 'It will be somehow.'

Mummy kisses her teeth. 'Daddy spoiled you, have I not been saying this? I told him that he was spoiling you, but he did not listen. Do you think it's every mother that will care about presenting you to society the right way? Do you think that every parent wants to push for what is in your best interest? I am trying to help you to help yourself, not to be expecting people to do things for you; today Daddy, tomorrow someone else. Without him, you cannot live?'

I am not talking back, but I am thinking that is not me that went to go and sleep for many many months after Daddy died. It was me that went to be looking for food, to be fetching water. It was me looking after Mummy and not going to school. Why is Mummy now telling bad words? I don' know when me I kiss my teeth.

Mummy gives me one kain detty look and says, 'I don't blame you, Treasure. It's me you're kissing teeth for? Me, Akuabata? So, because you are having breast on your chest nowadays, you now think the two of us are agemates?'

'I didin say that, Mummy.'

'Listen ma chérie, some people's mothers are only interested in what they can get from them. Some girls your age, their mothers dress them fine-fine and pass them from man to man to man, collecting petty-petty money, and nothing else – no schooling, nothing. Some girls your age, they have to fight, run comot to where they can have beta life, where they can use sense that they carry under their nails to make something of themselves, where they learn how to stand themselves up and be of good value so that they attract beaucoup husband materials, young and hardworking husband that will pet them and treat them like python's egg.'

Mummy is mixing Pidgin, English, French, and I know she has vexed finish, but me I don' tell her sorry again. I am using my tongue to count my teeth. Daddy used to tell me that I had so much sense that it entered under my nails, and one of my sense is telling me that Mummy is talking about herself, because since I was born, only Aunty Ojiugo is the person I know from her side, nobody else, not mother, not father, only Aunty Ojiugo, who has the same father with her but not same mother.

As we are coming near our house, Mummy begins to blow her horn, she blows it and the thing sounds all over the street, GRA or no GRA, she don' care. Gateman opens gate and salutes for her, and that is when me I say, 'Mummy sorry, I just don' feel like having party, but you are right because since we came here, nobody is coming to our house apart from Uncle Obi them. It will be good to know our neighbours.'

Mummy breathes out and adjusts her hair well. 'A small party then, because of your Daddy. Let it not be that me I am not listening to you.'

My mind is firing like bullet. 'You should tell our neighbours them to come with their children, so me I can know them too.'

I know they will come, because everybody likes gossip, and where Mummy goes, gossip pursues her. In my mind, I am seeing that stupid girl next door as she is collecting one seed during the party. My belle is sweeting me.

The ~~Second Bride~~ First Bride

Ogenna did not want to come with her parents to the party, especially as she knew they had not wanted to come either. She had listened to them badmouth their new neighbour – well, her mother had been the one talking, but her father had been a captive audience, laughing in the right places, prodding his wife along in others. It was the first time the girl had seen them both laugh with each other in a long time. Her father had been taciturn since his tenure as head of his department ended in balloting that had not gone in his favour.

While the adults spoke amongst themselves, Ogenna wandered about. There were no other children present, which she added to her 'against' column, but after a while she thought to herself that perhaps it was a good thing. She needed a juicy story to tell her friends, and what could be better than their unsophisticated, flashy, try-hard new neighbour with the daughter who stared everyone down so rudely? Her friends would need a good laugh. Ogenna snorted to herself, thinking about the cheap trinket that she had destroyed, how the daughter's expressionless face had cracked and crumpled as if she was going to weep. It had thrilled her, given her such a surge of authority and power.

She snuck away from the living room, with its Hi-Fi system blaring Bright Chimezie and his Zzigima Sound, the over-flowing glasses of Mateus rosé and Malibu rum, the hostess overdressed in a red sequined dress with a thigh-high slit, tossing her big hair, flashing with every over-the-top laugh and theatrical expression, her father growing steadily drunk on spirits as much as the hostess's attentions, her mother's pinched mouth, the other guests, laughing, relaxing, gradually embracing the charming outsider in their midst. Even if she did try too hard.

Ogenna tested several doors along the hallway. Many of the rooms lay unfinished, crammed with luggage and crockery. The kitchen was a marvel of polished wood countertops and varnished cabinets of rich reddish wood, but its pantry remained bare, its black and white plastic tiles stark from disuse. She found foodstuff in the next room, crammed floor to ceiling, bags and tubers and basins. From the middle of the room, the party and its throbbing brass sounds grew dim. The girl put a finger out, impish, and poked a hole through one of the bags. Salt. She made the hole larger until there was a steady flow pooling white and sparkling on the floor.

'What are you doing?' The daughter, bearing a plate. She had spoken in Igbo and hurried to repeat herself in her rough-sounding English. 'What are you doing here?'

'Why do you keep all your food in here and not in the pantry?' Ogenna countered, putting on the voice her mother often used for the help.

'You made a hole in that bag.'

'It was already like that when I came,' Ogenna replied, shrugging. The lie was thin, and in the silence that followed, Ogenna forced herself to meet the daughter's hard eyes. The room's lightbulbs, cupped in frosted glass shades, dimmed and brightened, as if they were blinking.

'They're going to take the light soon,' Ogenna said, staring at the light above the daughter's head, trying to break the tension without conceding defeat.

'We have gen. Come and see my room,' the daughter

replied, clamping a hard hand around her wrist. Any objections Ogenna had, she quashed under the weight of her guilty conscience; after all, she had poked a hole in the bag of salt and lied about it. And what's more, the daughter seemed to know. Instead, she concentrated on filing away as many details of the house as she could to regale her parents with over breakfast the next day.

The daughter's room was beautiful: peach walls and matching bedsheet and pillowcase. There was a silver blanket on the bed that looked soft and would feel divine on freezing Harmattan mornings, the girl thought. On the floor was . . .

'Do you have a bathroom mat in your room?' Ogenna snorted, scorn burning away the jealousy she was starting to feel. 'For wiping you feet after bathing?'

'No,' the daughter replied, setting the plate gently on a table. She stood with her back to Ogenna, fiddling with its presentation, but Ogenna heard the anger in her voice, the embarrassment. She feasted on it.

'Yes, it is.' She prodded a side of it with her foot, lifted it to reveal the rubber underside. 'Yes, it is. I can't believe you put a toilet mat in your room!'

'Okay. Whatever you say.'

Ogenna paused, changing tack. 'Why do they call you "Treasure"?'

'It's my name. God's Treasure. It means me I'm special.'

Ogenna snorted. 'It's a bush name.'

'Do you want chin-chin?' Treasure asked. She picked up the plate and proffered it with both hands, and Ogenna, all-powerful, smug, and enjoying herself, scooped up a handful of the fried snacks and tossed them into her mouth one by one. She did not break eye contact, relished this cowering daughter, who was clearly her inferior, did not waver – even when her teeth met a surface that was not quite chin-chin and cracked straight through.

It was only as Treasure began to smile that Ogenna felt the first pinpricks of alarm.

'What?' she asked.

Treasure began to laugh, a silent, painful laugh, clutching her stomach hard. Ogenna spat the globule of masticated chin-chin paste on to the floor, forgetting her superiority, regretting her earlier glee. Her throat tingled. 'What did you put inside that chin-chin?' She cleared her throat once, twice, and Treasure ceased laughing.

'I didn't do anything to the chin-chin,' said Treasure. 'It was already like that when I came.' She seemed to glide across the floor until she was standing in front of the door, blocking the girl's chances of escape.

'Come . . . out of my way.' Ogenna tried to regain her earlier authoritative tone, but her throat swelled and itched, and something unfurled inside her, bit by bit, like the digits of a hand. She tried to shout for her parents downstairs. Whatever it was blooming inside her pushed through her gullet and out of her mouth. Ogenna leaned over and retched, but her stomach contents hung from her in clumps and did not spatter on to the ground. Desperate, she attacked her own face, grabbing and pulling and coming away with long, whitish fibres from her mouth and ears.

She sank to the ground, pulling at her hair, her skin, trying to clear the web of cotton from her eyes. She pulled and pulled until her skin cracked and fibre spilled where blood and tissue and bone should be. Slowly, Treasure disappeared from the girl's view as she sank further than the floor and further still.

The ground burned cold on Ogenna's forearms and knees. She had stooped protectively around herself, but now she opened herself up carefully, stretched, stared at her hands and legs. One arm hung limply. Instead of the peachy pink bedroom, she stood under a sky the colour of poison, staring up at celestial bodies that appeared close enough to touch. Before her stood a tree trunk covered in spikes, with roots higher and deeper than her shoulders. From its branches hung large oval pods, spilling white fibres from between split seams.

Ogenna sat down hard on the ground. Wide-eyed, she stared and stared, and the wind sucked the wet from her unblinking eyeballs.

CHAPTER TWENTY-SEVEN

Ozoemena: Now

Soon you will become the thing that all other beasts fear.

Ozoemena tries to forget it, the sensation of not being in control, of being pushed into the ground by forces she could not see. She is a long way from anything being afraid of *her*. It appears she is an easy target, which is why *things* continue to test her. It is bad enough facing bullies like Ugochi, who are trapped with her in school all the time, but to now add unseen enemies? A shiver works its way from the base of her neck down. Outdoors, the air is motionless. The sweat on her forearms lies greasy, plastering the hairs. It is unusual for the dry season to be humid, and yet, she feels it, the moisture in the air. It creeps down her back under her school blouse, crawls along her scalp. Ozoemena licks her top lip, tasting brine. None of her classmates seem to be feeling the heat as she does. They are moisturised with various unguents, but nobody appears to be sweating.

Beside her on the bench, Nkili is focused on assembling the apparatus for their experiment, pouring out bicarbonate of soda into a beaker, tongue worrying at the corner of her mouth as she concentrates on the task. Not for the first time, Ozoemena considers confiding in her friend. Not for the first time, she remembers the whispering from back home, her mother's admonition to 'Stop all this nonsense'. What if Nkili thinks she is crazy – or worse, possessed? She imagines it;

being ostracised, having no friends, nobody to borrow so much as a pen from, or to lend one to. Ozoemena shakes her head.

No.

'Why are you sitting there shaking like a wet chicken?' Nkili asks. 'Help me grind the sugar, now.'

'Yes, okay.' All around her are sounds of grinding and scraping, girls chattering excitedly. Miss Uzọ, the chemistry teacher, walks up and down, inspecting the girls' preparation. She is shaped like an S, a petite woman whose outfits seem to involve an inordinate number of red roses, down to her high, high shoes.

'If you haven't got a lab coat, find one now-now,' says Miss Uzọ. 'You know where they are.'

Ozoemena's lab coat comes to the middle of her palms, but before she can fold it away, Nkili reaches for her hands and flicks up the sleeves. 'Thank you.' Ozoemena is embarrassed.

'What is even doing you? You've been doing like you're stuck in yesterday. Are you sick?' Nkili shakes the beaker to settle the bicarbonate of soda.

'No, not that.'

The class falls silent, and Ozoemena looks up. Miss Uzọ is raising her palms up to the class. She is one teacher that never needs to raise her voice or employ punishment to achieve authority. The girls adore her for all the weird and wonderful things they get to do in her labs.

'So, when you have finished measuring out and grinding, I need one person in each group to come to the front, pick up one of these aluminium bowls and go outside and fill it with sand.' There is a scramble before she has finished speaking, and she makes the volunteers stand in line and wait until they settle before letting them out of the lab.

Ozoemena assembles sugar cubes on the square of bathroom tile she has been given and covers them with a piece of scrunched up paper so that when she begins grinding, the granules do not scatter all over the lab bench. She ignores the sound of excitement coming from beyond the rectangle of the door, where the girls seem to have abandoned the simple task of filling their receptacles and are now playing. It is a compound full of sand, how hard can it be? Part of her wishes to stay suspended in this moment, weighing up whether to reveal her true self to her friends or not. Ozoemena does not know if she and her chi will accept the leopard, but does that even matter when whatever fought her clearly believes she is of significance?

A cube of sugar clatters to the floor under her counter and, startled, Ozoemena looks up. It is Thelma. The girl slides off her stool across the aisle from Ozoemena and crawls after it. She lumbers, clutching her stomach, her usual pink lips bloodless and pale. She smiles at Ozoemena, a tired thing, and Ozoemena, discouraged from enquiring, smiles back. She starts her task, pressing down on the cubes and paper with a wooden club she has been given. As the sugar crumbles, Ozoemena's heart begins to palpitate. It sets her teeth on edge. Saliva pools in her mouth. Ozoemena wipes the sweat from her top lip with the back of her hand.

'Any wahala?' Miss Uzọ stands before her, beaming reassuringly. Her eyebrows have been shaved into orderly strips, but Ozoemena can see the beginnings of growth flouting this order. One of her incisors nearly overlaps the other in the middle.

'No, Teacher.' *Yes, Teacher.*

'I think you should probably stop grinding now, abi? We are not making icing sugar.'

Have you ever slipped into another world and heard a stone-grinding machine, Teacher?

Ozoemena's hands are covered in white sugar dust. The paper is torn with the force of her crushing.

'It was smart of you to use the paper, but make sure you pick all the pieces out, otherwise it might change the outcome of your experiment, mm?' Miss Uzọ moves on to Thelma.

Presently, the girls come bounding in with the bowls of sand, and the experiment begins. Obiageli is the first. She winks at her friends, takes something out of her pocket and pops it into her mouth. Ozoemena and Nkili turn to each other, grimacing. Sugar.

Miss Uzọ raises her hand for quiet again and the noise shuts off.

'Today, we are going to perform abracadabra!' She pauses. 'I am going to teach you how to make snakes – like Moses.' Miss Uzọ grins widely, and this time when the wave of disbelieving noise comes, she does nothing to stop it.

They make snakes that writhe out of the beakers charred and blackened. Ozoemena is fascinated. She cannot look away.

'Who can guess what is happening? It's not something we have covered, but any real student of science will be able to tell me. Yes?'

Ugochi's hand is raised. 'A chemical reaction!'

At the back of the lab, Ozoemena rolls her eyes. Of course Ugochi would know; her brother probably prepared her for what is to come. She sits at front of the lab, turning back and smirking, as if she has said something special.

'Good!'

'Yes, but what kind of "chemical reaction"?' asks Nkili. 'We all know it's a chemical reaction – is it not chemistry we are doing? Fool.'

Ugochi glares at her, at the both of them, as if they conspired to steal her thunder.

'Excellent question. Does anyone know what *kind* of chemical reaction this is?' Miss Uzọ looks quickly around the lab in that squirrel way she has. 'Thelma? You are usually not this quiet. Do you know the answer?'

Ozoemena hears Thelma groan as she half-stands, and it unnerves her, the guttural quality of it, too low to be coming from a mouth such as hers.

'It's . . . a heat . . . reaction,' Thelma mutters.

'What did you say? Speak up. I can't hear you.'

'She said, "It's a heat reaction."' Ozoemena feels the need to talk for her classmate. She recognises the pained expression on Thelma's face. The girl has clearly got diarrhoea.

'Yes, she's right. It is a heat reaction', says Miss Uzọ. 'Your beakers should be cooler now, so they won't be too dangerous to touch. Can you see it is warm? And what can you see with your eyes?'

'The snake is hard,' someone pipes up.

'Yes? What else?'

'The sand is warm,' Nkili replies.

Thelma raises her hand. 'Teacher, please can I go and ease myself?' she asks, confirming Ozoemena's suspicions.

Miss Uzọ waves for her to leave and continues speaking.

'Very good! We call this kind of chemical reaction an "exothermic" reaction.' Miss Uzọ turns away from the class to write on the blackboard. '"Exo" means "out". This kind of chemical reaction gives off heat. What would be the opposite of this?' she asks, facing the class again.

Exoskeleton. Endometriosis. Word games. Ozoemena raises her hand. 'Endo . . . thermic?' she asks, tentatively.

Ugochi sniggers, scenting Ozoemena's confidence depleting.

'Yes! Fantastic! "Endo", meaning "in", because some chemical reactions need to take in heat for them to occur.'

Ugochi slumps on her stool.

Nkili gives Ozoemena a high-five under their bench, and Ozoemena resists the urge to stick her tongue out behind Ugochi's back.

Miss Uzọ bounces around in front of the board, warming to her topic. 'And what do you think you would feel if you touched the beaker during or after an endothermic reaction?' Hands go up.

'Can we taste the snake?' This from Obiageli, already reaching for her experiment.

'No!' cries Miss Uzọ. 'You never, never, *never* eat anything inside a lab.'

The girls titter nervously and Obiageli, chastised, drops the inquiring hand. She seems to be contemplating tasting it yet. Miss Uzọ, talking and walking, seizes Obiageli's experiment and dumps it back on her own bench at the front of class.

Ozoemena becomes aware of the quiet in her mind, the low whine building within it. The hairs all over her body rise and tingle. She shivers. The same thing happened before Madam Koi-Koi came to the front of their dormitory room last time. How does one fight an invisible foe? Ozoemena is all eyes and ears.

Nkili nudges her with her elbow. 'What is it?' she asks.

Ozoemena's eyes are stretched wide, and she feels her panic infecting her friend. She clutches Nkili's arm.

'What?' asks Nkili, a little too loudly. Heads turn.

'What is going on there?' their teacher asks.

Ozoemena sees Thelma reach the stairs leading up to the door and the pavement above. The rectangle of sunlight in which she stands appears, for one moment, to glow brighter than ever. Thelma begins to stumble. Ozoemena jumps off her stool without meaning to, her gasp alerting others to what is happening. Her wooden seat smacks down heavily on the concrete.

Thelma judders on the stairs, her legs apart, braced against the top step, confused, frightened. Urine pours out of her, brown and stinking of spoiled eggs. Her unfocused eyes wander around the lab. Her mouth opens and shuts, releasing unheard words into the air. Thelma locks eyes with Ozoemena, stares straight at her, and Ozoemena grips Nkili's hand tighter, their heads close together, sharing the horror unspooling before the entire class. Thelma's head falls back, her throat bulging, thickening. She strains.

A wet thing plops to the smashed concrete beneath her squatting thighs.

'Everybody back to your seats!' Miss Uzọ cries. She does not need to tell the girls twice. The overpowering odour works in her favour. The girls shrink as one, apart from Ozoemena, who pushes her way to the front, drawn inexplicably against her desires.

'Move back!'Miss Uzọ commands.

'Thelma is messing herself!' says one of the girls. Someone vomits, noisily on the floor. The girls scatter from it, a second wave within the original. Some of the mess has spattered on Ozoemena. Warm chunkiness slides down her leg towards the bands of her socks.

The mess that has slithered out of Thelma is a cake of sticky hair and viscera, with one eyeball plonked in the middle like a contaminated cherry.

Ozoemena cannot stop staring at it, even after Thelma passes out and Miss Uzọ, handkerchief over her mouth and nose, dashes to get help. Not when Nkili tugs at her blouse, hard, trying to pull her away. She stares and stares, certain that the answer to the mystery of whatever is happening to her in school lies within the blue eyeball staring up at her.

CHAPTER TWENTY-EIGHT

Treasure: Then

They cannot find her when it is time for them to go. The woman is shouting her name around the house, and after much, I hear Mummy coming out of the parlour, so I carry myself down the step.

'Is my daughter with you?' That is the first question the woman asks me, and now she is seeing me, because before-before when they came for the party, I was greeting her at the door, wearing this my fine flay-trouser that Mummy bought me, and she and that stupid child of hers were looking up-up as if she did not see me. I frown my face and tell her, 'No, Aunty.'

The woman is running everywhere, opening this place and that place, and Mummy is helping her be finding.

'Maybe she went home.' It's the professor-husband talking this one, falling side-by-side because drink is carrying him. 'She is a precocious child. And you know she didn't want to come.'

The woman cuts her husband one type of eye like this, and he closes his mouth sharply. 'She would not dare leave without my permission.' She turns to me. 'Are you sure my daughter did not come upstairs?' As she is asking, she is pushing me, as if I am one detty pant, chooking me with the wing of her hand, and going upstairs by herself.

When she comes down, she is sweating. 'She's not there.'

Mummy's face is muddy because our house is not complete and too, the woman will see everything inside. She is not minding something has happened, otherwise she will not be thinking all those ones. The woman is seeing as Mummy is keeping face so she does her shoulder like cash madam and says, 'Sorry, I should have asked. I was just worried. Perhaps she went home. Let us be going. Thank you for the party.'

Her professor-husband is still holding his glass as he is following his wife to go. At the door he embraces Mummy, using her body like cane to stop his leg from bending. His face is talking at her the way that Daddy's face used to some-times talk. Sweat is covering all his cloth and you can see his singlet through the shirt he is wearing. He carries his jacket in his hand, falling side-by-side and going out of the gate. Gateman salutes them.

The estate security turn the whole place upside down. When their power could not do the problem, they called police. After that, Prof and his wife wait for ransom phone call. The wife begins to sit by the phone and not be going out. Mummy goes one time, two time, to support as per neighbour, but the woman don' look at her or look at me, she is just sitting with red eyes and not talking to anybody, any of the neighbours. Mummy and the other women organise food for her and her husband, but she don' eat. Prof goes to TV, radio, newspaper, but nothing-nothing. Everybody begins to lock their gate extra.

Me, I'm happy the spirit is not coming, but my mind is telling me that I should not remove mind for his matter. What kind of trouble have I put my head inside? If he can be changing the numbers of the wives I am owing, how can I be sure he will not be using me forever? How can I know that he will show Daddy the way to come back? What if all the plan I am making is good-for-nothing?

But no. I know what he fears. He fears the Bone Woman,

and if he disappoints me, I will expose his matter to her. Is only to figure out how me and her will meet that remains, but that one is small. I will agree and my chi also will agree. If I want me and her to jam, we will jam. Then we will see between the spirit and me, who is using who.

But there is another problem. One morning, our new driver is going to wash car, and he starts shouting, 'Chei! Chineke-God!' and he and Gateman are making noise. I look outside my window, but the car is parked near my wall, and I don' see what they are using to disturb everybody. Then Driver start to shout, 'Madam! Chei, Madam come o! Come o!' So, me I go downstairs, even if it is not me they are calling, is in my house that the something is happening.

I bend under the car that Driver is pointing, and try to see the thing.

There is tortoise under Mummy's car. Somebody put it there, tied it with red string and feathers.

'Don't go there, Miss! That thing is medicine! Bad medicine!' Driver clicks his fingers, spits.

The tortoise is small like my hand. Is not only the string and the feathers of bird, is like it have eaten something. Me I have not seen tortoise except Mbekwu the Cunning in story book, but this one is falling one side-one side, as if it had drunk palm wine. After when Mummy comes down, she is angry enough to throw shoe.

'I know it is those useless men that tried it, those your father's brothers. Obi, may your big eye be pierced and blinded! Amos, may your longathroat be choked as you are trying to eat what is mine! Shuwa, slow-poison, it will not be better for you!' She calls them one by one and curses, and then she tells Driver to go and get her a strong dibia.

Gateman is saying he will use stick and remove it, and nothing will do him because the charms from his place are strong pass Igbo people own, but Mummy is telling him, 'You won't do the job you're supposed to do, it's now dibia wahala you want, you this man,' and they are laughing with side-eye and corner mouth. Is good that Gateman is funnying her, because it is making her not to be cursing, and Mummy is remembering she is madam and brushing her hair with her hand. She pulls the front of her boubou well and tells me, 'This must be why nothing has come for us this week, eh?' in a small voice so nobody can hear.

I answer her, 'Hio,' and my mind is turning. I have my own problem to remove from my head, and I am thinking that maybe there is a way, where before the way has no passage.

We have finished afternoon food by the time the dibia comes to the house. He use taxi to come, and the man is not looking like how me I am thinking dibia look. He is wearing shirt and trousers and silpas. He didin have powder around his eye and he is even wearing facing cap. I can see on Mummy's face that she is thinking what me am thinking.

'Good afternoon, sir,' Mummy greets him.

The dibia don' even look at her. He is going the car round. 'If you want to greet me, you hail me by my proper name, Agwọ nọ n'akịrịka. And I hope you are not menstruating near me.'

Mummy closes her face. Before, she was opening her teeth the way that people enjoy, but the man is doing as if she is an old broom on the floor. 'I'm not menstruating,' she says, but she shifts until she is on the first step leading inside our house and crosses her hands in her front.

The dibia is going round, and am counting without using my mind because I am good at that kind of a something. He does seven times and stops. He opens the bag he is carrying, like the type that businessmen use to do function, and brings out one container. He knocks it on the car, and black powder is everywhere. 'Move the car,' he says.

Driver makes In the Name of the Father on himself and enters the car. He moves it back so that all of us can see the tortoise. The dibia man takes another something from his bag and pours it on the tortoise, this time a white something. Then he plucks leafs from our house, picks up the tortoise and puts it in his bag.

'Agwọ nọ n'akịrịka!' Driver is hailing him.

The dibia answers him, 'Mm,' as if what he did is not a big something. As he was doing, Mummy went inside. Now she has come back, and she salutes him. She is smiling again, but not a real one. She tries to give the man envelope.

'Did you not tell her?' The dibia's nose is swelling.

'Ah, Madam,' Driver is begging. 'He doesn't take money, and not from women.'

'You will bring a goat, next Eke day, to my shrine. Your driver will bring you. That is my payment. For now, I will take only water, to wash my hands and to drink.' Mummy calls our new maid, and that is the only time the dibia looks at her. 'The water must come from your hand. Bring water, bring charcoal. After I wash my hands, you can bring drinking one. Boiled.'

Mummy is now vexing well. The way she turns and walks away is loud. She is saying, 'Charcoal from where, do we cook with firewood?' as if she is talking to herself but is the dibia she is telling. Driver don' know how to put his face, because is him that brought dibia and now the man is trying to shame his madam and too, Mummy will make him hear nwii for it. He rushes into the house to beg, maybe help her.

Am standing there where I have been all this time, when the dibia raises his head and looks me innermost my eye. He is not near, but is as if he is in front of me.

'Yes?' he calls me. I didin even know what to talk before he spoke, but as am walking to him, the question is there.

'Mazi.' I look to see if Gateman can hear me, but he has gone into his house. 'What can I do to stop someone finding me? Finding my trouble?'

He breathes out as if I am smelling him. 'Who is chasing you?' I open my mouth to answer, and he raises his hand. 'I'm not asking you. I'm asking your chi. It cannot lie.' He is listening, nodding his head. He breathes out, removes his facing cap and ons it again.

'You women and your trouble. You will have to pay what you owe, but I can give you small something so that you can rest and not have visitors when you don't want them.' The bag again, and this time, a small stick that is green and brown in the back. The dibia breaks some of it and chews fast-fast, talking. 'You are lucky that Agwọ nọ n'akịrịka is here.' The stick is foaming in his mouth. He spits the chewed thing in his hand and squeezes saliva from it. 'Bend down,' he says, and before I can say 'Jack Robinson', his hand is inside my shirt.

'Hei, oga!'

'Stop that thing. What do you have on your body that I have not seen?' He mashes my breast with his hand, saying something that me I cannot hear, and puts the chewed thing at the tip. Then he does it with the other one, rubbing and pinching. Everything in my body wants to jump up, run away, fly away. Am hearing Mummy's leg marching on the floor. If she sees me, what will she now say? How will I talk that I dinor listen and now the spirit is using me to play table tennis? Is as if Mummy them are on top of my back before the dibia removes his hand. Mummy touches her one knee to the floor and gives him water in a bowl. He is washing his hands, praying, when I go upstairs.

I remove all my clothes and tight them inside waterproof bag to throw it away after, then I baff myself and wash all the thing he mashed in my breast, wash everything well. But peradventure, the thing works, because one week, two week, I don' see the spirit, I don' smell any spoiled meat smell.

Am relaxing watching video cassette one afternoon like this when Gateman says somebody is finding me. I follow him outside to the compound. Ifeanyi is standing there, looking like a corpse that nobody mourned.

I say, 'Ifeanyi, what are you looking for?'

He don' say anything, only put his hand inside his short nika. I can smell it as he is bringing it out. He takes another seed and puts it in my hand, looking me with his eyes that are quarter-to falling out of his head. I blocked the spirit, and he found Ifeanyi to do his work. Ifeanyi's legs is elephant, as if he has been walking all over the whole world. Am sure Landlady dinor know he is coming here, because she will give him transport money or query because what is he coming to find us for?

Is after that I tell Mummy that me I must to do boarding, not ordinary secondary. She says me I should find where I want to go and tell her, that after all, I am big. I will go somewhere far, far, far. Let me see if Ifeanyi will follow me and come there. Should-in case, I ask for protection.

I make sure I lock my room door. I am thinking, the first time the spirit said me I called him because I was crying inside the market, but no tears is coming from my eyes. I am thinking instead of how the dibia put his stinking hand inside my breast and is paining my whole body.

I use heart pain to call her. 'Woman of Bone Piles.' In Igbo, like the spirit calls her name. I am saying it one, two, seven times, like the dibia going round the car.

I wait. Nothing.

'Woman of Bone Piles. Bone Woman. Please come, I am begging. Please come.'

Now crying is coming. I am thinking of if Daddy was here, will I be doing all this rubbish? Somebody will be asking me

'How are you?', not like Mummy that she wants me to be doing Daddy for her and looking after her. If my Daddy was alive, who will touch my breast anyhow? Who?

Still nothing happens.

The ~~Third~~ Second Bride

Thelma, Thelma, Thelma.

Thelma was an okay girl. She was light, the way some people appreciated. Her hair was blacker than charcoal and her lips were lined naturally. A bright student, she sat in front of class to prove it. A bit of a notice-me, but that was not a crime. Her greatest talent by far lay in her powers of observation. Nothing escaped her.

She had known her parents were unhappy before they admitted it to themselves, had seen things like the looks her father gave his official driver, a young graduate who spent what seemed to be hours washing and polishing the car. And when she was old enough, Thelma observed that she seemed to resemble neither her father nor her mother, but instead took after her Uncle Geoffrey, the kind and quiet man who had served as best man in her parents' wedding and remained unmarried himself. It was the sort of thing people would notice but not talk about, but in Thelma's mouth, it became a blisteringly hot yam, and she could do nothing but spit it out. Slyly, you see, so you weren't quite sure what she knew, what she was saying, but you also knew. Thelma menaced her parents into staying together.

Then there was the time she caught one of the senior girls inscribing her thighs with possible answers before a test, her back to the rest of the hostel. Thelma lay in her bed with her face under her arm, fake snoring, and watched in the grey light of dawn as the girl tattooed her skin with fine print. She let the day go by before approaching the senior. Thelma had a few seniors who gave her protection from chores and punishments. They hated her, but it was easy, in a school that valued academic achievement, to pretend that their shared interest in Thelma was because of her brains. They secretly wondered if Thelma had anything on the others, and what it was, but they did not dare ask. Those who lived in glass houses did not tend to hurl rocks.

And so, when Thelma saw her classmate sneak furtively into the long grass, Thelma leaped off the ledge of the platform where she'd been sketching in her notebook and followed on quiet feet. The whispering of the grass hid whatever small noises Thelma's feet made as she approached, and she watched them, her classmate and a tattered boy that could only be from the village – she did not recognise him – speak. Or rather, the girl spoke, and the boy gestured, sleepily. Two aces up her sleeve, then. The girl must be from the surrounding villages, or why else would she speak to the boy? Why would the girl hide that she was local, unlike the other scholarship students? It could only be for a sinister reason, and Thelma could not wait to find out what it was. The second? Girls and boys were not supposed to mix on school ground, even if the boys in question were not from school. It was grounds for expulsion.

A blast of wind on the grass, obscuring her vision. When she parted it once more, the couple had disappeared, but Thelma was not worried. She knew her chi would guide her once more. She would catch them both at it one of these days, and then she would strike. Thelma turned around to depart, and bumped into the girl, who had a wide smile breaking open her face.

'What are you doing in the bush?' the girl asked.

Flustered, Thelma dropped her pencil. 'I'm drawing the grass,' she said. Gathering her wits, she challenged back: 'And you, what are you doing in the bush?'

'Me?' replied the girl. 'I was following you now.'

Thelma swallowed her misgivings – not completely, but enough to allow herself to be walked out of the bush. Her classmate clasped her tightly around the waist, too tightly, really, walking fast and almost lifting her off her feet. Thelma would never have guessed from looking at her that she would be that strong, but brushing her off did not work. Thelma became anxious, kept casting her eyes backwards, wary.

'What are you looking for?' the girl asked.

'My pencil.'

'It's in your hand, foolish girl,' the girl said, laughing. She stopped laughing. 'Ey-ya, you're bleeding.' She pointed at a spot on Thelma's stomach.

Thelma raised her blouse, and examined the cut which appeared much smaller than the splotch of blood on her daywear implied.

'It's probably just the elephant grass that cut you, sebi?' the girl said, and Thelma did not know if she was telling or asking. She gazed steadily at Thelma. Smiled her cheery smile. 'Let me help you clean it.' She pulled out a slender packet from the pocket of her skirt, dabbed the wound and blew. Thelma winced as it smarted. More fiddling and the girl slapped a plaster on the wound.

At the porter's lodge, the girl abruptly departed, and Thelma had to stumble to regain her footing. She chewed her lower lip, regretful. She wondered what other discovery she had just been stopped short of making.

It took a few days for the normally sharp Thelma to notice the lump under the skin around her navel. It grew fast. She became listless. The cut. Something about the cut. As quickly as she remembered how she could have got the lump, it vanished again from memory. Besides, there were many who did not like Thelma. Who would listen if she told?

CHAPTER TWENTY-NINE

Ozoemena: Now

Ozoemena's head aches intermittently and often, without warning. She gets strange sensations, as if her head swells out of all proportion or shrinks until her eyes are one on top of the other. The night is relatively quiet – some animal clatters amongst the rubbish in the metal cans under the tree, looking for something to eat, but there are no footfalls.

It is funny, Ozoemena thinks, lying in her bed in hostel four, how her definition of quiet has changed. The night is full of insects and nocturnal creatures, but none of these noises faze her. She lies quietly on the aubergine sheets belonging to Mbu, chasing fugitive sleep.

Thelma. The gossip mill was abuzz with the scandal during the daylight hours. Thelma, pregnant! How? With whom? For Ozoemena, this is a Very Big Deal. She knows how women become *gravid*, studied illustrations in her father's many medical books while she was learning how to read, not discriminating between material. This is different. Pregnancy is not the same as being gravid. Gravid is bare, technical, non-judgemental. Pregnancy at their age is something else entirely, loaded with consequences, ruination, tarnish to the family name. Nobody will ever forget that Thelma got pregnant until everybody who knows about it is dead and has turned to dust. And even after that, her family will have a *reputation*, which will be worse for nobody knowing *why*. Thelma is rumoured to be in a coma. Ozoemena thinks it would be better to remain in such a state than face vicious gossip.

When it had happened, Mr Osugiri, the school's handyman-driver, had brought the bus around and, with Miss Uzọ tottering around him, managed to lift Thelma in. Matron had hobbled along behind them, giving instructions to Watch her head! And, Turn her left! And as they pulled away, Matron had placed Thelma's head on her bony thighs, signalling loudly how caring she was, how this had happened *in spite* of her leadership. How motherly she could be. Ozoemena grimaced thinking about it. Poor Thelma. She was already in trouble; she did not need Matron's noduled fingers clenching her jaw firmly to keep her head snugly resting against those skeletal hips. Miss Uzọ tried to maintain order in the lab afterwards, to act as if nothing had happened, but nobody could concentrate. By breaktime, the news was all over the school.

A purposeful squeak. Someone walks towards Ozoemena by the smoky orange light of a kerosene lantern.

'Ozoemena? Are you awake?' asks Senior Joy.

In response, Ozoemena sits up.

'Come and escort me outside. I want to ease myself.'

As soon as Joy draws their bolt back, other bolts clatter from doors all across the quadrangle, as girls rush out to relieve themselves in the company of others. Ozoemena holds the smoky lamp.

'Put that away!' Joy hisses. 'I don't want Matron to see my face if she comes out.' She sticks her bottom out over the pavement and empties her bladder on to the sand. All over the compound, there is the slap of water hitting earth, occasionally a hard shuffle as someone backs out further, mid-flow. Joy is tall, one of the tallest in school, despite only being in class four. Barely a senior. Ozoemena marvels at how she can hold the half-squat for so long.

Joy bobs on her tiptoes, shaking off the remnants of urine

before pulling her pants up and nightgown down. The junior students who made it out wander en-masse towards the bathrooms, in a show of obeying the rules before they take the same position. One junior girl has a bright lantern, and they rush towards her, moths to flame.

A familiar loud trumpeting in the night; an image forms in Ozoemena's mind of a bunch of feathers flying into her face. It is coming from the tree in the centre of the quadrangle, its call smashing against Ozoemena's eardrums. Goosepimples pop on her skin. The girls scatter. Ozoemena backs away into hostel four, tripping over her feet after Joy rushes past her for the door. The junior girl's bright lantern lies at the end of the pavement on its side, guttering, abandoned.

'Close the door!' hisses Joy. With shaking hands, Ozoemena tries and fails. There is a trick to the door, a lifting and sliding, but with fear surging through her body, Ozoemena is not strong enough. Joy bounds out of her bed, lifts, slides, and jumps back in. The lantern in Ozoemena's hand belches more smoke. It is burning wick now. The kerosene has been used up.

It is a dazed Ozoemena that makes her way back to bed. Her wrist hurts from when she landed on the floor, and she rubs it absentmindedly. She is certain that had she raised her lantern up towards the tree, she would have seen the creature, great wings folded, staring straight at her. She knows the sound. She has heard the bird once before, that afternoon during an unfair fight, when she slipped and fell into another world.

'It was only okpoko, a hornbill,' says Ugochi. She is extra snappy this morning. The Harmattan chill is biting, and they jog in place, trying to keep warm. Chinonso, the new girl, nods, agreeing with her.

'You have the answer to everything, don't you?' Ozoemena purses her lips.

'Not all of us are sheep,' says Ugochi. 'And my father is a lawyer. He studies things.'

Nkili snorts. 'What is a lawyer's concern with birds? Is he a bird lawyer?'

Ugochi stops jogging. 'And you, what does your father do?'

Nkili ignores her, stretching. She has on a pair of long socks that come up to her knees, along with shorts and running shoes that bounce when she moves. She wears a jacket, zipped up to her chin. Ozoemena thinks Nkili looks like a proper athlete. Unlike herself, shivering in her T-shirt, wishing they could get moving soon.

'I didn't know that's what it was. My grandmother told me a story about an okpoko once,' muses Ozoemena. 'That's the title-name of the Igwe of my hometown. But this story has to do with how the world was created.' She is interested in Ugochi's information, even if it is delivered with derision.

'I think I know the story,' Chinonso chimes in. 'If you see okpoko bird, it is good luck forever.'

'Oh, I wish I'd seen it.' One of Ugochi's triplets speaks up. All three comprising her entourage clutch and rub at their hands, and Ozoemena does not know if they are cold or overtaken by their desire to see a hornbill.

'Shut up,' Ugochi says. 'If you see a vulture, it's bad luck; if you see an owl, it's bad luck; if a bird shits on your head, it's good luck.' She counts on her fingers in a mocking tone. 'Birds are just birds. There's no such thing as good or bad luck, and only lazy people think there is.'

'I'm just saying that . . . there are some things . . . that . . . we can't . . . fashi it.' The triplet speaking trails off when Ugochi scowls at her.

Ozoemena seizes the opportunity to challenge her rival. 'But you believe there are witches?' she asks.

Ugochi sighs, exaggerating her frustration. 'If someone wants to kill you, that is a real thing. If they believe that *they* are a witch, then they will do things to prove it true; poison you or kill you . . . those things are real.' She turns away, disgusted at having to explain herself to a bunch of buffoons. 'Not this bird nonsense you people are talking.'

Mr Ibe blows on his whistle and the girls line up. He stares at Ozoemena and she hides her face, remembering the way he had pointed at her after she threw the ball at his star player's nose. He beckons, and Ozoemena drags her feet towards him. He places her at the front of the line, his hands strong on her shoulders. Ozoemena resists the urge to shrug them off. The games master gives her a pointed look, as if he can tell what she is thinking. She will be pacesetter, whether she likes it or not.

Ozoemena feels sick to her stomach. She is not an athlete, has never been one. Every Saturday, she vows to herself that she will complete the race. Ozoemena has got better at running over the past few weeks, but she has never made the entire cross-country trip before. On her first ever one, she stopped short of two miles and had to be walked back to Novus while the others carried on. Her top lip and nose grow hot from shame.

Many of the girls huddle in sweaters and wrappers on top of their sports gear. Mr Ibe travels the line, snatching wrappers and tossing them on to the porch of the tuck shop.

'If you're cold, move,' he says. His voice comes from deep inside his beefy chest, the mounds of muscle nearly horizontal to his chin. His sleeveless T-shirt is tight, his shorts sit higher than his knees, and Ozoemena thinks his black calf-length socks incongruous with his worn white trainers. The games master lines up the boys behind the girls, jogging all the while, moving in and out of the morning mist, which settles smoke-heavy in the grassy fields.

The newly born sun breaks through, and its light hits the shiny whistle on Mr Ibe's neck, winking.

'Jog,' he says.

A universal groan travels through the line. Ozoemena's spine tingles with unease, but she shrugs it off.

They break through the gap in the fence in relative silence, passing the manual water pump. A short line of villagers bearing water containers stretch out before the pump, awaiting their turn. Ozoemena tries not to look at them, but she thinks that many of them glare as the students jog past.

The path is only wide enough to let cars in and out in a single file. An old man in long shorts rings his bicycle bell. His two-handled containers and hoop of climbing twine denote his trade as palm wine tapper. Mr Ibe stops, and they exchange greetings in a melodious Igbo that Ozoemena does not understand. She gasps when she realises what this means. Mr Ibe is a local. Mr Ibe is a villager. Her unease grows.

Stop it, Ozoemena, she tells herself.

'Run!' commands Mr Ibe. The students' groans are louder now that the sleep has cleared from their eyes. They obey, picking up the pace. Ahead of them, the road widens, leading into the village proper. The ground is hard. Wearing plimsolls hurts the soles of her feet. A group of village children point, their hard, efficient bodies carrying loads that are twice, thrice their sizes. Ozoemena closes her mouth against the cold and the dust, but her nostrils have tightened, and the air is not enough. She wonders if this is how Mbu feels during her asthma attacks. A few steps further and her mouth drops open again. She hates the way her breathing sounds. It gets in her head, telling her that she is dying, any minute now she will *die.* Ozoemena wants to stop, to suck down cool oxygen into her deprived body.

'Left! Left! Left!' The message travels up the line. Ozoemena turns left, pumping her arms. Where are they going? They have never taken this route before. They turn away from the straight road leading to the massive Catholic church and the hospital, and hit another bush trail. The sand is cushiony underfoot. The tight arches of Ozoemena's feet thank her, but only for a moment. Running on soft sand is harder than on tread-hardened earth. Her thighs burn. The saliva in her mouth dries to cotton wool.

'Nwanyị di ya fụrụ n'anya!' A senior boy has started the song, his voice cracking like a whip.

'Onye ụjọ ọrụ!' the rest of them respond.

'Ebute akpa rice, orichaa!'

'Onye ụjọ ọrụ!'

Ozoemena stops responding after the second verse. It is hard to run and sing at the same time.

Vomit, vomit, vomit, she thinks with each step. She tastes acid in her throat.

Mr Ibe gives another command. 'Jog.'

There are sighs of relief as the pace slows. Ozoemena spits, trying to get rid of the sensation of suffocation. Her saliva is white. It hits the sand and curls the brown around itself like a blanket.

Ozoemena gulps down oxygen greedily, her mind whirring, seeking distraction from the pain. She tries to settle on a thought, the bird in the night, the breakfast she will eat once they return to school, her arts project, but the strain in her body draws her back to the path, to the present, to the pain.

They break into a forest of bamboo trees. The light is dappled and beautiful, the sun playing hide and seek, striking the trunks when they least expect it. A breeze blows, and in seconds, their sweaty faces and arms are dry.

Long live the Harmattan, Ozoemena thinks.

The song changes, and this time, she tries to join in between puffs, stomping her right leg hard on the beat.

'Ken-ken-ke!'

'Obi!'

'Ke-re-ren-ke!'

'Obi!'

'Nwoke ndi army!'

'Obi!'

'Nwanyi ndi army!'

Mr Ibe jogs up the line. The games master has a lighter tread than most, but Ozoemena can always sense him before he hots up her ear with his breath. She imagines his lungs are bellows, stoking the fire burning in his body. His skin pours sweat, and the earth drinks it up.

Ozoemena hears the swish of his switch before it stings her legs. She yelps, skips.

'Faster.' His voice has no inflection. 'Run,' he says.

Her stinging legs unlock a fury in Ozoemena. She picks up the pace. Her bra-top is not correct for running; the narrow elastic band rubs under her slight breasts, adding to her discomfort. Ozoemena supposes she should be thankful. A few weeks earlier, her inner thighs had chafed. She had treated her skin gently and it had recovered, just in time to do it all over again the next weekend. Now, though, the wind whistles though the gap between her thighs, a lack of food and an abundance of chores joining the constant exercise in whittling down the baby fat.

The sun hides behind a cloud and the temperature drops. They are deep into the bamboo, pockets of forest swathed in cobwebs, unreached by the sun. Dead leaves make for a springy, crunchy racetrack.

Danger, the silence screams. *Danger.* Ozoemena's natural caution causes her to hesitate. She turns her head, wanting the reassurance of those behind her.

The wind whizzes to her left and she catches a dark shape streaking faster than lightning through the bamboo grove. Ozoemena stumbles, alarmed, searching the shadows. There is nothing.

She races ahead. Her skin melts off her bones and spatters

with her sweat on to the leaves below. Ozoemena's chest begins to tighten once more as she struggles to breathe. Her muscles tense; she clenches her teeth, her fists; her knees begin to lock. She is in her own head again, back in her old school, not a runner, not an athlete, sitting on the pavement reading her books, balls thumping around her. Her vision begins to blur at the corners.

The shape again. Something is racing her in the bushes. Racing to catch her. Ozoemena cannot hear its footfalls, but she knows the leopard is there, just like it knows Ozoemena is on the path between the bamboo. It keeps time with her, a half-visible companion, like something out of a waking dream.

Breathe.

Ozoemena inhales hungrily and messily. A lightness opens up in her chest and begins to spread. The blurriness fades from her vision. The green flashes by, but she can breathe, nearly as easily as if she is walking. Surprise and pleasure. She barks out laughter. Her body is new, improved. Ozoemena knows if she stops, she will lose it.

Keep up, little leopard.

That voice again, speaking to the part of her that has begun to court wildness. Restraint flies off her, sails off the sweat. Ozoemena puts her head down and races, palms open now, fingers splayed, feet springing off the earth. The leopard glides ahead in her peripheral vision, taunting her. Ozoemena's mouth hangs open, gleeful. She races faster than she ever has in her entire life. Tears stream from her eyes.

She sees the opening in the earth, a gully, made in the rusty earth by erosion. Ozoemena is too fast to stop without hurting herself badly.

Jump.

She feels herself begin to slide. *Someone will find me,* she thinks. Mr Ibe, the students in the line far behind her.

Ozoemena has never broken any bones, but she closes her eyes now, prepared for the inevitable. Her friends who had broken bones before said it did not hurt, not at first.

Jump.

The gully is upon her. The gulf is vast; she is not going to make it.

Jump!

Ozoemena jumps –

– and lands on soft, loamy earth.

Her first impulse is to touch her head. The next one, once she catches sight of the vibrant violet skies, is to jump to her feet and look around. Despite her usual urge to stare at the entrancing landscape, Ozoemena knows what is coming. She is not in the leopard, and is aware of how weak she is, how soft and exposed. She looks around and notices that the tree in which she had first seen the weeping girl is some distance away, its boughs reaching to the skies in a dark, leafy embrace. At least, it seems to be the same tree. She tries to get her bearings, but she could be facing any part of it. Ozoemena stands as quietly as she can, listening. Her heart pounds in her fingers, in her toes. Her plimsolls are gone. She senses the earth underneath the soles of her bare feet breathing, surrendering under the pressure from her body. Blood thrashes against her eardrums like waves on a cliff face. She takes off running towards the tree.

A bird circles overhead, trumpeting a loud call. Okpoko. It flies ahead of her towards the tree, close to her, fanning her with the draft from its flapping. Ozoemena races in a messy sprint. Despite this, Okpoko gets to the tree before her and settles on a branch, trumpeting again. Ozoemena puts her chin down, arms cutting through the air. As she approaches, she notices a hillock through the amethyst luminosity of her surroundings. She reaches the tree, panting, and touches it. Nothing. She places her hands on various parts of its exposed roots. The bird honks at her, a sound like mocking laughter.

'Maybe you should tell me, instead of laughing,' she says, and is surprised to hear her voice sound firm, assured. Okpoko honks at her again and Ozoemena, understanding, walks towards the mound. It is bigger than she is, spired like a church and wide as the single wardrobe in her old room. Gooseflesh pops all over her skin. It is an anthill.

She does not like anthills, not since her former bully Benjamin once pushed her into one, cracking its structure with her body. Ozoemena had dusted herself off and stared as ant larvae were exposed, white and wiggling to the sun. Then agbusi came, soldier ants defending their young. They bit and clung so that her friends had to break their bodies off her. She had cried from the fiery anguish. The multitude of chambers gave her a funny feeling in her stomach, an urge to scream and throw up, a desire both to destroy it and to run from it. She fights the latter urge now, tamping down her disgust with logic. The anthill is silent, but so is the bird, and Ozoemena's eyes search in the bizarre glow.

There is a girl sprawled on the floor. Ozoemena reaches out a hand to touch her arm, and the skin under her fingertips is the texture of old yams. Ozoemena bends down and puts an ear to the girl's nose. A thin stream of air tickles her neck.

She taps the girl. The girl's eyelids flutter, showing the whites of her eyes. Then her eyes flash open. She lashes out with something, catching Ozoemena with a solid thwack. Ozoemena screams, clutching her right hand. The girl scrabbles to her feet.

'You're not one of them,' she says. 'You have a smell.'

'What?' Ozoemena tamps down the urge to retaliate, the pain dancing merrily up her right arm. 'One of who?'

'Whom,' the girl corrects. 'The spirits. You're not one of them. Are you alive?'

'Yes.' Ozoemena's eyes leak a few tears despite herself.

'Sorry,' says the girl. 'How did you come here?' She glances around her. 'Do you know how to get out?'

Ozoemena puts the most painful finger of her hand in her mouth and attempts to soothe it by sucking. She shakes her head. 'I just come and go.'

'Like the poem. Are you ogbanje?'

'What? No!'

'Can you take me when you leave?' the girl says fast, continuing to look about her.

Ozoemena examines her. She notices that the arm which had felt like an old yam hangs from the girl's shoulder, useless.

The girl observes her scrutiny. She folds her good arm over the dead one, hugging herself. 'I don't know what is happening to me. I just want to go home!'

'Where do you live?' asks Ozoemena.

'I don't remember.'

'What's your name, then?'

'Ogenna.'

Okpoko trumpets once, twice, and takes off, circling the tree.

'Okpoko says they are coming. We have to go,' Ozoemena interprets, pointing skyward.

'You understand birds?' the girl asks. She takes a step backwards.

Ozoemena knows what she is thinking. A simple equation would be 'Birds = witches'. She catches herself before she says the words, *I'm a bird lawyer.*

'It doesn't matter, it doesn't matter,' says the girl. 'It's not the strangest thing I've seen. But we can't leave her. Help me!'

'Who?'

The girl dashes back to the tree, flinging aside leaves, branches and mounds of white fibre.

'Thelma?' Ozoemena kneels, pulling her up. 'Thelma!'

'You know her?' asks the girl.

'She's in my school. How did she get here?'

'I don't know. She's like you, maybe. Sometimes she is here, sometimes she is not, and she's always asleep. I can never wake her. We can't leave her now that she is here.'

Okpoko trumpets again.

The ground begins to rumble. The girl grabs Ozoemena's arm, nostrils flared and vibrating. She picks up her weapon, the log of wood she had used to whack Ozoemena, and holds it like a machete. Despite her bravado, the girl's voice had cracked. The log shivers in her hand.

Ozoemena shakes Thelma, but as informed, nothing happens. She tries to move her, bending at the knees to support her classmate's limp, uncooperative form. Thelma flops to the ground. Ozoemena grits her teeth and begins to drag her by the legs. Immediately, Okpoko swoops, cutting them off. Ozoemena yells, slapping the air around her as the bird swoops and dives, the span of its wings terrifying and enraging her. Is Okpoko not supposed to be good luck? The bird appears to be against her, pushing her nearer to the dreaded anthill.

The girl collapses. She stares at her lower limbs in dismay. 'My leg!'

Before their eyes, the leg shrivels, taking on the same yam-skin quality of her useless hand.

Thelma is immoveable. Ozoemena begins to camouflage her as the girl had done, piling leaves, empty pods and the same white fibres over her. 'I'll find a way to come back, Thelma. I won't leave you here.' Ozoemena begins to grow angry at the leopard. Why has it not appeared to take over? She needs its strength.

The crushing, churning noise is nearby, and with it, something Ozoemena does not wish to encounter, vulnerable as she is. She grabs the girl. She is light. Ozoemena hoists her up. The hornbill's trumpeting is regular now. Behind them, the anthill is crumbling, chunks breaking off and rolling downhill each time Okpoko cries. Ozoemena stumbles backwards, dragging the girl with her. She waits for a wave of soldier ants to come flowing out of the damaged structure, but instead a finger of light shoots up.

Through it.

She welcomes the not-voice speaking calmly into her spirit. Fighting revulsion, she closes her eyes, clasps the girl to her and falls backwards on to the crumbling edifice of the anthill. Ozoemena expects a grainy resistance, but the anthill stretches, muscular, and begins to swallow her. A moist squelching fills her ears. The anthill is contracting, sealing up again, pushing them apart through the space between their bodies.

'Wait for me!' the girl cries. 'Please don't leave me here!'

'I'm not doing it,' Ozoemena shouts. 'It's not me!'

She tightens her hold on the girl's arm, determined to pull her through. A tug and give, the sound of cassava torn from dry soil. Ozoemena falls into the void and the aperture seals shut before her eyes.

She sits in the bottom of the gully, cradling the girl's arm, light and hollow as a paper tube, and stuffed full of cottony fibres. She is certain of something now.

Whatever the leopard is chasing is at her school.

CHAPTER THIRTY

Ozoemena: Now

Ozoemena surveys the gully, searching for a way out. She tries to clutch at saplings and their young roots, but they are dry and give way in her hands, showering her with a red, dusty mist. She takes off her plimsolls and her socks, stuffs them into the pockets of her sports skirt and begins to dig herself hand and footholds, gritting her teeth. If the leopard must take her, why on earth could it not simply return her to the path? Why leave her in a grave?

There is dirt under her fingernails and toenails when she finally makes it up and out. Ozoemena's whites are filthy orange, but she laughs, catching her breath in between each painful outburst of sound, ignoring the sand in her hair as she lies supine on the ground. She breaks a twig and cleans under her nails, wincing but laughing, amazed at her own strength, then begins jogging back the way she had come.

Ozoemena's return to the rest of the students almost goes unnoticed. Almost. Then someone shouts, 'Here she comes!' and her friends swarm her, all talking at once.

'Why did you run off?' Obiageli's eyes are wide as saucers.

'I didn't mean to,' Ozoemena says. She is aware of how dishevelled she appears, even compared to the rest of the school. The sun is out in force and sweat pours out of her friends.

'Mr Ibe will kill you,' Chinonso mutters.

Shouts of 'Here she is' and 'She's back!' ring out. Ozoemena wishes she could transport herself of her own volition. Anywhere would be better than here, at this moment, with the games master striding forcefully towards her. He reaches her, yanks her ear and gives it a mighty twist. Ozoemena feels a crack in the lobe, an ache inside her ear.

'Did you not hear me saying "On the spot"? You are supposed to mark time.'

'No, sir, I did not hear you.' Tears form in her throat. Ozoemena is humiliated. Her eyes downcast, she watches as more feet join them, Senior Nwakaego's famous red trainers amongst their number.

'Nwokeke, come with me,' she says, through clenched teeth. Ozoemena has never heard her so angry. 'And put on your shoes. You are not an animal.'

'Yes, Senior.'

'What about the other one?' Senior Ambobo this time.

Ozoemena frowns, raises her head. 'What other one?' she asks.

'Nobody was talking to you,' says Ambobo.

'One of the triplets,' Mr Ibe replies. 'The half-deaf one. She followed you.'

'Etaoko,' Senior Nwakaego clarifies.

'There was nobody with me,' Ozoemena says.

'We saw her follow you.'

'No, sir,' she replies.

Ozoemena is perplexed. Yes, she was pacesetter, but she had not heard anyone behind her. And *half-deaf*? Ozoemena had not realised this. She had assumed the triplets were simply quirky, speaking in their secret signs. Now, she feels thick, stupid. In her mind's eye, Mbu sneers at her: *Some leopard.* Frustration, anger at herself imploding.

'There was nobody behind me. I just turned and walked back.'

'Show us where you went,' Mr Ibe says. Ozoemena nods, finishes slipping on her socks and shoes. A handful of seniors accompany her and the games master as she walks back the way she came. She had not worn her wristwatch on the run, it tended to malfunction when her arm got sweaty. Ozoemena tries to estimate, keeping an eye out for the trees, for markers, but the entire bamboo grove looks the same wherever she turns. She remembers sliding to a stop and searches the earth for signs of this.

'Well,' Mr Ibe says when she stops once more to scrutinise the earth. 'Is this the place?'

'I think so,' Ozoemena says.

Senior Ambobo makes a sound in his throat that sets Ozoemena's teeth on edge. The tears sting under her eyelids. Anger, remorse, irritation. She must not cry. They search until they begin to wilt from the heat. Ozoemena is exhausted, stumbling on the second walk back. They meet up with the rest of the school and fall into haphazard lines. Mr Ibe runs ahead, leaving the prefects in charge. At the junction, they turn right towards the road leading to Novus, while he jogs left into the village, probably to the local police shack.

'What did you do to her, you witch?' Ugochi by her ear, speaking in low, menacing tones. 'You better pray she's alright. And when we get back to school, I will beat you tube and tyre.'

Ozoemena spins around, disregarding the presence of seniors, of boys. 'Why wait?' she challenges. 'Let's do it here.'

Ugochi shoves her. The blow glances off a breast bud, and Ozoemena grits her teeth, nearly doubling over.

'You think you are something, right?' Ugochi says. 'I will show you that you're nothing more than a hanging pant.'

Ozoemena shoves back, swift and sharp. 'Get your stinking mouth away from my face,' she growls.

'What is going on there?' shouts Senior Nwakaego from the end of the girls' line. 'Why is nobody moving?'

Ozoemena's anger grows until there is nothing else but the sensation feeding on her earlier unease and resentment.

'Don't the triplets always stay together?' she asks. 'Only God knows what you did for Etaoko to want to get away from you.'

Ugochi rears back. 'You're a stupid idiot!'

'You're a goat!'

'Go and die.' Ugochi appears to have grown to almost twice her size.

Driven by fear, Ozoemena throws a punch. It is clumsy but effective, catching Ugochi on the side of her head, whipping it to the side. Ugochi shakes her head to clear it and lunges, pulling Ozoemena to the ground in one movement.

Ozoemena has not yet been in a fight, not properly, and now she wishes that she learned from Mbu. She whomps hard into the ground. A piercing pain above her heart as though her ribs have stabbed through the flesh. She and Ugochi roll around in the dust. The girls roar. Mob mentality is sweet and heady and distracting.

They are on their feet again. Gritting her teeth at the déjà vu of it all, Ozoemena throws a punch with all her might, but something happens to it before it lands on Ugochi's shoulder, and the fist squishes up uselessly like a handful of fufu. An answering blow blasts into Ozoemena's face. She bites down on her tongue.

Ozoemena tries to disengage from Ugochi, but the girl holds on tightly and they sway in a parody of a waltz. The floor. Grabbing a fistful of sand and dead leaves, Ugochi attempts to compost them in Ozoemena's mouth, but the latter clamps her teeth shut and twists away.

'Why always sand?!' she cries.

The girls scream louder and some of the boys join in. Some try to separate them, and others to stop those people. Ozoemena grips Ugochi by the neck and tries to scratch the brown off her skin, but her nails are too short, and all it does is make Ugochi dump the sand in her eyes.

Ozoemena yells, hitting out at her opponent in messy slaps and punches, intending to do more damage than she actually does, getting more riled up each time.

Bite her.

Ugochi grabs her hair. It is short and she has to hold it tightly, but she does, and Ozoemena's new headache, never far away, returns with a slicing pain.

Ugochi slams her head on the floor.

'One!' the crowd yells.

Ozoemena weaves underneath Ugochi's hand and strikes, biting down on her arm.

Ugochi belches out an ungodly sound. Ozoemena turns her head to spit out the saliva in her mouth, and something small rolls in the sand, brown-on-red. A piece of flesh. Ugochi's eyes widen with disbelief. Ozoemena swallows hurriedly, licking salt from her lips without thinking.

'She bit me!' Ugochi screams, holding her arm to her chest. Her lower lip quivers from the horror. 'She bit me!'

The raised cords of her white polo shirt turn slowly crimson. The prefects flood the scene, amongst them Ambobo. He resembles a virility statue with his thickset build and wide nostrils.

'I'm sorry, it was an accident.' Ozoemena scoots away on her bottom. The anger has gone, leaving her deflated. She is dirty, streaks of rusty dust running in rivulets with the sweat. Senior Emeka, the boys' senior prefect, blows a whistle. The students fall into line. He examines Ugochi while Senior Nwakaego cuts a switch from the bushes.

'Quick march to school,' Senior Emeka shouts. 'Not you,' he adds to Ozoemena. 'You will go with Nwashike and her brother to the hospital.'

Ugochi is making a racket, slumping theatrically against

her brother, pointing at Ozoemena. Despite this, her tears are real. Ambobo carries her in his arms and marches, gritting his teeth.

The remaining triplets stare at Ozoemena. They seem scared. Lost. Afraid. Obiageli slips between them, leading them into the line.

'We can't go yet, Etaoko is there.' They stare at each other, communicating something silently between them. Their chins tremble, and one of one them begins to weep while the other hangs on to Obiageli's arm. Obiageli gives Ozoemena a smile, something small and supportive as they follow the rest of the students back. The mood is sombre, their chattering subdued.

Ozoemena stares at her feet all the way to the hospital. She bit someone and drew blood. Only children without home training bite.

Or mad people.

Oruke Nwosu had said she was a leopard, tasked to protect people and defend the land, but Ozoemena is beginning to think that her mother is right, and it is all wildness and nonsense. Maybe she is mad after all; maybe the leopard is some form of mental illness. She resolves to write to her mother as soon as she gets back to school.

In the hospital, she faces the scorn and derision of the nurses. They ask her who she is, who her family is, and is this how people from Anambra state behave? Ozoemena carries the burden of guilt for her whole state. Ugochi weeps when they clean her wound and give her an injection. Fresh guilt suffuses Ozoemena's being. Ambobo glares at Ozoemena. Never mind that she is a girl and smaller than he is, he wants to knock her down – that much is apparent. His biceps bunch whenever she looks at him. Ugochi develops a fever in the evening. The nurses make Ozoemena wipe Ugochi's brow with a clean, cool cloth after Ambobo leaves. Whenever she finds herself nodding off, they wake her up.

'Serves you right,' the staff nurse says. 'Next time before you bite somebody, you will think twice.'

Ozoemena is at the hospital when Uncle Fred arrives the next day. The school has called her mother to have her picked up. There is a letter of suspension waiting for her in the admin office when she gets there. Some members of staff, led by BC, grill her about Etaoko – how fast were they running? Did she see if anyone came out of the bushes? The implication is not lost on Ozoemena, despite her fuzzy head and parched tongue. Kidnapping. Election? Villagers? The teachers exchange looks with each other while Mr Ibe, the man-mountain, slumps on a bench, dejectedly picking at his well-used trainers. There is a man in plainclothes, his body language too studied to be casual, his eyes sharp, watching Ozoemena's every expression. Nobody introduces him. They let Ozoemena go. She has nothing to add. Nevertheless, she feels the weight of the things they did not speak: she is the reason Etaoko has vanished. She was the pacer for the group. She led the deaf girl astray.

Uncle Fred waits for her to pack her things. She has been suspended from school for one week. Ozoemena imagines Mbu crowing at her upon her return: *Kwa-kwa-kwa! You thought being in boarding school was all about eating Indomie, abi?*

She does not speak one word in conversation or explanation all the way home. Uncle Fred obliges her need for distance. It is a serious thing she has done. He slips his Father Edeh audio cassette into the van's player. Ozoemena falls into a restive sleep to the recorded preaching and cheering from crowds.

CHAPTER THIRTY-ONE

Treasure: Then

The last Sunday before I take exam for boarding is Harvest and Bazaar festival. I am happy because plenty things are going to happen. I will pass my exam because I have been cramming well for four months now and my English is getting more better. More best. Am doing reading comprehension, am doing spelling, am doing GK, am doing social studies, am doing maths so I can know everything I missed. Ever since I told Mummy that me, I want to do boarding, she went by herself and got me lesson teacher who finished from ASUTECH, and he is the one that has been teaching me. He is the one who is telling me to be speaking English more. After much, he now told Mummy that me I need separate English and verbal teacher and brought another woman that me I know is his girlfriend. The two of them will not let somebody rest, but her own matter is worst than his. She will be putting her nose up like she is a white person as she is talking hiọ hiọ hiọ even though she is from Owerri. It was her that told Mummy of the expensive private school in Imo State where they don' speak Igbo and English together, only English. She said her uncle in Lagos, his friend's wife's brother came back from America and opened a fantastic school. By the time she finished talking about the school, the thing is doing Mummy like malaria because they are plenty childs of ambassador and senator and oil and gas them. Me, I'm happy because it is far. Let me see which leg Ifeanyi will use to pursue me there. Whatever the dibia mashed inside my chest, it must be working, because the spirit has not been disturbing. It's like he cannot even find me sef. Not as if me I'm a promise-and-fail, but if I get all the girls finish before Ifeanyi can find me to give another stone, then I will have paid him his three wifes abi? Then he will not cheat me. He cannot be giving me more seed to be finding him more girls as if me am wife supplier. And too, me I am not following him to go anywhere.

If he cheats me, then I will play my last card. If the Bone Woman will even answer me, otherwise, I will be in hot soup.

Anyway, me I like Harvest and Bazaar. Not only me, everybody likes it. The men are carrying plenty bags of money and the women are dressing in whatever lace or wrapper material is reigning in August Meeting for that year. The canopies are already up all over the church compound and food is smelling everywhere. My stomach is sounding during Mass and me I'm coughing to cover it. Mummy is shining Bethlehem star. I'm thinking this life is just nonsense. Just yesterday-yesterday, hunger was using me to play football, my stomach sounding regularly as if it is another heart beating in my stomach. Now, I am coughing to cover something that is normal. Why? When all of us in church are hungry, some did not eat before Mass, some are looking for money, some for husband, and wife. Others are finding the reverend father's face. Me sef, I am hungry for when Daddy comes back. And yet we will wear cloth, tie scarf, cross leg as if we don' all eat, or pollute, or have bad heart for somebody.

I don' like the way my mind is talking to me nowadays. I think am just tired. And too, the Mass is too long. The reverend father knows that everybody is waiting for church to scatter so he is keeping us, preaching long preaching and doing plenty announcement. I can smell fried meat.

During the bazaar, they are selling plenty of the offering that people gave as harvest; new yams, fruits, Eva wines, plenty fat fowls and cocks, even goats sef. They will bring out the thing they are selling, group it, and people will start shouting how much they will buy, then the man talking will say, 'Last price, going, going, gone!' and everyone will clap. Plenty people are giving what they bought to the reverend father, Mummy is enjoying. She brought the last of the bags of rice, beans and yam the spirit gave us. I asked her, 'So how will we manage?' since the spirit is no longer bringing, only collecting, and Mummy said, 'God will provide,' and she was smiling her Bianca smile, so I know she is not worried. I want to ask her, which God is the one providing? The God that left us to nearly be dying of hunger? The God that saw me and allowed me to enter with a spirit?

Me, I am saving plenty things in my wardroom: garri, salt, palm oil, soap, eggs, beans, De Rica, St Louis, sardine, Omo. Once bitten, twice shy.

My heart is not feeling okay, and I don' know why, so I say let me go outside the compound. There are people selling ice cream, both the one tied in waterproof and Wall's ice cream. There are also people begging. I bring out money from inside my purse and share for them. Some of the beggars are taking the money from my hand fast and putting inside their trousers and bags and leaving their begging bowl empty. I know is so that other people don' think they have too much money and won't give them more. I know that thing.

There is a woman at the end of the line, but she is not sitting on the floor. She has one small chair like this, like nwanyịnọduluokwu, which women in the village use to sit down and cook. She is fanning herself with raffia fan. I come near and I don' know how to ask her if she is looking for money or whether I will give her and insult her. The woman looks at me and our eyes jam. Am seeing my mistake. No beggar can be looking someone in the eye like this. As I am turning to go back inside the church compound, she talks.

'Treasure.'

Immediately my whole body seizes. Her voice is sweet and shocking, like when you lick orange, and it shocks your teeth electric.

'How do you know my name?' Am not greeting her because anybody that calls my name like am owing them money cannot be good. The woman stands up. She is wearing necklaces and bangle and earring, thick and carved as if she is mourning somebody that is expensive because they are pure white—

'You are the Bone Woman,' I say.

'I was curious about your impudence, summoning me like that, so I came. Normally, I ignore. Who told you my name? What do you have for me?'

She is looking rich, and her rich is old and smelling. She is not wearing blouse but trying two wrapper, correct Akwete on her chest and her waist, big and thick. As am looking her, I see that the wrapper is moving as if there is something hiding under there. Her face don' move, but everything is inside her eyes, the korokoro eyes of an animal that is cunning, that swallows something bigger than itself and wipes its mouth. Am thinking me I've entered wahala because as I am seeing her, she is worst than the spirit. All the things he told me is going around my head. My mind is not there so I don' see when she moves to the front of my face.

'You are very pretty. The kind of prettiness that attracts spirits.'

Why is she saying that? Does she know is me that the spirit is using to plan, that he wants to come out from under her? The Bone Woman is looking me up and down. She moves fast like snake and holds my face tight, under my jaw. 'Pretty bones.' She opens my mouth. 'Pretty teeth.' She takes one of her long nails and knocks my teeth. 'Sound.' As she is in my front, I am seeing her teeth too, as she is talking. They are carved as well in different small animals: monkey, rat, goat, cat.

The Bone Woman sees that I am looking inside her mouth. She uses her tongue to lick her teeth. 'You like them, yes?'

I say yes, because I am not stupid. The teeth inside her mouth is not looking like her own, but like she is taking one-one teeth from different people and putting it inside her mouth. There are different sizes and colours of white.

The Bone Woman releases my head, flies her hand as if she wants to throw my head off my neck. 'I am more than man, more than spirit, something you cannot imagine. And I built myself; no help from any god or man.' She closes her mouth like is purse. 'You have been playing with things you shouldn't have, Treasure. When your life is over, you will come to me.'

My mind is disturbing me. So, she knows is me the spirit is using to plan all the things he is planning. What does she mean that I will come to her? The spirit said those with hard death that she takes. God forbid bad thing. It is not me that will die a hard death. Cold-skin is all over my body. I don' even have mind to ask her the thing me I want to ask again.

The Bone Woman is looking something in her hand but when I stretch my neck to look I don' see anything. She closes her hand and smiles. The cane she is using to walk away is white and carved also, with things tied on the head that shake and makes noise, and she is walking.

'If you're going to call for me next time, better bring me something that is worth it.'

Two things are coming out from her wrapper, brushing the floor, and after much, I see that it is two tails. What have I entered with a person that have tail?

In the morning, as am brushing my morning teeth, I see

that one of them, the one in front, is grey like inside pencil. No matter how many times I scrub it, with toothpaste, with salt, with soda, with charcoal and chewing stick, it stays like that.

CHAPTER THIRTY-TWO

Ozoemena: Then

Apart from school and church, there was really no place else to play, and Ozoemena was getting too big for running around. There was not much tolerance for her playing in school, either. She was coming up to her Common Entrance examinations, the popular consensus amongst her parents and teachers being that she would and could 'pass from five'. Ozoemena accepted this with equanimity – it was just how things were done. People believed in her ability to do well, and she would not let them down.

School examinations and now church ones too. Ozoemena was heading to St Faith's Pro-Cathedral to take her confirmation tests. If she passed, there would be first Holy Communion. Again, Prisca had assumed she would pass. It was a forgone conclusion. She had already bought Ozoemena's outfit for the special day: white, poufy dress, white knee-length church socks, white leather shoes – without a buckle, to denote grown-up status – white feathered hat, and white lace gloves without fingers. The shoes were her favourite thing, lined with a mauve the same colour as the bishop wore. And the gloves. Nobody would have her sort, she was certain. Prisca had a manner of ensuring her children stood out. Ozoemena really wanted to wear the clothes, but more than that, she needed to pass. She had already spent weeks memorising her catechism in Igbo, and it had been taxing. There had been the option to learn in English, but Mbu, uncharacteristically, had roused herself to suggest that Ozoemena not do this. The bishop did not have time to test individually, so rows of children were tested at once. Only the English speakers had individual tests. Mbu, of course, had aced hers – and in Igbo. Ozoemena would not be letting the side down.

She gripped her copy of *Ekpere Na Abụ*, trying to rehearse questions and answers in her head, but it proved impossible. Traffic was loud and demanded concentration, and there were what seemed like a thousand possible questions, with answers that had to be in very specific language. Ozoemena walked briskly, as though her mother had sent her on an errand. She was determined to have enough time to revise if she could, and had set out early.

There was an acrid smell in the air when she reached the market, thick and pungent, and underneath, the aroma of grilled meat. A pile of charred remains lay at one entrance, blackened coils from several tyres. Ozoemena had never seen a lynching up close, and for a moment, she forgot where she was going, forgot her anxiety over her exams. Her eyes followed the curled up blackened form, the red gashes in the corpse where the skin had split. A group of children gathered, gawking – the grown-ups having had their fill – at the embers of a fire.

One of the children spat. 'That's what happens to thieves,' he said, and a few other small kids followed suit.

A passer-by reached over and knocked the first boy on the head with his knuckles. The rest scattered. Around them, traders exchanged the story of the burning with newcomers, embellishing, relishing. The ease of narration told Ozoemena this was a story that had been retold often. She adjusted the scarf on her head and continued down the road, folded into her thoughts. The gashes of red had shaken her more than anything else she'd seen.

Ozoemena had seen corpses before: dogs knocked down by cars because it was good luck for a new vehicle; a cow hit by a trailer on the expressway; even a mad man whose body had lain on the roads for a while before his family was alerted and came by to move it in the middle of the night. But those had been seen at a remove, driving by with her parents. In the mad man's case, the parents in her school were most concerned that his penis had been on display. The cow had lain there until drivers no longer wound up their windows. Ozoemena had watched it swell, burst, and dry out into nothing but hide on her way to school and back. It intrigued her but did not disturb her, not as much as this burned corpse did. Her walk to church became sombre, reflective. Ignoring her peers playing in the ample church grounds, she went straight inside and opened up her *Ekpere Na Abụ*, but the words did not make it past her eyes. She was as yet pre-occupied with the corpse when a commotion, a rushing, informed her that the bishop had arrived. They arranged themselves in rows as they had practised, according to surnames. The Ns were plentiful and occupied at least three rows. She was one of many. Ozoemena shut her book. There was nothing more she could do. She watched with a crazy, thumping heart and shuddering limbs as row after row was examined. The bishop would point at one or two or three and ask them to remain standing after they'd answered a question, while the others sat after they had answered. Ozoemena realised she should have gone to the toilet.

The bishop stood in the aisle beside her row. 'Stand up,' he commanded.

Ozoemena obeyed, straightening her skirt and making sure her scarf did not slip off her head. The bishop's eyes blazed with holy fervour. Ozoemena held her breath.

'Gua ihe dị n'Okwukwe-gi?'

The Apostles' Creed. It was easy! She had been saying

the creed every Sunday in church for years. Ozoemena opened her mouth to speak, but a thick piece of cobweb landed on the bishop's shoulders like a shawl, breaking her focus.

A leopard balanced on a beam, high in the cathedral's rafters, suspended in a shaft of the multicoloured sunlight that filtered through the bodies of saints in the stained-glass windows. Ozoemena, mind in a frenzy, wondered why it had come. Was there danger? Would she have to fight? The leopard opened its mouth and, rather than the roar she'd expected, a short series of barks burst out of its throat and bounced around the church with the force of cannon fire. Ozoemena ducked involuntarily. When she was able to tear her eyes away, the bishop's gaze was cold as he regarded her. She forced herself to stand, to ignore the beast treading gracefully above their heads, now shadow, now all colours of the rainbow. *The Apostles' Creed*, she said to herself. *Now.*

Ozoemena joined in, stuttering, stumbling over her own tongue, reeling off words without paying heed to their meaning. The bishop frowned. Ozoemena struggled not to look up, tried to focus on her examiner's thin brows, his clean-shaven face, the cleft in his chin. Another cobweb floated down, draping over his caul, turning him into a true bride of Christ. Ozoemena swallowed the hysterical laughter in her throat, the terror that came with the realisation that only she could see the cobwebs.

The bishop motioned for her peers to sit. 'You, keep standing,' he said to Ozoemena in Igbo. He licked his index finger, turned the onion-skin pages of his book, and cleared his throat. Another question. Ozoemena froze. It was as if a giant hand in her mind had wiped the blackboard containing all the answers she had learned. She swallowed. Her eyelids twitched. Her neck felt thick and heavy from trying to hold her head steady and look the bishop in his already disapproving eyes. Ozoemena forced her mouth to open, a noisy ungluing that echoed in her ears.

'Erm,' she said. Tittering broke out immediately. The catechist standing behind the bishop raised his hands for quiet. Ozoemena could resist no longer. She looked up.

The leopard bunched itself up and leaped, sailing into the air above her. Ozoemena realised what it meant to do as if it had telegraphed its intentions. Panic seized her.

'No!' She threw a forearm up, but the leopard was strong and powerful. It jumped on to her back with two of its giant paws. Ozoemena heard breaking in her bones, a moist unfolding in her muscles. She fell to the carpeted floor, saliva pouring through gritted teeth as she tried to overthrow the leopard. She heard the bishop's voice, high and frightened: 'Give her room!'

The carpet was red, worn, embedded with sand from many dusty shoes, close to her face.

Then Ozoemena was no longer by herself, but ensconced inside the leopard, sensing the tremor that ran through its body before it landed in a body of water, barely breaking a ripple.

CHAPTER THIRTY-THREE

Treasure: Then

The goat is doing 'mkpaaa-mkpaaa' in the boot. Ever since we left it have been making noise, even though driver tight its leg and hand and opened the boot so that it can hang its head outside and be getting breeze. Goat is not cow; they are always making noise. There is go-slow all the way from Onitsha to Agulu upon it have not yet reached ten o'clock in the morning, and Mummy is fanning herself because Driver can only be putting on AC small-small so that battery will not die.

'I don't know why you had to get dibia from Agulu, are there no longer people in Onitsha, eh?' Mummy is asking Driver again upon she have already asked him plenty time and Driver is telling her that he knows the man because he is his brother from his mother's side, and his gift is pure from God; he is not a wayo man. This time as she is asking Driver is not saying anything again, only minding his driving business, because after all, is not as if Mummy is looking for answer, she just wants to bite somebody, because going to dibia house is paining her.

Is paining me too. Dibia said Mummy should bring goat, he did not call my name, why is Mummy forcing me to follow her and go as if me I did not see what I will be using my time for? I have to finish my revision. And this dibia man that put his hand inside my breast? Shame is catching me, I am just vexed completely. Am totally vexed and fed up, but nobody asked me my mind so I didin talk.

And too, who knows? The dibia man have strong medicine because I sleep well, baff well, no spirit coming excepting when he sent Ifeanyi message for example. If Mummy did not bring goat for him, who knows what the dibia will do? Is better that we do as he says so that the people we are owing will be lesser and lesser. As I am here now inside the car, there are whole two seeds inside my wardroom where I hide it, waiting for who will collect.

The go-slow is much, but Driver knows how to drive, how to put tyre inside small space until the body of the car enters finish. Sometimes he will cut hand, cut hand, Mummy will now use the China handfan she is using to be fanning herself to beat him as if he is a small boy, that he should stop dragging her new car; after all, he cannot buy it. Driver has full-stop his mouth. He is vexing.

As we are nearing Agulu, Driver is relaxing because it is his hometown, and talking small to himself. Mummy is fanning herself more-more.

'Treasure, we need to go in, give him his goat and get out fast. We don't want anybody to see us going to dibia before it will look as if we are fetish people. We are going up in the world,' says Mummy. She puts on her sunshades. Driver starts to be singing and I know he heard what Mummy said. Next thing, we drive into the small road and Driver stops the car in front of one old, falling-down house and says he is coming, that has to go and collect number.

'Number for what?' Mummy is winding her window and shouting him.

'Everybody coming must pick number. Please Madam, I am coming.' He enters the door of the falling-down house. It is quiet, as if main road is not in our back. Even the goat that was disturbing is now closing its mouth. Mummy fans her China fan fast.

'I need to do my hair today, this foolish man should not

waste my time. If I sweat too much, relaxer will pepper me.'
She looks inside the steering wheel. 'And he took the keys.
Imagine!'

Driver comes out, holding one yellow paper. He enters car,
gives the paper to Mummy. They wrote '52' on it with black
marker. On the back in pen, they wrote 'N20'. Mummy opens
her purse and counts the money, five-five naira and one ten
naira, and gives him. He goes back inside, comes out, enters
car again and starts it.

'He is not collecting the goat again?' asks Mummy.

'No, Ma. This is where we get ticket, not where we see him.'

I jus' said let me close my mouth and be looking. As we
are driving, see Agulu Lake moving like cloth that someone
is holding on one side and shaking. Driver corners again and
this road, even though it don' have kolo tar, is big and wide.
On one side is compound wall, high but no broken glass on
it; on the other side is a tree, which I am thinking is mango
but it don' look like mango, and the smell is like ugili. My
body is cold as I am remembering the spirit and his ugili.
There is bush on the ugili tree side, cleared and pushed for
all the plenty-plenty cars parked there to be parking. Small
cars, big cars, pick-up. Driver finds space under another tree
so Mummy will not be hot and offs the engine. He opens
the boot, carries the goat and tights the rope holding the neck
to one iron hook in the grass. There are plenty other hooks
there, like people are bringing goat always.

There is a gate, pure white, big, with Jesus on one side,
and on the other side, a woman I am thinking is Mary, but
there is no veil on her head and her hair is long, plaited and
tight all over her head, carrying one big snake on her neck.
As the gate is big, I can see the top of one white house inside,
bigger than the gate. Bigger than our house sef. Mummy is
no longer talking, and Driver is opening all his teeth as if he
is landlord.

'You see all the cars? He is very important, very good.'
Driver uses handkerchief to clean his face, his head.

'Why didn't you park inside?' asks Mummy.

'Madam, there is no space inside! People are waiting!'
Driver is happy like somebody gave him food and beer. 'That's
your number that I gave you, ma. You are number fifty-two.'

'I can't wait here that long. Treasure, go and see if anybody
will exchange numbers with us.'

Me and Driver knock on the big gate, and when they open
it, we go inside. In the compound is one canopy with plenty
chairs under, but I am counting and only eight people are
there, me I don' know how our number is fifty-two. Is like
Driver is seeing my face because he says, 'Some people are
by the water.'

There are people like church wardens, wearing white. One
of them, a man, comes to ask for our ticket. I give him and
he marks it in a book and tells us to sit down, or we can walk
around small if we want. I say I will walk because Driver is
like a dog that somebody gave meat. He is pointing here and
there, showing me all the moulded statues everywhere. Plenty
Jesus, big cross, then the woman with snake, then crocodile,
then hippopotamus.

'If he calls you to the water, be careful. There are plenty
crocodiles in there and they are not afraid of people because
he feeds them all the time.'

I don' know which god they are worshipping here, because
there are plenty moulded statues, Jesus and Abraham, all of
them. One is looking like Indian statue sef like I see in film
with six hands.

'Where is the water?' I ask Driver.

'You didn't see it when we were coming in? Great Agulu
Lake! The whole of the backyard is open to the water, but
you have to climb down.'

The sun is beating me, so I sit under the canopy, but

everybody sitting there is removing eye as if they don' want to look me or for me to look them too. We sit and sit, until my bum-bum is hot, so I stand up again and go to the car. Mummy is sleeping because the car is inside the shade so me I jus' leave her. The church warden man comes and shares water, shares Beck's biscuit. Am asking him, how long will it take before it reaches us, and he is saying small time, that I should have patience, that I should go and tell Mummy to come inside, but me I don' go. Driver has carried his legs to somewhere me I don' know. I keep waiting and waiting. After, Driver comes and give me Coke and Scotch egg and meat pie inside Den's Cook bag and am thinking, did him and Mummy drive to Den's Cook and jus' leave me here like that? And my mind is turning inside me because after all, is not me that dibia said I should come.

When they call our number, Driver runs outside the compound and brings the goat inside with rope, and Mummy is following. Her face, even as she slept and ate, is vexing very well. Only that the man is dibia that Mummy did not say let us go home. Only that he is dibia is why she is not insulting him. Her face is swollen like hot garri. The church warden leads us, circles the house to the back. Plenty trees and there is cool breeze, but it is smelling fish-fish. And then I see the dibia man, standing in white shirt and white trouser that he rolled on his leg. He says, 'Ah, she is Thanksgiving, not sacrifice, why didn't you tell me since?' Mummy's face is as if she want to slap somebody.

The dibia man says Mummy should off her shoe and come down the step that will bring her to the water so he can wash her and remove all the eyes of evil on her.

'You daughter, too.'

I curse him inside my mind. If he put hand inside my breast again, I will bite his hand, I don' care what power he have.

The dibia tell Driver to give the goat to the church warden man, and the goat is young and fat too, even it is tired, and it refuses to go and the man starts dragging it. Am tired. Mummy says me I should first go, so I off my silpas and go down the step to where the dibia is standing inside the water. Under my leg is like okro soup.

Dibia says I should bend. I bend. 'Not like that, bend like a woman.' I squat. He bends down, collects water with his two hands and pours it on my head. It is smelling. I am trying to see inside the water so that crocodile will not carry me away inside its mouth.

He pours, one time, two time, three times. 'Ngwa get up,' he says.

As I am getting up, I hear something moving in the water. Crocodile! There are plenty bushes and trees hanging near the water, thick-thick bush. It is through there that I see two eyes like a torch. As I see it, that's when the dibia turns and sees it. The shout he is shouting is what makes me to pick race. But the water floor is drawing like okro soup, and I am falling, the eyes are inside the water, the water is entering my nose, my mouth, like pepper, fire-pepper in my body, my chest. The dibia is dragging me up, up. He is shouting to the thing in the water:

'Please, I am not enemy with you! Please, I have kept my hand straight, I have not killed anyone!'

And Mummy is shouting, far away where she is standing. 'See, what you have done to my daughter? You bastard. I will sue you to court!'

And Driver is shouting, 'Chei! Chei! I saw it! Madam, I saw it.' Everybody is looking for the thing that wounded me, but the water is shaking cloth again like nothing is inside, not even crocodile. Dibia helps me to walk, dragging me up the stairs. Him and Driver carry me and put me on a mat. Am cold, my body is shaking and am crying, calling Daddy.

Dibia is saying, 'Eighteen years I have been working, and never once has leopard come to my shrine. Madam, take your daughter and go, don't come back. I don't want the thing pursuing you. Leave my goat for me.'

My dress has piececesed in my front and there is blood on my chest, on my stomach. There is blood inside the water.

Mummy's voice is high with anger. 'Who is going to marry her like this now?'

CHAPTER THIRTY-FOUR

Ozoemena: Then

Ozoemena watched herself motionless, surrounded by eager bodies, gossiping bodies; she watched the catechist slap her about the face a little too rigorously. Sweat shimmered brightly in the folds of the bishop's neck. The leopard had entered through one of the side doors. It approached Ozoemena's body and, bending almost double, hacked repeatedly. It spat, and she tumbled out into her own skin, wet and dirty. There were many feet, many eyes. The carpet beneath her head stank.

'Chukwu di ebube,' the catechist muttered when she opened her eyes. 'Why did you not tell anyone you were epileptic? You could have sat during your test.'

'Blood . . .' Ozoemena said, before realising she had spoken aloud. She snapped her jaw shut and the action triggered some reflex within her. She turned on her side and vomited, sour and hot. The carpet stank worse than before. They helped her up. The wet carpet taunted her, and the eyes of the saints dripped sorrows from the windows. The clergymen shepherded the children back to their pews, commanded calm. Ozoemena searched every inch of her person, looking for 'blood'. The bishop frowned his episcopal frown.

They made Ozoemena wait in the vestry so as not to distract the others from their tests. It was another two hours before the catechist drove her home in his rusty blue

Volkswagen beetle. Ozoemena slumped in its warm interior, watching the long, naked gearstick as the man changed gears. The floor of the vehicle was pockmarked, and Ozoemena spied the road pass by beneath her.

She recalled the rending of flesh beneath the leopard's claws, the rich taste of blood. Her mouth watered. She swallowed her spittle, shamefaced. Ozoemena pondered the rules of the leopard; how she could be affected by what the leopard did, despite not being in control of its will or actions. She wondered where it had taken her, and why. Ozoemena had squeezed her eyes shut when she had understood its intentions to attack, unprepared to have blood on her hands, literally, but she nonetheless heard the screams, felt the anguish. This was no dream. She had enjoyed it, and this new bloodthirstiness bothered her. The leopard was taking her over. Ozoemena knew she could tell no one – not M'ma, not Oruke Nwosu – about liking the taste of blood. She had to find her tether, and fast. Not for the first time, she wished her uncle Odiogo had done more than just mark her. Ozoemena needed structure, clarity. She needed to know the rules.

A familiar shape, and Ozoemena realised they were in front of her father's hospital-cum-their-flats. She could not remember telling the catechist who she was, or where she wanted to go. Nevertheless, here she was, at the last place she wanted to be. Already, she had begun to feel much better – and, consequently, to feel ashamed of her writhing and vomiting in church, imagining the stories that would be told. And had she passed? Was she confirmed now? Ozoemena did not know how to ask without making it seem as though she had been pretending in church, perhaps due to being ill-prepped. She stepped out of the Volkswagen with a bent head.

'Thank you,' she said, without meeting the driver's eyes.

'Greet your father,' said the catechist, before driving off, leaving Ozoemena to wonder how much of what had happened would reach her father, wherever he was. How long before Prisca heard? Ozoemena began to prepare excuses, each one more ridiculous than the next. The gate that would have allowed her access to the staircase leading up to their flats was locked. Ozoemena was forced to slink past the duty nurse behind her desk, through the waiting room packed full of the evening crowd, eyes turned upwards to face the blurry TV. She spared a glance for the door of her father's consulting room, where she knew someone else currently sat, and slipped through the door leading to the staircase where a pair of nurses gossiped angrily about a rude patient in the wards.

'Maybe that is why the crocodile got her,' one of them said, and their laughter vibrated low and dirty and forbidden. Ozoemena dashed up the four sets of stairs to their flats.

Prisca was on the phone when Ozoemena entered the parlour, let in by her sister, Mbu, who wrinkled her nose but said nothing else. Their mother raised a hand and Ozoemena froze where she was. Her mother's end of the conversation contained nothing but noises of agreement and incredulity. Ozoemena's spirits descended almost to her knees. She would tell Prisca the truth, she decided, since it seemed she knew what had happened, but she lost her nerve when Prisca hung up, clearly distracted by something else.

'Did you pass?' she asked eventually, and when Ozoemena nodded, she said, 'Good.' Ozoemena stood, balancing from foot to foot, ignored by her mother, until she risked Prisca's wrath by moving before she had been asked. Her clothes smelled even to her own nose, and she wondered why Prisca, with her acute sense of smell, did not say anything, only gazed past Ozoemena's head to the photos on the wall behind her. And yet when Ozoemena made a move for the kitchen and corridor that would lead her to the bedroom space she shared with her sisters, she felt Prisca's eyes following.

There were no burns on Ozoemena's hands as before, no welts or bruises, she was proud to note, and so, no need to reveal anything to her mother. At breakfast, she ate her corn-flakes, humming between spoonfuls although there were no voices in her head to hush.

'Here are your vitamins,' said Prisca, handing Ozoemena a coral tablet. She would not leave until Ozoemena swallowed it down.

CHAPTER THIRTY-FIVE

Treasure: Then

Hospital have one kain smell and that's how I know is where my body has landed. There is fan on the ceiling and another standing fan to the side, and they are both blowing me. The room is creamish and there is generator with deep throat shaking somewhere. My own throat is drying me; saliva is not in my mouth at all. There is bottled Swan water on the table, and cup, pink plastic, but where it is, my hand cannot reach. Am thinking where Mummy is, whether am in Onitsha, if me I can get up and get the water so I can drink it well.

There is bandage all over my chest, tight, and if I do breathe in, is paining, my chest and back. The bandage is cutting my breathing. The door to where am lying is closed and I'm hearing people walking up and down. I open my mouth to call somebody, but my voice is a frog's own. I sit up small-small in the bed, stretch my hand for the water and the cup falls on the floor under the bed.

'Leave it. Don't get up or you'll tear your stitches. Lie down!' The nurse that opens the door is shouting as if me and her have seen before.

'I'm thirsty.'

'Wait, let me call doctor. Lie down!' She is pushing my head. See this stupid woman. I beat her hand away with all my force, and she starts to be opening her eyes wide.

'I will slap you now o, don't give me problem. Lie down, I will call doctor.'

'Where is my mummy?' I ask her, but she does as if she is not hearing me and carries her tipper bottom out of the room. Sleep carries me again, and the next time my eyes open, someone is shining light inside it, holding my face. I draw my face away.

'You're awake. Do you want some water?' The doctor is one slim man with moustache, wearing suit. He have one golden pen in his pocket and his shirt is pure white, the neck is standing like there is starch in it. He looks like him and Daddy are mate, and his voice is quiet, as if he is talking inside church.

'Yes, sir.' My throat is paining more. 'Yes, doctor. Good afternoon.'

'Morning. Call me Emenike.' He pours the water in another cup, this one is colour green, not pink, and puts it on the table. He is touching my bed, doing something. The noise is loud, but the bed is moving as he is winding it like generator. The thing I am carrying in my mind is showing on my face and the doctor laughs small. 'I know. They say I have become too Westernised, especially the nurses. If they hear you calling me by my name and not "doctor", they might beat you.'

The water is not cold, but I am drinking like it came out of freezer. I tell the doctor that the nurse said she will slap me, and he laughs small again, but as I am looking at his eye I can see that he is not laughing real laugh, like he is trying to tell me something not good.

'Where is Mummy?'

'She comes every evening after work. Don't worry, she will soon arrive.'

Mummy don' work. Why is she telling doctor that she is working? Where is she going that she is only coming to see me in the evening? My stomach is swelling with badness.

Doctor Emenike pulls the plastic chair that is for visitors and sits inside it. He is reading one brown file, turning the paper inside, slow-slow.

'Can you tell me how you got wounded?' he asks, as he is reading the paper.

Am thinking what to tell him, what Mummy has told him. I don' want him to think we are idol worshippers or to talk the one that I will use to enter trouble, so me I just tell him that I don' know anything and close my mouth. He looks my face after I finish talking, looks me well-well innermost my eye and asks me.

'Are you sure?'

Nothing about Doctor Emenike has changed, but is like he is not the same person that entered to give me water. He is sitting on the chair, but his eyes are jumping electric at the inside of his glasses, as if wire in his head is touching. His shoe is knocking on the floor like to urinate is troubling him.

He says, 'Are you sure?' He pulls the chair again. 'Whatever you tell me, I will believe you. How did you get the injuries on your body? I'm the one that stitched you; I know what it looked like before. Tell me what wounded you.'

All of his face is torchlight inside my face. The way he is looking, am thinking he knows how me I got wounded, but he is waiting for me to say it by myself.

'It was a crocodile. I was playing by the lake . . .'

'Lake? Which lake?'

'Agulu Lake.'

'How did you come to be playing there?' He is talking church-church, but he is putting his whole face inside my own face.

'My mummy went to see her uncle. He lives near Agulu Lake.'

'I see.' Doctor Emenike relaxes inside his chair. He is looking me, waiting, but me I can wait too; if he thinks anything will come out of my mouth, both of us will be looking each other.

'I grew up in the village. I'm a good swimmer.' He removed the pen in his pocket and is using it to write slow on the paper inside the brown file. 'We used to prove how good we were at swimming, by diving down to the bottom of the river and coming up with a handful of clean sand from the riverbed.'

Am thinking, what is my business with swimming in the village?

'That's not what crocodile bites look like.' Doctor Emenike seizes my hand. 'Was it you it was after, or did you get in the way? It won't stop. If you or your mother have done a mortal evil, it will keep coming for you until you are dead. Or until you confess. In public.'

'Leave my hand!'

He is pressing it like something is doing him in his head.

'Leave me!'

'Just tell me where it went. Where did it go after it did this to you? Do you know?'

'Doctor! You came back!' The slapping nurse has entered. She is shining her whole thirty-two as if she have seen Father Christmas.

Doctor Emenike leaves my hand and arranges himself. His eyes are not torch again, and he is looking around everywhere like he don' know where to put hand or march leg.

'When did you come back? Nobody told me o,' says the nurse.

Dr Emenike says, 'I'm sorry, excuse me,' and runs like something is pursuing him. The nurse is looking for his face but he don' give her face, so she is questioning his back as he carries himself out of my room. Nurse looks me up and down, up and down.

'Only God knows what you said to doctor to make him behave like this. That man doesn't like trouble.' She put tamometa inside my mouth and winds the bed down. She don' even look at it before she put it inside her pocket, just shakes it one, two, three.

'Eh-he. Somebody is looking for you, a very dirty boy. Of course we did not allow him inside. He should bath first. Is he your boyfriend? When your mother comes, I will tell her. It's girls like you with torn eyes and big mouths that we have to watch out for. Next thing you will come back at sixteen to ask if we can do you abortion.'

Am not minding her. I am thinking everything that the doctor said, how he was looking like a mad person in his eyes, how he was talking, the white-white spit that gathered in his corner mouth.

Am thinking if I should have told him the thing I saw, because as he was talking, it was as if he knew what happened, as if he has seen something like this before.

Where is Mummy?

CHAPTER THIRTY-SIX

Treasure: Then

That I don' know something don' mean that me I don' know anything. Whenever there is problem inside my head, I will use my mind to think it and think it well, and this thing that Doctor Emenike said, I sleep and I wake up and am still thinking it.

What am thinking is this: one, the thing that wanted to carry me inside the water, two men now are fearing it. First dibia, then Doctor Emenike. It means that me, I have to be very very careful, because something that two strong men are fearing will use me to play.

Two, when I look Ifeanyi in his eyes, I see the spirit looking me. I know the spirit is inside Ifeanyi's body and that's the only reason why he cannot be coming out. If me I dodge Ifeanyi, the spirit will not find me.

Three, the spirit he said other spirits them pursued him because that stupid shaid spoiled one of the seed. But what if is this thing that teared my body that also did him bad thing? In maths, they teach us common denominator, and for me and the spirit to be tearing body, am thinking that this thing Doctor Emenike is talking is pursuing both of us because of the wifes that me and him are bringing so that Daddy can come back.

Four, they say give Siza what is his own. Because I have two seeds remaining, let me finish getting two wifes; then, I will know am not owing, and once Daddy is in front of me like this, everything that me I did, I will tell him, because he so much loves me and will take care of me.

Five, Mummy is getting money from somewhere, and that place, she don' want me to know, but me I am not a goat. I am seeing as people are making eyes for her all the time and I know if I don' do fast, somebody will just deceive her to forget my daddy, and all of us will not be living together like before.

Six, do me I do you, God no go vex. Once Daddy is in my very before, I must revenge what the spirit did to me. Now, me I know the Bone Woman her face and how me I can call her.

Seven, I will tell Doctor Emenike the truth when he comes for ward round, so that me I can know everything inside his head about this matter. If I know, then I can find how to make sure it don' kill me. Every sickness has medicine and me, I will find my own.

But is not Doctor Emenike that comes to do ward round for me, is another doctor, short with big bum-bum. I don' like how he is looking me, and touching my dressing around my breast. Am asking him, where is my doctor, and he is saying is him, that Doctor Emenike has gone for annual leave. After in the afternoon, I hear people talking in the corridor outside my room, that they saw Doctor Emenike walking up and walking down, talking to somebody that nobody's eye can see.

M'ma's Story

When the sacred bird, Okpoko, came out of its mother, it met the Earth at the beginning of creation. There was no light, no stars, no sun, and no moon. There was also no land on which to perch. The whole of the world was dark and covered with water. Nne Okpoko, the mother, was the first bird that Chukwu made, and she spent her time flying all over as the world was being created, reporting back to Chukwu's house with her mate.

Then Chukwu, the god of creation, sent the sacred hornbill in its turn, to go forth and see how the work was coming along (for the Earth took a long time to make). Okpoko and its blessed parents went, and all they saw in the great distance was a tree, straight and tall, growing out of all the water and the dark formlessness.

The birds decided to fly towards it and perch, but it was at such a great distance that Okpoko's aged mother, already worn out from eons of servitude to the creator, died. Since there was no land, Okpoko buried her on one side of its head and continued flying.

Soon, Okpoko's father died, too. Again, there being no land, the hornbill buried its father on the other side of its head. Now its head was heavy and lumpy on both sides. Regardless of the discomfort, it flew, bearing its parents' deaths and their bodies, until it reached the World Tree.

Upon perching, Okpoko laid a beautiful egg. It was its first, and so huge that it was awed at the sight of it. Immediately, Okpoko was carried away by a huge sadness. It thought, *Oh, if only my mother was alive to see such beauty.* Its sorrow became so great that it opened its mouth and cried, a loud, booming cry that shook the world.

The egg cracked. Its yolk rose up into the air and Okpoko saw that it was its mother, miraculously restored and transformed into the sun, roused by its cry. It flew up to meet its mother and, to its joy, found that the egg's shell followed and was now its father, the moon, glowing with pride.

Okpoko's parents embraced, thrilled to be reunited. As soon as they clasped one another, the Earth rumbled and shook, and the land pushed up from the water.

And that is why the hornbill is sacred in our culture, for not only was Okpoko there at the beginning of creation, but its devotion to its parents brought about the world as we know it.

CHAPTER THIRTY-SEVEN

Ozoemena: Now

In Ozoemena's absence, Prisca, Mbu and Baby have moved house. The new place is twenty minutes' drive away from the old one, but it might as well be in a different town. Ozoemena, in her sheltered existence, has not previously been aware of any areas away from the main commercial zones. New builds surround theirs, square mouths without glass in windows, mostly uninhabited. Streets bear no signs or names. Ozoemena perceives the area as unfinished, as though an illustrator or architect has run out of ink, or interest, or both.

New room. New bed. Ozoemena hates it all. Her mother is trying hard to erase her father, and Ozoemena finds herself growing increasingly frustrated. She wanders around for days, feeling an end that had not been present earlier. While they had been in their old house, living their old life, she could pretend to herself – no matter how her mother and Mbu acted – that everything was on pause and could be resumed, just as soon as her father returned from his *travels*. Was that not what he had said? He had a mission. One does not just give up on a person when they go on a journey. Their father is coming back. Why can nobody see that?

Her suspension seems benign in comparison.

Every morning, Prisca loads her with homework before leaving for a long day at the pharmacy. Apart from the maths questions, a lot of it is easy to Ozoemena, given her new deductive and analytical skills. Being overburdened with schoolwork every week appears to have done her some good.

Their new house comes sans Aunty Comfo, or any other aunties, so Ozoemena eats what she wants for lunch. Often, she does not eat at all, paying her penance even though nobody minds her. Mbu stays away as well. Upon her return from school the first day Ozoemena had arrived, Mbu had looked her younger sister up and down as if they were quarrelling. Ozoemena tensed, waiting for the abuse.

'You grew,' was all Mbu said, before sauntering off.

Ozoemena spends the week bored out of her mind. To make matters worse, the end of her suspension ties in to the start of the mid-term break. Is this on purpose? Two long weeks away from her friends. She does not know how she will survive in a house where her only constant companions are lizards and wall geckos. She wonders if she will be allowed to return to school when the holidays are over. Already, it is as if she imagined that life, those friends. She wishes she had been allowed to say goodbye and not rushed off like someone with a contagious disease. She speculates about Etaoko. How could she just vanish like that? Why did the leopard do nothing? Why pick and choose whom it could help? The guilt is intolerable. It is as if anytime she gives in to the leopard, something bad happens.

Ozoemena slumps on the front steps in the dry Harmattan heat. Perhaps she is contagious. For all she knows, her classmates are getting on much better without her. Ozoemena chides herself for being ridiculous. She hears Mbu's voice in her head – *The world doesn't spin around you* – but she cannot stop her thoughts swirling like dirty water around the drain of her mind. She surprises herself by looking forward to her sister's return every evening. Ozoemena discovers that she prefers her solitude to be by choice rather than necessity. She fills the space between homework with cleaning, dusting, mopping the house, which gathers more dust blown in from the Sahara minutes after she is done. She tries exploring, but the house is small and strange. There is not much to it: a living room, kitchen, toilet and store downstairs; three bedrooms upstairs, with a shared bath for she and Mbu and a private one for their mother. There is a tiny boxroom with high windows, painted pink and full of toys for Baby. There are no pictures of any of them on the walls. Ozoemena knows why. Most of them had their father in. She wonders what happened to those photos in their heavy hand-carved frames, but will not ask. To ask is to remember. No good comes from reminiscing.

On the weekend, the girls wake up to a list from their mother. They are to go to the market for the weekly shop. Mbu makes Quaker Oats with powdered milk so thick and creamy it almost becomes fufu. Ozoemena sweats through the heavy breakfast, then to the market, where Mbu haggles and bargains her way through. The market is hot and dense. Flies buzz around in the dried fish section, attracted by the smell, but staying for the taste of sweat. Mbu walks by the towers of fresh peppers with a handkerchief to her nose. Their spicy scent is enough to trigger her asthma.

'Stay here,' she tells Ozoemena, dumping her with the shopping.

The shopkeeper is a young man whose eyes eat up her sister as they talk. Mbu begs him to let Ozoemena stay. 'I am faster on my own, please Jekwu. Let her wait for me here.'

Jekwu's sorrowful eyes drip acquiescence. His shop is clean and fragrant, festooned with artificial flowers – plastic stems and leaves holding up fabric petals with clear wax droplets on them to simulate dewdrops. He sells frames, inspirational and plain, posed by mainly Asian models, delicate and petite, or soft-focused blue-eyed blondes. As Ozoemena watches, he pulls open a frame and inscribes on it in perfect calligraphic script: '*My love is your consign. Be my wife.*'

'Do you think your sister would like this?' he asks. Even his voice is soft and mournful, as if the rose-tint of the frames leached into his bones. Ozoemena examines the bouquet of red roses in the frame, the writing curling all over it like scrollwork.

'You spelt "concern" wrongly,' she says.

Jekwu sighs. He hands her a piece of paper. 'Spell it for me.'

'Also, the sentence doesn't mean anything,' she adds.

'How do I say . . .?' And he tells her something in Igbo that is nowhere near what he wrote.

By the time Mbu returns, Jekwu is happy to see the back of Ozoemena – she has gone about his shop, pointing out his incorrect spellings in the frames, and the boy, in all conscience, cannot envisage selling them now. He barely looks at Mbu as he waves them off.

'What did you do to him?' Mbu asks, a hint of laughter in her tone.

'Nothing,' says Ozoemena.

'Maybe you should do more nothing to him before you go back to school so that he can stop disturbing me.'

Ozoemena basks in her approval. They take their mother a lunch of pepper soup and agidi-white, the plain steamed corn starch pudding that Ozoemena dislikes. Baby is in the backroom, playing resolutely by herself. She jumps up when she sees her sisters. 'Mbu!' She stares at Ozoemena and says 'Sweet?' holding a palm up. Ozoemena pretends to search her pockets. Mbu picks Baby up and takes her away.

Ozoemena joins her mother, taking prescriptions at the counter and passing scripts over to be filled, taking the meds, passing them back. People stare at her and she fumbles, tension in her hands and shoulders.

'This one looks like her father, hewụ nwanne m,' they say, and Ozoemena sees her mother's jaw muscles pop from the strain of smiling, holding it together, swatting aside nosy questions with professional ones of her own. She manages to do it without offending anyone. Ozoemena is angry for her; she wishes, not for the first time, that she could turn into something monstrous, just for a split second. Just enough to terrify people into silence. *Leave us alone!* She has forgotten how weighty the scrutiny in this town can be, the busybodies buzzing with faux concern, searching for titbits to turn into gossip. The implied criticism of her father. The real underlying reproach of her mother as a woman who has lost a man to anything other than death. It is a relief when their mother sends them home, with Baby in tow.

After lunch, while Baby is taking her compulsory siesta, Ozoemena fills one of their mother's huge pots with water and sets it over the fire. Mbu sharpens a knife against the rough concrete ground of their backyard.

'Did you . . .' she starts hesitantly, 'see anything in the market?'

'See anything?' asks Ozoemena. She is so used to hiding what she is supposed to be that she slips and forgets Mbu knows. She observes the wrinkling of her sister's brow before it comes to her. 'No, nothing.'

'There are supposed to be all kinds of things in markets. You didn't see any?' She looks up at Ozoemena hungrily. Ozoemena considers lying for a moment – anything to keep the unusual peace between them – but she shakes her head, no.

Mbu huffs, looks away. Her burgundy polo shirt is stained with sweat at the armpits. 'I suppose you wouldn't tell me if you saw something anyway?' She does not wait for Ozoemena to answer, but draws her dwarf stool closer to where the three white chickens they bought from the market are huddled. She bares their necks one after the other and slices, quick and sharp, placing the limp heads back on the ground. The chickens jerk violently as they die, and Mbu restrains them, placing her feet on their wings until they stop moving.

'Are we expecting someone?' Ozoemena asks. They do not have electricity all the time. It does not make sense to store a lot in the freezer.

'It's almost Christmas,' says Mbu, shrugging. It is not an explanation that satisfies Ozoemena. Normally, Christmas Day is filled with bands of dressed-up, marauding children, going from house to house, eating, drinking, round bellies protruding through new clothes with shop creases left on – but Prisca cannot abide things like that. Mbu, seeing her confusion, adds: 'Mum will be working a lot, you know, since she's alone this year? There needs to be food.'

Inside, the pot is beginning to boil, fogging up the kitchen windows. Mbu raises her feet off the carcasses to go into the kitchen and get it, but one of the chickens is not fully dead. It lurches away, startling Mbu, who screams, almost dropping the knife on her foot. Ozoemena strolls along after the chicken silently, not obeying Mbu's instructions to, 'Catch it! Quick!' Where will a dead chicken go?

By the gate, it stops, its death finally catching up to it. Ozoemena takes it by its warm feet and holds it in place upside down until the little heart empties what is left of its blood. She returns the chicken to her sister.

'Some things don't always know they are dead,' Ozoemena says, as Mbu places the carcass in a basin with the others and pours boiling water under it.

Mbu waves away the steam from her face. 'You always say strange things.' She turns the chickens a few times, flapping scalded fingers through the air to cool them. Lifting the birds out, Mbu places them on a metal tray and begins to pluck handfuls of feathers. 'You don't want to leave them in the water too long, or the skin comes away with the feathers.'

When the chickens are clean, Mbu deploys the knife again

and pulls out their intestines. They are both girls with hard stomachs for blood; nevertheless, the hot smell of it triggers the memory of the night their uncle died. Ozoemena pushes it deep down inside before it draws out something of their father. Mbu will not tolerate her tears. She shows Ozoemena a green capsule, hiding in the mass of slimy guts. 'Don't let this burst, or it will make the meat bitter.'

The chickens are ready once Mbu has soaked their feet a while longer and pulled off a layer of hard skin and talons. She empties the crop of seeds and stones, pulls out the stained tissue lining and rinses the bodies under running water. She covers them in the clean basin. Their mother will see to them when she returns.

Mbu washes her nails clean and dries them. She puts lotion on her hands and applies a clear polish over her nails. The scent is pleasing, but Mbu neither does her sister's nails nor offers the bottle.

'I thought I saw Daddy once, you know,' she says, and Ozoemena knows that they have been thinking along the same lines. 'In Amaenyi, one day like this after school. I ran after him, but it was just one mad man like this. It wasn't Daddy.' She snorts. 'What kind of life is this when you think a mad man is your daddy? He was so dirty.'

Ozoemena bites the dry skin around her nails. They smell of raw meat. She swallows the skin. 'Mad people are people's fathers and mothers.' *And sisters.*

'That opened my eyes,' Mbu says. She blows on her nails and sneezes, a tight, cut-off sneeze. 'I don't want to eat the leopard or be linked to it, if there is a chance that I will become that way.' She looks at Ozoemena. 'Sorry. I don't mean to scare you.' She starts to rub her face, stops when she remembers her nails. 'I haven't been a very good big sister, have I?'

'What if Mummy is right? What if the whole thing is some sort of . . . nonsense?'

Mbu exhales. Ozoemena's body is tense, her everything waiting on her sister's response. They have never talked like this before, as equals. And she needs it, an answer. She has to know what her sister thinks.

'If you think it's nonsense, tell everyone to leave you alone. Even M'ma. What will they do to you?' Mbu asks the question as if she expects a detailed answer.

Ozoemena stares at her sister, lost in thought. She recalls the last time she had said aloud, 'Mbu is better,' to her grandmother. M'ma had chortled, disbelieving.

'Which Mbu?' she'd asked. 'The one we know or another? No. Mbu is too much like your mother's people, beating and stomping all the time. You see how your mother complains about her fighting all the time in school? How much it affects Mbu's health? Yet, your sister keeps going. She will destroy herself if it means getting her revenge on people. Her blood is too hot. There is more to being a leopard than that.' M'ma had touched Ozoemena's face. 'A leopard must be balanced. Justice, yes, but also compassion.'

She wonders what M'ma would say of this newer, coolheaded Mbu. Her sister does not seem nearly so angry.

Mbu catches her staring and rather than bark, she asks, 'Why did you bite that girl?'

It throws Ozoemena, and she ponders how much to tell her sister of the voices that are not voices, nor hers, even though they sort of are. She knows instantly that she must not. That part is private, sacred, as are her travels within the leopard. She settles for: 'She was smashing my head on the ground. I had to.'

Mbu nods, understanding. 'Well. Hopefully now she knows herself.' The sisters stare at each other and begin to laugh, Mbu's quickly developing a raspy edge. She pulls out her inhaler and takes two puffs, holding the vapour in her lungs before exhaling slowly. 'It's bad enough you have no wounds.

Mum didn't believe you. You are going to have to be more cunning than that.'

'Cunning as a tortoise!'

'More, even. Did blood come out?'

'Flesh too!'

Mbu mimes retching.

Ozoemena relaxes. Talking with Mbu like this soothes her mind somewhat, but her body remains tense, untrusting of the camaraderie. Ozoemena scratches her head. Her hair has grown, and this would be the time to get it braided with 'artificial' for Christmas, but she cannot bear to sit for hours while people tug at her scalp.

She decides to trust her sister. A severely abridged version, then.

Ozoemena exhales slowly. 'I have been having lots of strange dreams,' she says. 'Like when my hands got hurt.'

Mbu leans forward from where she sits on the back steps, waiting.

Mbu rolls the nail varnish bottle between her palms and the viscous liquid glides, coating the bottle, then receding.

'It sounds like you are looking for something in your dreams,' she says finally. 'Or somebody.'

'The crying girl?'

Mbu rubs her nose. 'Maybe, maybe not.'

Baby begins to cry upstairs. Mbu sighs a sound older than her fourteen years. 'I'll say be careful sha. Anything that can burn you in a dream and have wounds appear in real life is to be feared. Maybe M'ma is right, and war is coming.'

Ozoemena starts to nod, catches herself. 'You were eavesdropping.'

'I'm always eavesdropping.'

Baby howls louder.

'Do you think I will have to fight in a war?' Ozoemena

asks. Her blood has run cold. They have video cassettes documenting the previous one: children with swollen bellies and twig limbs. Corpses piled on the roadside. Ozoemena cannot imagine how she could help in such a situation, leopard or no.

Mbu stands up and begins to dust off her skirt. 'You probably shouldn't let Mummy know you're having dreams seriously again.'

Ozoemena does not know why she often needs Mbu to point out things she knows in her spirit before she takes any notice of them. 'Is that why she has been giving me the special vitamins?' she asks.

'Yes. For your mind. So that you can stop . . . seeing things that are not there.' Mbu swallows. 'And there are other ones. Worse ones. Better act normal.'

'But I am normal.'

Mbu sucks her teeth. 'Stop talking nonsense.' And she sounds so much like Prisca that Ozoemena smiles.

CHAPTER THIRTY-EIGHT

Ozoemena: Now

The leopard runs her ragged over break, but Mbu is now on her side. Somewhat. She asks no questions, especially when it is apparent to anyone with eyes that Ozoemena is having more than dreams, or when Ozoemena zones out during the day, caught between sleeping and trying to decipher the susurrus of voices, to catch the one that sometimes comes through clear as day.

Ozoemena is glad to return to school after nearly two weeks of fitful and cautious sleeping. Uncle Fred drives her back. Pulling on his own ear, he says, in lieu of a goodbye: 'Don't tala mmadụ alụ again o. Keep your teeth in your mouth.'

On the way down, Ozoemena counts twelve new police checkpoints from Owerri, sometimes nothing more than an old petrol barrel, garlanded by leaves. As they approach the village where the school is situated, there are fewer people milling about, but Ozoemena senses many eyes behind the façade of sleepy village life, watching.

Novus has gained a new gate, a blank, black, imposing thing thrusting up from the ground. The walls on either side have been built up to accommodate it, giving the effect of a crown encircling the school. There is a brand-new gatehouse to match, housing two policemen from the local precinct and the school's gateman in his plain khakis and beret.

The school has a shut-off, vaguely menacing air. Ozoemena

watches the men lounge, their obligatory transistor radio always on full blast in the shack, despite studies occurring in the classrooms. The school's domestic rota has a new role for girls and boys: collecting the policemen's food from the kitchen and serving it to them in the new gatehouse before any of the children eat. Ozoemena stares from her classroom window. Their soup is greener than what the students get, thicker too. The men leave late in the evening and the new gate is locked behind them. The opacity of the gate gives Ozoemena an itch in her chest. Its saturated blackness is a tear in the fabric of the world, leading in her imagination to somewhere unfathomable and perilous.

Novus has also gained its proprietor, Dr Vincent, forced back down from relative comfort in America by events surrounding his beloved institution. He can often be found hobnobbing with the media, reassuring parents, showing off the new police presence, tighter security. Camera persons spend time at his behest recording as new classroom blocks go up, sweaty masons working hard under the baking sun. Teachers are hushed, efficient. Students are hushed, cowed. There are staff meetings upon staff meetings. Those who would often sneak home to the village, or who used to ask favourite teachers to grant exeat notes in exchange for gifts from mummies and daddies, now stay behind and keep their heads down. Their proprietor has a habit of stopping anyone and demanding an answer to whatever questions he deems fit to ask, regarding everything from trivia and academic knowledge to physical appearance. Punishments are rife, fuses short.

Ozoemena starts out the new half-term getting into trouble with Mr Ibe. All she does is relay an instruction he gives during basketball practice to a classmate. He benches her, and afterwards she has to serve punishment. Ozoemena is perplexed by the way her teacher refuses to meet her gaze, until her friends inform her that Mr Ibe got in hot soup for losing a student. In the middle of a presidential campaign, no less. The newspapers, fatigued with political coverage, were only too glad to converge on their school. And that was excluding the meal she had made of Ugochi's arm.

Fortunately for her, she has company during her punishment – manual labour – in the form of students who have been caught talking or misbehaving in class, or who do not participate during lessons, or who keep falling asleep, like Queeneth. Most of the other students cut grass, blunted cutlasses fighting against the tough, fibrous plants and tangled roots. The class one students, however, have the worst of possible punishments.

The back of the hostel building is a mess, covered in heaps of rubbish, emptied out from the dustbins. The smell of ancient urine is sharp, and Ozoemena covers her nose, avoiding the bits of crumpled toilet roll that dot the grass like diseased flowers.

'Why are we the ones to clear this, kwanu?' grumbles Obiageli. Often teachers appoint secret class monitors to record names during their absence, and Obiageli has been caught clowning around. 'It's not as if class one girls urinate here.'

Every two or more paces, someone finds a black polythene bag, and flies rise up into the air, making them shriek.

Ozoemena spits. 'I hate this school, and I hate flyovers and everyone who does them.' She spits again. Ozoemena does not hate school. She is relieved to be back after the limbo of mid-term, and in spite of the polythene bags full of faeces, – flyovers – but any junior student who does not declare as much is treated as suspect and ostracised by the rest of the group.

Ozoemena has to be even more vocal than she would normally be. She has returned to stares and whispers. Ugochi

and her brother Ambobo seem hellbent on making sure
nobody forgets what she did. On the wall above her bed,
someone wrote: 'Beware of Dog', and even though Ozoemena
scrubbed at it with a rag, the ghost of white chalk mixed with
water still outlines the words on the green wall.

'Yes, God punish these shitters,' Obiageli adds. 'Me I hope
when they try to poo it's like rubbing pepper on their anus.'

Ozoemena snorts, and soon they are laughing. Obiageli
has a way of articulating horrors that they appreciate.

'I hear they are going to build latrines for us,' Queeneth
says. She frowns, concentrating. She is at her most alert, as
if being outdoors and in the sunshine has revived her.
Queeneth has a technique: prodding the bags with a long
stick before lifting them up and dumping them further away
in the bush. She has a small heap going, to which she adds
the toilet rolls that have not crumbled to fluff. The sun plays
on her head and her unusual hair – thick and curly, but
interspersed with naturally straight strands – lights up like a
disco ball.

'I hope that's true,' replies Ozoemena.

'It's now the school knows we need latrines,' says Obiageli.
'Only because all the press people are always here. They are
afraid some girls will be caught pulling down their pants in
the bush.'

Someone whistles from a window and the girls look up to
see a beckoning Nkili. Aware of the senior girl supervising
them, they sidle up to the window, pretending to be searching
for more bags.

'How is it out there?' says Nkili. 'Is it stinking?'

Chinonso pops up behind her. 'You people are really
smelling,' she says, pinching her nose.

Obiageli pretends to put a soiled stick through the window,
and they scream and duck.

'Give us water,' says Ozoemena. 'We are working hard.'

'It's not work, it's punishment. Work is what you do in class,' Chinonso replies. Obiageli looks taken aback.

'Have sweets,' Nkili says quickly, reaching into the pocket of her skirt. 'At least it will help you not to be smelling the poo.' She manages to slip TomTom sweets through the grid bars before the senior girl yells at them to get back to work. Obiageli pops hers in her mouth and chews through the wrapping, looking expectantly at Ozoemena, who hands over her own TomTom. It goes the way of the first. She hawks and spits out both chewed-up wrappings.

'You're an animal.' Ozoemena laughs.

'Friend of an animal,' Obiageli replies.

Queeneth wanders off, poking and lifting soiled bags without tiring.

'Latrines would be a good thing,' Ozoemena muses. The class twos are often responsible for keeping the toilets behind the bathroom cubicles clean: pounders and flushers, working in combination to get the excrement down clogged pipes with logs and violently hurled buckets of water. On pounding days, a vile fug lies over the entire compound.

'They should break down all the toilets before we get to class two. There's never any water to flush them anyway.' Obiageli lifts up one foot, scraping at the underside of her slipper with her stick.

Ozoemena has resisted asking, for fear of drawing attention to her part in the events, but she has to know. 'What about the triplets?' Ozoemena whispers to Obiageli. Lower still. 'Should we call them twins now?'

'They are not coming back,' Obiageli replies. 'Their parents pulled them from school. We are having a service for Etaoko later.'

'Service?' Ozoemena asks. Obiageli shrugs. Ozoemena has encountered death, but this liminality of neither life nor death is perplexing. Why hold a funeral service without a corpse?

Again, the twinge of guilt. Why had Etaoko followed her so closely? Ozoemena grits her teeth, irritated at the path her thoughts are taking. Etaoko vanishing is not her fault.

They set the rubbish they have accumulated on fire, watched by the prefect. Obiageli wipes smoke-induced tears from her eyes. She lowers her voice. 'I don't like that Chinonso you know. She is too overfamiliar.'

'Mm. "*Work is for the classroom.*"' Ozoemena mimics Chinonso's nasal voice. 'Who is she talking to like that?'

'I think she was the secret monitor. Nobody else would actually write names apart from Ugochi, and that one will tell you to your face that she was writing your name so you can beg her.'

Burning faeces turns out to be the only thing worse than clearing them, and many of the girls retch and vomit, but they must remain where they are to make sure the fire does not spread through the dry, flammable grass. They wash up before dinner, but no matter how hard she scrubs with Dettol and soap, Ozoemena can still smell the roasted faeces. It is in her nose, in her lungs, and when she eats her dinner, it contaminates everything. She abandons her food.

At the service for Etaoko that Sunday, they go to the church in town. Ugochi stands alone on the first pew, bereft without the triplets. She seems smaller to Ozoemena, shrunken. Ozoemena's heart clutches when she sees a wide plaster on Ugochi's arm. Her mouth fills with saliva as she remembers the salty, heavy taste of blood. She swallows it down, perturbed.

Nkili slips into the pew and sits to the left of Ugochi, holding her hand. Chinonso follows, sidling towards Nkili until their arms are melded.

'That girl behaves one kain,' Obiageli whispers. 'Can't she kuku sit by herself?'

Nkili turns to say something to Ugochi, catches Ozoemena's eye and gives a low wave from the front of the church.

Ugochi's frown is ferocious. She eyes Ozoemena up and down and up and down, cutting her eyes like a scythe. By the time she looks away again, all of Ozoemena's pity has evaporated.

'How come you didn't bring a candle for Etaoko?' whispers Obiageli, pointing at her empty hands. 'You don't want people to say you guys were enemies or something.'

'I didn't know about the candle thing.' Ozoemena is flustered.

'I thought I told you before?' Obiageli pretends to yawn and palms something into her mouth, chewing with barely moving teeth.

'Stop asking me. I said I didn't know.' Ozoemena is irritated, but not for long. An unusual flickering behind the candles at the altar, and Ozoemena sees the leopard, made out of shimmering heat, pacing slowly backwards and forwards behind the officiating priest.

CHAPTER THIRTY-NINE

Treasure: Now

I have paid what me I owe original, according to what me and the spirit agreed. I found him three wifes. I found Chinenye, whatever nonsense he says. Ogenna too. Thelma took in. In my very before. All of us in school saw it. Is it my fault the baby did not stay? Other wifes, they collect one-seed-one-seed and they go. I don' know why Thelma did not go, why her own was now different, but is not my consign. I have done my part. After all, is not as if the spirit them have tried to born theirselves before. All this time they have been dead, him and his friends, and he was hearing things of how to come back, planning, so he told me. How does he know there is not risk of miscarriage?

I will wait him and too, am not collecting any seed again. Frankly, fear is catching me. As I was sitting inside the church the other day, doing service for the three-twins and their family, my chest started to be paining me. Not my whole chest, but that part where I am carrying scars, where the thing Doctor Emenike is asking scratched me. All this time, nothing was pursuing me. I carried two seeds, waiting until I could go to secondary, until Ifeanyi could not see me to give another seed, but that one is forgone conclusion because he carried himself to come here. Now my chest is paining. Every day is getting hot. I am afraid because am thinking in my heart that the leopard has come. But why now when I have finished paying, now that Daddy can come back? Is not as if I can do anything with the remaining seed, I can't return it back, I must give it to somebody. And now, is like it was waiting for me to do another one before it comes.

Every day as we are praying stations of the cross, I am calling the Bone Woman to come. Every morning as we are doing devotion, or in the night as we are doing closing prayer, I will join my own begging to be calling her. I know she is not like the spirit. I don' know what she is, but she have power and power is what me I need. Anything that she wants me I will give her.

I pray her with all my heart and soul.

CHAPTER FORTY

Ozoemena: Now

Queeneth, it turns out, heard correctly about the latrines. The men arrive before noon the next day, a huge yellow digger clanking its way down the drive. It pointlessly circles both classroom blocks, goes round the boys' hostels, and from there to the girls' side. The driver is reckless. He parks diagonally between the two buildings and swaggers out of the cab. Other workers mill about, marking sections of earth for digging, sweat running down their backs and soaking tattered work clothes.

The yellow digger is clogged with old mud, its windows opaque with dust, but it seems to work well enough. Ozoemena hates the noise it makes, the loud, grating, in-need-of-oiling sounds somehow mingling with the cruel sun in a rhythm of agony. It reminds her of the *thing* in the other place, the thing she has not yet seen, but knows instinctively means her demise.

Ozoemena is anxious about falling sleeping that night. The leopard appeared in church. It is the second time it has appeared while she has been in school, unless you counted the force that shoved her into the ground in the generator house. Had it been trying to get her attention all this while before she could see it once more? She considers the medicine in her suitcase, her special vitamins which she took sporadically. Ozoemena had not been able to look her mother in the face after Mbu's revelations. She had felt betrayed, humiliated. Her mother had been drugging her, trying to rid her of 'madness'.

The air is peppery in her throat; her eyes water for no reason. Ozoemena attempts to immerse herself in the night's music, following one strain, one cricket, trying to predict when it will chirp again, trying to establish if she is listening to the same one. The bed presses its springs into the knots of vertebrae on her spine. Morning is both a pain and a relief. Ozoemena spends the day trying to keep awake.

It seems like no sooner than lessons are over, the students begin manual labour all over the school. The digger excavates the earth and students are delegated to haul the thick, heavy soil away, prefects directing them to an unused part of the spacious compound. They are not given tools; instead, they have to empty and use their water buckets for the work. The builders dig deep for the septic tanks. The children haul and haul. It is back-breaking work, but Ozoemena does not grumble. She is suspicious of everyone. It makes her muscles tight and unyielding, and an ache thumps in her clenched jaw. She works fast, trying to burn off the anxious feeling.

'Why are you working so fast? You're going to make it hard on everyone!' Obiageli whines during night prep.

'Have you seen,' Nkili says, 'how the school is using us as builders? Today, we are packing sand, then they are mixing concrete for us to carry on our heads. Today brikiler, tomorrow carpenter. Don't our parents pay this school lots of money? Where is it even going?'

Ozoemena hears Ugochi mutter 'It's "bricklayer" stupid.'

'Dr Vincent says it's to make us self-sufficient and independent,' Ozoemena answers Nkili quickly, trying to head off the inevitable quarrel, but neither Obiageli nor Nkili seem to have heard Ugochi.

'Rubbish!' Nkili's eyes flash. 'If the man and his family are just going to chop our parents money, they should tell us.

Look at my hands.' She thrusts them under Ozoemena's nose. 'Hard like a labourer.'

'Me, I've written my parents already,' pipes up another girl. 'They should pull me from this hell, please. My mum says she will send me to a federal government school once this term ends.'

'It's true, you know,' says another girl. 'Cutting grass for punishment, I can understand, but to be building latrine, building house? No biko.'

Chinonso, whose lips had been moving silently over the finger rosary on her index finger, breaks off to add: 'And upon that, we can just be kidnapped here anyhow.'

At this, Ugochi looks up sharply. There is an indrawing of breath, and Ozoemena expects her to explode at Chinonso. Instead, she lowers her head and continues studying.

Ozoemena doodles in her exercise book. 'At least we have a gate now.'

'That nonsense,' another girl adds. 'I can cross the fence just by tucking my skirt between my legs. A chicken can fly over our fence sef.'

'You know what people are saying, right? That Dr Vincent organised for Etaoko to be kidnapped by his fellow village people.' Obiageli this time. 'My brothers told me.'

Chinonso pulls a face. 'Your brothers are gossipers sha. How would he spoil his own business?'

'I thought you were talking about school being bad,' says Nkili. 'Which side are you on?'

'That school is not secure doesn't mean he used a student for juju. What will he gain from that?'

'Nobody said juju o,' Nkili replies.

'What else are they kidnapping people for? To eat?' Chinonso says.

'Ah, you never can tell o,' Obiageli says, 'I heard there was one man in America that was eating people.'

'But what if that's why Etaoko was taken during cross-country, so that Dr Vincent's hands will be clean?' asks the federal girl.

Ugochi bangs the lid of her desk down, padlocks it and leaves the classroom. The others watch her go in silence. Ozoemena considers going after her, but only for a split second.

'Dr Vincent's a knife with two edges,' says another student.

'That's why he is allowing them to keep a shrine on the school grounds,' someone adds.

'And nails,' adds Queeneth, waking up suddenly. The girls laugh at her.

'Oh, you're awake?' they jeer.

'The building site is covered with nails. One went through my slippers sef,' Queeneth insists. She lifts one of her slippers up and pokes a hand through a hole in the middle. There is a plaster on the underside of her foot. 'Matron took me to get injection.'

'There's just too much schoolwork for us to do, talkless of sports and now building. Ah-ah.' Nkili erases a mistake on her page, rubbing hard enough to wear a small hole in the paper. 'Let my dad hear this one.'

'Me I think they should close school so we can go home,' says Chinonso.

'Why?' Ozoemena asks, sitting very straight.

'Too many things. They kept Thelma's pregnancy quiet. If our parents knew that girls were taking in here . . .' Chinonso twiddles her rosary. 'The boys' and girls' school are supposed to be separate. This is not a brothel.'

'All of us are not opening our legs. Shut up,' says Obiageli.

The laughter ceases once they catch sight of Mr Ebiere's torchlight. He is the prep-master for the day. Ozoemena pretends to focus on a maths problem while the man walks around the classroom.

'Dundee United,' he mutters at her under his breath.

As soon as he leaves, Obiageli carries on. 'My brothers told me Thelma just can't wake up.'

'It will be better for her to kukuma stay inside that coma,' Nkili says, good-humouredly, 'than to face the wahala that is waiting for her.'

Silence greets her utterances. Ozoemena fidgets in her seat, full of knowledge and guilt. She had thought the same thing not too long ago herself, but when Nkili says it aloud, it stings the ear. Thelma being pregnant makes her a thing of ridicule, but a coma does not. Someone coughs.

'You are right about some things being kept quiet. I did not see Etaoko in any newspaper at home,' Ozoemena muses aloud. 'And I saw her only one time on six o'clock news.'

'Maybe that's Anambra State. She was all over the news here.' Obiageli, constantly chewing, is now biting her nails and swallowing them.

Sweat prickles under Ozoemena's skin. Surreptitiously, she casts her eyes about for the leopard, but does not find it.

'Who do you people think will win?' asks Chinonso, trying to change the subject, but they shush her as one. Ozoemena has been briefed to never repeat what she has heard her parents say regarding politics. The military has ears everywhere.

Bedtime is a sombre affair. Mummy the matron leads most of the call and response. The girls are recalcitrant Ozoemena tastes ugliness in the air. She observes the girls depart for their hostels and, after a while, goes into hers, hoping that if anything happens, the leopard will wake her.

CHAPTER FORTY-ONE

Ozoemena: Now

'Nwokeke, they've come for you!'

Ozoemena rushes out ahead of the end of this sentence, screaming her thanks at the unseen messenger. Out in the sunshine, she pauses and surveys the busier than usual compound. It is Sunday. A lot more parents come on a Sunday than any other day. Ozoemena waves at a few classmates, searching for Uncle Fred's white van or – her heart sinks – her mother's Honda. She does not register the man walking towards her. He is skinnier, scruffier than the last time she saw him driving away, his afro combed and levelled.

'Dad?'

Her father's smile is hesitant, but it need not be. Ozoemena's strides are long and forceful, leaving deep grooves in the sand. She leaps up into her father's arms and is surprised to feel her toes graze the floor.

'You have stretched!' Her father's voice is hoarse, as if he has not used it in a while. His breath wafts stale.

Ozoemena wipes her eyes, embarrassed by the tears tingling under her eyelids, in the corners of her eyes. Her father Emenike takes off his sunglasses and wipes his eyes, unashamed. Ozoemena has been raised by her mother, and even though she has cried a few times in boarding school already, it is never where anyone can see it. Crying always makes her uncomfortable. It feels indulgent. Her parents are alive, as are her siblings. She is in good health. What is there to cry for? Even as she thinks this, Ozoemena recognises that it is Prisca's voice she hears in her head.

'I came to see you,' says Emenike. 'How is your school? How are your studies? Are you enjoying it?' Emenike walks her back to the green Mercedes and Ozoemena has to stop herself from climbing on to its wide, high boot. Solid and spacious, the vehicle is the epitome of her father – as the Honda is of her mother – and she has missed it as much as him.

Now, she runs her hand over the tiny triangular grooves accentuating the creamy leather seats. They are darker than she remembers, dirtied from overuse. A few clothes are stuffed into the footwells, as are two big Swan spring-water bottles, one half-full of liquid.

'Have you gone home?' she asks, knowing the answer to be in the negative.

'Not yet.' Emenike riffles around the driver's seat. 'I just wanted to see you, make sure you were settling in alright. I am sorry that I was not there to take you to school.'

Ozoemena settles into the seat beside him. Emenike puts his arm around her, drawing his daughter close. His ribs press into her newly thin arms and the discomfort is divine. Here is her father. His smell is stronger, but it is he.

'Where have you been? Where did you go?'

'Tell me everything about school,' he replies. 'Who are your favourite teachers?'

And Ozoemena spills her guts. When she confesses about biting Ugochi, Emenike frowns. His forehead does not smoothen out, and Ozoemena watches him anxiously, waiting for his smile, his laugh; waiting to be validated. Emenike flicks his car keys around his finger. Ozoemena does not taint their time together with her dreams and the travels and the place with the violet skies, nor the girls who have dragged her there.

She says nothing about the trees or the smoky figures, for fear that now that Emenike is before her, he will somehow convince her mother to take her away from her new friends and her new life. She cannot bear that happening. Her parents are not friendly at the moment, but she will not put it past them to cooperate on this one thing.

Adult logic is infinitely confounding.

'Has anything else happened?' Emenike asks. The door on the driver's side is open, but the car is boiling hot. Emenike has parked under the sun, unlike the other drivers chasing scraps of shade around the school. Ozoemena flicks the sweat off her forehead and wipes her nose with the hem of her blouse.

'What kind of thing?' she asks.

'Have you seen your uncle, Odiogo? Has he come to you again?'

At the mention of his name, the spot where the boy touched on her back begins to warm, to itch. Ozoemena fidgets.

'Have you seen anything? Gone anywhere? Have you eaten the leopard yet?'

'No. Not yet.' Ozoemena pulls her legs up on the passenger's seat. Her knees nudge the gearstick. She pauses, panic-stricken, expecting the car to move. When it does not, she turns on her seat, eyes searching Emenike's face for reassurance, for understanding. 'Dad, I don't know how to . . . there are some things that are . . . happening here. I don't know what I should—'

'Why?' he asks. 'Why have you not eaten the leopard, Ozoemena?'

'I don't know how to. Nobody will tell me. Dad, I keep having these dreams, and it started the first time I went to the Purple—'

'The Purple?' Emenike's Adam's apple moves, but his eyes are sleepy, and this is how Ozoemena knows she has his attention. Her father always appears sleepy when he is at his most alert.

'Yes, that's what I call it, this other place that I sometimes go to, because the sky is purple.'

'"Oh Henny-penny," said Chicken-Licken, "the sky is falling down . . ."' Emenike smiles at Ozoemena. 'Do you remember? You used to love that book when you were a baby. What was the other one? Cocky-locky? Drakey-lakey?'

'Yes, Dad.' Ozoemena stops talking.

Emenike glances about as if he can hear something that Ozoemena cannot. She is losing him again.

'Odiogo liked to read it to you. It amused him to treat you like babies, because he missed so much of your lives when we lived abroad. Do you remember how he made you and Mbu pick his grey hairs for ten kobo each? Did he ever pay you?'

'No, Dad. He always turned his palm over and let the hairs float away before he could owe us one naira.' Ozoemena smiles, a minute tug at the muscles of her face. 'We used to make plans about how we'd spend the money. I remember.' The leather seats are scorching. Ozoemena sweats like grilled meat. 'Mbu liked being the only one to pick his hairs. She wanted all the money for herself.'

Emenike laughs, a sound untainted by madness. 'Odiogo did that on purpose, to keep you focused on each other. He was cunning. He made a great leopard. If not for the war . . . he lost so many lives! That is why he fell to ordinary robbers. Part-man, part-leopard, and they killed him with a gun. It makes me so angry. So angry.' His eyes are suffused with electricity. 'When you see him, when you eat the leopard . . . why are you delaying?'

Ozoemena's spirits sink. This is why her father has come. Not to see her, no, but to find out if, no, *when* she can reach her uncle.

'Baby is forgetting you,' she replies, trying to hold on to the nostalgia. Her displeasure is a finger of palm oil, staining the whites of her serenity.

'Who?' Emenike stares at her, a stranger. 'Oh, yes. I don't know why you people insist on calling her Baby, she is now . . .' He trails off, calculating. Quietly, Ozoemena opens the car door. Emenike returns from where he has gone to in his mind.

'Wait!' He grabs the car door, yanks it shut. 'Listen to me, Ozoemena. You have to eat the leopard; do you hear me? Many people are depending on you.'

'No, Daddy. I don't have to do anything. Mummy says—'

'Your mummy doesn't know anything! If you reject the leopard, you will not know peace, in this life or the next.'

'Oruke Nwosu says I can choose.'

'Choose? What does he know? Listen, find your tether, and do your job. You are not a child.'

'I *am* a child,' says Ozoemena. She grits her teeth. Her jaw aches and her eyes prickle from holding her father's gaze, but she refuses to flinch.

'Well,' he says at last. 'You are leopard as well. You don't have the luxury of being childish.' Emenike breathes hard. There is spittle at the corners of his mouth. He pops his sunglasses on and takes them off again; the whites of his eyes are bright and hard. 'Do you think your uncle had a choice? He did his job and paid for it with his life. If you are a leopard, it means there is something to fight, and you'd better wake up, Ozoemena. Wake up! You help me find Odiogo wherever he's gone, you can travel all the worlds! Odiogo can help you—'

The shrieking in Ozoemena's head threatens to blow out her eardrums.

'Don't you care about anyone?!' *Besides your brother?* Ozoemena would have baulked to speak to Prisca this way, but this is Emenike, her father, who encouraged her to express herself. And Ozoemena is disappointed, because for all her father has raised her to be, he is a man. Human. Ordinary. Small. His desires pale next to the vast incomprehension of this gift-cum-curse that she has been given, and what she must do with it. Disappointment twists in her gut. Ozoemena often feels her feelings in her stomach and this one is sour. In spite of her father's encouragement, Ozoemena regresses in his presence to dutiful daughter, and the truths she wishes to tell instead spill out within her like an internal bleed.

You don't even care about me, about us. Do you know what people are saying about us? About Mum? Instead, you are here, wanting me to help you reach Uncle Odiogo. It's as if nobody else matters to you, Dad! You think I am not worthy of being leopard? I will show you. I will show you all.

'Uncle Odiogo is not coming back, Dad,' she says. There is an excess of spittle in her own mouth, bitter from the bile in her stomach. Her words froth, much as his had. 'And even if I could, I wouldn't bring him. "For it is appointed unto man to die once, and after that—"'

Emenike seizes her by the arms. 'And after that, what?' His words run together: *Andafterthatwhat?* 'You have seen with your eyes that there are other places out there, and yet you sit here spouting Bible passages to me? You know there is not one way to God, nor one life! You are so stubborn, Prisca! Filling the children with garri and telling them that is the only food! Everything is one thing to you. What about beans? Rice? Banana? What about bananas, Prisca?'

Ozoemena's brains rattle in her head, and she grows nauseated. 'I am Ozoemena!' she screams, yanking herself free. Gritting her teeth, she hisses her rage at him, spittle collecting in the corners of her mouth. 'I hope I never ever find my tether if they are anything like you!'

She pushes open the door and bolts, hearing Emenike

calling behind her, not stopping, fleeing past the parked cars, the incredulous parents, her peers, eyes open, mouths wide, gossip forming. She runs, not caring where, only wanting to get away, away, tripping over the scales falling from her eyes.

Prisca and Mbu, melding into the same person, Ozoemena always on the outside. Cursory letters from home, stilted language. How she has waited for Emenike's return. What a fool she has been. Emenike can no more help her than Prisca or Mbu or anybody. They can no more help than Ozoemena has helped any of the missing girls. She has to be stronger, tougher. She has to do her job and stop waiting for anyone to tell her what to do or where to go.

Her country is a land of excesses. Excess sunshine, surplus heat. She runs into the shoulder-high grass, unheeding of the tough blades, the severe itching that besets her almost soon after, and sinks down into it, wanting to press herself into the very earth. Ozoemena swallows several times. She will not cry. She *will* try to think. She is not a dundie. There are many types of knowledge, and her uncle chose her. Not Mbu. Her. She must be good for something.

Ozoemena holds herself motionless, and the insects are emboldened. She turns everything she knows over in her mind. A few bugs settle on her skin, green, small, irritating. Ozoemena rips up handfuls of grass at the root, raising dust, white root tendrils like worms in the dry earth. She rips and tears until the blades of grass cut her palms; her rage swells, a tidal wave, taking her up with it until she crashes, panting on to the clearing she has made around her. Her bladder fills up, the pressure building in her lower abdomen. Ozoemena moves deeper into the bush, then squats and positions her underwear. She starts to relieve herself.

A hand grabs her ankle, causing her to jump. Someone moves fast through the bushes and Ozoemena gives chase, leaping and pinning the figure to the ground.

'You want to be peeping at me, eh? You want to peep? Come o! Everybody! Villager! I caught a villager!'

She raps the head with her knuckles and the figure howls, struggling and bucking to throw her off. Ozoemena holds on tightly, locking her hands around shoulders, under arms. Her thighs strain. A foul odour comes from the person beneath her and Ozoemena's mouth waters before she bites down hard on his ear, twisting.

The person flips over, and Ozoemena recognises his eyes. The same eyes she had seen watching her at ground level a few weeks prior. Pleading eyes. Ozoemena hits him weakly in the nose and, although his eyes water, he does not hit her back. He frees his hands and places them together.

'Op, op,' he mumbles weakly. 'Op-ee op.'

The boy does not possess a tongue. Ozoemena slides off him, watching as he pleads with her. She no longer has him pinned, but the boy cannot seem to move his head. His eyes roll to the side, where she is. Ozoemena cannot fathom how such a wretched body could possess such desperate strength, his pleading eyes at odds with the speed with which he ran from her. It is as if he is two separate people at the same time.

The boy is trying to communicate something.

'What are you saying?' she asks.

The boy repeats his sounds.

The noise has attracted students. There is a rush of foot-steps, and at last the boy raises his head. He pushes off the ground with his hands.

'Hey! You!' shouts Senior Emeka. The boy takes off running, and about thirteen boys give chase, whooping and hollering. The senior prefect pulls Ozoemena to her feet. He hands her over to the girls, who are thronging nearby with a few of their visitors. Ozoemena spits discreetly. Her insides feel soiled from biting the boy's ear. She allows herself to be transferred from hand to hand, the girls making comforting noises, asking what happened. Her knees are bruised and bleeding.

Her father is where she left him, pacing by his Mercedes, a frown on his face. He takes Ozoemena by the shoulder.

'Did you hurt that child?' he whispers. 'The leopard is going to overtake you, Ozoemena. Find your tether, or you will go to the beast completely and be unable to find your way back to yourself.' He hands her a parcel, haphazardly wrapped in newspaper. 'Take this. I got it for you.' Emenike puts it in her hand when she does not reach out to take it. He scratches his head as if plagued by lice.

Ozoemena slips free of him. 'Dad, bye-bye,' she says. Ozoemena is already consciously forgetting that he came. Instead, she replays the sound the boy made when she caught him: *'Op, op, op-ee'*.

Ozoemena misses her leopard. She has begun to think of it as hers. She needs all the help she can get to figure out who it is she is meant to be looking for. Why would the leopard abandon her now? Novus is not small; she could be looking for staff or a student. Whoever it is can go where the leopard goes, otherwise, how else are the human beings ending up in the purple place? And what of the boy in the bushes? Is she supposed to help him? Why did he come to her? Does he know her secret? Sweat pours out of Ozoemena's pores. The day's excitement is getting to her.

Over the following days, Ozoemena awaits the leopard's presence, turning suddenly if she spots a shadow in her periphery. Night sounds fail to lull her into complacency, and so do the days' routines. *Boy or girl?* she asks herself often. *Staff or student?* Ozoemena is paralysed by the enormity of the task ahead of her. The magnitude of the responsibility dwarfs her age. Ozoemena yearns to confide in her friends, but even considering the notion feels taboo. Mbu had found out by herself, so Ozoemena had broken no vows. She wishes

Mbu attended their school. She wishes her so-called tether would magically show up.

'Eyi! Eyi! EYI! WATCH OUT!'

A burst of manly shouting disrupts class. Ozoemena looks up, alongside the girls whose desks line the window, just in time to see the top of the tree-shrine at an odd angle.

'Jesus! It's falling! The tree is falling,' Chinonso exclaims.

Nobody seems to care about discipline or punishments, and finding her vision swamped by bodies, Ozoemena finally climbs on to her desk. Even BC has joined his students by the window, after instinctively trying to regain order.

'Oh dear,' he says. He works the chalk in his hand until his fingers turn ashy. Across the strip of green lawn separating them, Ozoemena watches the boys doing the same. The silhouette of an adult begins to whip the legs of the boys at their own windows, and they scramble back to their seats.

As soon as the bell rings for break, the entire school swarms to the back of the girls' hostels, or tries to, anyway. The boys stand behind their building, obeying the invisible barrier even though the chicken mesh fence falls short. Mr Ibe is already at the site, and he has cordoned it off.

The tree has fallen over the girls' B-side rooms, its underskirt of roots indecently exposed. It is difficult for Ozoemena to assess where exactly it has fallen, but listening to talk, it appears to be by the back door and WCs.

'Mr Ibe is sweating like a Christmas goat already,' says Obiageli. 'You know this means we are in hot water.'

'We don't need Mr Ibe's sweat to tell us that one,' says Nkili, subdued. 'The villagers will take heads at this rate.'

Ozoemena does not join in. She attempts to use the opportunity to read the assembled students and staff, but their voices are loud and varied, everyone talking at once under the midday scorcher of a sun. A few of the male prefects slip to the girls' side under the guise of authority. The workmen gesture amongst themselves, breaking off to communicate with staff. Mr Osugiri appears to be trying to organise some sort of correction involving rope looped around the tree trunk.

'What is that fool doing?' growls Ugochi. It is the first thing Ozoemena has heard her say since her return to school. She almost smiles at the return to form. The newly taciturn Ugochi had made her uneasy.

They all watch the teachers circle the scene, reading in their bodies apprehension, weariness, growing concern from the likes of BC and Miss Uzọ, and boredom from Mr Ebiere.

Mr Ibe claps for quiet and asks them to return to breaktime activities. Dr Vincent is on his way, he says. At that, they begin to disperse.

'Let me go and buy puff.' Obiageli rushes off to the tuckshop.

'God help us.' Nkili loops her arm through hers, but Ozoemena is slow to turn, distracted by her thoughts and lingering apprehension. She stumbles over the feet of the person standing behind her.

'Sorry,' she says, but Chinonso does not answer her. She stands under the sun, shielding herself with a splayed exercise book, utterly transfixed by the sight of the fallen tree in front of her.

God help us, repeats Ozoemena to herself, suddenly figuring it out. *Op-op-op-ee.*

Help. Help.

Help me.

CHAPTER FORTY-TWO

Treasure: Now

When I was small, Daddy used to sit me on his lap and tell me plenty stories. All his stories used to have learning matter. He told me the story of Tortoise and akidi, and said that when me I marry, I should know that a husband and wife is one person, that I should not do like Mbekwu and his wife, Anim, who each take akidi cooking on the fire to eat by their . . . themselves and jam each other in shame under the bed. That time, I used to cry and cry and cry when him and Mummy will go out leave me with house help, but I didin use to cry for Mummy, only him. Mummy didin use to like it. Ever since I was small, she will be asking if me and her are dragging husband.

The thing is that Daddy is not my real daddy. I mean, he is not the daddy that born me, but even though, he is my real daddy, because after he married Mummy, he did everything a father will do and more even. When Mummy was sleeping and Aunty Ojiugo taking care of her, that's when she told me. One day like this, she just started talking, that what will happen to me, that what kind of evil is this, the man that saved her sister from disgrace, how come he came to come and die echetaram echetaram.

My mouth opened. Aunty Ojiugo saw my face, then she stopped, shaked her shoulders, said, 'I will tell you the truth,

I won't pretend like my sister does. When you know the truth about yourself, nobody can use it against you.'

Is Aunty Ojiugo that asks me have I not noticed that there are no pictures from Mummy and Daddy marrying? They hid everything because me I was flower girl in their wedding. They did not want me to be asking them questions. Aunty Ojiugo is the one who was saying, 'Your Mama get sense. She married someone that resemble . . .' Then she stopped talking and said that me I should stop looking at her mouth, she has finished what she wants to say.

The thing did not move me, all the things she was saying. I don' care who the man that pregnanted Mummy is. I don' care if I was at their wedding. All those things are babash. Because whether or whether't, Daddy is my Daddy. If Aunty Ojiugo did not say anything, a day would never have reach when I ask myself that question of 'is Daddy my Daddy?'.

He is my Daddy, and I am his Dazzling daughter. Is him that started calling me Dazzling, because he said that since he was not there for my naming ceremony, he will give me his own name. Daddy is my daddy. Anybody that is his enemy is my enemy; anybody that is his friend, is my friend. Full stop. I don' care what all the uncles in this world say. I don' care if heaven and earth pass away. If I have strength, if I can find somehow to make Daddy alife again, to make it so that his name don' end in 'That Man', if I can make death turn back, then I will do, because Daddy did not make me suffer in this life, so he must not suffer in the next one.

My menses started today. As am looking and seeing as it stained my pant, I know that my own and the spirit have finish. I have seen first blood. Everybody's palm markings are various, and their destiny also. Am not for the spirit, is not me that will born him in this world and my stomach is sweet. My stomach is polina-polina. But Daddy also used to say if you're going to eat frog, you should eat the one that is fat.

Yesterday, Mr Ibe collected some of us to go and clean the Big House – that is what they are calling Dr Vincent's house. He said we should bring bucket and rag, and they gave us mop, Omo, water. There were boys there, cutting grass already, and we cleaned and mopped and used baby powder to shine-shine the windows. Some people were using kerosene, but me I don' like to use kerosene, because it makes me to be remembering somethings that I don' want. When we were coming back, all of us were tired and gisting, and as we cornered, I saw him. I saw Dr Emenike driving one green Mercedes Benz going outside the gate. I dropped my bucket fast and bend down as he drove past, but my whole body was shaking me.

The scars on my chest are peppering me. I don' know how Doctor Emenike used to find me, but now I know the thing chasing me is him. My cup has full, but I will not wait like a cockroach for him to march me.

Is time for me to do my own back. It is time for me to follow big masquerade, and I cannot do that with hands that are empty.

I take my blood to the bush, past the classroom and the hall, past the generator house. As am walking am praying. Praying not to see any eyes shining like torch, praying that the Bone Woman will hear as I am calling her. What if some of my class girls catch me, what will I tell them I am doing? Where will I tell my friends I am going, when I know plenty of us like to do things together? Am doing like I want to go to the games field, but I turn off the way, to the left side, where the bush is longer than me and thick. As am walking, I can see that the whole school sef, we don' even know half. Am walking and calling, am praising her telling her that she is powerful, that nobody can fight her, and come out alive, that all her teeths inside her mouth is special and beautiful, the same way Daddy used to hail Mummy is how am hailing Bone Woman. There is bush everywhere, but one small tree is growing and there is space near it, so I stand there and be calling her. Water is thirsting me, my throat is dry and the tree sef me and it are almost size and it don' have plenty leaves, so the sun is flogging me and am praying, praying, praying.

As me am calling the Bone Woman, wind starts to be blowing. Is not ordinary wind, is Ikuku Ndị-Mmụọ, the one that we used to run from when I was small in primary, the one that turns, the one that we used to say is spirits passing. There are three winds, turning aeroplane-turner, the san-sand is turning, the wind is growing big with all the dust it have swallowed. I use my hand to cover my eye and the wind falls down inside the grass and stops. I can hear it, like rain of sand falling all over the grass.

'My child, you have got your woman's blood.' The Bone Woman is sounding as she is walking, plenty small-small bones on her neck, her hands. I open my eyes. There are two monkeys smelling everything, walking on four legs with their bum-bums shaved as if they are having ringworm, their tails hanging up and hanging down. Then they stand up soja, opening their long-long teeth that is sharp.

She is saying, 'Woman's blood is strong medicine, but you are exciting my boys.' Am telling her that I have something to tell her, and she says me I should talk quick. The monkeys are opening teeth again. I tell her everything about the spirit, when we both made a deal, what he said about her, what he is doing, that he have mates: everything. The Bone Woman is not looking me. She is yawning as if to say sleep is catching her.

'I thought you had words. I already know all these things. Did you think I did not know what was happening in my

own domain? Your lover's cohorts have been dealt with. And
as for him, he is stuck where he is, in the body of that boy.'
She laugh like laughing jackass, and when she laugh, the
monkey them laugh like somebody is beating them.

'He is not my lover.' The way she is laughing is vexing me.
What is laughing her? My life is not laughing matter.

'Oh, see boldness. Why were you begging me, calling me,
if you can handle yourself?' She is laughing again, and the
monkeys are laughing and clapping, but their eyes is like
people own without laughter inside it. They are coming near
me and going back, coming and going, as if small thing they
will eat me like banana with their long teeths.

'Can you release my daddy to me or not?'

'You are ripe palm fruit, you. Who says I have your daddy?'

My mind is turning what she is saying. 'You have my daddy.
If you know everything that is going on in your house, then
peradventure you have him or you can get him for me.'

The Bone Woman yawns one big one and sucks her mouth.
Her walking stick she is using to walk, she is turning it in her
hand as it is standing on the floor. 'Just look at this one,' she
is telling the monkeys. 'Are you hungry? Do you want to eat
her?' They open they mouth 'waaaaaaaaah'.

I play my last card. 'I know where you can get bones.
Leopard bones. A man that is a—'

'A leopard-eater?' The walking stick is no more turning.
Bone Woman is trying to do as if am gisting ordinary gist,
but me I know I have got her.

'He don' eat leopard. I say he is—'

'Just say what you have to say.' She shakes her body and
the bones are sounding, the wrapper in her chest to her legs
is like Best Ink if you put it inside water and all the colours
come out, many-many colour like person pouring petrol on
wet kolo tar.

When I finish talking my own, she comes near and too,

the monkeys are coming, but she put her hand stop and they stop.

'Show me your scars.'

I raise up my daywear blouse. The Bone Woman is doing her hand waka and touching them, and they are paining small and hot. Her nails are long-long like the monkeys' teeth, and she is putting her face inside my own, inside my body, as if she wants to collect the scars from my chest.

'You are wrong about something. No full-grown leopard would attack you and let you live. Your doctor cannot be the leopard.' She is licking her mouth; sucking as if she is eating something. 'This is the work of a young leopard. A new one.' She pulls her hand away. 'Maybe not yet bound.'

'Bound?'

'You are alive, so I would say unbound.' The Bone Woman is holding my face, tighting it. 'Find him and bring him to me, and I will bring your daddy to you.'

Am thinking fast. If Doctor Emenike is not the leopard-person, that means he did not pursue me and come. And if he did not pursue me and come—

Am feeling the pepper in my chest. Wherever leopard is, I don' want to be there at all. 'I already told you what you need. Why can't you go and collect it by yourself?'

'Can you go and bring your daddy by yourself? No. I do my part, you do yours. A leopard would sense me coming, anyway.' The wind is starting again. 'I've already stayed too long in its vicinity.' The Bone Woman and her monkeys are standing inside. 'Be careful, though, with finding who the leopard shadows. An unbound leopard is unpredictable, dangerous. But you already know. If you want, I can help you make it easier. But you will owe me another thing.'

'When will I hear word from you?' The Ikuku Ndị-Mmụọ is making the grass to be loud and am shouting.

'You will know when it happens. A leopard will always go

where there is palaver.' Bone Woman is coughing her laughter. 'I *own* palaver.'

The wind blows, carrying dust, carrying the Bone Woman and her monkeys to where they take to come.

The blood inside my laps is sticking. I will like to baff, but is not dark. I don' like people to see my chest and my stomach. As am thinking how I will find the thing that wants to find me, I am remembering somebody that has brothers that are the biggest gossipers in Novus. I will ask if they know who Doctor Emenike came to see.

CHAPTER FORTY-THREE

Ozoemena: Now

At night, most of the girls from B-side bunk with their friends on A-side, more terrified of the tree now that it has been felled. They fear reprisal attacks by the villagers. They fear what evil the fallen shrine could release with its decades of alleged sacrifices and offerings. They all understand the power of belief. Everyone, no matter what they believe, knows to leave sacred things well enough alone.

The sleeping arrangements displease Matron. She shuffles along on mouse feet, knocking on doors and striking at slumbering forms with her cane.

'No, no.' Her voice shrills with age. 'Not allowed. You will not fox in my house,' she says. Ozoemena does not understand the term, but she presumes its meaning. Matron separates even siblings, pulling a girl out of her elder sister's bed. The girls wait for her to retire to her quarters and creep out again, their instinct for safety stronger than their fear of the dark, than the lashes from Matron's cane. This game of Ludo lasts all night, girls moving like tokens from dorm to dorm. The students from the village sleep without stirring.

It takes Ozoemena a while to wake, to decide if the ringing is in her dreams or not. She bolts upright. The bell ringing is frantic. In hostel four, students rush about, putting on shoes, pulling dressing gowns, wrappers, sweaters, cardigans, over their nightwear. Ozoemena's limbs are alive with adrenaline. She shoves on a long sweater.

'What's happening?' she yells over the noise.

'Emergency! Leave the hostel! Now!' Senior Akudo flings a wrapper around her waist, and, running, tucks it underneath her sweatshirt. Ozoemena starts making her bed unconsciously, then abandons it. Her armpits grow moist under her sweater.

The quadrangle teems with students, shivering, speculating. They heave towards the assembly ground in front of the girls' classroom block and line up according to their classes. At the end of the years, the boys begin to line up in the same order. The sky is only just beginning to open its lids, the day a promise to be fulfilled. Ozoemena looks around for her friends. She sees Nkili wave from the back of the line, next to Chinonso. Ozoemena waves back, searching for Obiageli. Queeneth yawns, stepping into the line in front of Ozoemena without asking. Ozoemena elbows her in the ribs until she moves over. The bells jangle, frazzling her nerves. When they cut off, the bell ringer Bobby drops a flat metal piece on the pavement and joins his class. The silence is brutal and startling.

Dr Vincent takes to the pavement, clad in a safari suit. *He has had time enough to digest whatever this emergency is,* Ozoemena thinks. *It cannot be that bad.* The teachers flank him on both sides, Mr Ibe, Mr Ebiere, with Miss Uzọ standing the closest. Matron hobbles up from the girls' hostel, supported by Senior Nwakaego, who helps her on to the stage. Mr Osugiri, the handyman, clicks on his torch and shines it from row to row, clicking it on and off in a kind of tic.

Somewhere in the bushes, the leopard barks. Ozoemena's head jerks up. She becomes alert. It cannot be a coincidence. Whatever the emergency is, she assumes it must be bad.

Dr Vincent clears his throat. He is a short, bow-legged

man, and the breeze, when it comes, flutters the fabric of his trousers between his legs.

'Good morning, Novus.'

'Good morning, Dr Vincent,' they chorus.

Dr Vincent clears his throat again. Out comes a handker-chief, into which he blows his nose. He replaces it in his trouser pocket and pats it as if to reassure himself that it has not migrated. He has an American twang that sounds as though the sounds are pinched off in his nostrils.

'We have an important announcement. As you all know, a student of this prestigious institution has been missing for weeks now, presumed kidnapped.'

A chill descends on Ozoemena.

'As a direct consequence of which, we lost two special members of our student body, the siblings Taiwo and Kehinde. What you might not be aware of is that the search for Etaoko never ceased. Our faculty were instructed to return to status quo by members of the Nigerian police force as they chased down various leads, so as not to alert any possible nefarious parties of their activities.'

Dr Vincent stands with his hands clasped around his midriff. 'Last night, I received a call from the commissioner of police, saying that, thanks to the brave efforts of officers, and following searches a mere twenty kilometres from here, Etaoko's body was discovered in an uncompleted building, missing certain parts of her anatomy. The owner of the house has been apprehended, as well as one other man—'

That is all Ozoemena hears before the wailing, shouting and fainting begins. The boys are loud and angry, their broken voices swelling with threats of reprisals, formless and without direction. Dr Vincent claps his hands, Mr Ibe shouts for calm; even Miss Uzọ, whose presence is normally so reassuring, is ignored. The leopard barks again. Ozoemena looks about her. Where is Obiageli? The assembly breaks up, but she cannot retain whatever else Dr Vincent says, and wanders from group to group, trying to glean additional information. Classes are supposed to carry on as normal, but the teachers disappear for a staff meeting, leaving Novus in the hands of the prefects.

Ozoemena is aware of her dry, worried eyes, and casts her head down. People are beginning to remember how Etaoko went missing, to look her way. There will be more questions soon, she can feel it, even though she has been cleared, even if she knows nothing. They will question her over and over. Ozoemena has heard the leopard; she does not wish to be tied up. She must get to it, fast. She does not know why it chose not to appear during the emergency assembly, but she is grateful. Ozoemena knows she must appear normal. All around, people are weeping, walking in clusters. Chinonso clings to Nkili, who appears to be struggling under the girl's theatrics. Ozoemena tries to lend a hand, but Chinonso attaches herself to someone else. Nkili wipes the corner of her eyes quickly. Ozoemena pats her on the shoulder, unequipped to deal with the display of emotions.

'Have you seen Obiageli?' Ozoemena asks.

'I was looking for her. I bet you Choco Milo that useless girl did not even wake up.' Nkili chuckles; a tense, dispirited sound.

The hostel is abuzz. Someone has thrown open the double doors to the porter's lodge and left it ajar. The girls automatically begin to congregate as if for prayer, standing like lost sheep, until Senior Chikodiri begins the rhythmic clapping for songs of praise. The church prefects take turns singing out their favourite songs, and the girls bring up the chorus. They hear a swell of altos and basses. From their side of the compound, the boys are singing as well. Ozoemena is pummelled by the melodic force of a choir united across denomination and sex by a shared tragedy. The Evangelical students raise their hands in the air and begin to speak in what Ozoemena has come to learn is 'tongues', and a few of them fall to their knees. Chinonso joins them, clutching a rosary in her fist without counting, and muttering fast prayers, swaying back and forth on her knees.

They all take turns praying; they are all invited to speak if they feel it in their hearts. Some pray for comfort, others protection. Senior Chikodiri says the Prayer for the Dead, and all the Catholic students chant the refrain.

Senior Joy climbs the pavement. 'May all those wicked people, the people that took our Etaoko's private part, took her breasts to do whatever rubbish juju they are planning, may they burn in hellfire, in Jesus' name!'

'Amen!'

'May all their plans fail, in Jesus' name!'

'Amen!'

'They will come one way and be scattered a thousand ways!'

'Amen!'

'As they live by the sword, so shall they die by the sword!'

'May they drown in their own blood!'

'AMEN!'

'Only you, Jehovah El-Shaddai, see all. Guard our country Nigeria! Guide us!'

The earlier mood of sombre reflection is disrupted. Senior Joy has the girls riled.

Ozoemena watches Ugochi sit down on the pavement, burying her head in her lap. Her shoulders shake with sobs. A few senior girls take turns stroking her back. Picturing Etaoko's family getting the news, her forlorn siblings missing a third of their number, Ozoemena finally begins to tear up. It is a ghastly way to go, ritual killing. It might have been she, had the leopard not been with her. Ozoemena is relieved, and guilty to be so relieved. She raises her head to the sky.

'I still can't see Obiageli anywhere,' Nkili whispers.

'What time is it?' Ozoemena asks.

Nkili looks at her Casio. 'Seven-thirty.'

Ozoemena is keeping her eyes on the sky. 'Have you noticed that the sun is not rising anymore? It's like someone pressed "pause" in a video.'

Nkili pulls her dressing gown tighter around her body as a wind starts up. 'Maybe we should say we can't find Obiageli.' The sky remains paused between dark and dawn.

'I'm going to find her. I think I know where to look,' says Ozoemena.

Ozoemena has only seen dust storms of this size in films featuring the deserts. Wooden shutters are slammed and secured against the dust. When she changes out of her pyjamas, Ozoemena notices her bed is covered by a layer of sand. *What is happening?* she thinks. Dread clogs her veins.

Nkili rushes out of her hostel as Ozoemena gets to the porter's lodge. 'Me, I'm coming. I don't know if the world is ending or what, but I'm not staying here by myself.'

Together, they push against the wind, which seems to come from all directions. Voices carry above the winds, drawing Ozoemena's eyes towards the gate, where a crowd of adult men, arrayed in typical village garb of singlets, shorts and flat caps, have converged, waving machetes and sticks. The school's khaki-clad security men are overrun, as though half the number at the gate had previously hidden themselves from sight. They motion for the men to remain where they are. A few young boys start to scale the fence. Ozoemena's fingers grow moist and cold.

'You!' Mr Ibe runs past them, making for the invasion. Senior Emeka and a few other boys, including Ambobo, are on his heels. 'Get back into your hostel.'

'But, sir,' Ozoemena begins to protest – but she is speaking to herself. Before her eyes, Mr Ibe throws his bulk on the men surging through the gates, pummeling with his fists. Nkili puts an arm around her, squeezes hard. Ozoemena feels the tremor run through her skin.

Shutting her eyes tightly, Ozoemena finds her way by memory to where she thinks she heard the leopard earlier. Grains of sand squeeze under her eyelids. Tears stream down her face. They push down the length of A-side, past the dining room's external door and the annexe containing the kitchen. The open metal water tank that serves both kitchen staff and girls buckles in the gale. As they round the bend to take the incline towards the latrines, Nkili taps her.

'Where are we going?' she shouts above the deafening noise. As Ozoemena points and turns to shout something back, she sees the first of the young men approach the tuck shop. She halts, hesitating. The porter's lodge door is still ajar. Her schoolmates are in danger.

The wind has a personal vendetta.

'Let's keep going, now,' says Nkili, pulling her hand.

Ozoemena pushes back to the dining room door. Grabbing a hunk of rock, she begins to bang out the emergency alarm she had heard that morning. The vibrations from the metal pole holding up the ceiling cause a soreness in her muscles, but she continues to bang until someone inside the hostel takes up the tune.

As they approach the bushes, the wind wails like a dying woman. Shivers cover Ozoemena from scalp to sole.

Where are you? She thinks loudly in her head. *What is happening?* She prays the leopard can hear her. Her legs tremble. She cannot look at the tree, its scant branches like staring down on an elder's head. The bushes are thicker, and she links hands with Nkili when her friend stumbles. Ozoemena has never ventured this far before, and yet when she looks behind her, the zinc roofs of the girls' hostels are still visible. She hopes her schoolmates are alright, but there is nothing to be done now. Ozoemena wonders if she has made the wrong choice. Obiageli could be anywhere on school grounds, but her schoolmates are in danger right now.

The gust scatters bits of green into the sky like confetti. Nkili squeaks as a leafy twig tangles up in her hair.

In the midst of her doubt, Ozoemena experiences the same tug in the middle of her chest that she had in the purple place, when she tried to lead the girl out. Three more steps and Ozoemena trips over something, landing hard on her hands and knees.

'Obiageli!'

Nkili falls to her knees too.

Obiageli is stiff and cold, and Ozoemena tries to feel first for her pulse and then her breathing, the way her father taught her, but the wind is too loud, and her hands shake. She is uncertain about whose pulse she can feel.

'Help me carry her, Nkili!'

Nkili remains frozen on the ground, staring at their friend.

'Nkili! Lift here, let us carry her down to school.'

Nkili reaches out both hands for Obiageli, grasping her shoulders. The light begins to dance, and the voices, never far away from Ozoemena, start up their whispering. Ozoemena can hear clearly: the grass, the flowers, the sky. The blood in Obiageli's veins thrashes with life, and she hears it. Ozoemena breathes a sigh of relief.

The leopard barks, three short barks. The air around Ozoemena's right ear heats up and she knows it has arrived. She crumples in relief. 'Thank God,' she says, turning to Nkili. 'Don't be afraid,' she adds.

Nkili takes her eyes off Obiageli's supine form. They widen, but even the flash of fear cannot mask her rage.

'You have been trying to kill me, shey?'

In the space above her head, three whorls begin to form. Nkili's hair stands up straight into the charged air.

CHAPTER FORTY-FOUR

Treasure: Now

When I know who Doctor Emenike came to see, my heart piececesed. They say is someone that know you that will be your downfall. I didin know that as I was shining my thirty-two, sharing biscuit, gisting, fetching water, helping her with maths, that Ozoemena was trying to kill me.

Me that Aunty Ojiugo named God's Treasure when I was born.

Me that my mother calls Nkili, a thing to behold, because I am beautiful.

Me that my father calls Dazzling. These are all my names. As Ozoemena is looking me, anger is carrying me. So many people love me, but even her and her sister, same mother, same father, are keeping malice always.

Even sef, I didin want to believe. I told Obiageli to come and escort me, that me I want to do flyover and she followed. I don' hate Obiageli because she didin do me anything. I was planning let me tell Ozoemena to escort me to find Obiageli. I will tell her that Obiageli said she was going to shit in the bush, then I will surrender her to the Bone Woman. But even, I was saying in my mind that no, it cannot be Ozoemena.

I didin even have time to do my plan. When she started walking to where Obiageli was lying that was when my heart started to tell me the truth, that this girl is not a human being. Does it mean that when she was taking exam, she already knew all the things that me I did? Because when the torch eyes inside the water scratched me nail, I have not start secondary. Ozoemena was just marking me and waiting till she can eat me and swallow me.

But is not me she will eat.

Me that have picked souls like corn, that have said who will go and who will not go.

Me, that have talked to human beings and talked to spirit.

Whatever Ozoemena is, me and the Bone Woman, we will deal with her, because never, never will anybody keep my daddy from coming back to me.

Do me, I do you. God will not be vex.

But first, me I will ask Obiageli to escort me somewhere. Is just snacks that the matter will eat. I will give her and I will tell her to escort me and she will follow.

CHAPTER FORTY-FIVE

Ozoemena: Now

With the leopard behind her, Ozoemena stands her ground – barely – when the whorls in the air touch down. The sky darkens, a portent to rain that is out of place given the season. The leopard nudges her in the back and Ozoemena moves forward – and yet, when she puts out a hand to stroke its body, to reassure herself of its presence, her hand meets only air.

A woman steps out of a dusty whirlwind, followed by two baboons that bound forward with teeth bared. The woman holds a chunky horsetail whisk over one shoulder, which would have probably belonged to some magnificent beast. It is thick and long, dappled brown and white and looped with leather around its hilt. She shivers with pleasure; smiles, impressed. The leopard rumbles in its throat but remains by Ozoemena's side.

'So, this is our lady leopard,' says the woman, baring her teeth like the baboons do. 'A girl! Live long enough and you will see everything at least once.'

Ozoemena is agog at the mismatched, awe-inspiring set of teeth.

'I am the Mother of Bone Piles. My supplicants call me the Bone Woman.' She beckons and the rings encircling her fingers clack, a melody played on the sun-bleached ribs of a carcass.

Ozoemena remains where she is. The baboons pace, snarling, and Ozoemena struggles to keep everyone in her sights. The leopard does not move from its position beside her.

'What is it they call you?' asks the Bone Woman.

Ozoemena thinks. A person's name is their destiny, their power. One does not offer it up easily. 'I will not tell you my name,' she says. In the stories M'ma recounts to her, naming oneself aloud means ceding control. Ozoemena is through with being controlled.

The Bone Woman frowns, resembling her baboons in ferocity. The leopard nudges Ozoemena forward again. The Bone Woman's gaze drops from Ozoemena to the space beside her elbow, then back. She steps backwards.

'Her name is Ozoemena,' Nkili says, getting to her feet. Ozoemena watches her, sees the slight movements she makes so as not to startle the baboons, who never stop snarling.

'Ozoemena,' repeats the Bone Woman, and Ozoemena hates the way she says it, the sucking she does at the end, as if her name has a taste. Ozoemena's skin crawls with the sensation of being licked, savoured. She grimaces, spits and wipes her mouth off with the back of her hand, trying to control her rising breathing.

'Nkili, what did you do to Obiageli?' Ozoemena hears the wobble in her own voice. The change in her friend's demeanour has shocked her; its implication, even as she refuses to acknowledge what all her senses are telling her, sinks in. Ozoemena fights the urge to bend over and bawl.

Nkili crosses her arms. 'Ozoemena, why are you trying to kill me since?'

'I'm not trying to kill you!'

In response, Nkili raises her T-shirt. Her chest has been slashed and healed in diagonal strips, disappearing where her shorts begin. The leopard breath rumbles again, and Ozoemena is in its head, seeing through its eyes, filling in the gaps from the morning it slashed the air before her and landed in a body of water. Ozoemena gasps, a strangled sound. She had closed her eyes, but she still remembers the give of flesh, soft and yielding underneath her hands like warm candlewax. Ozoemena wants to protest her innocence – 'It wasn't me!' – but was it not?

'The leopard doesn't go after the innocent. What did you do to Thelma?' Ozoemena asks, knuckling away moisture from the corners of her eyes, tears that have not yet formed. 'Don't lie. I know it's not just her. Was it you who caused Etaoko to disappear?'

'I had nothing to do with that one!' Nkili says.

Sound carries on the wind towards them, a clashing, clanging, shouting. Fighting in the school. Ozoemena glances quickly down at their friend's inert form on the ground. 'Then what did you do to Obiageli?' she says again. She cannot help the tears collecting in her eyes. Ozoemena is helpless, useless. All around her, a battle rages and all she can do is cry. 'Is she dead?'

'She's with me,' says the Bone Woman. 'Enjoying my hospitality.' She taps a piece on her necklace, and Ozoemena realises that all of her accessories are made of bones. 'Come with me, and I will release her soul back into her body.'

'Release her, and I'll follow you.'

The leopard snarls.

The Bone Woman's laugh is two dry planks being rubbed together. Instantly, her baboons start a ruckus. 'You must think I was born yesterday.' The Bone Woman flicks her whisk impatiently. 'I know you are unbound. A leopard *is* the leopard-eater. And yet, here you stand with yours beside you, hazy, yes, but there. A leopard wants nothing more than to be, to do the job for which it was made. I can kill you and make it all disappear.'

Ozoemena moves her shoulders in a shrug. She wipes her eyes hard, hurting her eyeballs, punishing herself for crying. 'You can't kill me.' She speaks slowly, enunciating every word. 'You have never seen anything like me before – you just said. I am special. You want me to follow you. Return Obiageli to her body. Every piece of her.'

Nkili's anger is hot, and Ozoemena imagines that she can smell smoke coming from the hatred burning in her. She searches the face for familiarity, for a sign that her friend is yet present.

'You too have power,' Nkili says to the Bone Woman. 'Power pass power. Just take her; what can she do? You can't see? It's not her that have the power.'

The Bone Woman raises a hand. 'Close your mouth,' she says to Nkili. Nkili draws in a breath to say something else, and both baboons turn liquid eyes on her, their snouts long and menacing. She steps to the side, watching them on her right, with the leopard and Ozoemena to the left of her.

'Okay,' the Bone Woman says. She plucks a small bone from her strings of necklaces and sniffs it. She slips it between her teeth and cracks it.

Obiageli coughs, long and strenuously, and when her eyes open, they are watery and red, as if she has been swimming underwater for a long while. Ozoemena kneels beside her again, clapping her on the back.

'You!' she huffs, staring at Nkili accusingly, but she is wracked by another bout of painful coughing, clutching her middle as if she is about to expire. Saliva drips in clear, unbroken strings from her open mouth.

Nkili ignores her. 'What about my daddy? You said if I found the leopard and brought it—'

'Oh, I did not forget.' The Bone Woman pulls out another bone, this time from somewhere in her bosom. She holds out a thumb-sized piece. Ozoemena watches the proceedings out of the corner of her eye as she helps Obiageli to her feet. The baboons snap at Nkili when she steps forward, and she jumps back again. The Bone Woman throws the fragment of bone in the grass, and Nkili scrabbles for it. She tries to break it, but the bone is irregular and small. It does not break.

'Nkili, please. Listen to me . . .' Ozoemena tries. Her chest heaves with the effort of keeping her sobs contained. Tears start again, and she wants to beat herself when her vision distorts, but she jerks her head to clear it and tries to continue. 'Listen to me. Are we not friends? Why are you—'

'He's not coming out,' shouts Nkili. 'Bring him out, bring my daddy out!' She offers the piece back to the Bone Woman, who waves her away as if she is a bothersome insect.

'You said I should return your daddy, but you did not tell me how. There. He is returned. Our deal is done.'

'You are trying to cheat me!' Nkili screams. Her face is twisted. Ozoemena thinks to herself that she has never seen anyone so ugly. Nkili puts the bone between her teeth like she had seen the Bone Woman do and bites down on it. There is a crack, and she grabs her face, howling.

'Obiageli, can you walk?' Ozoemena whispers to her friend.

'What is happening?' Obiageli's voice is hoarse and talking appears painful. She cries openly, tears and mucus streaming from her eyes and nose. Ozoemena pats her, turns her towards school.

'Go,' she talks quickly. 'Run. Hide in the latrines when you get there; don't go into the hostel.'

Obiageli asks no questions. She nods and takes off through the forest, stumbling rather than walking. She sounds like an elephant crashing about in the undergrowth.

'Now come, our lady leopard.'

Ozoemena feels the leopard brush her leg and stand before her, blocking her way as though to stop her going to the Bone Woman. The baboons go crazy, howling, snarling, pacing, jumping around. Despite the assurance of the leopard behind her, Ozoemena's heart jumps several paces up her throat.

The Bone Woman stares at Ozoemena and a look akin to pity crosses her face. 'You are too young. Don't you want to put this burden down? Don't you want to rest and let it go? The life of a leopard is tumultuous. I have known older, stronger leopards before you, and they did not survive. Come with me. Give your leopard in service to me, and you can life a long, peaceful lifetime.'

The sky is the colour of a bruise, and the wind, which had previously died down to a breeze, starts up again.

Nkili spits a bright crimson spark into the earth. 'You cheated me!' she shrieks. Maddened, she charges towards Ozoemena, forgetting the leopard, forgetting her terror of it. 'You can't take her unless you deliver my daddy.'

Ozoemena shoves her hard, anger and hurt and betrayal connecting firmly with Nkili's breastbone. 'Nobody is taking me anywhere.' She squares up. Her throat tickles. She breathes hard.

Sprawled on the ground, Nkili is too stunned to speak. She spits again, rubbing her chest. Ozoemena finds herself reaching to help her up. She halts, stops herself.

Now, she thinks at the leopard. If there is to be a merging, it has to be now, but the leopard is crouched down, motionless as a sculpture.

The Bone Woman eyes the leopard, but speaks to Ozoemena. 'You mean to revoke our deal?'

'You just did the same thing to her,' Ozoemena says, pointing at Nkili. There is blood staining Nkili's T-shirt, long unbroken strings of crimson drool linking her chin to her chest. Ozoemena wonders if she has damaged a tooth, or a few teeth. Nkili holds on to the bone protectively.

The Bone Woman thumps the earth with her stick. 'Imbecile child! I existed before your ancestors. I was there when your kind was made to satiate a god's vanity. What do you even know? Your life is like a mosquito's compared to mine.'

Ozoemena speaks slowly, half to herself. 'I know you cannot make me go with you. I must agree, and my chi must as well. Otherwise, why go through all this?' The truth of her statement sings in Ozoemena's heart, in her bowels, in her blood and mind. She had not been certain when she began to speak, but she is now. 'And don't think you can threaten anyone again.'

No doors are closed that a leopard cannot claw open.

'Or I swear on all my ancestors, I will hunt you through all the worlds and even the afterlife. That kingdom you think you have built for yourself; I will destroy everything.' Her throat again. Ozoemena coughs, and now she is certain the smell in her nostrils has nothing to do with Nkili's anger. It is the smell of smoke. Something is burning.

'You *will* come with me, or I will ask my hungry spirits to burn every last inch of this school to bare soil. If spirits cannot have living warmth, they will take it in fire. And these ones have been hungry and angry for a while.' The Bone Woman appears to be growing taller. Her chest swells like bread dough. She swings out with her carved bone cane and catches Ozoemena in the side of the face near her left eye. The leopard leaps and pounces on a baboon, crushing its skull between its jaws. The blackened sky opens up in pinpricks that reveal themselves to be more whirlwinds, dancing ever closer.

From her place on the ground, Ozoemena clutches her head, weeps, and tries to get to her feet. The cane has reminded her of how frail she is. Once again, she is facing Benjamin, and Mbu's callous indifference, and many of the ways in which she has been on the fringes, looking in. Her head is a bundle of shrieks. The Bone Woman is right. Any delusions of grandeur she might have had flee, and she remembers her age, how soft and useless she is. The leopard and the other baboon growl and snarl, dancing around each other, and Ozoemena knows she will die before she has had a chance to be leopard. She will be no help to anyone.

No, she thinks. Her sister is different now. Mbu is on her side and Benjamin was in the past. This is now.

The Bone Woman strides over to where Ozoemena lies and raises her cane.

'Nobody can climb a pepper tree,' she says, and swings. Ozoemena tries to roll, to avoid the worst of it.

The boy in the bushes dashes out of nowhere, stumbling over his feet as if controlled by another force, knocking the Bone Woman off balance. Her cane slices through the grass, unearthing a great chunk of roots. The boy opens his mouth wide in a strange exhale that is not quite a scream and ducks, his movements jerky, like a marionette hanging from broken strings.

Ozoemena crawls on her hands and knees, willing herself to stand. She tells herself that she has borne the leopard as it ripped her from place to place. Her bones have cracked, her skin has burned. She has endured pain like no other. Ozoemena is no longer the same person. She gets to her feet.

The leopard has dispatched the other baboon and now it turns, herding Nkili towards the Bone Woman. Ozoemena sidesteps towards it.

Okay, I accept, she thinks.

She stretches out a hand in the leopard's direction without taking her eyes off the Bone Woman. There is no pain, no resistance. Ozoemena is both girl and leopard.

Humanity spreads out before Ozoemena, and she sees all the worlds there are layered one on top of the other as onion flesh. She sees how thin, how permeable they are. And here she is, in the middle, solid and immovable. The leopard bearing Ozoemena hisses. Its tail whips in irritation.

The pinpricks of wind resolve themselves into faint, howling apparitions snarling in the gloom. The leopard raises its head and barks, its muscles rippling with impatience.

'Just give me my daddy back as he was.' Nkili is on her knees, ignoring the danger she is in.

Ozoemena wants to warn her about her bared neck. Ozoemena wants to seize her unprotected neck.

'Please. Don't let me have nothing. I did everything.'

The Bone Woman swishes her cane around her head, furious. The whirlwinds obey. 'Your cheating, lying, murderer of a father – how do you think he got so rich? But you were a child. You were not to know. Your father, the great businessman, made his money sacrificing apprentices to the old, blood-drinking gods, who rewarded his loyalty only as long as he kept them in drink. And then he got too comfortable and stopped. The night the vigilantes came for him I found him in my meanderings, hiding on the stairs to the roof. He knew a hard death was waiting for him, and his soul was in danger of wandering, being lost for eternity. So, he made a deal with me, for his reincarnation. He *gave* you to me. Like a chicken. Promised I could have your life if I kept his spirit from moving on to punishment. I already owned you, and your precious lover spirit knew that. Tried to steal from me! My property.'

The first of the whirlwinds begins to stretch wispy tails to the earth. The earth roars and heaves, but Ozoemena's leopard does not lose sight of its prey.

Nkili's eyes are wide. 'That's a lie. Daddy would never do that.' Veins bulge from her forehead and temples. The smoke is affecting her as well.

The Bone Woman's sigh is an exhausted sound. She lowers her cane. 'I would say ask your mother why she doesn't want her husband back. Ask her, if you can find whose bed she is in at the moment, how she is still getting money to keep you fed and clothed. But you are not leaving here today.'

She brings the tip of her cane to the earth and taps it, causing a dust cloud to bellow where she stands. The leopard pounces too late. The Bone Woman is gone. The leopard hisses again. It turns towards Nkili, who is trying to crawl away into the tall grass in the sudden brightening of the day. Nkili raises one hand. The other holds the bone that is her father.

'Wait,' she begins.

Wait, Ozoemena thinks. The leopard stops. Through its eyes, Ozoemena observes Nkili's crestfallen expression. She is bloodstained and crumpled, in a position of supplication. Her shoulders sag, the shoulder bones almost touching. The air thickens with smoke and the crackling of fire on the dry grass reaches Ozoemena's ears.

'So, what am I supposed to do now?' asks Nkili of the ground in front of her. She stares only briefly at the bone fragment in her hand before lobbing it into the bushes. When she does look up, Ozoemena begins to struggle to uncouple herself from the leopard, pushing out with all her might. Nkili is her friend, and she is in pain.

'You don't understand,' says Nkili to her friend in the leopard. 'He's my daddy. I had to try, to bring him back.'

Ozoemena feels her anger begin to cool. She could not fully comprehend grief, the power it had to make people act contrary to themselves. Emenike had abandoned his family to go in search of his dead brother, and now Nkili is hurting people for a father who does not deserve her devotion. Even now, as her heart breaks over their friendship, Ozoemena knows that she, nevertheless, will never give Nkili what she is asking for, any more than she will bring her uncle Odiogo back to please her father. When she tries to speak, the leopard barks, over and over and over, each one louder than the one before. Nkili cowers before it.

The boy leaps on Nkili and drives a sharpened stick through

her eye, pushes it deep until his fist rests on her eye socket. Instantly, the leopard surges out of Ozoemena, leaving her emptied and worn. She can no longer bear her own body up. The darkness takes her.

CHAPTER FORTY-SIX

Ozoemena: Somewhere

The trumpeting Okpoko is a welcome sound now. Ozoemena sits up, knowing what has happened, knowing she is somewhere else, and is completely unafraid.

There is no tree behind her, no trees anywhere that she can see. All around her is a sea of grass, gently undulating.

Ahead of her flies Okpoko, and Ozoemena follows. The path meanders in pleasing curves and her mind drifts. There is nothing to fear. The grass tickles her outstretched arms, licks at her armpits and she giggles softly to herself. The earth beneath her bare feet is soft sifted flour. It caresses in between her toes and Ozoemena considers resting, but Okpoko screeches, drawing her attention, and she sets off again.

The sun is rising to her right. It warms her skin. Ozoemena is aware of a mildly pleasant sensation on her back. She does not care that she is naked, that her thighs rub together here when she walks, that people called her plump as a child as a shorthand for rich and spoiled and all the things that she is not. She does not care about what could be happening to the body she left behind. Nothing matters in this moment but the path and seeing where it leads. Ozoemena is not even sure she is alive. How pointless her prior fear of death. She cannot remember now why she was so scared to die.

The tall grass begins to fade away, and now there are

trees. Flat leaves bearing yellow flowers cover the ground, velvety on her feet. The path ends in tall, square towers, two, three storeys high, covered in thatch and growing vines, marking an entrance. Gateposts. At first, Ozoemena assumes the buildings are trees, so well camouflaged are they. An old village. Homesteads of sun-baked or fired earth, smooth, patterned with animals and plants and abstract symbols; coloured, shiny stones inlaid in walls; roofs of thatch and clay. Clean. Empty. Ozoemena walks from house to house, and there is nobody in any of them. There are no pots, no mats or beds, no books or clothes. No sign that the village is a place of habitation.

Ozoemena backs out of the last hut. Loneliness presses down on her. Is this where she will spend eternity? Is *this* eternity?

Okpoko calls to her, perched on a high roof in the middle of the village, and she walks towards it, her dreamy state coming off her like a cloth.

The building on which Okpoko is perched is wide, with many eaves slanting downwards like the skirts of a masquerade. It is decorated in symbols, inlaid in white pebbles, marked in black and green, white and yellow clay. The house thrums with energy, and when Ozoemena crosses the threshold, it seems to exhale.

A man stands in front of her, the darkest person she has ever seen. He wears a cloth round his loins and not much else. On his chest are markings, one of which she has seen before. The man's eyes alight upon her, and though his lips remain unmoving, Ozoemena gets the impression that he is pleased.

She stops a few paces away from him. Fires burn deep in the four fireplaces set into each wall of the huge rectangular hall and Ozoemena sweats. The man is her ancestor, but she is at a loss. Should she pour libation? Break kola? Throw a

morsel of food at his feet? She has read the works of Chinua
Achebe, but has none of these things to hand. She shuffles
her feet.

'Blood smells,' says the man. He is tall and robust; his
shoulders block out the light from the fireplaces when he
moves to stands in front of her properly. Ozoemena swallows.

'Whose child are you?' he asks, and Ozoemena knows how
she should respond.

'I am Ozoemena, daughter of Emenike Nwokereke, son of
Irugbo, son of—'

'Nwokereke Idimogu, the leopard.' His chest widens. 'Yes.
I see that. You have come to eat the leopard.'

'I have,' affirms Ozoemena.

'N'eje. I am watching.' He moves out of her way.

Ozoemena stands in the middle of the great hall, with its
many chairs and drums of different sizes arranged in the
corners. Each fireplace holds up to three giant clay pots, as
high as Ozoemena's chest. The smell of cooking meat assails
her nostrils. She turns and looks at her ancestor, hoping for
clues, but all he does is regard her from where he stands.
Ozoemena turns in place. Dizziness overtakes her. She stops
and starts out towards the pots bubbling on the right. She
pauses.

'This one,' she says in Igbo, and the other two pots stop
boiling and are hushed. She peers at the surface of the pot
she has chosen. It is watery, unspectacular. A delectable aroma
pervades her nostrils.

'Eat,' says Nwokereke Idimogu. He has not moved, but his
voice travels to her from the doorway as loudly as if he is
standing next to her. Ozoemena looks around her for a tool,
for the sort of long-handled ladle with which women traditionally scoop things from deep pots.

'Eat,' Nwokereke says again. The pot glows faintly, made
from a yellow metal, bronze or copper. Ozoemena searches

for a bowl, for a shell, anything with which to scoop the soup.

'I can't find . . .' she trails off.

Nwokereke's eyes betray nothing, neither help nor condemnation. Ozoemena stares at her hands. She takes a deep breath, and her lower lip trembles. Closing her eyes against the pain, she reaches into the boiling pot and pulls out a handful of meat. She grits her teeth. She will not cry out.

The meat fights her, thrashing in her hands. Ozoemena stuffs it into her mouth and chews, swallowing it down, scalding her throat raw. She returns to the pot, grabbing the wriggling flesh and shoving it into her uncomfortably wide mouth. Her throat offers no resistance, and yet the meat fights her, climbing up inside her to get out. Ozoemena falls to her knees and the pot scalds her legs, her thighs, her chest with its buds knotted inside the flesh. She leans on its rim and smells her flesh burn. Ozoemena is in a place past anguish.

Nwokereke wears no expression. 'Eat,' he says.

Ozoemena pushes herself to her feet again. She grabs the meat and stuffs it down, grabs and stuffs. Her stomach distends. Ozoemena relaxes everything in her body and loses control of her bladder. Yet, she eats, staring at her ancestor, despising his impassivity, understanding it.

There is no more meat in the pot. Ozoemena hangs her head. She is sick and sweating. Her urine crackles under the pot, boils, evaporates, filling the air with the smell of ammonia. She crawls on the ground, faces her ancestor on shaky knees. The fire flickers off the taut skin on her stomach.

'Drink,' he says, in his monotone.

Ozoemena begins to cry hot, angry tears. Looking her ancestor in the eye, she scoops and drinks the broth, and scoops and drinks, and the broth goes nowhere. The meat she has eaten is cement, but she will not beg for a reprieve.

She needs a rest, but she will not ask for it, nor for a cup, nor anything. She grapples with the pot, tilting it. She enters it, head and torso, and slurps, telling herself that there is room in her stomach. She is the next leopard, not the last. There have been others before her. If there is anything left in the pot, she will eat it and drink it because she *can.*

Ozoemena lets go of the pot. It bongs, a dull sound. She lies on the ground, breathing like an animal in labour, taking little sips of air through her nose.

'You have chosen the east, Eke. The path of the rising sun.' Nwokereke nods. 'It is good.'

Ozoemena cannot speak. She is on all fours. If she throws up now, would it count as a rejection, she wonders.

A dark shadow winds forward between her legs, its width is the length of her arm.

She is looking at what created the path she walked to the hall. Eke Idemili, the royal python, Idemili's messenger. She has come full circle then, like her ancestor and her uncle before her.

What would have happened if I chose Afọ? Or Orie? Or Nkwọ?

'But you didn't,' says Nwokereke aloud. And he smiles, revealing a gap in the middle of his teeth. 'Whichever you choose; Nkwọ of the setting sun, Orie to the north or Afọ to the south, all are good.'

The python circles her, and she moves, crawling away. It is heavy against her thighs.

You will become the thing that all beasts fear, comes Oruke Nwosu's voice.

The snake winds itself around her. Ozoemena tries to struggle, but she is held fast. She can no longer move. It fastens her arms to her sides.

There is something you must do if you are to become leopard.

Her bones crack and splinter, and Ozoemena cries out. The python seizes her around the stomach and her bowels burst, scalding, liquefied torment. She struggles, but its grip holds. The python's skin is dry and warm, and when it crushes the breath from her lungs, it stares her down, its head as big as hers.

First, you will have to die.

Ozoemena: The beginning

Alive.

Tongue towel-dry. Throat moves. Nothing to swallow. Count teeth. Lose count. Start again.

'My eye.' No light in left eye. Don't like my voice. Small. Whining.

'Your mouth is booming,' says Mbu. Foot of bed. 'It's just a bandage.'

I want the green jelly from Leventis.

'Ehe, you're awake.' Mum, on a wooden chair next to my bed. Hospital bed. Antibiotic smell. Mbu moves. On window-sill. Brown mosquito net. Dust. Mum puts cup to my mouth. Milky smell. Water warm. Sun warm.

I want green jelly from Leventis.

'You did a good thing trying to save that Nkili girl from the riot,' says Mum. 'It's a pity the villagers killed her. You are lucky they didn't kill you too.' Mechanical sympathy face.

Mbu says, 'Thank god they've closed down that school.' Swishy green curtain. Government curtain. Teaching hospital. Dust dancing. Dancing dust. Happy dancing dust.

'Come out from that window before you start wheezing.'

'Green jelly. Please.'

Mum frowns. 'Your father spoiled you people.' More water. Don't like milk cup. Don't like water. 'I'm going to tell them you're awake. The sooner they can discharge you, the better.'

No green jelly.

'You got a letter the other day,' says Mbu, holding envelope. White. Red. Blue. Par Avion. 'It says from "Obiageli Maduewesi".'

Obiageli!

'She also keeps phoning to ask when you are back from hospital. Always chewing on the phone. She's annoying sha.'

'Green jelly?'

'Maybe I'll sneak some for you later.' Scratch, scratch. 'I hid some in my room. Not to eat. Just to . . . remember.' Sigh. Big sigh. Scrape. Wooden chair.

Mbu whispering. 'Can you see any ghosts in this room?'

'Two green jelly.'

'Okay, two, but no more. I don't have many. You know Mummy would die before she buys us more.'

I nod.

'How many ghosts?'

One finger.

'Where?'

I point. 'On chair. You sat.'

Laughing hurts. Good hurt. Itchy bandage. Itchy eye.

Tears coming. Turn away so Mbu can't see.

Nkili's eye. Nkili on the ground. So much blood. My friend. Everything hurting. Bad hurt. Bad, bad hurt. She was changing, I could see it. She was sorry. She didn't have to die.

Maybe.

I don't know. I don't know what I would have done if the boy—

I can't think of the boy.

Mbu coughing. Not real cough. Wipe my eyes. Pretend to yawn, do it naturally. Yes. Like that. Mbu cannot see. Real yawn. I am tired. Close eyes. Itchy eye.

I say, 'Daddy came to visit me in school.'

Mbu says, 'I don't care.'

I nod. Mbu in pain. Mbu lying. Everybody lies. Nkili lied. I am lying, because even if I don't want to think it, the leopard would have killed Nkili. That is its job.

That is *my* responsibility.

I am the leopard. The boy did my job.

Help me.

I must find him. I must help the boy.

Mbu is talking.

'Pardon?'

'I said, do you want me to read your letter to you?'

'Yes, please.'

Obiageli knows nothing. Doesn't matter if Mbu reads.

The leopard is calling me, and I must answer.

Close my eyes. Choose the right time.

The Departure

Something has happened to me since my last time in leopard. I feel older, more substantial. I have stood in the river of time, and its waters have flowed fast through me. I am who I was always meant to be.

Perhaps this is what it means to die. The old, passed away.

The boy's scent is strong, the odour of putrefaction and not merely of the flesh. A rot festers deep within his spirit, rot and despair and desperation, the smell of a carcass. Stalking the boy is easy, and so we do not run, not when the scent holds strong. He fled before us, and we chased him, feeling the minute vibrations of movement through the grass, our face abuzz with sensation. For a while he crawled, his legs dead and heavy and useless. Now, he tires; all movement has ceased.

We find him in the old burial ground in Amawbia, towards the back, well away from traffic on the old road. The leopard does not like to be so near traffic, especially in the day, unless it is absolutely necessary, and communicates this by the tremor running down our flanks, the twitching of our ears. The old burial grounds are red earth like most places, baked into a hard mass by the sun, by the rains, strewn with the broken crockery of tombstones and overgrown with grass.

The boy's chest barely moves. His shirt is torn, the xylophone of ribs painfully visible. He rolls his eyes at our approach, but cannot move on his wasted legs. His shorts hang off the sharp bones that should be his hips. We hear his heartbeat, slow. The skin at the base of his neck barely trembles. The boy's body lives, but it is not animated by breath, by food or water. The leopard crouches and I focus on what it is trying to say.

There.

Within the dying sheath of flesh, an essence, blurring the outline of the boy's body like waves of heat. He raises a hand and the leopard's growl rumbles in my chest.

It is you. You killed my friend. Not this boy.

The outline shimmers and blurs. A response, garbled. Within me, I struggle to comprehend, but the leopard's mind is quicker.

She promised me. Another chance.

The rest of it comes to me in waves of sensation: ecstasy, fear, loss, betrayal, rage. At the end of it, I taste something different to the rot.

We clamp on to the boy's throat and crush, ripping the parasite out of its spent host. Rage tastes of months-old water stored under the sun. No good for eating. I open our mouth and it crumbles to nothingness. The body breathes its last. A smell of wild mangos escaping as the boy stands before us the way he truly is, shiny skin, fat cheeks, a yellowish overbite that could do with thorough brushing. He smiles, nods, and takes off walking towards the road, whistling a discordant tune that we cannot follow.

We travel the byways and highways, slinking through doorways, taking shortcuts in back alleys of worlds until night falls. When I tire of my form, all I need do is think and I *unbecome*.

I carry the leopard on two legs for a while, its senses open to me, every feeling, every impression, every instinct. My footing is measured, my mind calibrated to the smallest movement. We are in synchrony. I have found my tether in the end – she is me.

Other leopards before us may have needed tethers to keep the animal within the man in check. I am starting to understand that I am not the same as they were. I am a new kind of leopard, for a new world, and my leopard answers to me alone. It must fall to me to observe this new world and re-invent the rules as I see fit.

The leopard wishes to hunt. I step out and watch as it ambles away into the bushes without a backward glance.

Acknowledgements

I would like to thank my agent Lucy C. Morris for her incredible support and dedication to this book, and my career, Caoimhe White, Liz Dennis, Luke Speed, and the team of super stars at Curtis Brown including Hillary Jacobson at ICM. I would also like to thank my superb editor Ella S. Gordon, Alex Clarke, Emily Patience, Serena Arthur, Zoe Giles, Areen Ali, Hannah Cawse and the greater Headline team for not only taking a chance on this book, but pitching it seriously and comprehensively, TWICE.

Tendai Huchu for waiting many years (patiently and not!), for always being in my corner and cheering me on – dude, you already know. Dr Carmen McCain and Dr Octavia Cade for reading this book in its very early stages and giving their notes. My love to Ann Orton, my *con madre*, and Jose Alatrista for their deep and abiding love and aid, Dr Claire Dempster, beloved god mum, for the space to write, boundless affection, presents, and a solid, dependable presence. My thanks also go to the Carrick-Davieses, who during Steve's birthday stood on stage and called me a writer while I was still dealing with imposter syndrome. My best girl Og Stella Okpala who has probably read everything I have ever written; her early observation of 'Why does she have no friends?' changed the way I approach my protagonists forever. That being said, come and collect your property, I don't run a storage company.

Vera Kwakofi for a long friendship and coming to wherever I am, Matthew 'MK' Kenyon and Heleen Arps ditto, and for loving my children as if they are yours. To the man who added to my interest in ghosties and spirits, Dr Rems Umeasiegbu, thank you and I hope this adds to the genre. Debi Mairesse and Jaime McKay for succour and friendship, especially at a difficult time.

For Nneka Arimah, for lifting me up and setting me down, for many things too precious to name in stark black and white. I've said too much already, and you mighn't let me live this down.

Thank you, Yuki Sawada-Lynch for being my friend and my light, and for the lovely flowers both literal and figurative.

To my sisters Ogbeishi Onyinye, Ifeoma Mgbogo, Abumchukwu Nyikwos, Posey Nkechi and my brother Chivovo Nwokeoma, for helping me remember things I forgot, and a wealth of shared experiences and nonsenses. I could not ask for better siblings – mostly because our parents have grown too old to comply and now I'm stuck with you goats.

And finally, for my dearest and best, my treasured offspring A and E, I am so happy that you chose me to bring you into this world. I am so proud of you both for teaching me every day.

I love you. Tidy your rooms.

Chịkọdịlị Emelụmadụ was born in Worksop, Nottinghamshire, and raised in Awka, Nigeria. A product of not one but two Nigerian boarding schools, she went on to attend Nnamdi Azikiwe University in Nigeria and the University of Newcastle upon Tyne. She was the winner of the Curtis Brown First Novel Prize in 2019. Her work has also been shortlisted for the Shirley Jackson Awards (2015), a Nommo Award (2020) and the Caine Prize for African Literature (2017 & 2020).